TANZI'S GAME

C.I. DENNIS

For Isabel

TUESDAY

ROYAL FINALLY WENT DOWN FOR his nap, and I flopped into my chair, totally exhausted from carrying him around, singing made-up songs, stroking the impossibly soft skin of his back and trying every trick I knew to get him to conk out. He had put up an epic struggle, but he was no match for me, Vince Tanzi, former deputy, retired private investigator, all-around tough guy and now stay-at-home dad. I'd spent my whole career dealing with badasses—taking care of my nine-month-old boy should be a lark.

Ha.

I was more tired and sleep-deprived than I'd ever been in my life. I could barely keep my eyes open. I needed my own nap, or a beer, or both, but I had a shitload of laundry to do, and Barbara would be home in a couple of hours. Wait—did I just say that?

Yes, I did. That was the deal now, whether I liked it or not.

I took five minutes to lay back in my recliner, which was one of the few pieces of my furniture that had survived the Great Purge when Barbara and I had combined our belongings. Everything else she had sold or given away. I wondered if she was trying to exorcise the ghost of my deceased wife by getting rid of all the stuff that Glory and I had accumulated during twenty years of marriage. "You need a reboot," Barbara had said, and she was right. It felt good to have a fresh start, and to be a new husband, and a new dad. Considering everything that had happened to me I was lucky to be alive at all, and I wanted to stay that way because I had a family to care for now.

I couldn't relax. There was still too much to do, and precious little Royal-napping time to do it in. I got up, padded quietly down the hall over the cool floor tiles and put a load of clothes into the washing machine, carefully measuring the detergent. I was becoming a whiz at laundry after learning about stains, shrinkage, color bleeding, over bleaching and other washday calamities, mostly the hard way.

1

Royal made a peeping sound, but it was a sleep noise, not a nap's-over-come-get-me noise. There was no other sound except for the whooshing of the laundry and the crunch of the mail truck's tires on the crushed-shell driveway outside. I decided to go out and pick up the bills and circulars.

The afternoon heat greeted me at the door. It was only May, but it was already sticky out, like midsummer when the tropical storms materialize out of nowhere. I don't mind the Florida weather as long as it's not a hurricane, but the greying sky and rustling palm fronds were hinting that something substantial was on the way. If it started to rain, I would back my car out of the garage and let the storm wash off the haze from the salt air—a free car wash for those of us getting by on a cop's pension.

I collected a clutch of magazines for Barbara, retirement planning flyers, hearing aid come-ons, and an invitation to a bra-fitting event that was addressed to me, not my wife. How did I end up on *that* mailing list? OK, in all honesty, I had put on a few pounds since my accident. A year's worth of physical therapy had gotten me back on my feet, but it might be another year before I could truly work out again, and in the meantime I was developing something approaching a B-cup. Maybe I should accept the invitation.

Roberto Arguelles was riding his bike down the street toward me. I waited while he pulled into the driveway and leaned it on its kickstand. He still wore his school clothes; it was our custom to hang out after school for a while before his folks got home and he had to knuckle down to his chores and homework. Roberto was crazy about Royal, and my little son was similarly enraptured with my teenaged friend and technology consultant.

"He's sleeping," I said, as Roberto entered after me and went directly to the fridge for a Coke. "I'll take one of those. The little guy wore me out."

"Heads up," he said. He tossed a can through the air, which I managed to catch.

"Thanks. Now I'll have to wait an hour to open this."

"Vince," he said, not smiling, "have you heard anything from my mom?"

"Your mom?" I could see the look in his face. He was scared.

"She took off. My dad won't talk about it. He's like, totally freaked out."

"Roberto," I said. "Sit. Tell me what's going on." I motioned to a chair across from me at the kitchen table. I cleared the mail away and set down my unopened can of soda. My young friend shrugged and took the chair.

"She was gone when I woke up on Sunday," Roberto said. "Dad said that she went down to Miami. You know, her family lives there."

"You guys stay at her sister's sometimes."

"My aunt is the only one she keeps in touch with," he said. "My mom and dad don't do much family stuff."

Lilian and Gustavo Arguelles had moved into my neighborhood in Vero Beach about ten years ago, back when Roberto was a tot. There weren't many Cuban Americans in Vero, and his parents had always said that that was how they liked it. Both of them had jobs at the hospital, they kept to themselves, and they accepted the close bond that had developed over the years between their brilliant, nerdy son and a washed-up ex-deputy and private investigator who was in the slow lane after taking a nine-millimeter slug to the head.

"So she's at your aunt's house?"

"No. She's on a boat. Or at least she was. I lost the signal."

"You tracked her? How?"

Roberto rolled his eyes.

"Sorry," I said. Of course he could track her. Adults with smartphones no longer had any secrets from their tech-savvy kids. "On a boat going where?"

"My dad said not to worry. He said married people need a break sometimes."

"But you think that he was blowing smoke."

"Yes," he said. "My mom would never do that."

"So where was this boat?"

"Key West." He was tracing a fingertip through the condensation that had formed on his can. "It was headed south, and then I lost it. She's bad about charging her phone. Or she could be out of range."

"South from Key West is Cuba."

"I know," he said. "But she can't go there."

"No one can just go there. You have to get a special visa."

"It's not that," Roberto said. "Her family was, like—they'd put her in jail."

"Where's your father?"

"I don't know. Probably still at work."

Royal began to howl in the background. "I think I have a diaper to change," I said. "And after that we're going to go find your dad."

*

I left a Post-It note for Barbara on the fridge and packed Royal into the backseat of the BMW. He had graduated to a forward-facing car seat, and we played little smiley games in the rearview mirror while Roberto sat motionless beside me. It was not like Roberto to be so worried, and his unease was contagious. Lilian Arguelles was one of those people where everything was on the surface. The idea of her just going off somewhere for whatever reason was a stretch. She was a dedicated mother to Roberto, and I'd never sensed any real friction between her and Gustavo, although there are people who can hide those things, even from me.

Like my first wife, Glory, who had become involved with somebody and had paid with her life.

So, it's possible that I'm a little quick to assume that pretty much everyone has a few dark secrets stashed away. Uncovering them had been my former business, before Royal had arrived and Barbara said no more snooping around. Not with a baby in the mix.

I'd had to dash through a torrential downpour to get across the parking lot of the Indian River Medical Center, and I was soaked by the time I got to the lobby. The heavy rain was an excuse to leave Roberto and Royal in the car, which was good, because I figured that I could get the full story out of Gustavo more easily without his son around if there was more to this than Lilian simply needing a "break".

I navigated through the hospital's halls to the accounting section where Gustavo sat in a windowless office. He glanced up from a desk that was covered in papers. His graying hair needed combing, and his eyes sagged. He didn't look very happy to see me.

"What are you doing here, Vince?"

"Roberto's out in the car. He told me that Lilian left. What's going on?"

"It's nothing." He turned away from my gaze.

"Do you know where she is?"

"No."

"Or who she's with?"

He hesitated. "Not really."

"Meaning what?" I took a molded plastic chair across from him and sat. The office was featureless except for a wall calendar and a photo of Roberto that was taped to the side of his computer.

"Meaning I don't know, Vince. I really don't. She left me a text. It said that she was going away for a few days, and that she needed a break. But she didn't take her car, or any of her stuff that I could see. I checked all the suitcases and none of them are missing. She even forgot her wallet."

Her wallet? I didn't like the sound of that. "Roberto said she has her phone with her."

"Yes, and I've tried calling, but she won't pick up."

"Gustavo...have you considered contacting the police? I don't want to frighten you, but this doesn't sound very good."

"There's no reason to," he said. "No police."

"Listen—"

"Vince," he interrupted, "I don't want to go all the way into this, OK? You'd just tell Roberto. Leave it alone." He looked back at me, his dark eyes pleading.

"I'm not moving from here until you explain," I said. "And everything stays between you and me. No Roberto, I promise."

Gustavo sighed and pulled his phone from his pocket. He tapped at it and handed it to me. "This is from yesterday."

On the screen was a text conversation. He had written: *Where are you Lil? Help me. I'm beside myself with worry.*

Please to not worry, the reply said. *I have met someone.*

"Please to not worry?" I said, looking up at him.

"Typo," Gustavo said. "Her English is perfect."

"So she's having an affair?"

"I guess so. Totally blindsided me."

"I'm going to call this in, Gustavo. I really don't like it."

"No, Vince. I don't want the police rousting her out of some hotel. No way."

"I—"

"You promised me."

"That was about Roberto."

"Take him home," Gustavo said. "I'm out of here in half an hour. And leave this alone. I can handle it, one way or the other."

Gustavo Arguelles is about five-five and is maybe two-thirds my weight. He's not an imposing guy. But he stood up from behind his desk and gave me a look that I'd seen before, back when I was a cop, on much tougher guys. The look right before they lose it that says: *Get out of my face.*

"Call me if you change your mind," I said, but I'd pushed him enough for now. If Lilian Arguelles had run off with some dickhead Romeo, I could find out on my own. I had the tools and the skills. I just wouldn't say anything to Gustavo. And I would definitely not say anything to Barbara, unless I wanted all hell to break loose.

*

"You're not going anywhere, Vince. And certainly not with our child." Barbara was carrying Royal in one arm and was trying to operate the blender with the other hand. The top had come off, and the machine was spraying gloppy red beetroot-and-fish-oil goo all over the counter and the walls. The kitchen looked like a set from a slasher movie. Royal had his mouth open so wide that I could see his tonsils, and his screaming was louder than the racket from the blender's blades.

"Just for a couple of days," I said. I had to yell, but my wife had already stopped listening. She said nothing and stomped off with the baby into his nursery. I grabbed a roll of paper towels and began to dab up blotches of Barbara's so-called health drink. Halfway through cleaning up the mess I decided to take a break for my own health drink, and I got a cold Negra Modelo out of the fridge. Our little discussion hadn't gone so well.

I had been on the phone and the computer since we'd returned from the hospital. Roberto had logged me in to his parents' Verizon account, and I'd gone back several months and had cross-referenced a few numbers, but I hadn't turned up anything suspicious. I could have had Roberto go through the family computer, but Lilian never used it, and as far as her son knew, she didn't even have an email account. I hadn't directly let on to Roberto about Lilian's possible romance because I'd promised Gustavo that I wouldn't, but my young friend no doubt knew what I was doing—he'd been helping me go through the digital equivalent of people's sock drawers since he was thirteen. Finally, I had called Bobby Bove at the Indian River County Sheriff's office and had asked a favor. Half an hour later Bobby emailed me the location records for Lilian's cellphone, which had made it as far south as Hialeah on Sunday, stayed the night, and then moved on through southernmost Florida and the Keys until the signal had abruptly terminated on Monday afternoon. The last known location was at an address in Key West on the Palm Avenue Causeway called Charter Boat Row. A quick look on the satellite map showed a marina full of boats. I had decided that it was time for a road trip.

I would take Royal with me, which might be good anyway, because this was Barbara's exam week at nursing school and she could concentrate better without the guys around. I would pack a load of frozen breast milk in a cooler. I'd tell her that the boys were going to have a little one-on-one time, no big deal. I had everything worked out perfectly, and it had all made complete sense until Barbara had come home, and I'd laid out the plan, and she had asked: *OK, Vince. Exactly what is going on here?*

I'd swallowed hard and told her about Lilian, and about the text that Gustavo had shown me. I wasn't going to lie to my wife, not even if all hell broke loose, which of course it did. You have to allow some hell to break loose now and then if you're going to be married.

You promised that you would retire, she'd said. *For the baby's sake. No more investigating. You almost got us all killed that time, and you promised me, and now you want to take a nine-month-old child with you to the Keys on some case?*

This is Lilian, I'd said. *Not just some case. Roberto's mother.*

Roberto is not your son, Barbara had said. *Royal is your son.*

I would have kept up my side of the argument, but she was right. In fact, she was more than right. I wasn't at all convinced that I would find Lilian Arguelles shacked up in a hotel, drinking champagne and running around in the sweet altogether with some loser. I had no idea what was going on, and until I did it would be foolish to have Royal anywhere near me.

It took me fifteen more minutes to finish cleaning up the mess from the blender. The house had gone silent by the time that I was done. I crept down the hall and peered through the partially open door to the baby's room. The shades were open, and the dying light of the early evening gently illuminated their motionless forms on the cot next to his crib. Barbara had one arm around Royal, who was asleep at her breast. A few strands of blonde hair were draped over her open mouth, and they fluttered each time she exhaled. Goddamn—I had a beautiful family. I gently closed the door and returned to the kitchen.

Between the demands of my physical therapy, Barbara's nursing school schedule, and Royal's needs, there wasn't much time left over for her and me. In fact, there was almost no time at all for just the two of us. Barbara and I had only been together for a few months before the baby was born. We didn't yet have the tightly knit intimacy of long-married couples, and you had to watch out, or the yarn could quickly come unraveled. I would need to do something about that, or one of these days I might be getting a text, too.

Please to not worry, Vince. I have met someone.

WEDNESDAY

MEGAN, MY PHYSICAL THERAPIST, always ended our routine with a massage, and today she had gone on for longer than the customary ten minutes. She mostly worked on my back, and then went deep into the muscles of my left leg. The left side was my bad side. I still had a noticeable limp, which my wife had dubbed the Vinny Shuffle.

"Are you going to charge me extra for this?" I asked her, my face buried in a padded ring. "Or maybe you just can't keep your hands off me?"

"Oh yeah, you hairy old guys are so hot."

I chuckled into the pillow. Megan was a good twenty years younger than me and was a looker, with vivid red hair that she usually tied up behind her head. She was muscular but still slender, and she had a bright, ready smile that defused her sometimes aggressive attitude. A physical therapist is supposed to be something of a drill sergeant if they are going to be effective, and in my case Megan had worked miracles. Nine months ago I could barely walk. After she'd relocated to Vero Beach from Vermont and joined the practice, she had insisted on being assigned to me as soon as she had learned that I was a fellow Vermonter. She had pushed me hard. If I were thirty-two and not fifty-two, I might be in even bigger trouble with Barbara.

"You're wicked tense, Vince."

"I have a lot on my mind," I said. Barbara had slept the whole previous night with the baby. We'd hardly spoken during the few minutes between coffee and when she'd left for her nursing classes.

"Like what?"

"You know how some dogs need a job? Like herding sheep, or retrieving tennis balls?"

"You wish you were back at work?" She was digging hard into the leg, and I almost cried out.

"I like being a father. And it's OK being at home," I said. "But, yeah. You can only do so many crossword puzzles."

"Why did you retire? You're what, fifty?"

"Barbara insisted, after I got shot. You can get killed in my profession. I almost did."

"Not doing the work that you love will kill you, too," Megan said. "It just takes longer."

She was right, and I knew it. I missed my job. Barbara had suggested that I use my retirement to write a how-to book for aspiring private investigators, insisting that "everyone has a book in them". I'd given it a try and had filled up part of a notebook, but all that I'd come up with so far was a tangled mess of random observations that had little or nothing to do with investigating and that no editor would ever be able to shape into something publishable or even readable. I called it *Tanzi's Tips*.

Tanzi's Tip #1: Some people will never have a book in them, unless they eat one.

I had turned my head sideways and was watching a flat-screen television suspended over a row of exercise machines. The news was on, from a Miami station. A group of cops and EMTs were loading a shrouded body into an ambulance, and a heavily made-up blonde woman was interviewing a plainclothes policeman. I recognized him: Talbot Heffernan, a pink-faced, patrician-looking detective lieutenant I'd once met when I had retrieved a teenaged runaway from a crack house in West Dade and hauled her back to Vero a couple of years ago. *The victim's name will be released shortly,* Heffernan was saying to the reporter. *After the family is notified.*

We understand that it was a shootout? The reporter said. *Did the victim shoot back?*

We can't comment on that, Heffernan said. He was dressed in a lime-green blazer, chinos and boat shoes, and he looked more like a prep school teacher than a cop.

The woman turned away from the lieutenant and addressed the camera as he walked away.

Jack, I'm outside of the Hacienda Club in Coral Gables, as you can see. Just hours ago a man was gunned down in his car outside the entrance. The police haven't officially released the name of the victim, but he was identified by several onlookers. He's a well-known figure in real estate in these parts. We believe that the deceased man is Raimundo Pimentel.

Raimundo Pimentel? I slowly rose from the massage table and swung my legs off the side.

"Vince?" Megan said, "I'm not done."

"I have to go," I said, as I collected my watch and my wallet. "I know that guy."

I didn't really know Raimundo Pimentel, any more than what everybody else knew about him. He was a real estate developer, and his net worth was in the many millions. But Pimentel hadn't gotten his start in real estate. He had come over with the first wave of refugees after Castro, and the word was that he'd run the *bolitas* numbers racket back in the days before Powerball. The Cubans were addicted to the game, and the odds were long unless you were the house, which happened to be the Pimentel house.

I also knew that Pimentel had a Vero Beach connection. His daughter lived here, although she seldom spoke to him. I had learned this from his grandson.

Roberto.

*

Gustavo Arguelles wasn't in, the receptionist said. He'd gone home sick an hour ago.

But he wasn't at home, as I found out when I arrived at his house ten minutes later. Nor was he answering his phone. I lifted the fake rock on the side of their porch that held a spare key and let myself in. No one was inside, and Gustavo's car wasn't in the garage.

I hadn't done any real investigating in well over a year. I didn't know where to begin. My present life was focused on being a good father and husband, and on getting my strength back. But Barbara was at school, Royal was at the sitter's, and it was Wednesday, which was my day off. Wednesday mornings were my physical therapy appointment, then I grocery shopped, and then I either went for a beach walk, or if the weather was bad, I stayed home and knit. I was partway through a sweater for my sister up North, my most ambitious project so far, and I figured it would be finished in no more than three years at the pace that I was going.

I needed to do what any experienced investigator would do: *Start with what you know.*

Lilian Arguelles was missing, last seen in the Keys, presumably with a boyfriend.

Gustavo Arguelles had gone home sick, but now he wasn't home.

Raimundo Pimentel was deceased, and he'd died the hard way.

Royal was all set until I picked him up at five. It was just before ten o'clock, so I had seven hours free. I took my phone from my pocket and called Sonny Burrows from Gustavo and Lilian's kitchen.

"Yo," he answered.

"How long does it take to fly to Key West and back?"

"Two hours each way, if I push it. We goin' fishing?"

"Sort of," I said. "Two friends disappeared."

There was a silence. "Does Barbara know what you're doing?"

"Not yet. No need."

"I can't be an accessory to that," he said. "I already done my time."

Sonny and Barbara didn't exactly get along. In fact, they could barely tolerate being in the same room together. It wasn't that Sonny had once been Vero's biggest cocaine dealer, now-reformed, nor was Barbara jealous over our unlikely friendship. They just didn't like each other—period.

"You're my only friend with an airplane," I said.

"I'm already at the airport. I was going to fly up to Sanford to see my little sister."

"Can you do this for me?"

"Long as you're paying for the fuel," he said. "Plus hush money, if your woman asks me about this."

"If you fly fast enough, she'll never know."

Sonny laughed. "Your wife? That woman already knows what you did *tomorrow*."

∗

The Vero Beach Municipal Airport used to buzz like a bee-filled orange grove in full blossom back in the days when the Piper Aircraft company produced thousands of planes each year at the factory next door. But the company had changed hands so many times and had weathered so many recessions that sales had dwindled to a trickle. An Indonesian sultan now owned it, and the few hundred locals who still worked there held their breath and hoped that their jobs wouldn't fly off into the sunset. In the meantime corporate jets whisked in and out of the airport all day, ferrying the One Percent in from points north to their estates out on the barrier island. The last thirty years had brought a crazy amount of wealth into Vero, and the Maseratis were starting to outnumber the Mazdas. Fortunately the rich folks lived in gated communities, which kept them at a safe distance from us normal, civilized people.

We were airborne not long after I had parked my car in the general aviation lot. Sonny's venerable 1964 Piper Comanche had a lot of hours on it but was well maintained, with a big, noisy Lycoming engine that made it impossible for us to talk to each other in the cockpit without using the headsets. Somehow Sonny had kept control of the plane even though it had a dubious past; it had gathered dust in a DEA hangar while he had served two felony-possession stretches over at Okeechobee Correctional. Technically, it belonged to his sister Myra who was a dispatcher at the Sheriff's office, although as far as I knew Myra had never flown in the aircraft, nor could she even squeeze through the cockpit door, as she weighed twice what her brother did, and Sonny was no shrinking violet.

He kept the cruising speed at about one hundred twenty knots and flew us south along the coast before turning southwest over the Everglades. Piloting small planes around Florida has always struck me as a mindless, expensive hobby—I mean, the whole interior of the state was basically the same topography: ranches, groves, shallow lakes, and swamps. You would think that the novelty would wear off after a while, but don't bother mentioning that to Sonny. I tried, through the headphones, and he gestured at the knitting project in my lap and laughed. He had a point; my own hobby wasn't exactly living on the edge, and half of the things that I had knit were probably languishing in people's closets.

But knitting was good for my dexterity, according to Megan, and it allowed me to think without distraction. And what I was currently thinking about was not pleasant. I smelled big trouble in the Arguelles family, and it felt like more than just a runaway wife and a jilted husband. The timing of Raimundo Pimentel's shooting death was unnerving. Even though I knew nothing concrete, I was tempted to check in with the police despite what I'd said to Gustavo. That would be the smart thing to do, promise or no promise. I would call Detective Lieutenant Heffernan in Coral Gables after we landed, I would find out who had been assigned to the Pimentel shooting, and I would try to get myself in the loop. Maybe I could pull it off without exposing Gustavo's and Lilian's dirty laundry, although that mattered less to me now, as I had been calling and texting both of them nonstop with no response, which was ratcheting up my blood pressure.

On cue, my phone buzzed in my pocket with a text from Gustavo.

Please take care of Roberto, OK?
Can't, I wrote back. *I'm in Sonny's plane. Where are you?*
Go home. Pick him up from school and keep him. It might be a couple days.
Gustavo, what the hell is going on? I saw the news about Lilian's father.
Under control, he sent. *Just get him. Please. Por favor, Vince.*

Got you covered, I sent back. But the truth was—I didn't. I was on the way to Key West, to locate his wife. And now Gustavo was worried about Roberto, too? Damn. What was I supposed to do about that?

I turned to watch my friend at the controls. He wore gold-framed Ray-Bans that were the only decoration on his shaved, walnut-colored head except for an earring in the shape of a peace sign. Sonny looked younger than his forty-three years, which was a miracle considering his former lifestyle, but he was nothing if not a survivor. "We have to turn around," I said through the microphone on my headset.

"No way," he said. "Not until I get my conch fritters from Sloppy Joe's."

I had promised Sonny a lunch at the iconic Key West hangout. "It's Roberto. His dad just texted. He wants me to pick him up from school."

"What time?"

"He has baseball until four thirty."

"No problem," Sonny said over the crackle of the headphones. He pushed the throttle forward, making the engine throb even louder as the plane picked up speed. "We can make that. This old bitch is faster than she looks. And I'm hungry."

*

The only taxi left at the Key West International Airport was a dented van that was painted nail-polish pink. You could rent a tandem bicycle for less, but I didn't think I could manage it with my bad leg, and Sonny wasn't about to pedal for both of us. We chose the van and ignored the nonstop commentary from the driver, a mature blonde who reeked of cigarettes and was dressed in a clinging blue tank top that would have looked considerably better on her granddaughter. A small dog sat on the seat next to her, yapping at Sonny whenever the driver paused to cough. The woman drove us past the beaches and low-rise condos along South Roosevelt Boulevard, which gave way to rows of small concrete-block houses as we crossed the island from south to north. I asked her to drop me off on the Palm Avenue Causeway, the last location where Lilian's phone had registered a signal. The causeway fronted on the Garrison Bight, one of Key West's principal harbors that sheltered a mix of houseboats, sportfishing charters, luxury yachts and anything else that would float. Even though I was working, I couldn't help but unwind a little as the day got prettier and prettier. If you enjoyed the sun, the breeze, the water, and oh yes, the rum, Key West was one of the most *chill* places on the planet, as Roberto would say.

Sonny continued on with the taxi, and the plan was that he would wait for me at the restaurant while I poked around on the docks. If I was going to get anything done, I would have to work fast. I had a two-hour window of time on the island if we were going to fly back in time to pick up Roberto, grab Royal at the sitter's, and slip back into my house before anyone was the wiser.

Charter Boat Row's faded blue sign said "historic" on it, but the marina looked like any other collection of boats moored to a network of aluminum and concrete docks. Perhaps it was historic because Ernest Hemingway had tied up there once. In Key West there are little brass placards stationed about every ten feet that commemorate the locations where Hemingway lived, wrote his novels, occupied a barstool, sneezed, cleared his throat, or paused to clip his fingernails. I found a low, gray-painted structure that was flanked by a Gatorade machine, a jumble of marine equipment, and a bait cooler, and I knocked at the threshold of an open door. A shirtless, middle-aged guy was inside, bent over a long wooden table and working on something. His underwear was riding up above the back of his shorts, not quite high enough to cover an unwelcome display of plumber butt.

He turned when he heard the knock, holding a knife and showing a smear of blood across his ample stomach. "Yeah?"

I wiggled a dog-eared business card out of my wallet and handed it to him. It had been a long time since I'd done that, and it felt strange. "I'm a private investigator from Vero Beach. Looking for a woman from there. She was here on Sunday."

"A lot of people were here on Sunday," he said. I saw a fat grouper on the filleting table behind him, half cut-up and still sleek from the salt water.

"She may have left on a boat," I said.

The guy took a look at my card and handed it back. "Sorry, man. Can't help you."

"Five-oh, maybe a hundred pounds, mid-forties, dark hair. She's Cuban American. She might not have left willingly."

"I still can't help. Lots of people come by here. I don't pay much attention."

"Mind if I scout around?"

"Whatever," he said. He turned back to his fish and resumed his work with the knife.

I walked out of the small building and into the bright midday sun. About thirty boats were currently at the marina, and there were several empty slips. Even if this was the right address, anyone who might have seen Lilian could now be out for the day, or just gone and not coming back—boaters came and went. I knocked on the doors of several of the houseboats, where I figured I'd find the more permanent residents, but I only succeeded in talking to one cellophane-skinned old guy who looked to be about a hundred and thought that I was his son. The whole exercise was a long shot, especially because it was just me and not a group of cops canvassing the waterfront with the potential threat of warrants and subpoenas.

What I needed was help—strength in numbers. It took manpower to knock on every single door until some unlikely person admitted to having seen something. All of this was yet another reason for me to call Lieutenant Heffernan, and despite what Gustavo had asked, I was getting close to going against his wishes. If Roberto's mother was at risk, all promises were on hold.

I left the dock and began to walk west along the causeway toward town. Barbara and I had spent several months here back when we first knew each other, before I'd suffered my accident. Walking around Old Town had been one of my favorite things to do, and I decided that I would hoof it to Sloppy Joe's, bad leg or not. I turned west onto Eaton Street, passing rows of clapboarded conch houses that reminded me of my native Vermont, although the thin-walled, uninsulated structures were built for the tropics, not the insanely cold climate where I had grown up. I was thinking about Roberto, and I was increasingly worried. The situation with his parents smelled fishier than the dead grouper on the cutting table. I decided that I would hustle to the restaurant, collect Sonny, grab a bag of fritters to go, and get the hell back to the airport. It had become clear to me that this trip was a dead end that would cost me a few hundred bucks worth of aviation fuel with nothing to show for it.

A blacked-out minivan pulled alongside me as I walked, and a man lowered the passenger-side window. He wore sunglasses, with a coffee-brown complexion and short, dark hair underneath a white rapper cap. I couldn't see past him to the driver, because Rapper-Cap was humongous enough to be blocking the view. I guessed that he wasn't a goodwill ambassador from the Tourist Bureau. He looked like professional muscle, and I absent-mindedly patted my side for the gun that I hadn't bothered to bring.

"Need a lift there, bud?" he said. I noticed a slight Latino accent.

"Just going to Sloppy Joe's. A few more blocks."

"You walk funny, bud." He wasn't smiling.

"I hurt my foot kicking somebody's ass," I said.

The man leaned forward, and I got a glimpse of his partner. The driver was also Latino, and was bearded, with a wreath of black hair around the back of his head that ended in a single, oily braid. The passenger must have been the little brother, because the driver looked like three people packed into one T-shirt.

"You're coming with us," the passenger said. "You gonna go peaceful?"

"No," I said.

He raised his hand from inside the car, and I flinched. Oh shit. I was going to get shot—again. Even if I had been carrying, he was too fast; I watched him pull the trigger, and I prepared to die, and then I realized that that wasn't going to happen because he wasn't holding a gun. He held a yellow Taser C2, and the twin electrode darts were headed for my chest with fifty thousand volts.

Back when I was a deputy, we all had to endure a Taser hit as part of our training, and it sucked. It didn't actually cause pain; you just felt like you were dead for a split-second, and then you lay helpless wherever you fell, tingling, and with your muscles bound up harder than a Genoa salami.

The two big guys loaded me into their van and one of them jabbed a hypodermic needle into my still-paralyzed thigh. By the time the Taser's effect wore off I was already halfway to Loopy Land. At least I wasn't dead, I thought, as everything slid out of focus.

*

My new amigos had dumped me in a parking lot next to the White Street Substation, behind a row of white rental trucks. My head was swimming and I felt like throwing up, but I was able to dislodge my phone from the pocket of my trousers and dial Sonny. The cellphone felt malleable in my hand like a damp sponge.

"Where are you, man? I been callin' your ass for an hour."

"Get a taxi and pick me up. I got mugged."

"What?"

"A couple of goons hit me with a Taser," I said. "Then they shot me up with something. I'm guessing it was ketamine. It's like I'm drunk out of my gourd."

"Ain't that the date rape drug?"

"Yeah," I said. "But I believe that my virginity is still intact."

16

I gave Sonny the address, and he pulled up ten minutes later in the exact same pink taxi that had taken us in from the airport. Granny Tank Top leaned out the window. "You're not going to throw up in my car, are you?" I got in the back without answering, and sat next to Sonny.

"Hospital," he said to the driver.

"Airport," I corrected.

"You look like you died, man," Sonny said.

"And you look fabulous. But that's probably the ketamine talking."

"So what the fuck was this all about?"

"Hey, no profanity in here," the driver said, glowering at us in the rearview mirror.

"Not a goddamn—I mean—gosh darn clue," I said to Sonny. "I'm guessing it was somebody trying to scare me off."

"You find out anything on the docks?"

"Nope. But I must have stirred the pot."

"Time to call the man," Sonny said. "You just got assaulted. That's a felony."

"Time to go home and take care of business," I said. "And then we'll do some assaulting of our own."

*

The drug had pretty much worn off by the time we landed in Vero Beach, and it had been replaced by a skull-crushing headache. Sonny offered me something from his shade tree pharmacy, but I'd already had a dalliance with painkillers a couple years back, and they were so addictive that I was now afraid to pop even a Tylenol. I would just sweat this one out.

I found Roberto outside his school, gym bag in hand. I hustled him into the car and sped off to Mrs. LaBombard's, back on the mainland on Old Dixie Highway, where we collected Royal. It was almost six PM, and Mrs. LaBombard was about to give me her punctuality lecture, but I made a quick apology, extracted Barbara's check along with an extra twenty out of my wallet, dropped them on her hall table, and ran. Barbara would be home in ten minutes unless she stopped for something, and I was determined to get to the house before her, even if I broke every traffic law to do it.

We pulled into the driveway, and I opened the garage door with the remote. Whew. No Yukon. Roberto helped me with Royal, hastily stashing him in his playpen, while I got him a Coke and poured myself a tumbler of water from the refrigerator door. We sat down in the living room as if we'd been there all afternoon. Ten seconds after we took our seats the front door opened, and Barbara came in with a grocery bag, which she put down on the kitchen counter.

"When did you get home?"

"Oh, a while ago," I said.

"Well I hope it wasn't too long ago," Barbara said. "You left the garage door open, and your car is still running."

"Jeezum crow," I said, shaking my head while Roberto smiled.

"I'll go turn it off," Roberto said. He was still a few months away from getting his license, but he took every opportunity that he was offered to sit at the wheel, and I indulged him whenever I could. Roberto went out the kitchen door, and Barbara scooped up Royal from his playpen where he had been happily gnawing on a blue plastic elephant.

"Roberto is going to stay the night," I said. "Something came up with his folks."

"His mother's still gone?" she asked. She was stroking Royal's soft cheek while she held him, and he inserted a chubby hand into her mouth.

"Both of them are gone."

"What's going on?" She was paying attention now.

"Sit down," I said.

"Just get it over with," she said, standing. "You're going to investigate."

"Yes. It may be a couple of days. I'll involve the police at some point."

"Why not now? You're still an invalid, for God's sake. You can barely function." Her voice was rising as her face reddened.

"I thought I was doing pretty well."

"Pretty well?" She was yelling. "You took a bullet to the head, Vince. You limp, you slur your words, and you forget things all the time. You're not up to it, and you'll put us all in danger."

"Roberto could be in danger—"

"And so you bring him into our house? Are you stupid or something?"

My head was throbbing even worse than before. Barbara's harsh words had lit my fuse, and the spark was burning just inches from the powder keg. I seldom lose my temper, but getting tasered, and drugged, and flying for four hours, and then busting my ass to get everybody collected and home safe just to be reamed out by my wife was too much for one day.

"Shut up, Barbara."

"What did you just say?"

"I said that's enough."

"What you said was shut up."

"That's right," I said. "You're correct."

Roberto came back into the house at that moment and froze in the kitchen, keys in hand.

"You and I are going to stay at your place," I said to him. "I'll pack a few things."

Barbara turned on her heel and disappeared into the nursery with the baby.

"I can stay at the house by myself," Roberto said. "You don't—"

"Wait in the car." I took a small suitcase from a closet and wheeled it down the hall to our bedroom. Three pairs of socks, some underwear, a few shirts, some trousers, something to sleep in, my knitting bag, and my toilet kit. I tossed in a fat paperback Dostoevsky novel that Sonny had lent me, and then reached under the bed and pulled out the gun case. I unlocked it and removed my Glock, a couple of extra clips, two boxes of ammo, and my waistband holster. It had been a while since I had handled a firearm, and the ugly black automatic felt heavier than I remembered.

I zipped it into a side compartment of my knitting bag and quietly hoped that it would be staying right there. The part that had upset me the most about my argument with Barbara was that she had a point. I had no business investigating anything, much less packing a gun. In my present condition I was more likely to shoot off a toe than take out some bad guy. That knowledge didn't make me any less angry, although I knew that there was nothing that I could do about it, because I would just make it worse.

Tanzi's Tip #2: Whoever said: "Don't get mad, get even," couldn't have been married. At least not for long.

*

Eighteen pages into *Crime and Punishment* I already knew that Raskolnikov was toast, and I wasn't going to wade through the next five hundred pages to find out why. Sonny was crazy about the Russians, but to me they were long-winded and depressing. I had enough on my plate without having to read about someone else's troubles.

Roberto had gone to bed, but not to sleep—I could see the light coming from under his bedroom door. I had told him about his grandfather, and we had had a long conversation about the Pimentel family. Roberto had seemed to shrug off the news of Raimundo Pimentel's death, but I knew that it would reverberate for a long time. He told me that he never saw any of his mother's family except for Susanna, his aunt, although he was aware that he had two bachelor uncles who were involved in the family real estate business. The much more immediate concern for him was that his mother had taken off, and his father was now out looking for her, and neither he nor I knew any more than that. In addition to my lack of knowledge, I had my wife telling me that I wasn't capable of doing anything about it, and two thugs threatening to break my legs if I did.

I don't usually care much about the *why*, like why Raskolnikov had killed the pawnbroker; my job as an investigator had been about uncovering the rest of it—the who, where, how, and so on. The why was for the courts. But in the case of Lilian's disappearance I was no longer buying what I had been fed about the why. No way would she take off with some guy. And I doubted that Gustavo believed it, either. A man usually knows when his wife's not happy. Just ask yours truly.

My body ached and my head still hurt from the combination of the Taser, the ketamine injection, and Barbara's stinging but accurate words. I doubted that I would get much sleep, especially since I had chosen to bed down on the Arguelles' too-short family room sofa. Just before I finally dozed off I had a moment of clarity, like the way the sun flashes just before it disappears into the water on a Key West sunset:

I am too old for this shit.

Tomorrow I would call the Coral Gables cops, and I would also drop in on Bobby Bove at the Indian River Sheriff's office. My task, for now, was to stick close to Roberto and make sure that he didn't disappear, too. That much I figured I could handle.

THURSDAY

ABOUT THE ONLY THING THAT I don't like about Glory's convertible is that if you drop something between the seat and the center console, it's gone. You are never going to see it again, even if you squeeze the bejeezus out of your hand trying to reach in there, and then dig around with a kitchen knife, or a coat hanger, or a chop stick (which will inevitably snap in two, leaving even more crap down there) and then move the seat forward and backward while feeling around underneath, only to come up with a half-chewed, rancid apple slice that had somehow worked its way into that dead zone from Royal's car seat. The space was the Bermuda Triangle of BMWs. But the spare key to Roberto's place had fallen in there somewhere, so here I was sitting in his driveway after having driven him to school, unable to enter the Arguelles house.

Of course, I could break in. That had been my specialty for years when I was investigating, and even back when I was a deputy. Shut out of your car? Call Vince. Need to investigate somewhere you might not be welcome? Give me two minutes while I do the lock. My talent had ultimately gotten me fired from the Sheriff's office after I'd blown a murder case by "discovering" a murder weapon via a warrant-free search, and the perp had walked after my cover story fell apart under cross examination. I had been a deputy long enough to be allowed to retire, but the lesson had been learned, and these days I used my lock-picking skills judiciously, if at all.

I had the right tool in my kit at home. Barbara hadn't called, or texted, and by now she would be in school. She would have made arrangements for Royal's care, probably with Mrs. LaBombard. I was in no hurry to reconcile, partly because I felt physically even worse than I had on the previous evening, and partly because I had some things to attend to before I turned myself in to the Warden, as Sonny called her, and reported for daddy-duty. I had a nine o'clock with Bobby Bove, and I figured that we'd call Coral Gables from his office.

I drove over to my own house and opened the garage. Hanging on the wall was a mechanical grabber with a flexible shaft and a tiny LED light that helped you see where you were going if you dropped a nut or bolt deep into an engine. I worked the device into the space next to the seat and came up with something: a credit card. I put the card on the seat next to me and tried again. This time I found the keys, and I pocketed them. I had no idea how long I would be staying at Roberto's, but I decided that it might be wise to get an extra set made while I was downtown.

I didn't remember losing a credit card, and I didn't recognize the bank. And then I noticed the name: Megan Rumsford. My physical therapist? What was her card doing here? Megan's office complex was not far from the Sheriff's. I would return it to her after I saw Bobby.

*

Bobby Bove peeled a tangerine over his wastebasket while we listened to Detective Lieutenant Talbot Heffernan talk via the speakerphone. Bobby silently offered me a slice, but I shook my head. I hadn't eaten anything since I'd been roughed up the day before, and I still wasn't hungry.

"The Pimentels moved over here from Hialeah around fifteen years ago," Heffernan said. "The old man ran the *bolitas* racket back in the day, and we pretty much looked the other way, although the game was fixed, not to mention illegal, but nobody really gave a shit unless somebody killed someone."

"How often did that happen?" Bobby asked.

"There was the occasional turf war," Heffernan said. "And he wasn't just doing the numbers game—his runners did some loan sharking on the side. Enough for him to buy two high-end shopping centers over here by the beach. He owns at least a dozen more of them, scattered around Dade."

"Who were his enemies?" Bobby said to the phone.

"That's what we're trying to find out," Heffernan said. "He's been legit for a while now. It looked like a hit, and maybe it was just an old score being settled. So who's the guy with you, Bobby?"

"Tal, it's Vince Tanzi," I said, leaning over the phone. "We met a couple years ago."

"I remember," he said. "That crack house on Sunset. You were after a runaway."

"Right. I'm friends with Pimentel's grandson—his mother is Pimentel's daughter. They live up here in Vero. The mother took off a couple of days ago, and his dad is gone now, too. Bobby is going to put out a missing persons, from here. But I saw the shooting news on TV, and I wondered about the connection."

"What does the daughter do?"

"She's a technician at the medical center. The husband is there, too, in accounting. Nice, stable people."

"There's a daughter down here, and two sons," Heffernan said. "I don't know much about the daughter up there."

"She doesn't get along with the family. Just her sister, Susanna."

"I went out to see Susanna yesterday. She wasn't too cooperative," the lieutenant said.

"How so?" Bobby asked.

"She wouldn't let me in," Heffernan said. "Said she never spoke to the old man, or the brothers. Slammed the door in my face."

"I hope you didn't get your feelings hurt," Bobby said, as he winked at me.

"Yeah, I already went to my shrink," Heffernan said. "He's going to help me work through it."

"What about the sons?" I asked.

"Tough nuts, both of them," Heffernan said. "Nobody showed any emotion, let alone grief. Javier and Segundo. I know the younger one—he's a lawyer."

"We'll send you the info on the missing couple," Bobby said. "Vince was in the Keys yesterday, looking for the woman. He got himself tasered by two big guys in a black van. It sounded like somebody didn't want him looking around."

"When you say big guys, how big?" Heffernan said.

"Like, somewhere between a Dolphins linebacker and a commercial freezer," I said. "I didn't get a plate number. Late-model minivan with all the chrome blacked out. I'm pretty sure they were Latino, and one of them had this little braid in the back."

"That sounds like the Iturbe brothers," Heffernan said. "Marielito gangbangers from Hialeah. They just got out of Dade Correctional last week. They worked for the Pimentels, collecting rents, and they got rough with one of the tenants. We've been looking for them since the shooting."

"OK, keep us in the loop," Bobby said, and he hung up. He turned back to me. "Your friends might be in a situation. You want us to provide security for the boy?"

"I got it," I said. "Thanks for taking this on. I need to go be a househusband."

"How's that working out, by the way?"

"Not so great. I'm currently living in exile."

"You fucked up?"

"Sort of," I said. "I'm sleeping on the kid's couch."

"Jeesh. You want to go get drunk and chase girls?" Bobby Bove was still single, even though he was near retirement age. "You probably couldn't make it any worse, right?"

"Oh yes I could," I said.

*

"Omigod, I've been looking for that everywhere!" Megan took the credit card from my hand and stared at it like it was a winning lottery ticket. "Where did you find this?"

"In my car, under the seat," I said. "How did it get there?"

"Barbara," she said.

"My wife?"

"Yes. She gave me a ride from the Treasure Coast Club last week. It must have fallen out of my pocket."

"You know Barbara?"

"I take her Pilates class," Megan said. She was smiling broadly. "I can't tell you how awesome this is. I really didn't want to go through the hassle of replacing it."

"She gave you a ride?"

"She was driving your car. She said that you guys swap vehicles when you take your trash to the dump. My Jeep died in the parking lot, and I had to get back to work. Oh, thank you Vince, you're such a boss!"

"You're welcome," I said.

"Is everything OK?"

"I guess so."

"You look awful."

"People keep saying that," I said. "I can't hide these things from you, can I?"

"No, you can't," she said. "Come on, confess. The full story."

We were standing in the lobby of the Seminole Rehabilitation Associates building, flanked by the receptionist's desk and a half a dozen clients in the waiting room in various states of disrepair. Megan took me by the arm and led me through a door to her workroom.

"Shirt off," she said. "Your neck and torso are all tightened up. I need to see what's causing this."

I removed my shirt, and she ran her hands across my chest. "I don't get it. You're like a brick. What did you do to yourself?"

"I got tasered by somebody," I said. "It makes you feel like you've been mummified."

"Tasered? How did that happen?"

"Work-related injury," I said.

"I thought that you were retired."

"Temporarily back on the job," I said. "I need to help out some friends."

Megan pointed to her massage table. "Pants off, dude. Lie down. I'm going to work out those kinks. You're a stress mess, and my next appointment just canceled, so you're getting a freebie today. And I want you back here tomorrow, too."

She started by working on my neck, and as she dug her fingers deep into the tendons and muscles, I began to float off into the ozone. It wasn't just Megan's fabulous technique—it was because I trusted her, and I had worked with her long enough that I completely gave myself up to her talents. The relationship was not unlike having a lover, although Megan was a professional and I was a married man who knew where the lines were drawn. Just relax, I told myself. She knows what she's doing. You're safe.

"It's not just the Taser thing, is it?" Megan asked, as she began to work her hands down my spine to my lower back.

"Beg pardon?" I said, my words muffled by the pillow on her massage table.

"Something else is happening. You're very upset."

"Yeah, I guess," I managed to say between grunts.

"Tell me about it," she said, making her hands stop. She rested them at my sides, and I could fell the warmth of her skin from the friction.

"Barbara. You two really know each other? You never said so."

"She and I kind of trade. She lets me take free classes, and I do her bodywork."

"Oh."

"Oh what?" Megan said. "What's going on?"

"It's...what we were talking about yesterday. I'm involved in an investigation. Not because I necessarily want to. It's for some very important friends. Barbara doesn't like that, but I don't really have a choice."

"You always have a choice," Megan said.

"You don't understand."

Megan stopped the massage again and leaned her face down to where her lips were right behind my ears. I could feel the warmth of her breath, and for a second I wondered—what the heck was she doing?

"Yes, I do understand, Vince," she said, in a half-whisper.

I waited for her to resume the massage, but it didn't happen. She was expecting me to say something in response. Nothing was going to continue until I spoke.

"I probably ought to get going," I said.

"Then go." She stood up and walked out of the therapy room, closing the door behind her while I dressed.

*

My appetite finally came back after not having eaten a thing since yesterday's breakfast before Sonny and I flew to the Keys. It was only eleven in the morning, but I knew what I wanted: red meat. That was a rare delicacy at home, since Barbara had all but banned it from the menu. I went to the reddest, meatiest joint I knew, which was Five Guys Burgers on the Highway 1 strip. The place was already full of people getting a jump on the lunch hour, and I stood in line trying to decide between the "little" cheeseburger and the regular one; I decided to go with the less humongous of the two. I was planning to take a beach walk afterward to clear out my thoughts, and hoped I could burn off some of the 550 calories, according to the nutritional information on the wall, plus another 526 calories from the "little" fries that I would inevitably order as an accompaniment to the burger. Sure, these things would eventually kill me, but when I go, I want to smell like a cheeseburger and not a bag of kelp chips.

I worked the phone while I sat at a table to enjoy my potentially fatal lunch. I had already texted both Gustavo and Lilian several times since daybreak, with no response from either of them. I was kind of annoyed that Gustavo would instruct me to take care of Roberto, and then wouldn't even text me back. Annoyed, and also worried. There was no reason that I could think of for him to ignore me. I'd given both of their cellphone numbers to Bobby Bove, who would try to locate them electronically and had promised to call me if he did.

I tried to compose an appropriate message to send to Barbara. You only get so many words in a text, so you have to make them count. I hadn't heard a thing from her, nor would I, as whenever we fought it was usually up to me to make the first overture toward reconciliation. No way would she back down first—that was just how she was, and I was used to it, even if I didn't like it.

Can we have a talk? I wrote.

If it begins with an apology, she sent right back.

Not necessary, I've already forgiven you. Haha. Needless to say, I didn't get a response. *Where's Royal?* I wrote.

At the sitter, she texted back, after a long wait.

I'll go get him. I just went 2 Sheriff's office. Turned it over 2 them. Not investigating this anymore.

That's not an apology, she sent back after another lengthy wait.

Bite me, I typed, and I came dangerously close to sending it. Instead, I slid the phone back into my pocket. Barbara was pushing my buttons, and I wasn't going to rise to it. I would pick up Royal, get in a beach walk, collect Roberto after school, and take some chicken wings out of the freezer when we got home. I would grill them over charcoal later tonight, and they would be crisp and succulent by the time that Barbara got home. Health-nut or not, my wife was powerless before my chicken wings, and I would thereby resume my role as her master and provider, and our argument would be quickly forgotten, right?

Tanzi's Tip #3: Women forget nothing.

Half an hour later I had Royal strapped to my back in an aluminum-framed carrier and we were crossing the warm sand of South Beach from the parking lot toward the water's edge. The surf was calm, and the afternoon was shaping up to be another hot one. By this time in May most of the snowbirds were back up North, and the natives had reestablished their presence on the beaches—real Floridians didn't go swimming during the "winter" months, but they were out today, and I passed several people who I knew. Royal and I trekked north to the Riomar golf course, which had sometimes surrendered big chunks of fairway to storms and erosion but had survived this year. Royal cooed and gurgled on my back while I navigated carefully across the sand, looking for the firmest path to support my uneven gait. The Vinny Shuffle had made beach-walking twice as much work, but I had 1,076 calories to burn off, my son was happy, and I began to relax for the first time in days. Megan's massage had helped, although she had thrown me something of a curveball at the end. I'm at the stage of life where young women look right through me as if I were invisible or potentially obscuring their view of a more suitable mate. I still have all of my hair, I'm not fat, I'm tall for an Italian American, and I keep myself well-groomed, but I have no illusions of being hit on by a thirty-something female, especially one who was pretty god-danged hot, like Megan Rumsford.

Nevertheless, it had been awkward when she'd said *yes—I understand*—and had practically kissed the back of my neck. That didn't feel like professional encouragement, or friendly affection.

It felt like a hit.

If that was what it was, I told myself, I should let it lie. Accept it as innocent, well-meaning flattery, and leave it at that. You're married, and oh-by-the-way, your marriage needs some work, and you are damn lucky to have what you have, so don't get distracted.

I could feel Royal getting antsy in the backpack, and I recognized the little leg-kicks that he does when he has a full diaper. I stopped near the surf's edge and put him down on the sand. There were extra diapers in the pocket of the pack. I had him wiped and changed in under a minute. If there was a diaper-changing event at the Olympics I just might take home a medal. I lifted him back into the pack and prepared to load it onto my back, when he pointed at a dark, oval-shaped object that was sitting in the shallow water a few feet from us.

The object was a deer cowrie. A spectacular, fist-sized shell, mottled with brown and white speckles across the top like a fawn. Cowries used to be fairly common back in the days when Vero Beach had been a sleepy Florida retreat, but they were rare now. I picked up the shell and handed it to Royal, who promptly put one end of it in his mouth.

When Glory and I had walked the beach, she would occasionally find a beautiful shell, and she would say that it was a gift from her dead relatives. Maybe this one was a gift from my deceased wife to my son. Glory and I had tried for children, but it hadn't been in the cards. The cowrie shell was Royal's now, and he cooed happily as he mouthed the salty brine from its surface while we made our way back to the car. I would find a safe place for it at the house, and I wouldn't allow it to become lost. I had lost enough already.

*

I was in the mommy line outside the entrance to St. Edwards School, waiting in a queue of vans and SUVs for Roberto. Royal was dozing in his car seat after polishing off a bottle of defrosted breast milk with the all the gusto of a parched tourist at Oktoberfest. I had my knitting gear out, but I kept making mistakes and was afraid that my cussing might wake the baby, so I put it back in the bag and surfed on the phone while we waited. There were several articles on the news about the Pimentel shooting, but they didn't tell me anything that I hadn't already heard from Tal Heffernan, except for one that had speculated about Pimentel's shady past and if the shooting was the start of a Cuban Mafia "war". I knew nothing about the mobster factions or rivalries in Miami-Dade County, except that with the Mariel boatlift of 1980 Fidel Castro had effectively emptied the jails of Cuba and had dumped twenty-five-hundred miscreants on our shores, to his eternal hilarity. There were lots of good folk who had come over during that exodus, but there was also a preponderance of bad actors and their offspring who had kept the Miami-Dade authorities busy ever since.

Roberto opened the door and got in the passenger seat before I'd even noticed him approaching. He didn't acknowledge me, and he wore the face of someone older than his years.

"I've got the Sheriff's people on it now," I said. "They know what to do. They'll find them."

"Whatever," he said.

"You holding up OK?"

"Barely," Roberto said. I had never heard him say anything like that. Roberto seldom expressed his emotions, not even to me.

"You want to go do something fun? Go for a swim?"

"I want my parents back," he said. "I'm scared, Vince."

Damn. I was scared, too, but agreeing with him wouldn't help.

"You drive," I said. That would distract him. "I'll pull over at the corner."

"Royal's in the back. Your wife would go crazy."

"You'll be fine."

"I don't think so," he said. "I—have a lot of homework."

"No problem then. We'll just go home. And your mom and dad are going to be OK, all right?"

"Yeah," Roberto said, just as Royal woke up and began to cry.

*

I had forgotten that Thursday nights were when Barbara taught Pilates at her club. So much for seducing her with my chicken wings. She had returned home from school, made a quick health shake, and had taken off again, barely acknowledging that I had moved back in with Roberto in tow. It appeared that we had a truce and that Roberto could stay, so I made up the sofa bed in my study for him before retiring to my own bed.

I lay awake wondering about what if any success Bobby Bove and Tal Heffernan might have had so far in finding Roberto's parents. I would check in with each of them in the morning. The longer these things went on, the more likely it was that they would end badly. I hoped that they had some good leads and they just hadn't gotten around to telling me.

Barbara was usually home from her class by ten, but ten o'clock came and went, as did eleven. First, I figured that she was trying to punish me, in her passive-aggressive manner that always bothered the hell out of me. Why not just sit down, hash it out and move on?

As the clock on the bedside table approached twelve, I started to worry for real. It was now two hours after her usual return time. She had school in the morning, and she'd need to be out the door by seven. I thought about casually checking in with the dispatcher at the Sheriff's, just to make sure that nothing bad was on the log. If Barbara was in a ditch somewhere...

The front door opened, and noises began coming from the kitchen: wife-noises, not intruder-noises, thank God. Barbara was home, and I was relieved—and seriously pissed off at the same time.

I heard her in the bathroom a few minutes later and rehearsed my opening line for when she got into bed next to me. *I'm sorry that you felt it necessary to stay out so late.* That would be the right combination of a sideways apology from me and a chastening for her misbehavior. Hell yeah, I can do passive-aggressive with the best of them.

I never got the chance. I heard the door to the baby's room close, just after the hall light went out. She would be sleeping with Royal again, not with her husband.

The truce was over, and the war would drag on.

FRIDAY

NOBODY EVER GETS A PHONE call at three thirty in the morning with good news, unless you happened to know someone who was expecting a baby. When I saw SHERIFFS DEPT on the caller ID, I prepared myself and reluctantly picked up the receiver.

"They found him," a tired-sounding Bobby Bove said. "Heffernan just called. Gustavo Arguelles is in the trauma unit at South Miami. They're putting his face back together, and one of his lungs is collapsed."

"Car accident?"

"Nope," Bove said. "No car, no accident. An ambulance driver saw it. He got dumped at the entrance of the E.R., out the side door of a black van. Nobody got a plate, but Heffernan is all over it, looking for those two guys."

"No word on Lilian?"

"Not yet."

"I'm going to go down there. I need help with the boy. He's going to need a ride from my house to St. Ed's in the morning."

"I'll take him myself."

"I owe you, Bobby."

"No, you don't," he said. "I tell you what. I don't like gangbangers screwing with people from Vero Beach. This isn't that kind of town."

*

You do what you think is best, because that's what you're going to do anyway. Those had been Barbara's only words when I had awoken her to explain what was going on. She pulled the covers back up, and I left the nursery shaking my head, realizing that I was strictly an amateur in the passive-aggressive department. I wiggled Roberto's shoulder before I left and told him that his dad had been in an accident, and that he was going to be OK, and that I would get him home from the hospital, all of which had just barely enough truth in it to not be total bullshit,

31

but I doubted that Roberto would get any more sleep, no matter how I tried to spin it.

The drive to Miami is a grind in normal traffic, but at this time of the morning I could make it in two hours. The Beemer likes to cruise along at around eighty on the highway, and the Highway Patrol guys left me alone—they were too busy pulling over the various carloads of kids who would fly past me at a hundred-and-something in their jacked-up compact cars. Where the heck did they get the money for a $400 ticket, not to mention the points? At that age you don't think about those things until it's too late, because you are invincible.

The dawn began to lighten the eastern sky as I passed through Fort Lauderdale, and by the time I parked on the top level of the South Miami Hospital garage, a fat, liquid sun began to wobble above the rim of the horizon. Another beautiful day in South Florida, unless you happened to be lying in a hospital bed with the shit kicked out of you.

I made my way to the trauma unit and negotiated with a sleep-deprived nurse at the desk about the visitor's protocol: you had to be immediate family, and you needed the doctor's permission, period, no exceptions. I would have continued to haggle, but Lieutenant Tal Heffernan came out into the lobby and met my glance with his piercing grey eyes. I tapped him on the shoulder and extended my hand.

"I'm Vince Tanzi."

He squinted as he examined me. "You—"

"Look different?" I said. "I got shot since the last time you saw me. I'm missing a few pieces."

"I read about that."

"You're up late," I said. His fair complexion was streaked red with the telltale broken capillaries of someone who enjoyed his evening cocktail.

"Another all-nighter. My wife says I'm a vampire."

"So, how is he?"

"He can't talk, but he's awake. They have his jaw all wired up. I got him to blink yes or no, and I asked him a few questions, but he's pretty far out there on the pain meds."

"Did you find out anything?"

"Not really," he said. "I asked him if it was the Iturbe brothers. Blink once for yes, twice for no."

"And?"

"And, he didn't blink."

"He doesn't want to say?"

"Hell if I know," the lieutenant said. "Nobody's volunteering anything on this case. A well-known rich guy gets gunned down in broad daylight, and nothing, not from his kids, not from any of our regular sources. His daughter's missing, the son-in-law gets the crap beat out of him, and even some nosy P.I. gets his knuckles rapped."

"Can you get me in to see him?"

"Sure," he said. "I can use all the help I can get." He took out a card. "My cell's on there. Call my office if you want a look at the file. And please don't text me anything, I don't do that."

I got a nurse to lead me to the room where Gustavo Arguelles lay in a bed, surrounded by blinking lights and readouts. Tubes and probes were attached everywhere, and the lower half of his face was swaddled in bandages with only a small slit for his mouth. His eyes opened when he heard me approach.

"Roberto is fine," I said. "He's staying with Barbara, and I have a deputy friend looking after him."

Gustavo's eyes showed his appreciation. He tried to lift an arm and grimaced in pain.

"Don't move," I said. "We'll do the blink thing, same as the guy who just left. Once for yes, two for no, OK?"

He blinked once.

"Was it the Iturbe guys? They look like football players? Black van?"

One blink. Yes.

"But you didn't want to tell the cops."

Two blinks. No.

"So I shouldn't either," I said. "For whatever reason."

Gustavo blinked once again. Yes.

"I haven't heard from Lilian. Did you find out anything?"

One blink.

OK, great. How was he going to tell me what he'd found out? Gustavo tried to move his arm again, and I pulled the cover away to expose his hand. He extended his middle and index fingers, and looked back at me.

"V?" I asked him. "Somebody whose name begins with a V?"

Two blinks this time.

"Two? The number two?"

One blink. Yes.

"OK," I said. "Number two. Something about the number two?"

He blinked once again. Goddamn. I'm no good at this kind of thing. I didn't even know what to ask him to help me figure it out. I was wishing Roberto was here—he'd be all over this, but I was glad that he didn't have to see his father looking like he'd been run over by a cement truck.

The nurse returned to the room. "You have to let him sleep. Please."

"Understood," I said. I moved closer to the bed and took my friend's hand. "I'm back in business, Gustavo. I'll find Lilian. You just get better, OK?"

He managed one more blink, and then his eyes closed as the pain drugs carried him away.

*

The Coral Gables Police and Fire building on Salzedo Street was a brick-and-glass behemoth built to replace the classy old Mediterranean-Revival police station a couple blocks away that was now a museum. The heart of Coral Gables is a little like the old business district of Vero Beach, but fancier: beautiful stucco and limestone buildings that had been the center of commercial activity in the '30s and '40s, then declined as the strips and malls had arrived in the '60s, and had been rediscovered in the '80s and '90s, as smaller merchants and businesses found affordable spaces in the fabulous old buildings.

I was escorted to the C.I.D. office and given a file by a no-nonsense sergeant in uniform. "You can use one of the interrogation rooms over here," she said. "Don't take anything, and don't make copies."

"Thanks," I said. I flicked on a light and sat at a metal desk facing a mirror that was actually a one-way window leading to where the spectators sat while somebody was getting grilled. I had been on both sides of those mirrors many times, and today I would be on my best behavior. It was something of a breach of protocol for Heffernan to allow me a look at the file, but it sounded like he'd been stonewalled so far, and there had to be a ton of pressure from his superiors to find the killer—daytime shootouts in front of country clubs didn't do much for a city that depended on tourists and conventioneers.

Heffernan and his people had filled a green Pentaflex hanger with an inch-thick sheaf of ballistics analyses, field measurements, coroner's reports, neighborhood interviews, and some of Heffernan's own jottings as he tried to connect the dots. I was particularly interested in Pimentel's family: who the lieutenant had spoken with, what they'd been asked, and what they'd said. I learned surprisingly little from the notes, but I took out my phone and entered the contact information for Lilian's two brothers and her sister. Raimundo Pimentel's wife was deceased, and I didn't see any notes about girlfriends, or even friends. Heffernan had talked to some of the administrative people at Pimentel's downtown office, which was also where Javier Pimentel worked; he ran the real estate business with the old man. The younger brother was listed as an attorney, and I wrote down both his business and home addresses.

I returned the file to the sergeant and made my way out to the street. Javier Pimentel's office was on Ponce De Leon Boulevard at the other end of the block that I was on, so I walked without calling ahead. It was still early in the morning; I took the chance that he would be at work. The building was prominently situated on a small park and looked glitzy enough to suit a real estate mogul like Raimundo Pimentel. The lobby directory listed Pimentel Holdings, LLC as the sole tenant on the top floor, and as soon as I stepped off the elevator I was greeted by a sweeping view to the north that encompassed the whole Coral Gables skyline and beyond to Miami.

Impressive. I couldn't imagine Lilian Arguelles fitting into this kind of wealth. Maybe she hadn't. Maybe that was why she had kept her distance.

A stunning young woman with long black hair rose from her polished-aluminum desk. She was the only person in the reception area, which was the size of a squash court. "Can I help you?" she asked, advancing toward me with a smile. Her navy blue dress was snugly cinched around her tiny waist and revealed a slender, hourglass figure: Business Barbie, Latina Edition.

"Is Javier Pimentel in? I'm a friend of his sister."

"Susanna?"

"No, Lilian," I said. "I just came from the hospital. Her husband is there, and he's in bad shape. I'd like to speak with Mr. Pimentel."

"And you are?"

"Vince Tanzi." I decided against digging out one of my cards; they were way too dog-eared for an outfit like this, where the business cards on the receptionist's desk appeared to be hammered from platinum. She disappeared behind a door while I waited. One side of the reception area held architectural models of groups of buildings, complete with trees made from lichen and parking areas with tiny little Ferraris and Range Rovers.

These must be the high-end malls that Heffernan had described. There was a place like that on the other side of the interstate in Vero, with stores like Ann Taylor and Polo, but shopping is about as fun for me as being waterboarded by the CIA. Barbara had dragged me there a few times, and I had sat obediently in the car with the windows cracked open, like an overheated Labrador retriever. Stay, Vince, stay. As painful as it is for me, shopping is like fresh oxygen for my wife. She has made it clear that if she were to punch out unexpectedly she would like her ashes to be scattered in the T.J.Maxx parking lot.

Javier Pimentel rounded the corner with his hand extended. He was about five-five, slim, and he had a perfectly smooth, circular face, framed by close-cropped dark hair that was thinning in front. I guessed that he was older than Lilian, although I hadn't bothered to check the stats in the police file.

"Vince," he said. "Welcome. I know all about you."

I shook his hand, making a cluster of gold bracelets jingle on his arm. He wore a braided gold chain around his neck, and a hoop earring in each lobe. He reeked of no-doubt-expensive aftershave, and I backed up a step to get away from the smell. "How?" I asked. "I thought you and Lilian didn't talk."

"Roberto tells me things. I believe in family. I call the boy sometimes, on his cell. He's a good kid."

"Yes, he is."

"He mentions you a lot," Pimentel said. Unlike his receptionist, he was casually dressed in a patterned golf shirt and light-green slacks. His shoes were buff-colored alligator, and I guessed that they were the real item. Latinos don't skimp on footwear; in fact, you are pretty much judged by your shoes anywhere south of the Tropic of Cancer.

"You heard about Gustavo?"

"Yes. This way, we'll talk in my office." He led me beyond the aluminum door to another space that dwarfed the reception area and held only a few pieces of furniture: a white leather couch, a modern walnut slab desk, and a few chairs. One wall had a gas fireplace, and two of the walls were open to the view, which extended all the way to the Atlantic.

"You people must be claustrophobic," I said.

"We're in the business. It's important to make an impression."

"It's been made."

He took a seat behind the desk and motioned me to a chair. "I'm going over to see him at lunchtime. How bad is he?"

"Bad. He may be asleep."

"I can't believe any of this," Pimentel said. "He and I used to fish together when we were kids."

"You have any idea where the Iturbe brothers are right now?"

"Who?"

"They worked for you," I said. "Muscle. Rent collectors."

Javier Pimentel eyed me cautiously. I obviously wasn't interested in small talk and had gotten right to it, and the partitions were being raised. "I remember them. They went to jail, and my father fired them."

"They're out now," I said.

"They don't work for us."

"Who would hire them to beat up Gustavo?"

"No idea. Like I said, all of this is unbelievable. My father, my sister, and now Gustavo."

"Any idea where Lilian is?"

"No," he said.

"Did you see Gustavo recently?"

"The day before yesterday. He said that Lili was having an affair, but he didn't believe it."

"Do you?"

"You don't always know about those things. People are unpredictable when it comes to their love life."

He was right. My first wife had carried on with one of my best friends, and I would never have believed it, but it had happened. "Where was he staying while he was here?" I asked him.

"At my other sister's. Susanna's. She's out on Key Biscayne. You want the address?"

"I have it. Is your brother in his office today?"

"He's away. On vacation."

"Where?"

"He didn't say," Javier Pimentel said, and I saw the tiniest bit of fear creep into his expression. "Roberto thinks that you are, like, Superman," he continued, changing the subject. "I wish I could see him."

"Maybe sometime. Here's my card. Anything at all, call me."

"Of course," he said as he rose and escorted me out. "Just unbelievable, all of this."

Yes, I thought, as I waited for the elevator. Unbelievable was exactly the right word.

*

The next stop on my bullshit tour of Coral Gables was Segundo Pimentel's law office. It was the opposite of his older brother's digs: a squat, one-story concrete building with a faded red awning that gave shade to the front windows along Alcazar Avenue, ten blocks north of Javier's place. I already knew that the lawyer wouldn't be there, but that was OK—at least I wasn't going to be lied to. I had believed pretty much nothing that I'd been told by Javier Pimentel, and I had put him at the top of the list of people who were neck-deep in whatever was going on.

I thought that I would at least question the younger brother's associates, assuming that there were any. Somebody had to know where he had gone on his ill-timed "vacation". Most people would cut their vacation short if their father had been gunned down in front of a country club. The fact that Segundo hadn't done so had earned him a place on my list right up there with Javier, even though I hadn't met him yet.

The interior of the office wasn't intended to impress anyone. It smelled like damp carpet, and the potted plants that were scattered around were frayed and neglected. No one was at the reception desk, so I had to lean my head into a side room where I saw someone at a desk behind a mostly-closed door. "Anybody home?" I asked a thirty-something blonde dressed in a floral print top and wrinkled khaki pants. Must be a casual day, I thought. The girl was as pretty as Javier's receptionist, but she was dressed from the Old Navy rack, not from Armani like her Business Barbie counterpart.

"Oh, sorry," she said. "I didn't hear you come in. We're closed, actually. I forgot to lock the door."

"Closed?"

"Mr. Pimentel is away. I'm just doing some catch-up." Her desk was covered in papers, and files were strewn all over the floor.

"Can you tell me where he went? I need to reach him. Something of an emergency."

"Who are you?"

"I'm a friend of his sister's," I said. "Lilian Arguelles. Her husband Gustavo is here, in South Miami hospital. He was attacked last night."

"Oh, no." She looked shocked, and she wasn't faking it, which made a nice change. "I don't have any way of reaching Segundo. I'm sorry."

"You don't know where he went?"

"Not really," she said.

Damn. The honesty streak hadn't lasted long, and I was back in Bullshitville.

"Ms.—"

"Heffernan. Chloe, actually." She stood and brushed a lock of strawberry blonde hair from her forehead. She was almost as tall as me and had a fresh, freckled complexion.

"Chloe," I said. "This is very important. Not to be dramatic, but people's lives are in danger. Lilian has been missing for days, and her husband got very badly beaten when he went to find her. You know about Raimundo Pimentel's murder."

"Yes."

"Why would his son be on vacation?"

"Who are you? Are you with the police?"

"Vince Tanzi," I said. "I used to be a private investigator. I'm a friend of Lilian and Gustavo, like I told you."

"I—really can't help, Mr. Tanzi. I'm so sorry."

"Here's my card," I said. "I know that you can help. Just take some time and think about it, OK? Then call me. I don't want anyone else to be hurt."

"I don't want to be involved."

"I think that you already are. Are you related to Talbot Heffernan by any chance?"

A slight flush rose in her cheeks behind the freckles.

"I'm his wife," she said.

*

So, Lieutenant Tal Heffernan's wife worked for one of the Pimentel brothers? And, she was holding out on me. The crazy part was that if she was stonewalling me, then she was doing the same to her husband, because he must have already asked her if she knew where her boss was. I would have to figure out how to work that little quandary into my next conversation with the lieutenant.

Susanna Pimentel had answered her cell when I'd called and had saved me the trip out to Key Biscayne. She was at South Miami Hospital at Gustavo's bedside, and her voice had cracked with emotion. I'd met her once years ago at Roberto's when Glory and I had been invited over for a drink during the holidays. I remembered that she was a professor somewhere, and was quieter than Lilian, who could go on about any subject at all, and always knew what she was talking about. Roberto had inherited the family brains, but he was more like his soft-spoken aunt than his mother.

Gustavo was asleep when I entered the hospital room, and a nurse was adding something to his IV drip. "He won't be awake," she said. "We're keeping him asleep for a while, maybe a couple of days."

"Pentobarbital?" I asked.

"You're a doctor?"

"I had a brain injury. They kept me in an induced coma for a while. Did he have brain damage?"

"Just a bad concussion, they think," the nurse said. "The lung is better though. The jaw is going to take some months to heal. It was broken in half a dozen places."

Susanna Pimentel entered the room with two cups of coffee in her hands. She passed one to me.

"Vince," she said. "I'm so glad you're here. Where's Roberto?"

"With my wife. Barbara. You haven't met her."

"I haven't seen you in a long time. I'm so sorry—about everything. Glory. Lots of water over the dam. But you have a baby now, right?"

"Yes. Roberto is crazy about him."

"So Roberto is safe." She put her coffee down on a side table and took one of the visitor's chairs, while I sat down in the other. She was bigger than Lilian, with wide hips and strong shoulders, but the family resemblance was still there.

"Yes, he's OK," I said. "Of course he's worried sick, though."

"So am I. Who did this?"

"You don't know?"

"Gustavo was at my house most of yesterday. He was frantic about Lilian. He'd talked to my brothers, and he made a lot of calls, but I don't think he found out anything."

I made a mental note to get a hold of Gustavo's phone and see exactly who he had called, if the police hadn't already. "He was awake when I saw him this morning," I said. "I think that it was two guys named Iturbe. Gang members."

"Pepe and Lalo. My father's henchmen. I thought they were in jail."

"They were, until a week ago. Your brother Javier said they don't work for the family anymore."

"My brother is full of shit," Susanna Pimentel said, her face darkening. "Don't believe anything he says."

"I already came to that conclusion. You don't get along?"

"I stay away from him. And from my father. He was a crook, and he abused my mother, and she's dead because of him. Needless to say I'm not going to the funeral."

"Do you talk to Segundo? Do you know where he is? His secretary won't say, and Javier says he doesn't know."

"Chloe? She's a paralegal," Susanna said. "And I can assure you, she knows."

"It felt like she did."

"No, I don't know where he is, Vince. I'm sorry."

"Where did he get that name? I've never heard it."

"Segundo? It's very Spanish," she said. "It means "Second". He was the second son. Not too creative, I know."

"How long are you going to be here?"

"I canceled all my classes. I'm just going to stay put, even if he's asleep."

"I forget where you teach."

"I'm an adjunct professor of Russian literature at Miami Dade."

"Really? I can't get through that stuff," I said. "But I have a friend who is crazy about it He runs a book group for African American boys up in Gifford. Street kids reading Tolstoy."

"There's a lot to learn from those books. Mostly about what not to do."

"That's what Sonny says."

"Are you any closer to finding Lilian?"

"No. I wish I was."

"She's not having an affair. You knew that."

"Yes."

"Talk to my brothers. One of them is behind all this."

"Javier wouldn't tell me anything."

"Put his balls in a vise," she said. "He's a wimp when it comes down to it."

I almost spat out my coffee. What was that I said about her being soft-spoken?

"Javier?"

"He's gay, if you didn't notice. Closeted, of course, because we're Cuban. My father used to call him *maricón*."

"I know plenty of gay people who aren't wimps," I said.

"I don't have a problem with gay men. But Javier is a liar, a crook, and a slimeball, and I wouldn't doubt it if he had my father killed."

"Other than that, he's a great guy, right?"

She smiled as she took a sip of her coffee. "Be careful, Vince. Gustavo said that they already went after you."

"I can take care of myself," I said.

I looked at Gustavo Arguelles lying in his bed and hoped that I was right.

*

My phone buzzed with a text just as I was getting back into the BMW in the hospital parking lot. It took me a while to retrieve it from my pocket—the drive south to Coral Gables in the wee hours was starting to take its toll, and my bad leg ached.

The text was from Barbara.

Where R U?

Coral Gables. Back ASAP, I wrote. *So sorry about everything*, I added. The shock of seeing Gustavo in his hospital bed had brought back the memory of my own months-long stay in a hospital in Vermont not so long ago. Barbara had been at my side the whole time. I hoped that we would get through this rough patch sooner rather than later.

We really do need to talk, she wrote. *And I realize that what you're doing has to be done.*

Thank you, I sent back.

Royal misses you.

Isn't he at the sitters?

Just finished all my exams. I picked him up already. I'll go get Roberto when school's out.

Thank you again, I sent. *And congratulations.*

You're a good person, Vince. I wish I was half as good as you.

What? That didn't sound like Barbara. She must be feeling beaten down by the nursing school exams, combined with everything else. I was suddenly worried about her.

I love you, I sent, but she didn't answer. Maybe she turned off her phone.

*

I had the choice of returning to Javier Pimentel's office to compress his testicles, as his sister had suggested, or going back to Segundo's place to grill Chloe Heffernan a little harder. She didn't have any body parts that I could squeeze without getting my face slapped, but I sensed that it would be unnecessary as she was probably carrying a burden that she didn't want, and would tell me where her boss was, sooner or later.

It was sooner. My phone buzzed before I even left the garage.

This is Chloe. Please call.

I dialed the number and waited. Maybe I was going to save myself another trip.

"Mr. Tanzi?" she said, as soon as she picked up.

"Vince," I corrected.

"I'm going to tell you where he is. But there is a condition."

"Go ahead."

"It can't come from me. You don't tell Segundo, and you don't tell anyone else. Especially not the police."

"Why?"

"Those are the terms," she said. "Don't make me regret this."

"I accept. And you won't."

"He's at his fishing camp on Blue Cypress Lake. Just outside of Vero."

"I know it," I said. "I've fished there before. Is he at Middleton's?"

"No, he parks there and takes his boat. He has a place at the northern end of the lake, out on its own. They call it the Moonshiner's Camp. It's been there since the Prohibition days."

"What's he doing there?"

"Getting away—from all this," she said. "I'm not going to go into it."

"Fair enough," I said. "And thank you. You're doing the right thing."

"God, I hope so. I'm scared. Be careful."

"I will," I said, for the second time this morning.

*

I had decided to take U.S. 27 through the Everglades so that I would avoid the heavy daytime traffic along the coast. It was a lot of two-lane traveling, but it only added about twenty minutes to the trip and was far more pleasant. The highway follows the eastern shore of Lake Okeechobee for about twenty-five miles and would ultimately lead me to Yeehaw Junction, slightly west of Blue Cypress Lake. There's not much to look at along the way, but I was contenting myself by listening to Vince Gill's guitar pickin' on the car stereo, and he made me proud to share the same first name.

It would be another hour's drive before I got to the lake, and I wondered what I would find at Segundo Pimentel's cottage.

Segundo. Second brother.

It hit me just as I was crossing over Taylor Creek into the town of Okeechobee. Gustavo had held out two fingers, meaning *second*, not the number two. That's what he was trying to tell me. I suddenly realized that I was on the right track. I would locate the younger brother, and I would finally have a handle on what was going on.

Gustavo was leading me to the person who would explain everything, who might even tell me where Lilian was.

It could have also been a warning, as in: *watch out for Segundo*. I had my Glock in the back seat and a sawed-off in the trunk, and I thought about taking one or both of them with me as soon as I figured out how I was going to transport myself out to the Moonshiner's Camp. I knew that you could rent boats from Middleton's, the one-and-only settlement along Blue Cypress Lake, and I should be able to make it there by five PM, so with any luck they would still be open.

Five PM—oh shit—I had made a follow-up appointment with Megan Rumsford for today at five, and had completely forgotten about it in the confusion of my whirlwind trip to Coral Gables. I had her personal number, which she'd insisted that I have in case I ever had a severe problem. I dialed it.

"You're not going to be happy about this," I said. "I'm blowing you off. I can't make my five o'clock."

"No worries," she said. "What happened?"

"I'm in Okeechobee, headed for Blue Cypress Lake," I said. "I have to go visit a guy. It's part of this thing I'm working on."

"Blue Cypress Lake? Like, Middleton's Fish Camp? I go there all the time."

"Really?"

"Where does this guy live?"

"They call it Moonshiner's-something," I said.

"I know it," she said. "It's about a mile up the shore from the launching ramp, tucked way back into the swamp. I take my paddle-board up there."

"I'm going to rent a boat, if I can get there before they close."

"Do you have a bathing suit with you?"

"I keep one in the trunk," I said. And I did. It was wrapped around my sawed-off, and it probably smelled like gun oil.

"Stand up paddling is the best core therapy you could get," she said. "You'll love it. You should be doing it every day."

"Megan, this is business, not—"

"No excuses, dude. You just blew off our appointment, so you're going paddling with me instead. I'll meet you at Middleton's at five. Don't worry, you can do your business."

"I've never even tried it," I said. "What if I fall off?"

"Then the water moccasins will get you."

"That's a pretty good motivation to not fall off," I said.

*

Middleton's Fish Camp is at the end of a long rural road that winds through the citrus groves and farms west of Vero. It's a throwback to the days before most of the state's wetlands were drained to make way for roads, houses and agriculture, and is surrounded on three sides by the Blue Cypress Conservation Area, with the shoreline of the lake to the east. The settlement consists of a few dozen houses and trailers, an airboat tour company, and the Fish Camp, which rents boats, fishing tackle, and cabins for those who want to stay the night. The sportsmen get up early to go after the big bass, and when I pulled into the lot the place was deserted except for a line of pickups with empty boat trailers, waiting for their owners' return.

Megan's yellow Jeep was already parked alongside a concrete ramp. She was dressed in a plain white T-shirt over a powder-blue bikini, and was unstrapping two paddleboards from the roof of her car. I parked next to her and got out to help.

"Perfect timing," she said, smiling.

"What exactly are these things?" I helped her lower the boards. They looked like fat surfboards with padded foam tops. "This is one of your P.T. torture devices, right?"

"Just what the name says. You stand up, and you paddle."

"I knew there was a catch."

"This is really good for you, Vince. Go get your suit on. There's a portable john over there."

I disappeared into the portable toilet booth and struggled to get into my bathing trunks within the confined space. If I could change my clothes in one of those things, then I could probably handle one of Megan's boards. When I came out she was standing on hers at the bottom of the launching ramp, and she beckoned me down to where she was tending mine. I had my automatic rolled up in a hand towel and wondered where the hell I was going to put it. Megan showed me a dry hatch that unscrewed, and I slipped the weapon inside, concealed by the towel. I didn't want to worry her, but I also had no idea what I was about getting into, and I wasn't going to go unarmed.

My board was wobbly at first, but I quickly got used to the long paddle, and followed Megan's instructions on how to steer. You used a J-shaped stroke to go forward and not veer off to one side, and after a while I was keeping up with her as we paddled through dead trees and water lilies. If we stayed close to the western shore of the lake we were in the shade, which was welcome in the late afternoon heat. No one else was out except for a pair of ospreys and a bald eagle that swooped down twenty yards from us to snatch a bass from the water's surface. Sometimes I forget how beautiful the undisturbed Florida landscape is—as do many of the state's residents who only know the strip malls, burger joints, beach condos and the other encroachments of civilization. Nature is no different from anything else that is precious: if you start taking it for granted, it will disappear.

Megan took us north along the shore, and after we had paddled more than half a mile she led our boards into the mouth of a slow-moving stream that fed the lake. In the middle was a small island with a miniscule clearing and a three-sided cabin that was covered in moss but looked serviceable.

"It's another quarter mile to the Moonshine Camp," she said. "Let's rest here for a sec, OK?"

"What is this?"

"This is my happy place," Megan said. "Just a little shack that nobody cares about. I come out here all the time to do yoga. Be sure to check for alligators before you land."

"Oh, I will," I said. I found a good spot to beach the board and pulled it out of the water. Megan had a rolled-up rubber mat strapped to her board, which she removed and spread out on the floor of the cabin. Inside the mat was a large brown bottle of beer, and she popped open the lid and took a big swig.

"Funky Buddha, from down in Oakland Park," she said. "Want a sip? It's still cold."

"I'm working. You really come out here a lot?"

"Yeah. I can get naked, and it's just me and the gators. Hold this, OK?" She passed the bottle to me and pulled off her T-shirt, and then began to unfasten the top of her bikini. Oh lordy. This time it wasn't just a hit. It was the invasion of Normandy.

"Megan—"

"What?" she asked, raising her eyebrows. Somehow, I actually managed to look at a half-naked woman's eyes instead of her chest, a feat that required a superhuman effort for any male with a sperm count above zero.

"I'm not immune to this," I said. "You know—"

"Oh for god's sake, Vince. It's just a set of tits. If you've seen two, you've seen them all, right?"

My field of vision slipped ever-so-slightly lower and I took in the view. Hers were tangerine-sized, with tiny nipples that were saying: *Go ahead. Make my day.*

Tanzi's Tip #4: Behind every temptation there is a nun waiting with a ruler.

I composed myself, at least partially. "Megan, I'm a guy, OK? You need to put your shirt back on. And I can't have a beer. I'm going out to question somebody, and I need to keep my head on straight."

She made no move to get dressed. "What's this about?"

"He's my friend's brother. The woman who's missing. He may or may not have something to do with it. Their father was murdered a couple days ago, my friend's husband is in the hospital, and things are getting worse by the minute. Plus, you're twenty years younger than I am, I'm married, you're my physical therapist, you're friends with my wife, and—" I stopped, having exhausted the reasons why she should get her admittedly spectacular gazungas out of my face before someone put an eye out.

She frowned. "You go on ahead. Do your thing."

"That's probably a good idea anyway," I said. "I don't know this guy."

"It's the only place along the shoreline. You'll see it—it's up on stilts."

"OK."

"And Vince," she said, taking back the bottle. "I'm not really friends with your wife, OK?"

*

The stretch of shoreline between Megan's lean-to and Segundo Pimentel's camp was a part of the lake that I was unfamiliar with. It wasn't really shoreline, it was a classic Southern swamp complete with giant cypress trees draped with Spanish moss and stumps poking out from the water every few feet. I was starting to get the hang of the paddling; I could get the board to go in a more-or-less straight line after a while. The temperature must have been in the nineties, but the moss canopy provided some shade, and I wasn't uncomfortable, although my shirt was soaked through. I wondered what Segundo Pimentel would think when a sweat-drenched, two-hundred-pound ex-P.I. pulled up to his hideaway on a surfboard, wanting to ask a few questions. With any luck he wouldn't shoot me, which under the current Florida law you are entitled to do if anyone so much as threatens to give you a noogie.

I was huffing and puffing my way around a bend in the shoreline when I spotted it. The house was about twenty feet long on each side, and was built on stilts above the water, like Megan had said. It wore a fresh coat of beige paint, and an expensive-looking bass boat with a big Mercury outboard was tied up to a dock that ran along the near side. That was good—if the boat was there, then somebody must be home.

As I paddled closer to the dock I noticed that it was already occupied. Two young alligators, one about eight feet long and one slightly smaller, were sunning themselves on the floating structure. They eyed me as I approached, and then lazily slid sideways off the low dock into the murky water. I ceased paddling and froze, but the momentum of the board was carrying me forward, right toward them, so I carefully dipped a blade in the water and attempted to steer away. Gators generally won't bother you if you leave them alone, but my wobbly paddleboard suddenly felt way less stable than it had before, and I was praying that I wouldn't end up as someone's chew toy. Eventually they swam off, and I was able to land the board on the dock and carefully pull it up out of the water.

"Hello? Mr. Pimentel?" I called out, before climbing the steps from the dock to a deck that surrounded Segundo Pimentel's camp. The close encounter with gators had somehow relieved me of any concerns about being shot. "It's Vince Tanzi—I'm a friend of Lilian and Gustavo. Anybody home?" I climbed up five steps and found a screen door. It was wide open, and I could see inside all the way across a single, open room. A gas stove was to the left of me, with a sink next to it that was fed by an old-fashioned hand pump. Kerosene lanterns hung from the ceiling, and fishing tackle was everywhere. In the center of the room a rattan sofa and two chairs surrounded a glass coffee table, and to my right was an alcove that held a built-in double bed. The only sound was the low hum from a small refrigerator that I figured must be hooked up to a propane tank—the nearest power line was a mile away. The house was definitely a man's getaway, but it was clean and tidy, and I noticed a cluster of women's magazines to one side of the coffee table, so the inhabitants hadn't necessarily been exclusively male.

Segundo was nowhere to be seen. I peeked into the alcove, where the bed was unmade. No clothes were strewn around, no food on the counter. I opened the fridge, which contained a bottle of milk, a carton of eggs, a big jug of water and a six-pack of Bud Light. I sniffed the milk, and it was fresh—Pimentel may not be in the house now, but he had been recently. I wondered how he had managed to leave without his boat, but perhaps he owned more than one. Or maybe he was out on a paddleboard with his own bare-chested amazon.

It was the open screen door that was bothering me. There was no spring on it, but when I shut it, it stayed in place. The weather was still, and there had been no breeze to blow it open. The biting bugs don't come out in force until after sunset, but there was no sense inviting them in whatever the time. People on these lakes were in the habit of keeping their screens shut.

I didn't like it.

I walked to the back of the house along the wraparound deck. Someone could probably drop a line from right here and snag a nice bullhead. I continued around the perimeter until I returned to the steps and saw that the larger of the two alligators was back on the dock. Damn. How was I going to get back down there? I looked for something to throw at him, hoping that I could shoo him away before he knocked my paddleboard into the lake.

And then I noticed from above what I had missed from below. A man's shape was curled up on the floor of the bass boat, wedged in between the control console and the seats. The alligator was nosing at the side of the boat, hoping to draw it closer, but the sleek craft was fastened to the dock with two mooring whips, keeping it just out of the ugly beast's reach. So that's what the gators had been doing there: hoping to come aboard for an evening snack.

I went back into the house and found an oar, which I used to poke at the alligator from the steps until it slid off and swam away. I didn't see any motion in the boat, and when I got down the steps and climbed aboard, I confirmed that he was dead: part of his skull was gone, and a pool of dried blood had spread across the dark green carpet under the helm. The man's face was turned upward, and I saw his bloated features, frozen in death.

I was looking at the male version of Lilian Arguelles—just bigger, and with several days of razor stubble on his chin, and I knew that this was her brother. Segundo Pimentel was gator bait, and he wouldn't be telling me a thing.

*

Bobby Bove's theory was that the victim had been shot from above, and he was positive that the ballistics report would bear him out. The blood spatter pattern was right, and so was the position of the entry wound. Pimentel had been hiding on the floor of his boat while somebody had been upstairs, and they had seen him just as I had—down there, curled up into a ball. It was a homicide, not an accident or a suicide, and it had the hallmarks of a pro hit, or at least the work of somebody who was a damn good shot.

We were in the parking lot next to Middleton's, and the medical examiner was packing up. He told Bobby that he would have an autopsy and a report by the morning, but he could already say that the body had been there for at least twelve hours, which put the time of death sometime in the early morning before dawn. Other evidence was corroborating that: the police divers had found a flashlight in nine feet of water near the end of Pimentel's dock while looking for shell casings, so the killing had been done in the dark.

I had offered to drive Megan home, but she insisted that she was all right and had gone home soon after they'd taken her statement. She had been shivering under the lights of the parking lot even though she had dressed back into her clothes and the evening was warm. I made a note to call her when I got to my house, just to make sure that she was OK. She hadn't seen anything directly except for Segundo Pimentel's shrouded body being loaded into an ambulance, but just being in the vicinity of a sudden, violent death was a bad shock to people who weren't used to it, and even to some of us who were.

I wasn't in shock. I was angry. Segundo Pimentel had been my best lead to Lilian, and he was now on the way to the coroner's fridge. I decided that I wasn't going to wait for Bobby Bove or Tal Heffernan to dribble out information as they found it, as if they were doing me a favor. I was the one who had discovered the body. I was the only one who was getting anywhere at all, even at a frustratingly slow pace. To hell with those guys.

I drove east on Highway 60, back toward Barbara, Royal, and Roberto. Royal would be asleep, which was too bad because it meant that I would miss him—I was planning to be up and on the road well before he woke up. I knew exactly where I was headed—back to Coral Gables, where I would be seeking out Mrs. Chloe Heffernan. I could have called her husband and had him ask the questions for me, but I had told her that I would protect her as a source, and I don't renege on my promises. Tomorrow was a Saturday, and it might be tricky finding her since she wouldn't be at the office, but I would take my chances because I didn't want to give her advance notice of my visit. I didn't want to give her time to come up with some kind of story—I'd heard enough of those already.

And if I failed to find her, I had a back-up plan. I would locate Javier Pimentel, and this time I might just do what his sister had suggested earlier in the day.

*

"You were on the eleven o'clock news," Barbara said, as I closed the front door. "You missed it."

"I wish I'd missed the whole goddamn thing."

"Oh, Vince," she said. "You look awful."

"It's been a crazy day," I said. "And I have to go back to Coral Gables first thing tomorrow morning."

"Are you any closer to finding Lilian?"

"Yes and no. I think I'm starting to narrow it down. Or maybe it's being narrowed down for me. The dead man was one of her brothers."

Barbara was dressed in her workout clothes and was sitting on the floor on a rubber mat like the one that Megan had rolled up on her paddleboard. Barbara liked to work out in front of the TV before she went to bed. I liked to lie in my chair and watch: her, not the television. My forty-four-year old wife was one of those spectacular human beings who makes the rest of us look like factory seconds, although everybody has a few nicks in the finish whether they are visible or not.

"I'm going to bed," she said. "I wanted to wait until you got home."

"OK."

She rose from the mat and kissed me on the forehead. "'Night."

"Megan Rumsford has been hitting on me," I said. "In the spirit of full disclosure."

Barbara's eyes widened. "She was on the news, too."

"I may have to change physical therapists."

Barbara turned her head and looked away, down the hall toward Royal's room as she spoke. "Megan has helped you a lot, Vince. She's really good at her work."

"I know that."

"I was going to sleep in Royal's room again," she said. "But I don't have to. I just thought you might want the rest. You look exhausted."

"The truth is, I'm—"

"I know," she said.

But she didn't. She turned away, walked down the hall to the baby's room, and quietly let herself in, carefully shutting the door behind her while I wondered what was going to happen to the two of us. I hadn't been trying to say that I was exhausted. Nor was I unwilling to sleep in the same bed with her. I just hadn't been allowed to complete my sentence.

The truth was that something was starting to go very wrong in my marriage, and I had no idea how to fix it.

*

The skin of my back was freezing cold, but I couldn't do anything about it, because I was unable to move. I couldn't open my eyes, or even make them twitch. It was like someone had turned off the switch that controlled all of my muscles. I couldn't even feel my heart beat.

Maybe I was dead.

The cold, hard sensation under my back and legs must be a mortuary slab. Somehow my number had come up without me even knowing it. Damn. I wasn't even close to being ready to check out. I still had to find Lilian. And I had the sweater to finish for my sister. Is this really how it works? You're just—gone?

I felt the hands on my chest. Warm, with a light touch, but strong. Massaging my pecs, and then working out to the deltoids, then slowly down my arms and underneath my sides and torso.

If this was death, it wasn't half bad.

The hands were behind my lower back now, kneading, gaining intensity, and they slowly worked their way up around my waist and moved down toward my crotch.

Now I could feel my heart beat, goddamn it. It was pumping the blood through my veins like someone had opened up a fire hydrant, but I still couldn't move an inch.

Barbara? Is that you?

I jerked convulsively under the bed sheet, and my eyes popped open.

I was at home in my own bed, alone. Just your basic horny dream, with a little weirdness thrown in. It had been weeks since my wife and I had made love, and when we'd had gaps like that before, my subconscious would sometimes treat me to a sideshow. I was still aroused, and I thought about waking Barbara, but it was late, and she wouldn't appreciate it even though we were way overdue.

Leave me alone, dreams. Please. I have enough on my mind already.

SATURDAY

THIS TIME I WAS GOING to take everything I had.

I gathered up my collection of listening devices, GPS trackers, and cameras with long-range lenses, my cellphone reader, my locksmith's tool bag, my knitting, my trusty MacBook Pro that Roberto had kitted out for me, both of my Glocks, the sawed-off, and plenty of shells and ammo, and loaded it into the trunk of the Beemer in the wee hours before anyone was awake. I wanted to get on the road by six, and maybe catch Chloe Heffernan in her housecoat, sipping coffee and surprised enough by my sudden appearance to tell me everything that she knew.

I had already decided that I would keep it under eighty on the way down to Coral Gables, because if I got stopped and they looked in my trunk, I would be detained, concealed-carry permit or not. I could storm the Bastille with the stuff that I'd packed—but it was a long drive down there, and I didn't want to have to come back to Vero just because I'd run out of bullets.

I was outside of Fort Pierce and was just getting onto I-95 when Roberto popped his head up from the back seat, causing me to swerve two lanes to the left and almost go off the highway. He looked sleepy-eyed, and a blanket covered his shoulders. I hadn't noticed him back there when I had been packing my gear into the trunk in the semidarkness of my garage.

"What the hell are you doing here?"

"I fell asleep," he said.

"In the back seat of my car? I can hardly fit a bag of groceries in there."

"It's not so bad if you curl up."

"I'm turning around. Shit. This is an hour out of my way."

"I'm going with you," he said. "I heard you talking last night. I wanted to go see my father, so I got dressed and crawled in here."

"You can't Roberto. Things have gotten—bad, OK? I can't take you along."

"Just drop me at the hospital. I'll stay out of your way, I promise."

I groaned, but my stowaway was right. I could drop him off and go about my business. "All right. But first you have to earn your keep. I need to find out where someone lives."

"You can do that on your smartphone."

"She's a cop's wife," I said. "They don't list home addresses."

"And?" he said. "Give me the phone."

Smug little bastard. I couldn't help smiling, despite the fact that I'd hardly gotten any sleep and had awakened in a grumpy mood. Roberto had a way of erasing all that.

*

Lieutenant Talbot Heffernan's place in Coconut Grove had frontage on one of the canals that led out the Coral Gables Waterway to the ocean. Not bad, on a detective's salary plus a paralegal's. Maybe there was some family money—Talbot sounded like a boarding-school name.

I had left Roberto at his father's bedside, after coming clean about Gustavo's actual condition on the trip down. The doctors had taken him off the coma-inducing drug, and he had acknowledged us when we arrived—in fact, I saw a definite spark of joy in his eyes when he saw his son, and it gave me hope that he was on the mend. Bringing Roberto had been a good thing, I realized. I hadn't said a word to him about his dead uncle, but I wondered if he'd already seen the news on the Internet. Probably. Roberto didn't miss much.

I had made the drive from the hospital to Coconut Grove in a few minutes, as the traffic was sparse. The shops weren't open yet, and the doctor's offices and banks were closed for the weekend, keeping much of the usual morning traffic off of the road. If you were Floridian and of a certain age, you checked in regularly with both your doctor and your broker. I mean, what good was it to be rich if you were sick? Or healthy if you were broke? These philosophical matters were pondered daily at the Aquacise classes and bridge tables, and in a few years I would be pondering them myself, but for now my philosophy was simply to stay alive, and not bounce any checks if I could help it.

Chloe Heffernan met me at the door. She wasn't in her housecoat. She was fully dressed, and she looked awake and properly caffeinated.

The house was one of those open-plan jobs furnished with glitzy, Pier One-type decorations that had the longevity of a mayfly. Mrs.

Heffernan showed me to a blue wicker couch with a thinly-padded seat that would keep any guests from lingering. That was fine—I planned to be in and out as soon as I could, as long as I was getting the straight story.

"Your husband?"

"In bed," she said. "He finally got some sleep last night. What are you doing here?"

"You heard about Segundo?"

"What?" Her face changed suddenly from that of a woman ready to start her day to someone who had had a brick dropped on her toe. I hated to say what I had to say next.

"He was killed yesterday."

She buried her face in her hands and began to make noises that sounded like she was going to be sick to her stomach. I rose from my chair and tried to put an arm around her, but she pushed it away. "What do you want to know?" she said, gasping for breath.

"Take your time." I waited, while she alternated between labored breathing and stifled sobs.

"Just—tell me what you need to know. I knew this would happen."

"That he would be killed?"

"He was a good man," she said. "Not like the other two."

"You mean Javier? And his father?"

"I—I don't know everything. Just—"

A bedroom door opened beyond us, and Talbot Heffernan entered into the big living room, dressed in a plaid bathrobe. "Vince? Something wrong?"

"Segundo Pimentel got shot," I said. "He was at his weekend place. Blue Cypress Lake, outside of Vero."

"Dead?" Tal Heffernan said.

"Yes."

"I'd better get to the office," Chloe Heffernan said. "The phone will be ringing off the hook."

"Stay here," her husband said. "We'll have to seal it off. We'll be getting a warrant, for sure."

"No, you won't," she said. "The court will appoint an attorney to take the practice over. That's how it works." She had quickly composed herself and was looking directly at her husband.

"This is a murder investigation," he said. "It was a homicide, right Vince?"

"It looked like a pro hit. Sometime the night before last."

"No one's going through his files, Tal," she said. "You know that. They're confidential."

"Chloe, whose side are you on here? The man just got killed. He was your boss."

I watched the husband and wife go back and forth, but she was right. A lawyer's practice records are laden with client confidentiality issues, and in this case there would be some give-and-take between the cops and the courts. Ultimately, the chief judge of the Superior Court would make the call.

"I'm going," she said. "At the very least I need to clean up. I left files open all over the place."

She left us, and the detective turned to me. "You came down here to tell me this?"

"I'm going to make a few more stops," I said. "Javier, and maybe the sister."

"Javier's gone," Heffernan said. "We were looking for him yesterday afternoon, after you saw him. His secretary said he'd left on a trip, but she didn't know where."

"That doesn't sound good," I said. "We're starting to run out of Pimentels."

"I should probably put someone on the sister," he said.

"I'll take care of her," I said. "I'm headed there next."

Which wasn't entirely true. Lieutenant Heffernan hadn't seen it, but his wife had given me a head fake from the hallway just before she'd left. I didn't think it was because she thought I was cute. She was sending me a message, and she didn't want her husband to know:

Follow me.

*

Now I might make finally some progress, I thought. Chloe Heffernan had just handed me the family jewels.

I was in the car, crossing over the Rickenbacker Causeway toward Key Biscayne with a slim, new-looking tablet computer on my lap. I didn't dare put it down on the seat next to me—it wasn't going to leave my hands until I saw Roberto and we got the slender little machine to spew forth the things that Segundo Pimentel had most wanted to keep hidden.

These aren't client files, she'd said when I had met her at his law office. *This was for his personal correspondence. He kept it in his safe. It has a password, so you'll have to find a way to open it.*

No problem, I'd said. I had tried to get her to answer a bunch of questions. *What did Segundo do for the Pimentels? Any legal work? Did he have enemies? Drink a lot? Was he a risk taker? A Don Juan? Did he owe people money?* But she wouldn't say anything.

Just take it and go, she'd said. *With one condition. If there are pictures of me on it, I want them deleted. I don't want to see them on the Internet.*

Pictures? I suddenly remembered the stack of women's magazines that I had seen next to the coffee table at the Moonshiner's Camp.

She had shown me out of the lawyer's office and watched as I got into the BMW. I knew exactly where I would go from there: across the bay to pick up Susanna, and then back to South Miami Hospital to collect Roberto. From there, the three of us would return to Vero Beach. Susanna would stay at my house and could sleep in the study with Roberto—I had quite the refugee camp going. I would greet my wife and child, and then Roberto and I would sit outside at the back patio table drinking Cokes while he hacked into the tablet.

Chloe Heffernan had actually answered one question for me, just as I was going out the door. I had paused at the threshold to ask her how long she and Segundo had been together. She'd looked me in the eyes, and for a moment I thought that she would come completely apart.

Nine years, she had said. And she had understood that I wasn't asking her how long she and Segundo had worked together. I was asking her something else.

*

"Backgammon?" I asked Susanna Pimentel as we passed through South Fort Lauderdale on the interstate. This time I was taking the coastal route, and we had traveled in silence while she finished her yoghurt. I had grabbed a quick calzone from Au Bon Pain at the hospital, and my stomach was now doing a triple salchow, followed by a double axel. I don't speak French, but I'm guessing that *au bon pain* means: this is gonna hurt.

"Segundo was one of the best players in the world," Susanna said. "He got into betting at Harvard, and he dropped out in senior year to go play all over Europe. My father finally persuaded him to finish college, and then go on to law school."

"Why would Gustavo want me to know that? It's just a game, right?"

"Segundo told me that he could make a hundred thousand dollars in a single match," she said. She was riding shotgun and Roberto was squeezed into the back, quietly working on the tablet. He had hooked it up to my MacBook and had said that he'd have it hacked before we got home.

"So he made a living playing it? He won more than he lost?"

"Yes, for about a year. He lost some matches, I'm sure. But he was so good that nobody in the country would play against him. He had to go to Monaco, or to Egypt, where the best players lived, and even they wouldn't play him after a while. So he went back to school."

"A backgammon hustler," I said. "I didn't know they existed."

When I had arrived at the hospital to collect Roberto, Gustavo Arguelles still hadn't been able to utter a word, and had been drifting in and out of sleep. But he'd had a brief waking moment, long enough for me to tell him about his dead brother-in-law, and he had waved his wrist as if he were holding a pencil. I understood, and found him a Sharpie and a scrap of paper, and he wrote it out, letter by letter in labored, uneven handwriting: *This is about backgammon. That's what Segundo told me.* Roberto's father was giving me all the help that he could, even in his heavily medicated state.

"I always thought that backgammon was luck," I said to Susanna. "There are only a certain number of moves, right? It's not like chess."

"My brother used to say that the game itself was eighty percent luck. Everybody who is any good knows the moves. It's the doubling die that is the secret."

"Doubling die?"

"You roll the regular dice for the moves," she said. "But there's a special die that has a 2, 4, 8, 16, 32, and 64 on it. When you think that you have the advantage, you can double the bet. So in one game a thousand-dollar bet can become sixty-four thousand dollars."

"So don't both players have the same odds? Especially if everyone knows the same moves?"

"We started playing when we were kids. He could beat me every time, because he played so fast, and he would rush me, and I'd make a mistake. He does that to his opponents, and after a while he wears them down. He goads them into playing faster than they should, and they screw up. He's like a machine."

"I still don't get why Gustavo would have written that. What would this have to do with Lilian?"

"No idea," Susanna Pimentel said. It was only two in the afternoon but she already looked tired, and her makeup was streaked from when she'd seen Gustavo and hadn't been able to hold back her tears. "Lili doesn't even play anymore. Not since we were all children."

"Lilian played backgammon?"

"Oh yes. She could beat Segundo, and it drove him crazy. It's probably what motivated him to get so good at it. The poor kid could never keep his allowance for more than a day."

*

Susanna and Barbara hadn't met before, but they settled onto two barstools at the kitchen counter and began to talk with the intimacy of old friends. At face value it was an unlikely combination: the Russian literature professor and the forty-something nursing student who had traveled a bumpy road through life. Barbara had grown up dirt poor in Jacksonville, and had only made it as far as high school, but she was an avid if slow reader, and if you read like that you can hold your own in a conversation with anybody. Susanna took an immediate shine to Royal, and the three of them were settling in nicely on the couch while Roberto did his computer forensic work on the back patio. I sat with him at the glass table and worked on my sister's sweater, which was starting to look like an overgrown potholder, and I wondered if I had been too ambitious.

So far the tablet hadn't revealed Lilian's whereabouts, but it had definitely revealed some interesting shots of Chloe Heffernan, who was a very attractive woman. The photographer had used a decent camera and a professional lens that had kept her features in focus while blurring the background in an appealing way: it directed the viewer's attention to the model, not the setting, and the result was breathtaking. It was also highly educational for Roberto, as many of the photos of Mrs. Heffernan's "features" had left little or nothing to the imagination. Roberto was trying his darndest to be cool about it, but I decided that it would be prudent to take the tablet away from him and have a look myself before his hair spontaneously caught on fire.

"Can you sharpen up the background?" I asked him. "I want to know where these were taken."

"Buzzkill," he said, grinning.

"This is work, dude. Not recreation. You can look at titties on your own time."

"Porn is for losers, anyway," he said. "There's an EXIF file in the images. It has the geodata embedded in it. Give me a sec."

He tapped at my MacBook, which was tethered to the tablet. "West of here. It's on this map."

He passed the computer over to me, and I saw what he was look-ing at. A red dot pulsed at the northwest corner of Blue Cypress Lake—the Moonshiner's Camp.

"I figured," I said. "Now I need you to delete all these."

"Seriously?"

"Yes. I made someone a promise."

"OK," he said. We liked to joke around, but he knew when I meant it.

"Next up is backgammon," I said. "I want to know if there's any-thing in there that mentions it."

Roberto tapped at the keys for several minutes. "Yeah, it's in here," he said. "My uncle was way into that. There are some websites he went to, and a bunch of emails. This is weird though—let me check this out."

"What is weird?"

"One sec," he said. He tapped at the keys. "OK. He was emailing somebody in Cuba. Not through Nauta."

"What's Nauta?"

"That's the Cuban telephone company's Internet service. Most traffic routes through there. But this is different."

"How?"

"It's a diplomatic email service," Roberto said. "And it's encrypt-ed, big time."

"Can you get into it?"

"I don't know."

"There's a six-pack of Cokes in it for you. Maybe a whole case."

"Forget that. If I can hack this, you owe me a six-pack of PBR."

"Pabst Blue Ribbon?" I said to my underage friend. "No way. If I'm buying you a six of beer, I'd just as soon not poison you on the first outing."

*

The whole house was asleep at ten thirty except for me. I was sit-ting in my recliner, trying to put everything together. Lilian was gone and quite possibly kidnapped, and we were coming up on a week with no real leads. Gustavo Arguelles was laid up in a hospital bed, barely able to communicate. Susanna and Roberto were safe in my house but were essentially hostages to the events. Roberto's uncle and grandfa-ther were dead.

So far, I knew that Segundo Pimentel had been having an affair with a police detective's wife for nine years. I also knew that he had been a backgammon sharp, and he might have made a few enemies in the process. What did that have to do with his sister's disappearance? Nothing? It didn't seem relevant, despite Gustavo's scrawled message. Maybe I just didn't get it. I still had very little hard evidence to go on, and I had checked in with Bobby Bove earlier in the evening to see if the missing persons search had turned up anything, but it hadn't. Lilian Arguelles could be anywhere.

She could also be dead, like her father and brother, although I couldn't allow myself to even think about that. I needed a break in this case. Yes, it was a *case*, and I was back on the job. I wasn't happy about the circumstances, but I also felt more alive than I had in months, and I knew that this was perhaps the most important part of my recovery—the mental part, in addition to the physical. Megan Rumsford could work me over and massage me all she wanted, but the real progress would only be made when I was back to being myself, Vince Tanzi, the guy who could solve other people's problems—albeit, while avoiding my own. Megan had nailed it when she'd said that you could die from not doing what you loved to do.

I thought about Megan, and what I was going to do about her, and how I should handle what I felt would be a healthy, necessary separation from her services, for both of us. She had crossed the boundaries of our friendship, for god-knows-what reason. Why would a babe like her even bat an eyelash at someone my age?

And I also had to keep my libido in check, or I would risk everything. Sure, Barbara and I had hit a speed bump, but things now seemed to be on the mend. I might even knock on the nursery door to see if I could entice her back to our matrimonial bed. Even though we would both be tired, we might still summon the energy to make love while being quiet enough to not wake the baby, or the Pimentel family refugees. It had been way too long.

My cellphone buzzed in my pocket, and I drew it out for a look. *I'm in trouble,* it said. The text was from Megan Rumsford.

Where are you? I sent back.

21st Street, she sent back. *I'm outside Cunningham's.*

Cunningham's Pool and Darts was arguably Vero Beach's finest dive bar, for a variety of reasons: the music was loud, the beer was cheap, the pool tables were level, and everybody was your friend, even if you were an Italian American like me, not an Irishman, and you couldn't tell a four-leaf clover from a cannoli. I'd hoisted a few PBRs there, back in my deputy days.

Five minutes, I sent. Whether or not I needed to fire Megan I still liked her, and I would do anything for her. She had been a huge help to me, like Barbara had said. I opened the door to the garage, started my car, and sped out of the driveway into the damp, moonless night.

*

"Get yourself a cue and let me give you a thrashing." I had hustled to get downtown to the bar, and was sweating when I entered. Megan Rumsford stood by the side of a pool table, wearing a sleeveless green top with tight denim shorts and holding a cue stick. She didn't look like she was in distress—she looked like a million bucks, after taxes.

"That shouldn't be too difficult," I said. "Do you want to talk first?"

"Afterward."

I took a cue stick off the wall while she racked the balls. "Nine ball?" she asked.

"Sure." I dabbed at the end of the cue with blue chalk as if I knew what I was doing.

"You can break," she said.

"Got it," I said. I positioned the cue ball and hit it hard, into the group of balls. The nine ball obligingly rolled into the far corner pocket, which was an automatic win.

"Dumb luck," she said, laughing.

"That's the only kind I have."

Megan re-racked the balls and took the break. Her shirt draped open at the front as she leaned over, and I glimpsed her bra. She took her attention away from her shot, momentarily, and smiled up at me. Then she gave the cue a fierce thrust and knocked in two balls on the break. Within a couple of minutes she had run the table, ending with the nine ball, and a guy in a Florida State hat at the next table gave a whistle of appreciation. Her game was fast but deliberate, and I figured that she could beat anyone in the place, especially if she flashed her lacy black bra at them like she had at me. Some people sure know how to ruin a guy's concentration.

"Where'd you learn how to play like that?" I asked. "That was amazing."

"We had a table, growing up. Tie-breaker?"

"That's enough for me."

"Let's find a seat at the bar," she said. "I'll buy you a beer and you can continue telling me how amazing I am."

"You said you were in trouble?"

"We'll get to that part."

*

One beer became a pitcher, which in turn became a series of pitchers, and the two of us exchanged our increasingly incoherent life stories at the bar while we drank. I knew that I had absolutely no business getting hammered with a vivacious young woman on a Saturday night in plain sight of anyone who might wander by. You do that and you might as well take out an ad in the morning paper: *Attention Gossips! Vince Tanzi was all over some babe last night at Cunningham's, and it sure wasn't his wife!* People liked to talk, and I saw several people who I knew. But I didn't give a damn, and it wasn't just the beer. I was enjoying myself, even though I was wondering why I'd been called out in the middle of the night.

Megan had grown up on a farm in northern Vermont, where her father dabbled at raising sheep but mostly watched the stock ticker on CNBC. She had quit college and had bounced from one job to another until she'd taken a massage course, which had convinced her to get her P.T. degree from the University of Vermont. She said she'd moved to Florida because she was tired of the northern winters, which was also a part of the reason that I had quit the Barre, Vermont police force almost thirty years ago.

We swapped details about our Green Mountain upbringing—I was the son of a blue-collar stonecutter, and she was the daughter of a blue-blood heir to a company that manufactured tractor wheels. Megan liked to smoke pot, and I liked my beer. She listened to Lady Gaga, and I listened to every possible kind of music except Lady Gaga. I'd been married twice, and—she refused to answer the question, when the subject came up. In fact, the conversation stopped dead.

"You OK?" I said. The third pitcher was now down to about an inch of beer, but I was sober enough to know that I'd stepped in something.

"This is the trouble part," she said. "I think I made a big mistake."

"How so?"

"You'll hear about it, sooner or later," she said. "Probably from your wife."

"Barbara?"

"Goddamn, Vince, you are so sexy," she said, slurring slightly. "And I'm not saying that because I'm drunk. The alcohol has nothing to do with it. You just are."

"Megan—"

"You want to fire me, I know."

How did she know that? "Listen, I—"

"Let's go outside," she said. "I'm parked in the back."

She took my arm and steered me between the pool tables, which were all busy with players, and we had to jostle our way through the onlookers. Megan pushed open a metal door that said "Emergency Exit", and we were suddenly thrust into a quiet, sultry Florida night, the only noise being the rustling of palm fronds. "My Jeep is over there," she said. "Come on."

"Do you want me to drive you? My car's out front."

"No."

"I should drive you," I said. "I know all the cops, if we get stopped."

"Get in the car, Vince." She gave me her P.T. drill sergeant look.

I climbed into the passenger seat and she got in next to me. "You can fire me," she said. "You're right. I got too close. I could lose my license for the shit I've done."

"You're good at what you do," I said. "Barbara thinks—"

"Would you just shut up about Barbara?" Megan said, her voice rising. "Come over here."

She put her arms around my neck and pulled me close to her, across the center console. Our faces were inches apart. "I'll let you fire me, but I want a kiss," she said. "Just a friendly little kiss. Because we're friends."

What do you do in a situation like that? Jerk your head back and say no? Rejecting her would only make it worse.

I closed my eyes and let it happen. She thrust her tongue deep into my mouth, aggressively, and grabbed my wrist, pushing my hand up under her shirt and over the lacy black bra. "Touch me," she said. With her free hand she unsnapped the bra from behind, and she pushed my fingers over her nipple.

"Megan," I said, trying to break free, but she kissed me again, hard. I felt like I was going to explode unless she let me go—partly from the shock, partly from the guilt, but also partly because I had never been kissed like that by anyone.

Tanzi's Tip #5: It's not just a friendly little kiss when the other person is licking your tonsils.

She had covered my hand with hers and was making me massage her breast, and then she began to convulse, and her arms and legs started to flail wildly. What the hell?

I'd had EMT training as a deputy, and I tried to remember what to do when someone had a seizure. You weren't supposed to restrain them, you cleared away the furniture, you kept them from falling, none of which applied. I was scared out of my wits, and I took the phone out of my pocket to call an ambulance.

"What are you doing?" Megan said. She had stopped shaking, and was staring at the phone in my hand.

"Calling for help," I said. "You had a seizure."

"That wasn't a seizure, you idiot," she said. "That was an orgasm."

Oh my god. Was that possible? "Look, Megan—"

"Just go," she said. "Get out of the car." She was trying to refasten her bra behind her back.

"I'm—"

"Get the hell out of here before I smack you," she interrupted. "You're firing me, so you can just fuck off."

I climbed out of the Jeep and limped across the parking lot. My shuffle had gotten noticeably worse, no doubt because of the three pitchers of beer. But any buzz that I'd had before was gone now because of what I had allowed to take place: I had just done the dumbest thing ever. God help me.

Maybe not the dumbest, God might have responded, but it had to be in the top ten.

∗

Getting home was something of a challenge seeing how I had lubricated myself enough at Cunningham's to allow the car to easily glide past a red light or a stop sign, and I crawled along at twenty miles an hour. That was always a giveaway back when I was patrolling the bars as a deputy—the drunks overcompensated, going way under the speed limit, and we would nail them. I knew better than to drive in this condition, but I wasn't about to call Barbara, or anyone else. If I got popped for DUI it would serve me right for being such a complete jackass with Megan Rumsford. I was still in shock over the whole thing, and I was especially disgusted with myself about one aspect in particular:

It had felt good.

Which meant nothing now, seeing how I had dumped her as my P.T., and then she had nearly kicked my ass, after nearly jumping my bones. Talk about conflicting signals—from both of us. In my next life I want to be a starfish: they can reproduce asexually, so there is no need to hang around in bars, get all hot and bothered with a potential mate, and then weave home, three-quarters in the bag just because nature made you do it. Everything would be so much simpler without sex, although if sex didn't exist, neither would most of the world's great literature, theater, art, film, photography, music, or strip clubs, and that would be a shame.

The houses on my road are modest by Vero standards, and my development hadn't spent a lot on amenities. The nearest streetlight was several houses away from mine, so when I approached the parked van I almost ran into it. Instead, I swerved, and I continued on beyond my driveway because I recognized the vehicle. The Iturbe brothers' blacked-out minivan was parked across from my house, where they could see anyone who was coming or going.

I drove down the street and rounded the corner. The house on the block that was directly behind ours was vacant, and I quietly pulled the BMW into the driveway. It was too dark to proceed without a light, so I used the one on my phone, which was one of the most useful features on the device. I crossed the backyard and swung my legs over the low wall that divided the properties and led into my own yard. I quietly let myself inside my house through the patio door.

First, I checked the bedrooms and the study to make sure that everyone was still there and to confirm that the two gangbangers hadn't already done something awful. Royal was asleep at Barbara's breast, and Susanna and Roberto were slumbering on opposing couches in the study. After that, I carefully entered the garage and selected a crowbar from the tool rack. I left the house from the back door, the same way I'd come in, and returned to my car, where I removed a GPS tracker and my sawed-off shotgun from the trunk. I called the gun my *lupo*, like they did in the mobster films—it was an intimidating weapon with an eighteen-inch barrel that measured just long enough to make it legal in Florida. Legal, and lethal.

I decided that the best way to do this would be from behind, so I rounded the block on foot from the other direction and proceeded up my street toward the rear of the van. If they happened to look in their mirrors, they would see me. Fine. Anyone who was dumb enough to stake out my goddamn house had it coming. If they got out of the van, I would shoot.

Nobody got out. Stakeouts are mind-numbingly boring, and I'd dozed off more than once while doing them as a P.I. The Iturbe brothers were probably in dreamland. I quietly snapped the GPS tracker's magnets onto a U-Haul hitch under the back bumper, and crept along the side of the van until I reached the driver's window. An XXL-sized human being was seated in the front with his head leaned back against the headrest, and I could tell that he was asleep. I didn't see anyone in the passenger seat, so maybe I was dealing with one brother, not two. Either way, I wanted them gone.

My left side may be messed up from my accident, but my right side works fine. I swung the crowbar in a wide arc and slammed it into the driver's window, creating a shower of fragments that covered the sleeping figure in broken glass. I shifted the shotgun to my right hand and pointed it at his face.

"What the fuck?" he screamed.

"You can leave," I said. "But if you come back here, I'll kill you."

"Fuck you, man," he said. I could see him now—he was the one with the braid. No one else was in the vehicle.

"Drive safe," I said. He started the ignition and stomped on the gas, making me step back, but I was able to swing the bar and take out a taillight before he was gone.

I got my phone and dialed Lieutenant Tal Heffernan's number. The detective would probably be asleep, but if he had been looking for the Iturbes, they were now found, and I would be able to track their whereabouts on my MacBook thanks to a GPS program that Roberto had installed. I would ask Heffernan to book them for the assault in Key West, not to mention Gustavo's injuries, and then sweat them, hard, because I wanted to know who they were working for if they were truly no longer in the employ of the Pimentels. I was thinking that I might return to Coral Gables yet again, to watch the interrogation from behind the mirrored glass. I had questions for them, and I wanted answers.

I also had a question for Heffernan, although I wasn't going to ask it, because it was none of my goddamned business, but still...

How can a police detective not know that his wife has been carrying on with another man for nine years?

SUNDAY

ROBERTO HAD A FORK IN one hand and was working at my open MacBook with the other. He hadn't said a word about the made-from-scratch waffles that I'd served him, topped with fresh strawberries, real maple syrup and whipped cream, because he was preoccupied with trying to hack into Segundo Pimentel's emails, and so far he hadn't had any success. His preoccupation might be a good thing, I decided, as today made a full week since he'd last seen his mother, and that had to be weighing on him. It was certainly weighing on me.

Barbara, Royal, and Susanna had left to go grocery shopping before I'd been awake, and I wished that I'd known—I would have kept them home. Nobody was going anywhere until the Iturbes were found. I'd been up until five AM sending location coordinates to Tal Heffernan, but when they'd finally spotted the van in a vacant lot in Hialeah it was unoccupied. I was angry with myself for not having just held the guy until the cops arrived, but with all that beer in me it had been too risky.

I'd had a slight hangover that had been tamed with a couple Motrins, but the drugs couldn't do anything for my guilt. Barbara might not have even noticed that I had been gone, but that was beside the point. The point was that I had sinned, big time, and playing pat-a-cake with Megan's womanly attributes on a warm Florida night was surely a mortal one, not the lighter, venal kind. Twelve years of Catholic school had drilled that into me. Messing with Megan was a felony, not a misdemeanor, and I was eventually going to have to turn myself in. She and Barbara knew each other, and things like what had taken place out behind Cunningham's didn't stay quiet for long, so I would have to get it out in the open if I wanted to have any chance to put my spin on it. And just exactly *how* I was going to spin it I didn't know yet, but I was already thinking about borrowing a SWAT vest from Bobby Bove before my wife and I had our little discussion. My three-pitcher hangover was nothing compared to what I knew her wrath would be.

Sonny Burrows pulled his Subaru into the driveway just as I was cleaning up the breakfast dishes. I met him at the door.

"Is the Warden home?"

"She's out shopping," I said. "You want some waffles? The griddle's still warm."

"I ate. Just checkin' on you."

"Let me pour you a coffee. I need to practice a confession."

"Uh-oh."

We adjourned to the back patio, out of Roberto's earshot. I sat at the glass table and motioned Sonny to a chair. "You ever hear of a woman having an orgasm just because you touched her? Fondled her breasts?"

He smiled. "All I have to do is walk in the room and they have an orgasm."

"I'm serious."

"Google it, man."

"It doesn't matter." I said. "I fucked up."

"So, confess," he said, taking a sip of his coffee.

I explained what had taken place the night before, and caught him up on the events of the past few days, including Gustavo's hospitalization, Megan's topless paddleboard tour of Blue Cypress Lake, and Segundo Pimentel's murder. I described my earlier visits to Javier and Segundo Pimentel's respective offices, and my subsequent meeting the next morning with Chloe Heffernan and her husband. I spilled the beans about the paralegal's affair with her boss, and told him about the pictures on the tablet computer that Roberto was now working over. I also told Sonny about the braided goon who I had found waiting outside my house.

"Same guys?"

"Just one of them. The same van. I ran up his insurance bill some, with a crowbar."

Sonny smiled. "Hoo boy. I'll work security for you if you need it."

"I need it. I'm going south again, to poke around. I want to talk to the Pimentel brother who's still alive, if I can find him. He knows more than he's telling me."

"I can stay right here," Sonny said. "And you can let that thing with the woman slide. Everybody makes those mistakes."

"Barbara will find out sooner or later."

"Don't you worry none about Barbara." He gave me a look that said: *There's more to that, but don't ask me.*

"Sonny? What are you not telling me?"

"I just have a problem with your wife sometimes."

"I know that. Why?"

"She rubs me the wrong way, that's all."

"How so?"

"You're my friend, man."

"Yes," I said. "And you're mine. So you can stop bullshitting me."

He waited for a long time to speak. "Vince—when you do your work, how do you find out when somebody's steppin' out?"

I put down my coffee a little too hard, and it made a loud noise on the glass top of the table. "The phone bill. I look for texts or the calls at three in the morning. You don't call your hairdresser at three in the morning."

"Uh-huh," he said, nodding.

"So what are you saying?"

"Dude's name is Angelo." Sonny looked away from me, back toward the house. "He may be full of shit, but he works as a trainer at that club your wife goes to. Says he has a white girlfriend, bragging about it all over Gifford. Says she's married to an ex-cop."

I had nothing to say back, and I felt the blood rush to my face. Barbara was cheating on me? Nine months after giving birth to our son? I had to laugh at what I'd thought about Talbot Heffernan being clueless for so long. This made twice for me—it had happened once with Glory, and now with Barbara.

"You want me to school him?" Sonny said. "I got two strikes already, but I know a guy."

"No. I don't want you to do anything. Nobody's getting schooled. I have to think this through. What makes you think he's not just running his mouth?"

"Check your phone bill, man."

I would, I thought. But not now. If Barbara was having an affair, it would explain some things, but I had way too much going on at the moment to have anything explained. I would just let it fester back there in my mind somewhere, while I did my job and found Roberto's mother. That was probably not the healthiest course of action, but frankly, I didn't care. The task at hand was more important than whatever drama my wife might have cooked up.

And I forgot all about my guilt over getting drunk and fondling Megan Rumsford's naked breast. That was ancient history now.

*

I had decided to take the back route to Coral Gables and was on U.S. 27 nearing Lake Okeechobee from the opposite direction that I had come a couple of days ago. The day had turned out to be partially overcast and was nearly as glum as my mood. Why was it that I could attract a beautiful, younger, single woman, but I couldn't keep a wife? Sure, that was some guys' fantasy, but all I can say is try it. It sucks.

Barbara had hardly reacted when I'd told her that I was leaving again. Maybe she would text her lover boy the gym-dildo, and they would arrange a hasty tryst. Christ on a pogo stick. I was letting this fester, all right. The farther I drove, the more righteous my indignation became, until I had fully and completely absolved myself of any lingering shred of responsibility for what had happened the night before with Megan Rumsford. That was no big deal. Hey, everybody makes those mistakes, like Sonny had said. I could let it slide. In fact, the Warden had just handed me a get-out-of-jail-free card. I could go out and do whatever I damn well pleased with Megan, or any other young babe who was crazy enough to think that a graying, semi-disabled goombata like me was still sexy. Had Megan really said that? It seemed like a dream now—a nice one, not a nightmare, as it had seemed earlier today, before my debriefing with Sonny Burrows.

My first stop would be at South Miami Hospital where I would consult with Gustavo, my bedridden oracle and clue-dispenser, when he was conscious. Maybe he'd throw me another tidbit, and I had promised Roberto that I would check on him anyway. After that I was going to find Javier Pimentel and put him through the paces, with or without the nut-vise. He had mentioned that he and Gustavo used to fish together, and I wondered if he had a boat. If you were stupid rich in Florida, you owned some kind of boat, whether you used it or not. Before I left Vero I'd called Bobby Bove and had asked him about my hunch, and sure enough there was a Mikelson 70 Sportfisher in the DMV records registered to Pimentel Holdings, LLC, with Javier as the contact person.

Whoa. A seventy-foot Mikelson wasn't something that you took out to the Gulf Stream to snag a couple of bonito while you quaffed Miller Lites from a cooler. A sportfishing boat that big was like a five-star hotel, with an Orvis store attached to the stern. The fish didn't stand a chance, unless the ship's occupants were too blitzed on champagne to bother to cast a line.

I also called Tal Heffernan on the way down to ask him if he knew where Javier moored the thing, and if anyone had gone looking for him there. No, and no. I was starting to have my doubts about the

Detective Lieutenant. He was a nice guy—nice enough to keep me informed to the point of allowing me to look through his files—but so far he had come up with diddlysquat about the Raimundo Pimentel murder, or the Gustavo mugging, or Lilian's kidnapping. That, and the fact that he was clueless about his wife, made me wonder if he wasn't one of those boobs who had somehow climbed the ladder when he should be writing out parking tickets. I'd known a few cops like that, and they just made everything harder for the ones who knew their jobs.

My phone buzzed, and I pulled over into the parking area of a fried chicken joint to read the text. Roberto.

The person calls himself Pescador, it said.

Who?

The one my uncle was emailing, he wrote back. *In Cuba.*

Good work, I wrote. *Anything else?*

Yeah, he said. *Spreadsheets. But they're way coded. I'll keep on it.*

You da man, I texted. *Back soon. I'll be seeing your dad in an hour.*

Tell him I love him, Roberto wrote.

Shit. I had to sit there by the side of the road for a while to get the lump out of my throat. How could a fifteen-year-old kid deal with all this? It made my own problems seem ludicrously overblown.

You know what? To hell with my romantic peccadillos. I was back to work now, and I was going to find Lilian Arguelles, and damn soon. Roberto needed his mother, and a week was already way too long.

*

Gustavo Arguelles had gotten his color back, but he still couldn't talk. They had stopped giving him the pentobarbital because his concussion was clearing up, and he looked alert as I entered the hospital room. He couldn't smile when he saw me, but I could see it in his eyes.

"Roberto sends his love," I said. "He's at my place. He's doing OK."

Gustavo raised his hand and made a writing motion. I saw a clipboard with a pencil attached next to his bed and passed it to him.

Tell him I love him too, he wrote.

"I'm looking for Javier," I said. "He's gone off somewhere, and the cops don't know where he is. I found out he has a boat, but I don't know where he keeps it."

Gustavo scribbled on the pad. *Key West. Big boat. Mamarta.*

"Mamarta?"

Is name of boat, he wrote. *After his mother.*

"Do you think he might be on it?"

Don't know.

"Did you find out anything about where Lilian might be? Before you were attacked?"

Maybe Segundo knew, Gustavo wrote. *Wouldn't say. We had a phone call. Said he was working on it.*

"Segundo knew? Is that why he was killed?"

Don't know.

"Would his paralegal know where Lilian is?"

Not sure, he wrote. *Segundo kept his secrets.*

"Why would someone kidnap Lilian?" I asked him.

Money, he wrote.

"You mean a ransom? You found out about a ransom?"

No, he wrote. *But Pimentels are all about money.*

"Have you ever heard the name Pescador? Somebody in Cuba?"

No. Pescador means fisherman in Spanish.

Fisherman? Hmmm. Maybe I was finally on the right track.

"You take care, Gustavo," I said. "I'm going back to Key West."

*

Once you're off the Florida mainland and out on Key Largo, it's about a hundred miles of the most beautiful scenery imaginable out to Key West via the Overseas Highway. Some of it is no different from the rest of the state, with white stucco condos, trailer parks, and tourist traps, but every few miles you hit a stretch of causeway between the string of islands, and it's just you and the perfect green-blue of the waters on each side, bordering the Florida Straits. I had the convertible top of the BMW down and was blasting out a Glen Campbell compilation CD loud enough for the rest of the traffic to hear me if their windows were open, but I didn't care because I was singing "Wichita Lineman" like it was me who had written it, and not Jimmy Webb. There's something about that stuff that goes right to the deepest, most unknowable part of my soul, which is what music is supposed to do when it's done right.

It would have been a perfect drive if I hadn't managed to get stuck behind an endless continuum of retirees in luxury RVs that looked like glitzed-up Greyhound buses. I would just get rid of one, and then another one would lumber out of nowhere and take its place ahead of me. Theoretically it's a three-hour trip from Miami to the very end of the highway, but it can be considerably longer if you're on Grammy-and-Grampy-time.

It was fully overcast and threatening to rain when I got to Key West, so I pulled over to put the top up. I took North Roosevelt Boulevard around the northern perimeter of the island, toward my destination. There are only two places to keep a boat that big: the Garrison Bight, where I'd already been and had subsequently been mugged, and the Key West Bight next to the ferry terminal. I decided to try the former, and if ol' Plumber Butt was in the fishing shack cutting up a grouper, I would grab the back of his undershorts and give him a wedgie to remember for ratting me out to the Iturbe brothers on my last trip.

I parked off of the feeder road to the Palm Avenue Causeway and got out my pocket Swarovski binoculars. The marinas were populated with houseboats and sportfisherman rigs of the forty- to fifty-foot variety—no luxury seventy-foot types in sight. I got out of the car and stretched, which felt good after the three-plus-hour drive from the hospital, not to mention the drive before that from Vero to Miami. If this was an actual case and I was getting paid, I might have just racked up a sizable mileage bill. But it wasn't, and I was exhausted, and hungry, and I needed to pee.

I found a floating Thai restaurant on the other side of the cause-way, and used their bathroom while I waited for an order of *bibimbap* to go, which is Korean, not Thai, but they didn't care and neither did I. I found a shady bench beside the water, where I ate the delicious rice and vegetable dish from the paper container, drank water from a plastic bottle, and kept an eye on the harbor's comings and goings. There was nothing I could see that looked remotely as elegant as a Mikelson—I had done an image search on my phone so that I would know what it looked like, and it was a boat that you wouldn't miss. I decided to pass the time by catching up on my correspondence—Barbara had texted me several times during the day, but I hadn't felt like answering. The last message that she had written said: *Where are U? They said U left the hospital hours ago.*

Key West again, I wrote.

She texted right back. *So we're stuck with your friend here?*

Sonny? Yes.

What am I supposed to feed him?

Supposed to feed him? What did she think he was, a zoo animal? *I believe he eats normal food. You could ask him.*

He's not what I'd call normal.

At least he's loyal, I wrote back.

A minute passed until her reply came. *Come home soon, Vince.*

Got to get this done, I wrote, and I snapped off the phone and put it in my pocket.

*

At four thirty in the afternoon I was all set for my nap, having digested the *bibimbap*, read the paper, done the crossword on my phone, checked my email, and finally gotten out my knitting, out of sheer, desperate boredom. Waiting around has never been my strong suit. I wanted to knock on a few doors, or maybe knock a few heads, but I didn't want to end up in the hospital alongside Gustavo Arguelles. *Time is on your side, Vince,* I told myself. You know that the boat lives here, somewhere. This is where Lilian's phone had last given a signal from land. Then, Roberto had tracked it offshore; south, until it either went out of range or the battery died.

Or, it went over the side of a boat. I was hopeful that it hadn't been in Lilian's pocket at the time, if that was what had happened.

My cellphone rang. "Tanzi."

"Tal Heffernan. I think we just figured this out. The Pimentel brother who died was cooking the books."

"Segundo? He did the accounting?"

"I just got off the phone with the other brother," Heffernan said. "He confirmed what we knew. Segundo did all the financing for the family's real estate projects, and he must have got in with the wrong people."

"Where did you find this?"

"We went through his office today," he said. "The Superior Court sent a chaperone, but we still scored. There were accounting records. The family coffers were millions of dollars in the red. Their lenders were in the Caymans, and we're guessing that they got fed up and took out Segundo and the old man."

"What about Javier?"

"Javier? He's more like, sales and marketing," Heffernan said. "He stays out of the finance side. He's all about the show. You've seen his office."

"My whole house would fit in his office. So you talked with Javier?"

"Yeah, and I laid it all out for him, but I figure he knew most of it already. I almost feel bad for the guy, losing half of his family over some shitty mall deals. Apparently the old man went on a buying spree in '07, at the top of the market, and Segundo had been trying to dig them out ever since, but he couldn't pull it off. He was making it look like they were solvent, but they were bleeding cash."

"So his bankers had him killed? That's crazy. There's bankruptcy, for god's sake."

"You don't know these Latinos," the detective said. "I deal with this crap every day. You look at them cross-eyed and they start a blood feud. No, this one's all done."

"What about Lilian Arguelles? My client?"

"Vince—I wouldn't get your hopes up, OK? I pressed Javier pretty hard, and he doesn't know anything about her. My guess is that she was collateral damage."

His words hit me like a sucker punch, and for a second I didn't think that I'd be able to keep the Thai food down. Lilian, dead? In a fight over who owed who? No. Not possible.

But it was possible, very much so, and I wondered what the hell I was going to say to her son.

"So, how are you going to go after them?"

"We're not," Heffernan said. "We're turning it over to the FBI. But they won't find anything. Basically, if some bad-guy lenders in the Caymans want to punch a few tickets here on the mainland, they call in a pro, and unless we happen to catch the shooter in the act, there's no way that anybody's going to find them. Don't expect the Feds to put a lot of resources on it."

"I have a teenage kid whose mother is missing. And you're telling me that nobody gives a shit?"

"I'm telling it like it is," he said. "You know. You were a cop."

Yeah, I knew. I knew that whenever a case led overseas, the locals bailed. That was somebody else's turf. Pass the buck. Call the FBI, the Border Patrol, the CIA, or Spider-Man. Whatever it had been before, it was now a lost cause, and there were a hundred other cases in the hopper that needed attention. Move along, nothing to see here, have a nice day.

Detective Talbot Heffernan had found out what was going on with the Pimentel family. Obviously he was better at his job than I'd given him credit for. Some unknown entity had made a phone call and had had Raimundo and Segundo Pimentel murdered, and Lilian might have been killed as well. Heffernan was telling it like it was.

But that didn't mean I had to accept it.

After twenty-five years of being a deputy, and then five more as a P.I., I know when I'm being told to go away. Sometimes it's obvious, like when two mugs shoot me up with a tranquilizer and then toss me out of a van. That's one way to tell me to mind my own business.

Another way is when a colleague, whom I have no reason to not believe, calmly and professionally explains that everything has been taken care of, and it's out of everybody's hands now, and, oh yes, keep your expectations low. That's the more subtle way, and it would usually be very convincing.

Except that it sounded like bullshit, and I didn't know why.

As if to prove my point, a big, expensive-looking sportfisher reflected the afternoon light on the side of its polished white hull as it slowly entered the Garrison Bight from the channel at Trumbo Point. Whoever was at the helm knew how to handle it, and they carefully maneuvered the boat alongside the far end of the row of slips, a hundred yards from where my bench was. I picked up my binoculars and adjusted the focus, just as the captain swung the big craft around so that I could make out the dark-blue letters that were painted across the transom:

MAMARTA.

Ten minutes later I watched from my bench as Javier Pimentel walked up the steps from the dock to the parking area, got into a taxi, and drove away.

I could get in my car and follow him. Or, I could wait for him to return. And while I waited, I could check out his boat. Javier had no doubt locked the Mikelson up tight, but I had my lock-picking kit in the trunk.

Popping a lock of the quality that I would find on a million-dollar yacht requires a high degree of small-motor control, and my inadvertent meeting with a bullet had taken much of that away. For the first couple of months after coming home from the hospital I had barely been able to open a beer. My hand functions had come back painfully slowly, and I'd had to completely relearn how to fasten a button, or pick up a coin off the floor, or zip up my fly without accidentally circumcising myself. Everyone agreed that I had made a lot of progress, and now all I needed to do was open a lock, on a boat.

Piece of cake. I'd be inside in five minutes, max.

*

Tanzi's Tip #6: When you meet someone from a foreign country, always ask them to teach you the best swear words, because you might need them when you run out of good ones in English.

The piece-of-cake door lock on the Mikelson had refused to yield after half an hour of coaxing with a short hook and my best tension wrench. I had skinned my knuckles twice and had broken two of the hooks, leaving me with a third one that had seen better days and might get me into an accidentally-locked bathroom but wasn't about to let me inside the sliding glass door of the boat's main saloon. My angry epithets in Norwegian and Portuguese weren't helping, and I was about to take a nearby fire extinguisher from the wall, dispense with subtlety, and heave it at the glass, when I saw someone approaching down the dock. I quickly ducked out of sight.

Javier Pimentel was leading the way toward the boat, and behind him were the Iturbe brothers, each carrying one end of a white plastic box that appeared to be a gigantic ice cooler. Uh-oh. Somebody was going to go fishing, and I was wondering if I would be the bait. I could jump off the side into the water, but I wasn't about to leave my tool bag, and it would make me sink to the bottom like a stone. Going back onto the dock wouldn't work either—there was only one way out, and it was blocked by the two massive guys who were quickly approaching behind their leader. It was apparent that what Javier had told me a few days ago about the Iturbes no longer working for the Pimentels was false. He looked like the boss here—the rock star, and the other two were the roadies. I set that thought aside to process later.

I gathered up my tools and scrambled around the deck of the boat for a hiding place. Lashed to the foredeck was a Zodiac inflatable tender, protected by a rubberized canvas boat cover. I peeled back one side of the cover and climbed in with my gear, hoping that I wouldn't have to spend the night there. The space inside was large enough for me to lie down comfortably, but if the warm evening cooled off, I would be in trouble. I was wearing a short-sleeved polo shirt and lightweight pants, and it could get surprisingly chilly on the water, even this close to the equator. I held my breath as I heard the voices getting nearer, and I opened up a corner of the boat cover to peek out.

Javier Pimentel was directing the other two men as they shrouded the big cooler in what appeared to be plastic wrap, and then attached pieces of foam to the sides with a tape gun. They bundled the whole thing in a heavy fishing net and left it at the stern of the boat. The two brothers cast off the mooring lines as Javier fired up the Mikelson's engines and then carefully piloted the craft away from the dock's perimeter. In less than a minute we were motoring back out of the channel past Trumbo Point toward the Fleming Key Cut. Not long afterward, the Mikelson rounded the western shore of the key past the

Truman estate, and I took note of our heading, which was made obvious to me by the passing landmarks and the position of the descending late afternoon sun:

South.

Javier Pimentel was steering his million-dollar fishing boat out into the Florida Straits, the hundred-mile-wide body of warm, shark-infested water that separated the Pimentel family's adopted state of Florida from their native country of Cuba. And it was a little late in the day for fishing.

*

By the time I had decided who I should call, we were out of sight of land and the cell signal was almost gone. I had eliminated Tal Heffernan, and even Bobby Bove by association. I didn't think that I was getting the straight story from the authorities for some reason and had decided that I would be better off on my own. I couldn't call Barbara, or Roberto—that would worry the hell out of them, and chances were that we'd be back in port after some evening fishing, and I could then slip away unnoticed. The person to call was Sonny, but it was too loud on the deck, even under the cover of the Zodiac, so I sent a text instead:

I'm a stowaway on Javier Pimentel's boat. Heading south from Key West. He's with the two big guys.

What? He sent right back. *You crazy? They catch you and you'll walk the plank.*

That's what I'm afraid of.

You want me to fly down?

I need you at home, I sent. *The cops say it's all over, but I don't agree. Still no Lilian.*

Maybe she's in Cuba?

Sonny had made the same connection that I had. *Maybe you're right.*

You speak any Spanish?

I can order a beer, I wrote.

Will fly to Keys tomorrow unless I hear from you, he sent. *Don't worry about your family.*

Thanks, I sent, and I turned the phone off. It had about an hour of battery life left, and I figured I might need it.

*

A couple of hours later, I used up some precious phone voltage to rummage around in the Zodiac with the benefit of the flashlight app. I was shivering from the chill, and if there was a blanket in here, I wanted it, plus I was thirsty, and I didn't want to get dehydrated. Wadded up near the motor mount was a pink sweatshirt with ELLE emblazoned on the front in block letters, and I wrapped it as far as I could around my shoulders, as it was about sixteen sizes too small to pull over my head. It helped. A small cooler in the bow of the Zodiac held about an inch of water, probably from melted ice, and I drank a few sips, knowing that I should ration it if I was going to be stashed in here for longer than I'd hoped. I lay on the bottom of the inflatable as comfortably as I could, and I began to add everything up.

Javier Pimentel had a boat in the keys, moored at exactly the same location where his sister's cellphone had last given out a signal. But according to Tal Heffernan, Javier was clueless about Lilian's disappearance, or his family's financial ruin. Javier had told me when we'd met in his office that all of this was so—*unbelievable*. Right. That one had pushed the needle on the bullshit-o-meter into the red zone.

And he had also said that the Iturbes no longer worked for the family, but here they were, and they seemed to be working pretty hard.

What had also gotten my curiosity was the "square grouper" on the rear deck, wrapped up and ready to go overboard. A square grouper was a term that was used to describe a rectangular bale of marijuana that had been dropped off the Florida coast by boat, or by plane, and then retrieved by the locals and smuggled into port. You could make a lot more money angling for weed than for amberjack. In recent years the same technique had been used to bring in cocaine, usually wrapped in a water-tight container and carrying a GPS device so that the retrieving boat was certain to find it, because a sealed-up cooler full of coke was worth many times more than a bale of brine-soaked pot and was something that you definitely didn't want to drift off into the sunset. The Coast Guard and the DEA kept watch on some of this activity from overhead, but there was just too much coastline and not enough resources.

My question was—why was Javier sending his package in the wrong direction? The stuff was supposed to come *into* the United States, not go out. The cooler was maybe five feet long and a couple of feet wide. That would hold enough cocaine to keep the entire country up until five AM watching Steven Segal movies. The box was also long enough to hold a small body. I shivered, even with the sweatshirt wrapped around me. Lilian? If she were inside there, she would be dead. The Iturbes had sealed the thing up tight.

We had been underway for nearly four hours, according to my phone. I estimated that the boat was making around twenty knots, which meant that we would be in Cuban waters very soon, if we weren't already. My calculations were confirmed when the engines were suddenly cut, and there was some activity aft of my hideaway, though I couldn't see what because my view was blocked by the pilothouse.

But I did hear the splash, just before the engines were restarted, and someone steered the boat in a slow arc north, back into our wake. We had dropped off our package and were heading home.

The sun had gone below the horizon an hour before, and the water and the skies were now nearly the same deep-blue tint, with a couple of stars out as early sentinels of the night. I had a good vantage point from underneath the boat cover, and I made out a boat approaching—fast—from the south. It was much larger than the Mikelson, and was festooned with gear. Not fishing gear—it looked like military rigging, and I took the binoculars from my bag.

The approaching boat was definitely rigged for patrolling, not fishing. The giveaway was a naval gun protruding from a turret on the front deck, and the large array of radar and communication devices that were strung along the tower. I could just make out a number in the nearly-gone light, painted in white on the side of the hull: 202. When I got back to civilization, assuming that I did, I would look it up, but my guess was that it was one of the ships that had been provided to the Cuban Navy by the Soviets, back in the day. Most of those were rusting hulks now, but this one was moving right along at full speed, directly toward the zone where Javier had dropped off his parcel.

A military vessel? Picking up a drug drop from a rich guy's sportfisher? That didn't make sense. We were cruising at twenty knots again, and I was able to watch the other boat slow down, and then turn back toward the south. It stopped, a bank of floodlights came on, and grappling hooks were dropped from the stern. I watched as they winched up the cooler, shrouded in the fishing net.

Package delivered. Sign here, please.

Everybody knows that you can't even scratch your privates anymore without some overhead satellite getting a shot of you. No doubt the area between Florida and Cuba had more cameras focused on it than a bra-less celebrity at a film premiere. Big Brother knew who was where, and when, and there were algorithms, patterns, and red flags that would set off alerts, and the Coast Guard would respond. The good guys, with the help of high-tech surveillance, were gaining ground on the bad guys. That was fine, though you also had to hold your breath and hope that this wasn't the beginning of 1984, just a generation later than Orwell had predicted.

But nobody would be paying attention to a sportfishing yacht that had casually crossed wakes with a patrol boat. A military ship was supposed to be the good guys, right?

The drop had to be something else. Javier Pimentel could surely tell me, if I was able to get him alone and ask him nicely—while hooking him up to a car battery. But I doubted that I would be given the opportunity, and that wasn't my style anyway. My best lead so far was the tablet computer that Chloe Heffernan had provided and that Roberto was now busy hacking. Once he got past the codes I had a feeling that the device would lay it all out for us, and that there would be a lot more to this than what I was being told.

MONDAY

I MANAGED TO SLIP OFF of the boat a few minutes after we docked. Javier and the Iturbes disembarked shortly after we'd returned to Key West, but they left lights on inside the main cabin of the boat, so I knew that at least one of them would be staying aboard for the remainder of the night. I watched them disappear down the walkway, and then I scooped up my knitting bag and wobbled unsteadily and not-so-stealthily down the dock toward my car, but no one saw me. The marina was dead quiet, the only sound being the metallic pinging of rigging wires against aluminum masts in the night wind. The BMW was where I'd left it, undisturbed except for a light coating of salt haze from the sea breeze. I was so glad to be back safe inside my nice little car I felt like kissing the steering wheel.

The ride back to Vero Beach took less than five hours, as the road was clear of traffic. I stopped twice for coffee, and when I rolled into my driveway I knew that even though I was dirty, smelly, unshaven, sore, and completely exhausted from sailing to Cuba and back underneath a tarp, it would be a while before I was able to calm down enough to get to sleep. The caffeine would rob me of that.

The drive had given me some time to process all the information that I had taken in during the previous twenty-four hours, and I had come up with something of a plan. First, get my exhausted ass to bed—until I was rested I would be useless. Second, work with Roberto to mine whatever information we could from the tablet computer. If our efforts came up empty, I would revisit Chloe Heffernan and ask for her help. If she had been Segundo Pimentel's paralegal—not to mention his lover—for nine years, then she must know plenty about his secret ways. And finally, I would locate Javier Pimentel again, and we would have our little talk. If Roberto could crack the tablet's defenses beforehand, I figured that I would have some leverage to make him open up.

My plan also included a couple of things that I would *not* do. One was to involve the police. I could finger the Iturbes right now for my assault, and probably for Gustavo's, and with their arrest record they would go directly to lock-up and would no longer be part of the equation. I decided that it could wait—the brothers could get their justice later, but for now it might be to my advantage to let them run free in case I wanted to follow their trail.

The other thing on my not-to-do list was to deal with Barbara, or Megan. That could also wait, as I needed to be single-minded about my investigation if I wanted results. Barbara had finished her exams and was out of school until September. She could take care of Royal, run the household, and do all the things that I usually did for the family. Megan wouldn't be expecting me for our next P.T. appointment because she had been fired. "Fired" was the wrong word; it was way too harsh, and I should never have said that to her. It was just that she had developed an inappropriate whatever-you-might-call-it, and it had gone well beyond the boundaries of a professional relationship. The obvious thing to do was to part ways and find a qualified replacement. Meanwhile, I felt terrible about the whole thing—Megan was a good kid, and she had worked miracles for me, and I owed her something more than *you're fired*.

I was so tired when I put my key into the door that I didn't know if I would make it across the living room to my bedroom door. My worries about the coffee keeping me awake were unfounded. It was starting to get light out, and it was a school day, so Roberto would soon be up, and one of us would need to drop him off, but my eyelids were so heavy I could barely see to open the bedroom door. I turned the handle, careful not to wake my wife, but a female form sat up in the bed, holding the sheet to her chest.

"Vince?"

"Yeah," I said. "Can you deal with Roberto? I've been driving all night. I have to get some sleep." I took off my watch and began to unbutton my shirt.

"Vince," she said. "It's not Barbara. Turn on the light."

I reached for the wall switched and flicked it on. Megan Rumsford was in my bed, naked except for the sheet. "Megan?"

"She said I could use your bed," she said, blinking in the light. "She's in with your son. Let me get a shirt on and I'll explain."

*

Megan was making coffee in my kitchen as if she lived here. She had put on one of my T-shirts, a light-brown one that had a hole in one side that was flashing me peeks at the skin underneath. "You weren't answering your phone," she said.

"The battery was dead."

"There are like, five texts from me. I gave up and called Barbara. I thought she might know where you were."

"What happened?"

"I was so scared, Vince. I completely freaked out. I'm sorry. I had no idea that you had all these people here. Barbara told me to come over, and that I could stay."

"Megan, what happened?"

"Two men were outside my place. In a van."

"A van? What color was it?"

"I don't remember," she said. "You want some of this coffee?"

"Yes, but I'd never sleep again. You saw the van, right?"

"Sort of," she said. "It was behind a big palmetto bush. But the men got out and were walking around my place. I was in bed, with all the lights off."

"What time was this?"

"About eleven o'clock. I probably should have called the police, right?"

"You can call me anytime, Megan. I was in Key West though." And so were the Iturbe brothers, so whoever had been prowling around Megan's house, it wasn't them. But was it connected to me? Was someone trying to get at me, through Megan? The last thing that I needed now was more bad guys stirring things up.

"Here," she said as she put a cup down in front of me. Maybe I would just skip sleeping—I'd done that plenty of times when I'd been working, and I was working again. Megan raised her arms up and fussed with her hair, and the big T-shirt suddenly outlined her woman-ly shape. This was beyond awkward, and if Barbara came into the kitchen right now...*Oh, hi honey! I was just having an innocent conversation with the young woman who was flossing my teeth with her tongue a couple of nights ago...*

Maybe I was delirious from the fatigue, or maybe this whole thing was nuts. My modest, three-bedroom house had turned into a full-fledged refugee camp, occupied by my wife, our baby, a teenager, a Russian literature professor, a retired dope dealer, and now my unpredictable physical therapist who was making coffee and busying herself around my kitchen wearing one of my T-shirts and nothing else.

"Where is Sonny?" I asked Megan, looking away from her in case she tried to flash some more skin or perhaps moon me.

"He and Susanna were going to take a beach walk," she said. "Then they were going to drop Roberto at school. Nobody got much sleep last night. I'm sorry, Vince, I really didn't mean to lay this on you. I guess I should just call the police."

"Not yet. I'm going to leave them out of it for now. And you can stay here for the time being."

"OK."

I took a sip of the coffee and pushed it back toward her. "I really have to sleep."

"I'll get my stuff and you can have your bed back."

Our master bedroom has heavy curtains that shut out all the light inside if everything is closed up, even in the middle of the day. I shucked off my clothes in the dark and slipped into the bed, which was still warm from where Megan had slept, and I could smell her scent lingering on the pillow.

What was that I had said about *not* dealing with Barbara and Megan right now? It seemed that I wasn't being given a choice.

In less than a minute I was out cold.

*

Sonny was at the kitchen range making grilled cheese sandwiches while Susanna sat at the counter, adding spoonful upon spoonful of sugar to a cup of tea that she had just poured. I came out of my bedroom dressed in my bathrobe after the soundest sleep that I'd had in years. I took a stool next to Susanna, but it was like I wasn't there. Neither of them acknowledged me because they were too busy arguing.

"The man was gay," Sonny was saying. "You can't write shit like that and be straight."

"That's ridiculous," Susanna protested. "Lermontov was a womanizer. He would meet them at a ball, seduce them, and then dump them. Gay? Not a chance. Lermontov was just nihilist melancholy at its best."

"Don't you go using those big words on me, "Sonny said. "I ain't got a problem with him being gay. But my boys will. They gonna be all over me about this. We goin' back to Tolstoy, soon as we finish this one."

"*A Hero of Our Time?*" Susanna said, arching her eyebrows. "You must be joking. Lermontov practically invented the modern novel. And he was killed in a duel. What more could your boys want?"

"Exactly what is going on here?" I asked, limping toward the coffee pot. "And why is there no more coffee?"

"The coffee is gone because you just got your white ass out of bed at four in the afternoon," Sonny said. "We were discussing literature. Shit you wouldn't know nothin' about."

"I beg your pardon?"

"Your friend has a remarkable grasp of the Russian classics," Susanna Pimentel said, "if a bit flawed." She wore a shy smile, and when I met her gaze, she blushed.

"Where's Roberto?"

"Out back," Sonny said. "Working on that tablet thing. He's been on it since he came home from school."

"And Barbara?"

"I dropped her and the baby at her club. The red-haired woman, too. I got somebody in the parking lot, don't you worry about it."

"What do you mean 'somebody'?"

"I know some people," Sonny said, as he flipped over the sandwiches. "Backups. I can't be everywhere at the same time."

"Thanks," I said. "I'm hoping that we won't need them for long."

"I've already subbed out my classes for the rest of the term," Susanna said. She was beaming a grin at me, like her captivity was a good thing.

"I'm taking Susanna to my reading group tonight, if that's OK with you," Sonny said. "You going to be here?"

"Probably."

"My kids are gonna freak when they meet a real live Russian professor," Sonny said. "Long as she don't say some dumbass bullshit about Lermontov being straight."

"What, gay people threaten you?" Susanna said, looking at Sonny.

"I'll be out back," I said. "I don't have a dog in this race."

*

"The encryption is controlled from the other side," Roberto had said. "Cuba."

He had explained that he'd gotten into the email exchanges by remotely hacking into Segundo Pimentel's office computer in Coral Gables. The computer was poorly protected, and Segundo had kept a master list of usernames and passwords on it, in a "secure" password-keeping program that my young techie friend had penetrated with his usual aplomb.

There were pages upon pages of correspondence between Segundo and the other side—the one who called himself *Pescador*—but the body of the text was gibberish. Roberto said that the messages were set up so that they could be read only once after logging in, and then they would be scrambled. The only way to unscramble them would be to gain access to the program via the sender's computer, which had an IP address originating from Havana and was tightly protected. Roberto confessed that he might have already tipped someone off because of his activity, if they were paying attention.

So, we weren't getting very far, despite Roberto's expertise. Were we missing something? Chloe Heffernan had seemed to imply that the tablet held something more than a bunch of racy photos of her—something that would lead us to Lilian. If so, it wasn't telling us.

"How do you look up a ship's registration?" I asked him. He still had his school uniform on, and was seated next to me at the patio table, under an awning that shielded us from the hot afternoon sun.

"What kind of ship?"

I told him about my stowaway trip on his uncle's sportfishing boat. His eyes widened when I got to the part about the package drop-off, and the retrieval by a military boat. "Describe it," he said.

"Over a hundred feet, a single gun on the foredeck, lots of communication gear on the tower. It had a number on it: 202. It looked old, but it was pretty dark out."

Roberto tapped at my MacBook, which was strung together with the tablet. "This was on my uncle's computer. The one at his office. I saved the image, because somebody in Cuba had sent it to him. Not Pescador."

He showed me a photograph of the same boat that I had seen the night before. The number 202 was clearly visible on the hull.

"I already looked it up," Roberto said. "It's called a Pauk-class Corvette. Given to Cuba by the Soviets in 1977, and it's still in use."

"This is the boat that picked up Javier's package."

"OK," he said. "There was a tag on the file. It said *Ministerio de Finanzas y Precios*. That's the Ministry of Finance. They control all the money and prices in the country."

"Why was a picture of a naval ship tagged by the finance ministry? Don't tell me they're in the cocaine trade?"

"My dad says that Cuba is about to change. Castro is like, ninety or something. My dad says that once he and his brother are gone, the socialism part will go away too."

"And?"

"People will be allowed to have money again. Some of them already do. There's a lot of corruption."

"I don't get where you're going with this."

"My Uncle Javier's box," Roberto said. "How much money could you fit in that box?"

"In bills? If it was in hundreds, they don't take up a lot of space. We dug up four million bucks in somebody's backyard once, when I was with the Sheriff's Department, and the box was about half the size of Javier's."

"So, eight million dollars."

"Possibly," I said. "But why?"

"If you're rich and corrupt, and you live in Cuba, you want to own dollars. Especially if the whole economy is about to change."

"Maybe. But I'm guessing that there's more to it."

"Me too," he said. "And you're going to have to go there to find out."

"To Cuba?"

"Yes. You need to find Pescador. Then maybe we can find my mom."

*

I had made a big batch of chili for my refugee camp residents. Sonny and Susanna were out at Sonny's book group, Roberto was in my study watching a documentary, Megan was rocking Royal to sleep in his nursery, and Barbara and I were outside on the patio at the table, drinking mojitos. I poured an extra shot, hoping that it would give me the courage to bring up a certain subject with Barbara, and would also loosen her tongue enough to give me an honest answer. We had already talked about Gustavo, and my investigation so far, and how long everybody might be staying here, and why I had decided that I needed to go to Cuba. I took a big swig of the drink and blurted out what was on my mind.

"So, you're having an affair, right?"

The first few seconds after a salvo like that are the most telling. People only get a tiny sliver of reaction time to let me know if they're going to start lying, or if they will come clean. I call it the Eyeball Test—you watch, and they blink, or they don't.

"An affair?" she said. "Vince, what are you talking about?"

She was stalling. Throwing the question back to me.

"I'm talking about a guy named Angelo. You might want to speak with him. He's told anyone who would listen that he's screwing you."

A wave of relief seemed to come over her, and she smiled. "Angelo? That's ludicrous. Have you met him?"

"No."

"He's—oh my god, Vince, how could you even *think* that? He's black, for one."

"White people have been known to sleep with black people."

"It's not that. He's just—a nice guy. He trains people at my club."

"I know."

"So who told you this?"

"Like I said, he's telling everyone in Gifford."

"It was Sonny, right? He can't stand me."

"Barbara—"

"It *was* Sonny then," she said. "What an asshole." She was angry now, having quickly made the transition from shock to indignation.

"You have to admit—you and I—"

"What? You mean we hardly sleep together anymore? We have a nine-month old baby, Vince. He nurses three times a night. I don't see you being able to help there."

"Barbara—"

"You have no idea what I've been going through, do you? I just finished working my ass off at nursing school, and by the way, I got my exam results back, and it was straight A's."

"Congratulations."

"And then you get yourself beat up, and Roberto moves in, and then the whole fucking world is living in our house, and I'm scared about my own safety, and the safety of our baby, and—"

"Look, Barbara—"

"No. No more look Barbara. I've had enough. You go to Cuba, I'm checking out. You can stay here with all your castaways."

"What?"

"Royal and I are leaving," she said. "Right now."

"Where are you going to go?"

"I don't know yet. Probably my sister's."

Barbara's sister Vicki lived two hours north in Jacksonville. Maybe that was for the best. She would be out of harm's way there, and we both needed to cool off.

"I understand," I said, but she had already gone inside, and I heard her taking her suitcase out of the hall closet.

Fair enough. A little time apart could be a good thing. Or maybe not. One thing was for certain:

She may have aced her nursing school exams, but she had just failed the Eyeball Test.

*

I hadn't done a head count, but to my knowledge Roberto was in the study on the pull-out bed, Megan was in the nursery, Sonny was on the couch, and Susanna was in the spare bedroom. I was in my own room, wondering what I was going to do about my marriage. Barbara and I had been husband and wife for a grand total of nine months—our ceremony had been held in my backyard only a few hours before our son had entered our lives. Having Royal was the best thing that had ever happened to me, and it had followed directly on the heels of several of the worst things that had ever happened to me. I thought at the time that I had turned a corner, and that I might live out the rest of my days being a dad and a husband, and would not ever again be surrounded by some kind of crazy shitstorm like the one that I currently found myself in, both personal and professional. Wrong.

I had the bedroom TV on and my knitting out, but I couldn't pay attention to either one. Distractions were not what I needed right now—I needed solutions. I had to go out and find Lilian Arguelles and solve the case. Then, I might solve the curious and enduring mystery of my marriage. Maybe marital mysteries were not to be solved, and the point was simply to persevere.

Endurance. That was what marriage was really about. There was no guaranteed happy ending, no permanently blissful state. Married people were like Sisyphus, who was condemned by the gods to roll a huge boulder up a hill every day, only to have it roll back down again. You did your job, called it a day, sat down in your favorite chair with a beer, and you hoped that you didn't get run over by a gigantic rock. From the outside it might look futile, absurd—even tragic. But men and women feel compelled to do it anyway, and there are those times in a marriage when you welcome the repetition and routine, and it's sweeter, cozier, and more satisfying than anything else. This was not one of those times.

I heard a soft knock on the door, and someone pushed it open. It was Megan, in my light-brown T-shirt that she had apparently adopted.

"You can't sleep?"

"I haven't really tried yet," I said. "Just thinking about some things."

"Barbara?"

"Yeah," I said. She crossed the bedroom and sat on the mattress, near me. Too near.

"It's none of my business, but I can't believe she left. You need all the help you can get right now. I don't know what you guys fought about, but that was wrong."

"She had her reasons. It takes two with these things. It's not just her."

"You don't just leave like that though," Megan said.

"She's a little impulsive sometimes."

"Do you like that? Is that what you find attractive in a woman?"

Megan was now about a foot away from me, and I could not only smell her, I could feel her warmth as if she was some kind of heating pad and I was a guy with a sore back.

"I—"

"You are *so* stressed out," she said.

"Yes."

"Roll over and I'll do your shoulders."

"Megan."

"Vince."

We looked at each other for a long time. I'm of the male persuasion—meaning, normally oblivious to the wants of those of the female persuasion—but it was crystal-clear to me that Megan Rumsford wanted to give me a back rub, and then she wanted to rub the rest of me.

It would be so easy. Some bad guys in a van had practically delivered her to my doorstep, although I suddenly wondered if that had actually happened or if Megan had made it up.

"I can't do this," I said.

She smiled. "Warm milk. You'll be asleep in no time. You stay right there."

I lay back on the pillow, relieved. She really was a good kid. She came back into the bedroom after a few minutes with a glass, and held it to my lips. I hadn't had warmed-up milk since I was five years old and my mother had made it for me when I'd been home with the measles.

"This is nice," I said.

"Everything about you is nice, Vince," she said, taking away the glass. "Now, sleep."

*

My phone buzzed on the bedside table with a text from Robert Patton. Patton was a friend in Vermont who was in charge of the state's Border Patrol, and he seemed to know anyone and everyone in law enforcement and beyond, since the Border Patrol was part of Homeland Security and interacted with the FBI, the DEA, the CIA, the TSA, the ATF, the Coast Guard, the State Department, and Brownie Troop Number 415.

You can pick up your visa in Coral Gables tomorrow, he had written. *Your charter leaves the Miami airport at 1 PM. You're going with a church group from Minneapolis.*

Seriously?

Yes. You're Father Vince Tanzi. You're accompanying a group of nuns.

You're kidding, right?

No, I'm not. You'll need to wear one of those dog collars.

Me? Anyway, thanks for pulling the strings.

No problem, Patton wrote back. *Behave yourself now. No lap dances.*

God forbid.

You can get into Cuba fairly easily these days if you fly in from Cancun or Montreal, but it takes longer, and there's a lot of red tape. Certain church groups can fly directly from the United States on a charter, provided that they are going to visit shrines and so on, and not just to travel for tourism. So Father Tanzi wasn't going to be hitting the beach. In fact, the good Father had already worked out a preliminary itinerary with his technology consultant, and the two of them had spent part of the evening outfitting his suitcase with a few items that would hopefully make it through security.

A group of nuns? I'd gone to Catholic school in Vermont, and I still had to cross myself when I thought of some of the sisters who had taught there. They were good people, but they didn't put up with any crap, and the wiseacres like me who got themselves sent to the Mother Superior's office usually toed the line after the first visit. As far as we knew, her authority came directly from God, and she might have even outranked the Pope.

The warm milk that Megan had poured me was taking effect, and I put down the phone. I had slept so long the previous night that I still wasn't sure that I could drift off, but as soon as I darkened the lights I knew that I was about to fade, which was good. I might need the sleep.

*

I was in Vermont, lying on the cold stone slab. Barre Gray is what they called the granite that was quarried from my hometown; it was the same stone that my grandfather and my father had fashioned into gravestones at the Rock of Ages monument company. Almost everyone I had grown up with had a family member who worked there, if not several.

Two warm hands were working my back, pressing upward from underneath. It was my dream again. The soft, sensuous, erotic movie that my subconscious had drummed up to entertain me. I might as well enjoy it. I was asleep, and no harm could come to me.

Wait a minute. My eyes were closed, but I could see, and a topless red-haired woman was leaning over me as her strong hands kneaded my lower back, and then slowly migrated up toward my chest.

No.

I forced myself to wake up, and saw that I had scattered the bed sheets everywhere. I flicked on the bedside lamp, remade the bed, and then went into the bathroom for a pee.

Goddamn. It wasn't even midnight, and I was wide awake again. I padded out of the bathroom into the hall and checked on everyone in the house. Sonny was on the couch, snoring lightly. Roberto was asleep in the study, Susanna was in the spare room, and Megan Rumsford was on the cot in Royal's nursery, lying under a single sheet. I quietly shut the door.

Everything was fine. My refugees were safe, and nothing crazy had happened. My subconscious had just conspired with my libido and had put on a show, that was all. I returned to my bedroom to try to get a few more hours rest, careful to avoid the full-length mirror that I had installed for Barbara on the closet door.

Because I wasn't one hundred percent certain that I would pass the Eyeball Test, either.

TUESDAY

I STOPPED AT ST. John of the Cross on the way out of Vero Beach to pick up a couple of tab-collared shirts from a priest I knew who was about my size and who was willing to help me once he heard that I was going after Lilian. She was a member of his congregation, and he said that they would be praying for her. I asked him what the penalty was for impersonating a clergyman, and he laughed and said that it would remain between us and the Lord.

Two hours later I was in Coral Gables, where I made a stop at the Border Patrol office to pick up my paperwork. I decided to double back and visit Gustavo Arguelles at South Miami Hospital, to see how he was doing and if he could shed any more light that might help me on my trip.

Gustavo was sipping water through a straw with the help of a nurse. "He still can't talk," she said. "But they want to release him soon. Maybe at the end of the week. Do you know anyone who can care for him? We know his wife is missing."

"He can move into my place. I may have to add a new wing."

"That's good," she said, and Gustavo appeared to smile behind his bandages. He waved his hand, signaling for a pencil and paper.

Roberto?

"In school. He's still at my house, and Sonny and Susanna are looking out for him. Those two are getting along pretty well, by the way."

Crazy, Gustavo wrote.

"Yeah," I said. "And I'm going to Cuba. I leave in a couple hours."

Why?

"I'm looking for a guy who goes by Pescador. That's who Segundo was emailing, but the emails are scrambled. Segundo's paralegal gave me a tablet computer that belonged to him, and Roberto hacked into it, but that's as far as we got."

You think he's in Cuba?

"I found Javier's boat in Key West the day before yesterday, after I saw you. I stowed away on the boat, and Javier and the two guys who beat you up came aboard and sailed us to the Cuban coast. They dropped a big sealed-up cooler off the side, and it was picked up later by a Cuban Navy ship."

Gustavo wrote down his thoughts after a pause. *Efectivo. That's Spanish for cash.*

"Roberto thinks the same thing."

They owe somebody. Segundo was a gambler.

"And Lilian is collateral?"

Hadn't thought of that, he wrote. *Maybe.*

"Can you think of anything that I should know before I go there?"

Eat the buñuelos, Gustavo wrote. *And don't forget about backgammon. That's all that Segundo cared about.*

Actually, I knew that there was something else that Segundo Pimentel had cared about—a detective lieutenant's wife. But there was no need to bring that up.

"I'm assuming that buñuelos are fattening, whatever they are?" I asked.

God's gift to the Cuban waistline, he wrote. *Good luck, Vince.*

*

Miami International Airport is one part crying baby, two parts European tourist sitting next to me who doesn't believe in deodorant, three parts unintelligible-but-loud P.A. system, four parts clueless business traveler sitting on the other side of me and talking on his phone louder than the P.A. system, and a dash of every other personality-type and nationality on the planet. Today it was mostly occupied by students in baggy outfits, lying on the carpet and plugged in to one electronic device or another via white headphone cords that stretched like vines upward to their ears. I spotted the Minneapolis sisters as soon as they got near the gate. They looked like a vision: a heavenly horde of angels—with roller bags—who had come to take me away. I had my dog collar on, but it didn't feel like I was fooling anybody, and so far no one had approached me to ask for forgiveness or to hit me up for a communion wafer. I wondered how long it would take until the sisters exposed me as a fraud and I would be excommunicated, or whatever they did these days.

"Father Tanzi?" A cherub-faced woman of around sixty tapped on my shoulder from behind. She had gray hair cut in a pageboy, and she wore a trim blue Ralph Lauren shirt over black slacks.

"Yes?"

"I'm Sister Mary Carelle," she said, "from the Visitation Monastery. It's so nice to meet you!" She extended her hand.

"You're not wearing—"

"A habit? No, we don't all do that when we travel. But please, you do as you like."

"These are the only shirts I brought."

"We'll dress when we visit the holy places," she said. "Oh, I'm so excited! Aren't you?"

"Oh—yes, I am." I gave her a weak smile.

"That was so nice of your friend—Mr. Patton? He said that you know a lot about Cuba."

"He did?"

"Yes. And that you speak perfect Spanish. That will be *so* helpful."

"He said that?" Holy crap. What was I supposed to do now? I didn't think that the nuns would appreciate the fact that I could order them a Dos Equis in Spanish, and that was about it.

"We arrive at two thirty, local time," the sister said. "What do you think we should do first?"

Heaven help me, I thought. Maybe I could read a tourist guidebook on the flight over, and simultaneously take a twenty-minute language immersion course. This was hopeless. I wasn't going to be excommunicated, I was going to be burned at the stake like the godless heretic that I was.

"Father? What would you like to do first? After we arrive?"

"Get a nap," I said. "And then we're going out for buñuelos."

*

The charter plane was a Brazilian Embraer short-hopper with about fifty seats. The Minneapolis sisters and I brought up the rear, and the front of the plane was divided equally between a party of Mormons and another one of Pentecostals. Everyone, thankfully, had the good grace to keep to themselves, thus averting a possible holy war. I was seated next to a nun who looked to be closer to my age than Barbara's, and had shoulder-length curly black hair, vibrant green eyes, and a light tan. Too bad she had taken her vows, I thought, because she was—OK, I was going to say cute, but in my role as Father Tanzi I didn't dare, lest I be struck down by a celestial Taser. She had been thumbing through an *Elle* magazine, and I thought of the wadded-up pink sweatshirt in Javier Pimentel's boat that had kept me from freezing. The nun tucked the magazine into the seat pocket in front of her and turned to face me.

"So, Father. What do you think of the von Balthasaar theology? In light of what the Pope has been saying?"

"I—don't have an opinion." Uh-oh. Whoever this woman was, she was about to blow my flimsy cover wide open. I needed to shift the conversation to small talk, fast. "What's your name?"

"Rose," she said. "So you don't think that bad people should go to Hell?"

"I think that—bad people should do their time. A lot of them can be rehabilitated. I've seen it."

"You don't really know what we're talking about, do you?" She smiled. It wasn't the kind of smile that you'd expect to see on a nun. More like the one on a hooker who had just taken your money and was about to skedaddle.

"Excuse me, Sister?"

"I'm not a sister. Rose DiNapoli, Immigration and Customs Enforcement. Robert Patton sent me to babysit you."

"Jeezum crow."

"Question for you," she said. "Did you bring any electronics?"

"Just my phone."

"And what else?" Ms. DiNapoli gave me a penetrating look. "Spill, Tanzi."

"I have a few items in my bag. Very small things."

"They'll rip you apart at Cuban customs. They X-ray everything, and if you have so much as a flash drive, they'll detain you and hassle the shit out of you. And then they'll confiscate it."

"That wouldn't be good."

"Get your bag out of the overhead bin. I can fit a few things in my bra. That's off limits to Latino guys, especially since I'm a nun."

"So why is ICE interested in this?"

"Because we've been after the Pimentels for eighteen months now," she said. "You can buy me a Cuba Libre and I might tell you more. I know where they make the best ones in Havana."

*

A little over half a millennium ago, Christopher Columbus described Cuba as "the most beautiful island that I have yet seen". He wasn't so far off—even though he believed that he was in India at the time. And Havana, the capital city and the Caribbean's largest at two million inhabitants, is a spectacular, if somewhat tarnished, architectural mix of nineteenth-century grandeur, run-down neighborhoods with music coming from everywhere, and the odd Soviet-era monstrosity like the Russian Embassy, a bizarre, Lego-like structure that pokes out of the landscape like the hilt of a sword. Our cab driver had decided to give us an impromptu tour of the city on the way to our hostel, no doubt in hopes of a tip, and he pointed out things along the way, which the three nuns riding with me expected me to translate. Some of it I could guess, like the park dedicated to John Lennon with a bronze statue of the musician seated casually on a bench, and the rest I made up. According to Father Tanzi we had just passed the Jalapeño Building and were now crossing Avenida Huevos Rancheros, and the sisters hung on every word. Maybe I could get a job doing this. I was almost starting to enjoy myself.

The driver dropped us in the center of Old Havana on a relatively quiet street in front of the Convento Santa Brigida, a mid-1800s structure that functioned partly as a home for the nuns who lived and worked there, but mostly as a "casa particular", which operated under the Cuban system that allowed people to open their homes to tourists and make more than the $20-a-month official salary that most of the island's inhabitants earned. The hostel was clean and tidy with a spacious interior courtyard, and the rooms were large although somewhat spare. I didn't expect to find a Jacuzzi tub and a mini-bar in a convent bedroom, and I was fine with the monk-like simplicity. It was appropriate to my cover, and to my mood as well. I hadn't come to Havana to guzzle daiquiris at the Tropicana, although that didn't sound like a bad idea after having traveled all day.

Someone knocked at my door, and I got up from the single bed to open it. Rose DiNapoli stood at the threshold, dressed in a floral print top with white linen pants and matching shoes. She had her curly black hair tied back and wore oval-shaped sunglasses, perched above her forehead. Any traces of the nun identity were gone.

"About that Cuba Libre?" she said. "Or are you busy?"

"I was praying," I said. "But I think that my prayers have been answered."

She smiled. "We're going to Lluvia de Oro. It's only a few blocks from here."

Ms. DiNapoli led us down the stairs and onto the street. This part of Old Havana was a mix of offices, private homes, shops, and restaurants, and the streets were filled with the smells of spicy food, flowers, the nearby harbor, and exhaust fumes from the mufflers of the venerable, brightly-painted mid-century Fords, Buicks, and Chevrolets that predated the revolution. Our taxi from the airport had been a '52 Studebaker Commander that looked like it was pointing backward and had over 300,000 miles on it. I had forgotten how cavernous those old cars were, and how my brother, my sister, and I used to romp around in the back like drunken chimpanzees in the days before you had to wear seat belts.

"How long have you known Patton?" Rose asked me as she steered us through the commotion, occasionally taking hold of my elbow. She seemed to know exactly where she was going.

"About a year," I said.

"I know who you are," she said. "The national ICE headquarters is in Vermont, outside of Burlington. I'm there a lot, and I read the papers back when you were shot."

"It was no big deal."

"Hell yes it was. You shouldn't be alive."

People kept bowing and waving to me as we passed. Huh? Did I look like someone they knew? And then I realized that it was the clerical collar, and they were just being good Catholics and saying *buenos dias* to a passing priest. I wondered what they thought about the dark-haired babe who kept taking my arm.

"I was lucky," I said. "And I've had a great physical therapist."

"Patton told me why you're here. What's your strategy? How are you planning to find this guy?"

"I'm not sure yet. How did you get involved in this?"

"Patton called me when you said Cuba. I know it better than any of the others—my mother is Cuban, and I've visited a lot. I'm kind of in love with the place."

"I can see why," I said. "So why is ICE after the Pimentels?"

"Because Javier Pimentel bought a boat a couple of years ago in the Caymans. He bought it for cash, and some of the hundred-dollar bills were marked. By us. We traced them back to a laundering racket where we'd been trying to set up a sting, but we got screwed out of fifty grand in cash. Not one of our more successful operations."

"So you think that Pimentel was laundering money?"

"We had him audited by the IRS last year, and the brother, too. They were squeaky clean. Like, too clean, and they had way too many toys, like the boat. But we kind of let it slide, and then I heard that the father and the other brother got killed."

"By pros, according to the locals."

"Yeah, I talked to your friend there in Vero, Bobby Bove. He said that you've been avoiding him, and to tell you to perform an unmentionable act on yourself."

"So what are you going to do now?"

"You tell me," she said. "I'm just the babysitter."

We were walking along the Calle Obispo in an area of stately buildings and hotels. Across the street was a Greek Revival structure that looked like the New York Stock Exchange, only smaller, and with an immense front door made of dark, highly-polished wood. At the top of a row of Corinthian columns the edifice's name had been carved into stone:

Ministerio de Finanzas y Precios.

I stopped and took a long look. Someone from inside there had sent Segundo Pimentel a photograph of a boat. A boat that might have picked up a few million in cash.

"Do your people ever track Javier's yacht?"

"We used to, a while ago. But he never puts in anywhere. Just in and out of Key West or up to Miami."

"He has a friend right over there." I pointed across the street. "And last Sunday he dropped a big cooler full of something a few miles off the Cuban shoreline. It was picked up by a Pauk-class Corvette. Segundo had a digital photograph of the ship, and the file originated from here."

"How the hell do you know that?"

"There's a Hemingway novel," I said. "It's called The Old Fart and the Sea. We old farts know where the big fish are."

"You don't look so old," Rose DiNapoli said. "In fact, you look kind of cute in that priest collar." She smiled.

"Hey, no flirting," I said, smiling back. "Remember, I took vows. Plus I already have enough trouble at home."

"That wasn't flirting. I was just being nice."

"Sorry. I've—kind of been under attack lately."

"Well you can relax then," she said. "If I was going to flirt with you, you'd know it."

*

The Cuba Libres at the Lluvia De Oro were good, and they got better with each one that we ordered. I drank the regular ones, made from Havana Club Blanco, Coca-Cola—from the fountain, not the bottle—and two halves of a fresh Key lime. The bartender admitted that he also had added a secret ingredient, which I suspected was some kind of hot sauce as the drink had a slight zing to it. Rose was drinking a variation called the *Cubata*, which used the darker Havana Club Especial—otherwise it was the same as mine.

The woman could put them away. We talked shop while we drank: law enforcement, crazy things that had happened in our careers, the tribulations of dealing with bureaucrats, and even our favorite weapons and other hardware, as her training for customs had included that, and she knew her way around the basic cop gear. Three or four Cubatas and Cuba Libres into the evening we ordered some food that I can barely remember except that it was some kind of gumbo-ish mix of pork, chicken and beans, which would describe ninety percent of Cuban cuisine. It was tasty but forgettable, mostly because I was enjoying my time with Ms. DiNapoli so much that for once I wasn't paying attention to the menu. It wasn't that she was some kind of supermodel, because she wasn't, just as I'm not some kind of muscle-mag beefcake. Sure, she was attractive, but she was a real person, and I liked her, and it was something of a relief to be with her after all of the anxiety that I'd experienced over Megan's various maneuvers. It was deliciously relaxing to spend some time with a woman my own age who shared some common interests and had a brain and a sense of humor.

"If we don't stop drinking these, we'll be in trouble," she said, draining her glass. "You'll have to sneak me back into the convent."

"That sounds like a Shakespeare play."

"Shakespeare would have loved Havana," she said.

"How so?"

"There's so much going on here," Rose said. "It's kind of a train wreck, but the people are so smart, and so proud. They still believe in the revolution, and it's held them back in a way, but it has also kept them—uncorrupted? There's no fast food, you can barely get Internet, and people don't walk around shopping malls like morbidly obese zombies. Do you know what I'm talking about?"

"Yes."

"Maybe Cuba should annex the United States," she said. "Not the other way around."

"Too late," I said. "We Americans are so sure that we're right about everything."

"It should be mandatory that everyone in the U.S. does some kind of work overseas. It would open peoples' eyes."

"We prefer to keep them shut."

"The whole U.S.A. is turning into one of those gigantic chicken farms," Rose said. "We're being fattened up for the slaughter."

"Jeez. This is getting depressing."

"Sorry," she said. "Maybe we should order another round."

"No way. I'd have to crawl back to the hotel, and these are my good pants."

She excused herself to go to the ladies' room. I did some people-watching while she was gone. The restaurant was full, and the diners were a mix of gringo tourists in Hawaiian shirts and logo-emblazoned casual gear, along with the natives, who were dressed like the inhabitants of a sophisticated if warm European city. I took notice of two men at a corner table who were drinking from tall glasses like ours, and had a board game open on the table, set up between them. One of them was scowling, and I heard him say: "*Doble.*"

Double? Backgammon.

As I got up and walked over to them, they looked up from their game.

"*Padre?*" one of them said. They wore tropical business clothes: expensive-looking guayabera shirts, dark trousers, and perfectly-shined leather shoes.

"*Hablo inglés?*" I said, attempting some Spanish.

"Yes, you do," the one on the right said. He had a smooth forehead and ears that were too long for his face. The two men looked amused.

"So you speak English then?" I said.

"No, you do. You said: I speak English. *Hablo inglés.*"

"I meant—"

"We know what you meant," the other one said. "No harm intended. *Bienvenidos a Cuba.* Welcome to Cuba."

"I was wondering—about your game," I said. "I'd like to play someone."

"We're about to leave," Long Ears said. "So sorry."

"Maybe you know him. He calls himself Pescador."

The expressions on the two men's faces changed suddenly, as if they'd just been informed that someone close to them had died.

"We can't help you, señor," the other one said. "Lots of people in Havana."

"No problem," I said. "*Vaya con Dios.*" I'd learned that one from a John Wayne movie.

"*Carajo,*" Long Ears said, under his breath.

I would have to look that up when I got back to the hotel.

*

Rose DiNapoli led me to the Malecón, a pedestrian thoroughfare that stretched along almost the entire coast of the city, wherever it hadn't been bashed by recent hurricanes. *Lovers and prostitutes*, she said. *That's what you find on the Malecón at night. This is where you come when you want a kiss.*

I was pretty drunk at this point. Despite my pitcher-fest with Megan Rumsford and my overindulgence tonight I seldom drink to excess, and since my injury I have been even more careful to not overdo it—with my limp and my sometimes-slurred speech I could already be mistaken for one of those people who started tippling before lunchtime. But arriving in Cuba, and knowing that I could finally make some progress on the case, and the companionship of a fellow professional—who happened to be unexpectedly attractive—was having an effect on me like a gust of warm Caribbean air. We stopped at an area that overlooked the Castillo de San Salvador, a sixteenth-century fort that had once protected the Havana harbor from various invading nationalities and was now a tourist site.

So, she wanted a kiss? What the hell, one more wouldn't hurt. I was already going to be barbecuing in eternal damnation for the Megan fiasco. I took her arm, and she turned to face me. "Don't get your hopes up," I said. "I'm not much of a kisser."

She gave me a puzzled look. "Vince? I wasn't talking about you and me."

What? Oh shit.

Tanzi's Tip #7: Your foot does not fit in your mouth. Believe me, I've tried.

"Rose, I had no business saying that," I said. "My life is a mess right now. I'm way off on reading the signals."

"I'm getting married in three weeks," she said.

"Really?"

"Yes," she said. "I might even go through with it, if he behaves himself."

"I'm sorry. About what I said, I mean."

"Don't worry about it. I like you, and I'll help you. We have some work to do if you're going to find your friend."

"I appreciate that," I said, and we turned back on the walkway in the direction of the hostel.

It's easy to get carried away in the tropics. The balmy nights seem to make it happen, which is why so many people leave their offices, their homes, and all of their obligations to escape to the sand, the sun, and the rum. That, plus I have always had a black belt in making an ass of myself, but as Rose had just said, I probably shouldn't worry about it.

But I did worry about it, because I suddenly didn't want to go home.

*

We were passing the Plaza de Armas and were almost back to the convent when a small white Lada sedan with a big blue light on the roof pulled up and stopped in front of us. Two uniformed men in berets got out, and Rose grabbed me by the elbow. "I'll handle this," she said.

"*Documentos*," one of them said. I took my wallet from my back pocket and opened it, upside down, causing the entire contents to rain down onto the sidewalk.

"*Está bien borracho, este*," one of the cops said to the other. He turned to me and gestured. "*Ven con nosotros, padre*."

I looked to Rose. "They're saying that you're shitfaced, and they want you to get in the car," she said. She talked to the two cops for a while in fluent Spanish, but they ended up putting me in the back seat and left her standing on the curb. We sped back in the direction of the waterfront, and the car slowed as we passed through the raised iron gate of a gigantic stone fortress surrounded by curtain walls, battlements, and corner towers. I wondered if I was being taken to meet Ivanhoe. A sign near the entry said *Policía Nacional Revolucionária Comandancia General*, which I took to mean: the cops.

I was going to lockup, to sleep it off. Oh boy.

Fifteen minutes later I was stripped down and was given a cavity search by one of the officers, which has never been my idea of a fun first date. They took my clothes, my shoes, and my phone, and put everything in a bag, leaving me in my underwear. I was smart enough to not say anything at all, and nobody questioned me, though I was pretty sure that none of them spoke English anyway. I ended up in a holding cell so bare and dank that I was already sobering up. The cell had a cot that squeaked, with a single, coarse blanket and no pillow. By the time that I was finally left alone, I was ready to wrap myself in it and attempt to get some sleep.

Suddenly, going home didn't seem so bad after all.

WEDNESDAY

SOMETIME AFTER DAWN A GUARD unlocked my cell and gave me the bag with my clothes. Nothing had been disturbed, and I checked the time on my phone: seven AM. Shortly afterward I was escorted out of the building, past the medieval-looking iron gate, and out into the already warm morning sun. I had worked up a pretty good hangover, and I found a peso stall on the street and ordered a coffee while I unfolded my map. The hostel wasn't far away, and I decided to walk, although what I really wanted to do was to crawl into a real bed with a real pillow until the construction worker in my head turned off his jackhammer.

The strong coffee helped, and I mingled on the streets with smartly-dressed business people and government workers as I navigated my way back to the convent. A few minutes later I was in my room attempting to wash away my sins of the night before in the primitive-but-functional shower. I dressed in fresh clothes and went downstairs to the courtyard where a breakfast buffet had been laid out. Rose DiNapoli was seated at a table reading a Spanish-language newspaper. She was the only person in the courtyard except for one of the resident nuns who was scraping food off of plates into a plastic bin.

"Where is everyone?"

She put down the newspaper. "The tour guide took them out to El Rincón on the train. There's a shrine out there. Kind of a mixture of Catholic and Santería. The people dress in sackcloth, and they crawl on their hands and knees and push rocks around with their foreheads."

"That's about my speed right now."

"You OK? Did they hassle you?"

"The accommodations were a little lacking," I said. "So you didn't want to go to the shrine?"

"I told them that you and I were both sick. Food poisoning. They're very strict about attending these things. We're supposed to be in our rooms, recovering."

106

She had two figure-eight-shaped pastries on a plate in front of her. "What are those?"

"Buñuelos," she said. "Kind of like your fried dough, up in Vermont. Want one?"

My stomach said no, but I was curious. I picked one up and took a bite. She was right—it was a lot like the fried dough that you could get from a booth at the Champlain Valley Fair, except sweeter, and with a hint of anise. "Saints above," I said, as I finished it. "I believe I've just made a miraculous recovery from food poisoning."

"They're pretty addictive," she said. "That one would have been my tenth. There are more in the kitchen."

I sat at the table across from her. She looked like she had slept just fine, and her dark hair was tied back into a bun, exposing her neck. She wore a light-green shirt that matched her eyes. "You don't look too bad, considering how much we drank," I said.

"I don't get hangovers."

"Are you really getting married in three weeks?"

She picked up her paper and pretended to read. "Maybe."

"Who's the guy?"

"We work together. He's in the Plantation office with me, near Fort Lauderdale. He's a lot younger than I am." She wrinkled her nose like a six-year-old might.

"Is there something wrong with that?"

"No," she said. "He's just—very serious and ambitious. Hard core, if you know what I mean. Shaves his head, works out a lot, big into martial arts."

"A guy's guy."

"Yes."

"And you're getting cold feet?"

Rose DiNapoli looked up from her paper with an assessing glare. "You hardly know me, Vince."

"Have you been married before?"

"No."

"And so you're getting cold feet."

"Go get us some more of these," she said, handing me the empty plate.

I rose up from the table just as a man entered the courtyard, wearing tinted glasses and dressed in a dark suit. He came over to us, and addressed me in slightly accented English. "Mr. Tanzi?"

"Yes?"

"Please come with me," he said. "I have a car outside."

"And where are we going?" The man didn't look like a cop, and I hoped that I wasn't headed back to my dank cell.

"To the Ministry. My employer will see you there."

"Who is your employer?"

"Her name is Maria Inés Calderón. She is the Minister of Finance and Prices, and she is a vice president-elect. She will assume the office next week. Come with me."

"I need to freshen up first," I said, and I walked up the stairs toward my room. I could hardly contain my excitement—I was making real progress now. I was about to meet with a Cuban bigwig, who might lead me to Pescador, who might in turn lead me to Lilian Arguelles, wherever she was hidden.

I quickly used the bathroom, brushed my teeth, and then unzipped a pocket of my suitcase where I had stashed a few things. One of them was very small, and had made the trip through customs in Ms. DiNapoli's bra. I slipped it in my pocket, and unhooked my phone from the charger, pocketing it also. Ready or not, here I come.

The man was waiting outside next to a shiny black Geely CK, a Chinese import that looked like the bastard child of a Mercedes and a Honda Civic. I got in on the passenger side, and neither of us spoke. My hangover had disappeared, and it wasn't because of the coffee and the buñuelos.

It was because I was finally getting close.

*

I had to cool my heels in the huge, echoing reception hall of the Ministerio de Finanzas for over an hour until a young woman in a Business Barbie outfit like Javier Pimentel's secretary came to fetch me and lead me to yet another waiting area, up a long flight of marble-clad stairs. The Cuban government hadn't spared any expense in the construction of this building back in the day, when sugar was king and the money had flowed. Today, this was the place that set the prices for everything, and in a socialist economy that would be equivalent of a partnership at Goldman Sachs. Whoever was pulling the strings here would wield a lot of power. I was looking forward to meeting Ms. Maria Inés Calderón, and I wondered if there was such a thing as a One Percent in Cuba. The whole idea of the revolution had been to eliminate that, but plutocrats were like cockroaches, and no matter how much poison you scattered around, they tended to sneak back in when you weren't looking.

My heel-cooling time left me with some room to think about things, and I realized that Barbara and Royal had hardly crossed my mind since I had boarded the plane in Miami. I had left somewhat of a mess behind. I was doing my best right now to help Roberto—getting his mother back was of primary importance. I felt a little guilty about forgetting about my family, but when I'm on a case everything else seems to fade away.

Royal would be fine with his mother—I liked to think that I played a big role in his life, but that wasn't the way it was with a nursing baby, and I figured that our relationship would expand as he got older.

Barbara would be at her sister's. That was probably good for a couple of days, max. Vicki was a controlling, clueless shrew; I could barely tolerate her, and even Barbara got burned out after a day or so. The sisters had grown up poor, neglected, and abused, and one of them had risen above the misery while the other one still wallowed in it. Even when you got kicked in the teeth, you still had choices, but some people were simply unable to make them.

Barbara might even be back home by now. She might be thinking about what she had done, and about this Angelo guy, and whether that was what she wanted in life, or if she could accept my admittedly flawed love. I felt a little strange pondering my wife's infidelities given my own behavior over the past week, but I still felt like I was holding the higher ground, and it was a lonely place. I would need to do a better job of talking with her about it when I got home—we had a baby to care for, and when that's the case, mom and dad can't just toss a relationship like ours into the trash like a soiled Huggie. Not that some people don't, but I didn't want to be one of them.

A cinnamon-haired woman of about fifty came around the corner of the reception area, not smiling. She wore a gray business suit with a purple satin blouse underneath, just enough color to be womanly, and her mottled skin showed the signs of too many years on the beach. On her feet were a pair of black Manolo Blahnik flats that I recognized because Barbara owned the knock-offs, and they were her favorites. These were probably the real thing.

"Maria Calderón," she said, extending her hand.

"Vince Tanzi," I said. She had a politician's grip: firm and fast.

"This way," she said, and she led me into an office that held a small rainforest's worth of dark mahogany furniture and was adorned with polished brass fixtures and paintings of hunting scenes.

"How are you enjoying Havana?" she asked. Her accent was one hundred percent American, as if she lived in the same Vero Beach neighborhood as mine.

"It's a beautiful city," I said. She motioned me to an upholstered chair in front of her desk, and I sat. "Nicer than I expected."

"You *yumas* think that we're going down the tubes," she said. "Meanwhile, our kids have better math scores than anywhere in the U.S.A." She took a seat in a high-backed leather chair behind the desk and let go of a sigh.

"Yumas?"

"Gringos," she said. "But it has a more negative connotation."

"You didn't grow up here."

"Hialeah. I went to Bryn Mawr, and then MIT Economics, and then I repatriated myself, to the great disapproval of my parents."

"And now you're going to be the vice president?"

"One of them died," she said. "We have five vice presidents in Cuba."

"Just in case you ever run out of Castros."

"That will be a sad day," she said. "The man is like your George Washington, Lincoln and Kennedy to us, in one person."

"So—why am I here?" I said. "I didn't seem to have a choice."

"Well, let's see." She picked up a page from her desk and looked at it while she spoke. "You're not a priest, although you are a Catholic. So you're here on false pretenses."

"And the Finance Ministry is worried about that?"

Ms. Calderón scowled. "The Ministry worries about a lot of things. Like why you are in the company of an ICE agent. And why you were bothering two citizens in a restaurant last night."

So they knew about Rose. Bad. And, whomever I'd asked about playing backgammon with Señor Pescador had also raised an alert. Good.

"I'd be grateful for an introduction," I said.

"An introduction?" She looked off-balance, and I decided to make my move.

"Pescador," I said. "He plays backgammon. I'd like a game."

Maria Inés Calderón knitted her fingers together on the surface of the desk. "Do you really play backgammon?"

"It's all in the doubling," I said. I met her glance and held it.

"I am Pescador," she said. "And now, I need to know how you know that name."

What? Pescador was a man, I was sure of it. Or maybe I had just assumed that? Damn. I needed to backpedal, fast.

Or, I could fast-forward. This might be the opening that I was looking for. I decided to double the bet.

"I'm here to negotiate," I said. "I represent the Pimentel family, and they want to settle this."

The finance minister said nothing. Instead, she got up from her chair and crossed over to the window that looked out on the busy street below. I waited, knowing that if I said anything more I might blow it. When you are negotiating you have to know when to shut up.

"It's still sixty million," she finally said. "No negotiation, no write-offs."

"And Lilian?" I said. That was risky, but I desperately needed to get somewhere.

"Nothing is going to happen until I see the money," she said. "You can tell Javier that he has until the weekend. And you are flying out this evening. Don't come back."

I began to cough, violently, and Ms. Calderón gave me a worried look. "Water," I managed to say, between my increasingly dramatic coughs. It sounded like I was about to die, and she rushed out of the room.

I retrieved the tiny device that Roberto had given me from my pocket and plugged it into an empty USB slot on the back of a computer that straddled the side of the Minister's mahogany desk. Then, I removed my phone from my pocket and stuffed it into the folds of the slipcovered chair that I was sitting on, just before she entered the room again with a mug full of water. I began gasping again and accepted the water, which "cured" me after a few sips.

"Thank you," I said.

"Don't miss your flight," she said. "And you can tell Javier that he's a stupid *palestino*, and if he tries to fuck me on this I'll kill him."

Whoa. Not only did I have another choice Spanish word to look up, but I also knew that I had just gazed into the eyes of the person who was responsible for Lilian Arguelles' captivity.

Fuck you too, lady. You might think that I'm just some errand boy, but if you're holding Roberto's mother somewhere, then you shouldn't worry about Javier Pimentel. You should worry about me.

*

The dark-suited guy dropped me off at the hostel, and I looked around for Rose but she wasn't there. No matter—I found one of the

English-speaking resident sisters and got directions to the nearest Internet access point. Roberto would be in school, but he watched his phone, and I was eager to get a message to him and get the ball rolling. I had been taken by surprise when Maria Calderón had told me that she was Pescador. But I had been able to switch gears quickly, and had set the bait, according to Roberto's instructions. Now, like a good fisherman, I had to wait. We would see who was the real *pescador* here.

The Nauta office had a line out the door, and I waited for forty-five minutes to send my three-word message to Roberto. "I miss you," I typed, after forking over the equivalent of five dollars and signing a form pledging that none of my web activity would hurt the State. I had to cross my fingers on that one. "I miss you too," Roberto sent back, via the Gmail account that we had set up for the occasion.

Meaning: Message received. The game was on.

*

When I got back to the convent, a nun knocked on my door and handed me an envelope. It held a boarding pass and a stamped departure tax receipt. My flight left at five in the afternoon, and I would have to change planes in Cancun and get into Miami shortly before midnight.

"My friend?" I asked the nun, hoping that she spoke English. "Has she come back?"

The young nun hesitated, and then spoke. "They told us not to say," she said. "But you are a man of God."

No I wasn't, but I nodded. "Where is she?"

"*Policía*," she said. "She was very upset. Big fight. They had to use—how you call?" She held out her wrists.

"Handcuffs?" I said, and the sister nodded. The cops had taken Rose DiNapoli away in cuffs? I had been wondering if they were going to deport her along with me, seeing how Ms. Calderón had known that she was with ICE. They might be sweating her right now in some dark cellar back at the police castle. I also wondered how much training a customs enforcement agent was given for a situation like that, where they might be interrogated in a not-so-friendly country, and my overactive imagination began to conjure up various torture devices, but this was the twenty-first century, and those things weren't supposed to happen anymore; all the bad stuff ended up on the Internet within minutes, and governments couldn't get away with that kind of crap. The Internet had made the world smaller and more transparent; it was harder to operate in the dark.

But Cuba had the distinction of having the worst Internet service in the western hemisphere. It was scarce, slow, expensive, and they monitored everything. So if the police wanted to beat up on Rose DiNapoli, a U.S. customs agent, no one might ever know.

*

A twenty-minute taxi ride later I was back on the Malecón in front of the U.S. Interests Section building, a concrete-and-glass architectural abortion that made the wonky Russian Embassy appear tasteful by comparison. If we ever really wanted to reestablish diplomatic relations with Cuba, we would need to start by knocking it down and putting up something that didn't look like a seven-story cheese grater. Since the U.S. had no ambassador in Cuba, the Interests Section functioned as a de facto embassy, and I figured that it would be the best place to get some fast help.

"Fast" is not a word that is well known in diplomatic circles. Despite my pleas to whoever would listen, I had been there for almost an hour before I was granted an audience with a deputy-deputy-assistant-somebody who looked like he had just graduated from high school and didn't know how to tie his necktie properly. He had called me "dude" twice now, and I was about to smack him, but instead I demanded to see his superior. He left me waiting in his office while he went to find his boss, or maybe, to get a security guard and throw me out. Either way, I was ready to unload on somebody. A U.S. agent had been snatched off of the street, and no one seemed to give a shit.

Eventually I was ushered into the slightly more spacious office of someone named "Tim", who was a couple of years older and pay grades higher than the first one, but no more helpful.

"We're not going to intervene in a police matter," he told me from behind a well-worn veneer desk. "I'm sure that they'll sort it out. This isn't the Cold War."

"They cuffed her," I said. "I was a cop. You don't handcuff people unless there's trouble."

"They do what they want," Tim said. "We don't have any clout with the Cubans. They ignore us. They enjoy thumbing their noses at us."

"Who's your boss?" I said.

"This is as high as you go," he said. "Look, we'd help if we could, OK?"

"Can you call the States directly from here?"

"Yes."

"I want you to make a phone call."

"Mr. Tanzi, I've—"

I slammed my fist down hard on the cheap desk, making his phone and a row of framed family photographs jump. *"That's enough!"* I yelled, and he drew back. I was expecting a security guard to rush into the room any second, but nothing happened. "You need to call Robert Patton, head of the Border Patrol in the Burlington, Vermont office. Look him up and call him. I'll wait."

The bureaucrat's hand was visibly shaking as he searched on his computer to find Patton's information. He found it, dialed the phone, and handed me the receiver. Fortunately, Patton was there.

"It's Vince," I said.

"Where are you calling from?"

"The so-called U.S. Interests Section in Havana. Rose DiNapoli got taken out of our hotel by the police a couple of hours ago, and everybody in this place has their head up their ass."

"They won't do anything?"

"No," I said. "They say they can't."

"Bullshit," Patton said. "Are you with somebody right now?"

"I'm in the office of a fellow who introduced himself as Tim."

"Put me on speakerphone," Patton said. Which was kind of like saying: *Here, take this match and throw it in that barrel of gasoline.*

I listened in admiration as Robert Patton ripped my junior diplomat friend a new one, threatening him with angry calls from the State Department, reassignment to Antarctica, and an imminent F-35 air strike if he didn't toe the line, and fast. When he was done, Tim hung up the phone and turned to me.

"So what do you suggest we do?"

"Whatever it takes," I said. "I'll be waiting for her at the hotel."

*

I had the cab driver drop me at the Nauta office and waited in line again to send another five-dollar, three-word email to Roberto. Actually this time I didn't even have to send a message, because when I signed into Gmail, I saw that he had already left one. *Good fishing today,* he had written. That was all that I needed to know.

Unless my diplomat friends had worked at lightning speed, I figured that I had enough time to complete the next step of my Roberto-mission, and I put myself through various scenarios as I walked to the Ministry of Finance building, only to find that it was *cerrado hasta las 14 hras.*, which I took to mean closed for lunch. I hadn't had anything to eat since the morning's buñuelo-fest with Rose Di Napoli, and my stomach was growling. I turned the corner and found a street vendor selling *pizza hawaiana* from a cart, which was a small ham-and-pineapple pizza that you folded and ate like a taco. I was about to order another one when I saw a woman approaching the side door of the Ministry building and recognized her—she was the Business, or rather, Bureaucrat Barbie who had led me to Maria Calderón's waiting area. I jogged toward her as quickly as I could.

"*Mi phono,*" I said. "*Es losto, en el office-o de la señora.*" I had practiced that line about a hundred times, and hoped that I might be understood.

"Excuse me? Your what?" The young woman's English was perfect, with a slight hint of Valley Girl.

"My cellphone," I said. "I left it in Ms. Calderón's office. Is she in?"

"Come with me," she said. "She's not here. I'll get it for you."

She led me into the building, which had gone semi-dark as the lights were out. These people took their lunchtime seriously. We climbed the polished marble stairs, and the young woman led me into the waiting area. "Stay here," she said. "I'll find it."

I knew that she wouldn't, but I did what I had been asked to, and she came back out after a few minutes. "It's not there, sir. Sorry."

"Please let me look," I said.

"You can look, but be fast," she said. "I shouldn't be doing this, but I've lost my phone before and they're, like, totally expensive."

"You're a doll," I said. I crossed the floor of the office and plucked my cellphone from the folds of the visitor's chair.

"I really didn't see that," she said. "I looked there."

"No problem," I said, and she led me back down the stairs and out the door that we had entered from. No problem at all.

Your boss is the one who's going to be having a problem.

*

Visitors were supposed to be captivated by Cuba: it was a place to hear some great music, enjoy the local cuisine, relax on the beaches, and get away from all of the numbing sameness that you found in the States. But this was hardly a vacation—it was an assignment, and the only captives were Lilian Arguelles and now Rose DiNapoli. I had returned to the convent and was worried sick. Despite Robert Patton's tirade I wondered if the consular staff could actually do anything—they had seemed so sure that they couldn't. There wasn't much to do except wait, which I was doing in the courtyard, hoping that Rose would come through the door at any moment.

The only positive was that I had made some real progress in my investigation. The task that Roberto had set for me was complete. Also, I knew for certain that Lilian Arguelles was being held as some kind of collateral—for a debt of sixty million dollars that was due by the end of the weekend, according to the Minister of Finance, and soon to be vice president. Due to whom? To the government of Cuba, of which Maria Inés Calderón was a high-ranking official? Or was this one off the books, and it was a debt owed directly to her? Either way it was a lot of money, especially if the Pimentels were as broke as Talbot Heffernan had determined that they were from Segundo Pimentel's financial records. The cooler that Javier had dropped off of the stern of his boat the other day would only hold a down payment, if it had indeed been packed with hundred-dollar bills. That would be nowhere near sixty million.

I would have to lean on Heffernan some more to do some better forensic accounting and see if he could trace anything to Cuba, or to Ms. Calderón. He had said that they owed some bankers in the Cayman Islands, but that could easily be a front for Cuban interests. The money people in the Caymans were notoriously unconcerned about those things as long as they got their cut.

It was three in the afternoon now. I would have to leave within the hour if I was going to make it to the airport in time for my deportation. I had already packed, and was now pacing the halls of the convent, planning my next moves to keep my mind off of my worries about my friend the ICE agent. I would drive to Vero as soon as I got back and would deliver my cellphone to Roberto, who would hopefully work some magic. I'd check in with Bobby Bove and Tal Heffernan and would share what I knew. This thing had now gone way beyond some private eye looking for a missing woman, and any resources that they could add might help. I would contact Robert Patton and see if he could bring in the cavalry: if Lilian Arguelles, a U.S. citizen, had been kidnapped and was being held in a foreign country, that should be something that would get some serious attention, and Patton was the right person to make that happen.

And I would find Javier Pimentel, and we would have a little talk. No—we would have a big talk. I didn't think that I was going to have to lean on him very hard; I already knew about his financial condition, his massive debt, and the fact that his sister had been held hostage for nearly two weeks. Assuming that the guy wasn't a complete psychopath, he had to be feeling the pressure, and I would now have some leverage to make him tell me everything that he knew, and to possibly help him get out of this mess. I just hoped that he was still alive, because the Pimentel family survival rate hadn't been all that impressive lately.

I also needed to check in on my refugee camp. I wondered what I would find there, and if Barbara and Royal might have returned during my absence. I badly wanted to see Royal, although I wasn't as enthusiastic about seeing my wife. We had a lot of heavy lifting to do, and I knew that it was important, but—

Rose DiNapoli staggered through the convent door and nearly fell at my feet. When I rushed to her side and picked her up, she collapsed into my arms and began to cry.

"Are you all right?" I asked her, as I held her as tightly as I could.

"No," she managed to say between sobs. "Don't let go of me."

The agent's hair was a tangled mess, and her clothes looked like she'd been dragged through the streets behind a bus. We stayed like that for several minutes while her breathing slowly returned to normal, and she finally looked up at me. Her makeup had run down her face in black streaks, and her eyes were swollen and red. "Those bastards," she said. "They'll never let me come back here now. Which is lucky for them, because I'd kill them."

"What happened?" I said. She had stopped crying but was still shivering in my arms.

"I—can hardly talk about it."

"I'm so sorry," I said. "They did some shit to me too."

"Oh yeah? Four of them?" Her voice had become a thin shriek. "Four guys stripping you, and you're naked, and they handcuff you to a table—"

"They raped you?"

She stepped away from me and looked around the tables until she found a plastic bottle of water, which she held to her lips and drained.

"Sorry, Vince. I just—"

"Did they rape you?"

"Nobody took their pants off," she said. "But yes, they raped me."

"I have a flight to Cancun at five. We'll get you a seat."

"Let's get the hell out of here," she said. "I hate this place."

.   *

To get to Miami via Cancun you begin by flying in the opposite direction, to Mexico, and then you retrace your path, flying almost directly over Cuba again to reach Florida. It makes no sense at all, but the only direct flights were the sanctioned charters, and we had already ditched our little group of nuns. I was looking forward to being home and getting rid of my clergy shirt, which chafed at my neck and fit me about as well as a size-six Speedo on a sumo wrestler.

Rose had spent the first leg of the trip alternating between shivering and retching with dry heaves into an airsickness bag. A few minutes into the Cancun-to-Miami flight she fell asleep, and her head lolled into my lap. A flight attendant draped a blanket over her, and now and then she would make a snorkeling noise, but otherwise she stayed silent while I read an article about the origin of Bermuda shorts in the in-flight magazine. Honestly, how did they come up with that stuff? The inanity of the reading material was in stark contrast to the seriousness of the case that I was now deeply involved in, and which included yet another casualty—the sleeping ICE agent with her head on my thigh. We had kidnapping, murder, and now rape. The felonies were piling up, and the source of it all appeared to be a middle-aged politician with sun-damaged skin and six-hundred-dollar shoes.

Rose was definitely in shock, and I hadn't had the heart to ask any further questions about what the Cuban police had done to her. Save that for the therapist. I presumed that the Customs Bureau had people who could provide those services when things got unbearable for their employees, just like we'd had when I was at the Sheriff's Department. Most cops retired after twenty or thirty years, but if they always held the bad stuff in, they would never make it that long. It's part of the job, and you kind of get used to it, but not really. Remember that, the next time a deputy pulls you over—he or she may have just scraped some unlucky soul off of the pavement, or worse, so don't get too worked up about your lousy speeding ticket.

We landed in Miami at ten thirty, and I offered Rose a ride, but her car was in the garage, and she said no. Her fiancé would be at her house, she said, and it wasn't a long drive to Fort Lauderdale where she lived. She had regained her color. I walked her to where her car was parked and held out my hand, which felt a little silly seeing how she'd had her face in my crotch for the past hour.

"I'd give you a hug, Vince, but I don't feel like touching anybody."

"Does ICE provide counseling? Someone you can talk to?"

"I keep my own counsel," she said.

"Not this time, Rose. That's not healthy."

"You go on along," she said. "I wish I could say I enjoyed it."

"Call you tomorrow," I said, and she got into her car and drove away.

I found the BMW and put the top down. It was still in the eighties, and I needed some fresh air to keep me going. Tomorrow would be a school day for Roberto, but things could no longer wait, so I would wake him up when I got home so that we could work. He would have to miss school for a day or two. The situation was suddenly about twice as bad as I had thought it was, which meant that I would need to work twice as hard, and get half as much sleep.

THURSDAY

ROBERTO HAD MY PHONE PLUGGED into his laptop and was sitting on a stool at the kitchen counter. There was nothing that I could do to help him, so I got out my knitting and sat in my recliner. My sister's sweater was looking less like a piece of clothing and more like some kind of bizarre woolen plant hanger, and I was about ready to chuck the whole goddamn thing in the trash. Knitting used to be good for helping me relax, but at two in the morning there was no relaxing; there was only fatigue, and anticipation, but so far Roberto hadn't said a peep.

I liked to watch him work—his fingers would dash around in a blur, and he would have several windows open at once, one of which was a chat portal that connected him to his hacker buddies. They all helped each other, and I didn't see a lot of difference between them and the fraternity of stonecutters that my father had hung out with at the Knights of Columbus in Barre, except that the stonecutters had probably never broken into some theoretically secure website just for the sheer hell of it. They were too busy downing Budweisers and coughing up granite dust.

I had taken inventory when I'd entered the house: no Barbara or Royal, Roberto was in the study, and I assumed that Susanna was in the spare room, as her purse was in the kitchen. Megan Rumsford's car was parked outside, and I didn't dare peek into my room but I figured that she was in there. No sign of Sonny, but he might have gone out, although the hour was late.

I interrupted my young friend. "Getting anywhere?"

"Yeah," he said. "But I need to generate a soft token code. I think Pescador has the program on his computer, but I can't find it."

"Pescador is a she, by the way. Her name is Maria Calderón. She's the Minister of Finance."

"Nice," he said. "How'd you get to her computer?"

120

"I can't share my methods. Not unless you want to teach me how to hack."

"You're way too old for that," Roberto said. He was right—I could open a lock, but this would be like learning Chinese. You needed a young brain, and preferably one that hadn't already taken a bullet.

"So tell me how this works again?"

"The thing you plugged into her CPU was a keystroke logger. It sent the info by Bluetooth to an app on your phone. After you emailed me I sent her a message using my Uncle Segundo's account so that she'd read it, and then I'd have her logon information, because it would be relayed to your phone. I told her I was Javier, using Segundo's email program."

"What did you say to her?"

Roberto blushed. "I was trying to stir her up. I thought she was a guy. I needed to get a reaction, or I wouldn't get the logon."

"So, you said...?"

"I called her a *pinguero*. It's not in the dictionary. It means a male prostitute."

I had just taken a sip of water and nearly spit it out. "So what did she write back?"

"Something not very nice. But it worked. And now some of my friends are all over the soft token thing. We might have it by the morning."

"I'll stick around until you do."

"You should go to bed, Vince. You look really tired."

"Is Megan in my room?"

"Yeah."

"Then I have nowhere to sleep," I said.

"You could hit the couch."

"But Sonny will be back, right?"

"He's upstairs with my aunt," Roberto said. "He moved his stuff up there last night."

Oh *really*? Hoo boy.

Tanzi's Tip #8: Cupid may look like a fat little baby, but he's one hell of a good shot.

*

We had stayed up until five AM and still no luck on the codes, so I took the couch and Roberto flopped into the pullout bed in my study. It dawned on me just before bedding down that I could take the cot in Royal's room, but when I opened the door it was gone, as was his folding crib. Huh? The bureau remained, along with a couple hundred stuffed animals, but the rest of the baby furniture was missing. Even the diaper pail had been taken. I didn't have the energy to ponder that one.

Three hours later I woke, showered, shaved, and lumbered into the kitchen looking for coffee. Susanna had already made a pot, and she handed me a steaming mug.

"Everything going OK?" I asked her.

"Oh yes," she said. "Sonny went out to run some errands." She was wearing that unmistakable just-got-lucky smile that people wear when they have a new flame and can hardly leave the bed. I was glad for her, and for Sonny, too. I knew nothing about his love life except that he didn't have anyone steady, and Susanna was a catch.

"What happened to the baby furniture?" I asked.

"Oh," she said, and the smile evaporated. "Your wife came over yesterday with a friend."

"A friend?"

"He had a pickup truck. She didn't say anything to you?"

No, she didn't. I sipped my coffee and began to smolder. The "friend" had to be the Angelo guy? Jesus W.T.F. Christ. Barbara comes over to the house and starts hauling away the furniture? What kind of bogus move was that? I had been thinking while I was shaving that maybe she and I should be going to counseling, but right now I felt like finding her new boyfriend and counseling him with the butt of my Glock.

"When did this happen?"

"She got most of her clothes on Tuesday night," Susanna Pimentel said. "They came back for the other stuff yesterday. Vince, I'm so sorry. I thought you knew."

"It's not your problem," I said.

Tuesday night? That was when I had a wicked buzz going, and had gotten fresh with Rose DiNapoli while strolling on the Malecón. And, oh yes—last Saturday night I'd had my hand up my therapist's shirt in a darkened parking lot out behind a pool hall. And that was after going topless paddle boarding with her on the previous afternoon. So now I was freaking out about my wife's possible infidelities? One thing that I had learned over the years of my P.I. career: it was never just one person who was responsible for the problems in a relationship. Love takes effort, and if you sit around and lay blame, you're only making excuses for your own bad behavior.

I spent the next hour on the phone catching up with the various authorities. Bobby Bove listened attentively but didn't have anything new to tell me. The Sheriff's Department had decided that the Segundo Pimentel murder was definitely a hit, and they'd pulled most of their resources from the investigation. Talbot Heffernan said that the Feds had made no progress on the Raimundo Pimentel shooting either, and had also called it a pro job. The one useful piece of information that Heffernan had was that Javier Pimentel was back in town, although the Iturbe brothers hadn't been seen. Neither of the two cops had found out any more about Lilian's kidnapping, and both of them were shocked when they learned that I'd been to Cuba and was pretty certain that she was there. I briefed them on my meeting with Maria Inés Calderón, including her reference to the sixty million that she expected to collect from the Pimentels.

What I didn't tell them about was Roberto's and my electronic snooping. I have always tried to keep Roberto insulated from these things as much as I could. If we found something out, and I believed that Heffernan, or Bove, or Robert Patton could use it, I would pass it on. For now it wasn't necessary seeing how Roberto and his friends still hadn't managed to get access.

Robert Patton wasn't answering the phone, and neither was Rose DiNapoli. I hoped that she was still asleep. She had had a horrible experience, and, with apologies to the male half of the planet for generalizing, I have to say that I don't believe that a man can really understand what a woman goes through when she is raped, groped, or whatever madness had happened to Rose. No matter the degree, it's all bad, and it is difficult for a man to truly understand what it's like to be victimized like that. I had seen it countless times as a deputy, and for many of the women there was no "recovery". They had lost something, and they weren't ever going to get it back.

Megan Rumsford came out of the bedroom—my bedroom—and took a seat at the kitchen counter. "When did you get home?" she asked me.

"Late."

"I didn't mean to take your bed," she said. "I thought you were going to be there longer."

"So did I," I said. She was wearing another of my shirts: a threadbare Red Sox jersey that barely covered her behind.

"Did you make any progress?"

"Yes," I said. "Roberto and I are working on some things."

"Vince, did you notice that Barbara—"

"Stole my furniture? Yeah."

"I told her not to do it," Megan said.

"Where did she go? Back to her sister's?"

"She's in the same development as me," Megan said. "Some snowbird who wanted his place watched for the summer. Free rent."

"You arranged this?"

"She did," Megan said. "She found it online. She was going to talk to you. She just wanted to try it out for a while. Nobody knew that you'd be home so soon."

"I'm about to be gone again. I'm going back to Coral Gables to find Roberto's remaining uncle."

"What are you going to do when you find him?"

"I'm not sure," I said. "That depends on how cooperative he is."

*

Javier Pimentel's house in Coral Gables was in one of those gated enclaves where the guards would wave you in so long as you drove a nice enough car and you smiled like you belonged there. I had run the Beemer through a car wash and it sparkled in the noontime sun, and I happened to be dressed in one of my WASP outfits: a navy polo shirt that so far Megan Rumsford hadn't slept in, and rust-colored pants that Barbara had found in a second-hand store in new condition. If you didn't mind wearing the clothes of deceased people, the thrift store pickings in Florida were without equal.

I had thought about stopping to see Gustavo, but I really wanted to grill his brother-in-law first, if I could find him. After that I would head to the hospital to see if they would release Gustavo and I could bring him back to my place to join in the fray. I was thinking that I might rent a hospital-type bed and put him in what used to be Royal's room. I was still reeling from the fact that my son was gone and I hadn't been given any notice. I hadn't received a single call or text from Barbara, and even if I had, I wasn't in a mood to answer.

I did receive a text from Rose DiNapoli, just as I was turning onto Javier's street: *Thank you, kind sir, for rescuing me.*

You feeling OK? I sent back, after pulling to the side of the road.

I guess so.

You really ought to go see somebody, I wrote.

Two minutes later, as I pulled up in front of Javier Pimentel's driveway, I received a reply: *Stop nagging me and I might.*

Off to visit Javier P, I wrote. *Will call you afterward, OK?*

OK, she replied. *Watch your back.*

The Pimentel spread had its own private gate within the gated community. I stopped and lowered the window. There was a call button under a speaker, and I pushed it.

"Yes?" a female voice responded in accented English.

"Vince Tanzi," I said. "I'm here to see Javier."

"*Momentito*," the voice said. Thirty seconds later, she said, "So sorry señor. Mr. Pimentel is no here."

"Tell him that this is about the sixty million that he owes Pescador," I said, and I waited.

Miraculously, the gate swung open.

*

If Javier Pimentel's Coral Gables office was over the top, his house might have offended the sensibilities of Louis XIV. Stone gargoyles adorned the roofline, and the entrance walkway wound around a green marble fountain that could have accommodated the entire FSU water polo team. Gurgling mosaic crocodiles spewed fresh water into the bowls, which also featured cast bronze mermaids, evenly spaced between the crocs. Watch out girls—you could lose a finger to one of those things.

A dark-skinned woman met me at the door with her hair wrapped in a black do-rag. "You can come in," she said, heaving a sigh as if she'd been letting people through all day. I was shown into a two-story entrance hall with bamboo side tables along the ochre-painted walls and a round black leather settee in the center that matched the black velvet drapes. The decorating scheme could be described as Gothic Revival, or perhaps Early Halloween. I took a seat and waited until Javier Pimentel came around the corner.

"Vince," he said, extending his hand. "Nice to see you again."

"You may want to reserve judgment on that," I said.

"Come with me. Something to drink?"

"No," I said. "But you go ahead." And you'd better enjoy it, because if you don't come clean you're going to be drinking out of a sippy cup, like your brother-in-law in the hospital.

Javier led me to a parlor adorned with portraits on the walls, dark mahogany side tables, an old Victrola phonograph, and Persian rugs. I sat on a fainting couch, across from the chair that my host had taken. I pointed to one of the portraits. "Is that your father?"

"That's Raimundo," he said. "The old son-of-a-bitch, captured for posterity."

"You didn't get along?"

"We had to get along, because we worked together." Javier had swapped out the gold loop earrings that he had worn the other time I'd met him for a pair of simple diamond studs. "My father referred to me as the *maricón*. I won't miss that part. He was an old-school homophobe."

"Who's the woman?" I gestured to another life-sized portrait across the room from Raimundo's.

"My mother," Javier said. "She passed away ten years ago. Maria Marta. We called her Mamarta."

"Like your boat?"

He gave me an appraising look. "How do you know so much about us?"

"It's my job. I'm here to ask you some questions, and I don't want any bullshit. Clear?"

"I'm on your side, Vince. I want to find Lilian just as much as you do. Maybe more."

I saw a hint of fear in the expression on his round face. That was good—I can work with people who are already scared.

"Let's start with the money," I said. "How much was in the box that you dropped off on Sunday?"

"Box?"

"Off of your boat. It was picked up by a Cuban Navy ship."

"What? Who do you work for?"

"Myself," I said. "Answer the question."

"Six million," he said. "A loan repayment, that's all."

"In hundreds? You're kidding me. That kind of money gets sent directly from bank to bank."

"They want dollars in Cuba," he said. "People are hoarding them. When the Castros are gone, everybody's going to want U.S. currency. The peso is no good."

"So your lender marks them up and sells them?"

"That's right."

"And you get a markup on this side, because you're laundering somebody's money, so you buy at a discount."

"No comment," he said. "You wearing a wire?"

"I'm not a cop, Javier," I said. "Not anymore."

He winked. "Let's just say I won't do anything for less than twenty points."

Twenty percent? Twenty percent of six million dollars was one-point-two million. Not a bad day's fishing.

"So this was ransom money? For Lilian?"

Javier shook his head. "That's something else," he said. "This was for Segundo. He got the money together before he got killed, and I had to drop it off or they'd kill me, too."

"But six million isn't sixty million," I said.

"Sixty million?" he said. "I don't know anything about that."

I looked directly at him and said nothing. The Eyeball Test. He didn't quite fail, but it was a D-minus at best.

"Pescador told me about the sixty million when I was in her office."

"You went to Cuba?"

"That's right," I said. "She asked me to tell you that you were a Palestinian, and that if you screw around with her, she'll kill you."

"You mean a *palestino?*"

"Not the same thing?"

"It means peasant," he said, "which is ridiculous. It's a socialist country. Everybody's supposed to be a peasant there, but they still use it as an insult."

"If everybody's supposed to be a peasant, why is the finance minister collecting six million in cash?"

"Backgammon," Javier said. "It's not a game, it's a curse. You play?"

"No."

"Segundo thought he was unbeatable. Lilian could beat him, but she quit a long time ago. Before she stopped talking to us. You get to be a big-shot gambler like Segundo, and you make stupid bets. Your ego takes over, and you make mistakes. Segundo got the crap beat out of him, and he owed her six mil."

"He owed Pescador?"

"The money was my father's emergency stash," Javier said. "Segundo took it out of the safe, after Raimundo was killed. Some of it goes back years."

"He bet six million dollars? You said it was a loan."

"We owe her money," Javier said. "Other money. He was trying to reduce the debt, and it got worse. Segundo was a financial genius, but he had too big of an ego. He couldn't stand being beaten by his own sister."

"You mean Lilian? Or Susanna?"

"Neither," Javier said. "I mean Pescador. Segundo gave her that name. He used to complain that she played backgammon like an old fisherman. Slow and smart."

"Maria Inés Calderón is your sister?"

"Half-sister," Javier said. "My mother had her when she was fifteen, and they put her up for adoption. It was a *vergüenza*, a shameful thing. My half-sister used her adopted father's surname—Calderón. In Spanish you use your mother's surname as your second last name, but she dropped it when she repatriated to Cuba, for obvious reasons."

"Like what?"

"You don't know?"

"No."

Javier breathed a sigh. "My full name is Javier Pimentel Batista. My mother is the daughter of Fulgencio Batista. She grew up in Spain, when they were in exile. We are all his grandchildren."

Fulgencio Batista? He was the dictator who had turned Cuba into a police state back in the '50s, and by the time he was ousted by Castro he had killed tens of thousands, and had also emptied the state coffers. No wonder Roberto had told me that he couldn't go to Cuba. Being a member of the Batista family would be like being named Mussolini.

A large shadow passing through the hallway caught my eye. It was a human shadow, although it was the size of a Volkswagen. "Is somebody else here?" I asked Javier.

"Just the housekeeper."

"Somebody bigger than that."

"*Carajo*," Javier said. "I didn't know they were back."

"You didn't know *who* was back?"

"Pepe and Lalo."

"I thought you said they didn't work for you?"

"They don't," he said. And if he had looked scared before, he looked terrified now.

The two brothers entered the room, and the one with the braid looked at Javier. "What the fuck is *he* doin' here?"

"We were chatting," Javier said. "He was just leaving."

"You got that right," One-With-The-Braid said. He reached into his jacket pocket and took out a Taser C2—the same one that they had already zapped me with, less than a week ago.

Not again. Please.

"How's the insurance claim coming, Lalo?" I asked Braid.

"I'm Pepe, not Lalo," he said. "Lights out, motherfuck."

In the split second before the darts hit, I imagined myself in a saloon, drawing my Colt revolver with lightning speed after some bad hombre had pulled on me. Bang! He'd be dead on the floor, and I would blow the smoke from the barrel before slipping it back into the holster.

But I had left my Glock in the car, and this time the bad guys won.

*

The smell is what woke me, not the light, because it was pitch dark. Whatever the Iturbe boys had injected me with this time hadn't just made me drunk; it had knocked me out cold, and all I could feel was a bunch of sticks jabbing into my face. I tentatively put my hands around the rectangular object that was functioning as my pillow and determined what it was: a hay bale. I was in some kind of barn, although it had nothing like that nice, bucolic barn odor. It smelled like someone had died in here.

My phone was gone, although my wallet was still in my back pocket. I remembered that I had left the cellphone in my car, in Javier Pimentel's driveway. Fuzzy images began to filter back to me—being stuffed into the back of a silver Honda Fit, with the two gigantic goons taking up the front half of the tiny car. Being driven somewhere, while I gurgled and sang Beatles songs and the brothers took turns laughing at me and smacking me—I could feel the sore places on my face. Sometime before we had arrived at wherever I was I must have passed out for good. I got up off of a pile of what I imagined was loose straw and tried to make my way through the blackness around the perimeter of my cell. It was quite large—twenty feet by twenty feet, according to my pacing, and there wasn't the faintest shred of light. If there was a window in here, it was boarded shut.

I found the door and felt along the edges for the lock. There was a knob, but the door wouldn't budge when I turned it, and I figured that there had to be a sliding deadbolt on the outside. With the right tools I might be able to rotate it and slide it out, but I had nothing with me except for my wallet and a whole lot of hay.

I was going to be here until someone came to let me out.

"Goddamn it," I yelled in frustration.

"*Agua!*" someone yelled back. "*Dame agua, puta de mierda!* There's nothing left in this bottle!" It was a woman's voice, and whoever it was, she was on the other side of one of the walls that surrounded me.

"Who is that?" I yelled back. "Who's there?"

"*Agua,*" she said. "Please. I mean it, Pepe. *Ten piedad.*"

"Lilian?"

"What? Who's there?"

"Are you Lilian Arguelles?"

"Yes," she said. "Who are you?"

"It's Vince," I said.

"Oh—dear God," she said, and I could hear her burst into sobs.

"Everybody's OK," I yelled through the wall. "Roberto is OK. He's at my place. Gustavo got beat up, but he's going to be OK. Thank god I've finally found you."

"Oh Vince," she said. "I have been waiting for so long. I gave up, really. I thought I was dead."

"You're going to be fine," I said. "Where the hell are we?"

"We're in a slaughterhouse," she said. "It stinks, but you get used to it."

"What part of Cuba is this?" I asked her. "They put me under. I don't remember the trip."

"You're locked in too?"

"I guess so," I said. "They tasered me, and then they shot me up with something. I don't remember much."

"We're not in Cuba, Vince," she said. "We're in the middle of the 'Glades somewhere. I've tried to find out where, but they won't say."

"The Everglades?"

"Yes," she said. "Can you hear me OK?"

"Pretty well," I said.

"Then get comfortable," Lilian said. "You and I have some catching up to do."

FRIDAY

I WAS WRONG ABOUT MY prison cell being sealed up from the light. It was now spilling into the building from over my head, and I took in my surroundings. I was inside a metal-walled holding pen, probably built to keep cattle in before they faced their demise. The walls reached up about nine feet, and then the building was open all the way to the corrugated metal roof. The morning sunlight was spilling in from above and from gaps between the wood slats that made up the siding. It was going to be a hot day outside, and the heat of the sun on the metal roof was making the stench of the place even less tolerable than before.

Lilian and I had stayed up late into the night while I filled her in and she told me more about the Pimentel family. She had shunned them, except for Susanna, ever since her mother had died ten years ago, for which she blamed her brothers and her father. They were rich, arrogant, and crooked, and Lilian couldn't take it any longer, so she and Gustavo had moved to Vero to get some distance. Gustavo still occasionally went fishing with Segundo at his camp on Blue Cypress Lake, and the family also went to Key Biscayne now and then to stay with Susanna, but that was all the family contact they had.

I couldn't see Lilian in the darkness while we had talked, but I had felt her bristle when I'd mentioned her half-sister. *She's the biggest capitalist pig of any of them*, Lilian had said. *It's bitterly ironic that she calls herself a socialist.*

You don't communicate with her?

She's the reason why I'm here, Lilian had said. *This is about money. That's all I know.*

So that meant that the Iturbes were not working for Javier Pimentel—he had been telling me the truth. They were now working for Maria Calderón, a future vice president of Cuba. The Iturbes were the enforcers –the debt collectors—who were making sure that Javier somehow came up with the sixty million that he owed his half-sister.

And anyone who got in their way would be beaten up like Gustavo, and me, or maybe even killed, like Raimundo Pimentel and his second son.

My face was sore from where the thugs had pummeled me, and all of my muscles ached from the few hours of sleep I'd had on the lumpy straw bed. There was a small stack of hay bales in the center of my room, and it dawned on me that if I piled them up I might be able to climb the partition wall high enough to see Lilian, who I presumed was still asleep, as it was dead silent in our shared, malodorous jail. My Vinny Shuffle had gotten far worse, and if I ever got back to civilization I would have to surrender myself to Megan Rumsford, who had better be wearing something other than my T-shirt when I next saw her.

I stacked a column of bales four high, and used the remaining six to make a staircase. I was pleased with my ingenuity, and just hoped that the bales weren't supposed to be what I had been given to eat. If I did get out of here, I would go find a roadside joint that sold draft beer by the bucket and fried oysters by the cubic yard, and I would have a little snack to celebrate staying alive. *If.*

I managed to make it to the top of the hay bale staircase despite the weak leg, and I peered over the top of the wall.

Lilian was gone. And her door had been left open to the outside.

Now, all that I had to do was to swing the weak leg up and climb over the wall, and then drop nine feet to the floor. Hello, concussion. There was no way that I could do that. But there was the open door, with the light spilling in, and somewhere outside of that door there was a big plate of oysters and curly fries with my name on it.

Now that's motivation.

I must have looked like a pole-vaulter who happened to be giving birth while in mid-jump, but I made it, and landed in a sore but uninjured heap on the floor of Lilian's former cell. I limped outside and surveyed my surroundings.

I was in the middle of goddamned nowhere.

*

It was a sweltering, two-hour limp down a gravel road to the Tamiami Trail, the highway that crosses southern Florida from Miami to Naples. I waited for an eastbound trucker and stepped onto the pavement, waving my arms wildly to flag him down. He hit the airbrakes and pulled to a stop in front of me, and I climbed up the step to the lowered passenger-side window.

"I need your phone," I said. "I have to call the police."

The truck driver had long, orange-colored hair that spilled out from underneath a railroad cap. He spit a tobacco wad out of his own window and turned back to me. "I ain't callin' no po-lice," he said. "I'm five tons overweight, and my insurance is lapsed."

"Just take me to the nearest place with a phone," I said. "I don't have a car. I got hijacked. I'm on foot."

"Well you sure picked a hot one, didn't ya, bud?" he said, giving me a brown-stained smile. "Hop in."

Tobacco Teeth ended up taking me all the way to Westchester, one town over from Coral Gables, where he had to turn north up the Palmetto Expressway. He dropped me at a tire store near the on ramp, and I borrowed a phone and called Talbot Heffernan in his office.

"Where the hell are you? You wouldn't believe how many people have called here looking for you," he said.

"Send someone to pick me up, and I'll explain when I see you." I gave him the address.

Ten minutes later, Lieutenant Heffernan himself pulled up in an unmarked cruiser, and I got into the seat.

"I need a beer," I said. "And some food. Let's stop somewhere."

"You need a bath," Heffernan said. "You stink to holy hell."

"I spent the night in a slaughterhouse."

"We'll get takeout. And then you're going to my house, and my wife will throw those clothes in the nearest dumpster."

*

Heffernan had dispatched a team to the slaughterhouse that was following my directions: six miles west of the Indian casino, as I had measured from the truck's odometer. Then, south on a deserted dirt road. Maybe they would find something that would lead them to wherever Lilian was now, but I doubted it. The Iturbes were smarter than they looked.

The detective and I drove to Javier Pimentel's house to get my car and my phone. I didn't expect to see Javier there, or the Iturbes, and we didn't, but Heffernan requested another team to watch the place. He also had the whole state looking for the silver Honda Fit, which would be distinguishable by the fact that the tightly packed-in occupants might burst out like a two-headed jack-in-the-box if you opened the door. I glanced at some of the several dozen texts and calls that I'd missed and put the phone back into my pocket. Before I tackled any of that, I needed to finish off the container of fried oysters that we had picked up at a joint on the Miracle Mile. Priorities.

Chloe Heffernan looked shocked to see me when I pulled my car into the driveway behind her husband's cruiser and got out. Or maybe it was the smell. She led me inside and made me shuck off my preppy red pants and blue polo, and she handed me a bath towel as she gathered the clothes. "Take your time," she said, pointing to the bathroom. "You may need more than one shower to get the stink off."

"That's the last time I stay at the Hotel Abattoir," I said.

*

Chloe had set me up on the back patio under a row of leafy palms that rustled in the sea breeze. I was wearing a borrowed pair of workout pants, which had a stretch waistband to accommodate my larger frame, and she had found an XL shirt that someone had mistakenly bought for her size-L husband. She made me a pitcher of sweet tea and left me alone to make my calls. I started with Rose DiNapoli, who had left the most recent message. I had promised Rose that I would call her back more than twenty-four hours ago, and she'd left one voicemail and six texts. I got her on the first ring.

"Vince? Where were you?"

"I got hijacked by the Iturbe brothers," I said. "I found Lilian, too, but they took off in the morning, before I woke up."

"Oh my god."

"I think I'm figuring this out," I said. "It's about money, and there's some bad blood mixed in."

"Where are you?"

"Detective Heffernan's house. I'm catching up on my calls. Where are you?"

"I'm—in bed," she said.

"Are you OK?"

"Yeah," she said. "Just beaten down. You know."

"You mean the, um—"

"Partly that, and partly because my boyfriend is an asshole. When I told him what happened, he said that I should go to his club and work out with him. *Be strong and get over it.* Those were his words. What a fucking jerk."

I knew better than to pick sides, so I said: "Uh-oh."

"Uh-oh is right," she said. "The wedding is off, as of last night. He went ballistic, probably because he's put down ten grand in deposits."

134

I decided to stick my neck out. "Rose, you have to go talk to someone. That's the only thing that will help. Your boyfriend is wrong."

"What do you do when bad things happen to you?" she said. "Is that what you would do? See a therapist?"

"Not really," I said. "I go out for oysters. I just polished off a quart."

I heard her laugh for the first time since we'd left Cuba. "You've ruined me, Vince. You know that."

"Beg pardon?"

"You spoiled my would-be marriage, thank god," she said. "I didn't think that there were any decent men out there. I thought I had to settle, but I won't now. You gave me hope. Too bad you're married."

"Um, Rose—"

"Relax, my friend. When you're done with this you can take me out for some red snapper. I hate oysters."

"I knew you had a flaw," I said.

*

Neither Sonny, nor Barbara, nor Megan, nor anyone in the house answered their cellphones. Royal didn't have one yet, because the trend among parents these days is to not get a phone for their children until they can actually form words. Once that happens, it's a free-for-all.

I reached Roberto, who was thrilled to hear that I had at least seen his mother, if briefly. Aside from that he sounded glum. *We can't get past this stupid token code thing,* he had confessed. It was unlike Roberto to not be able to hack into anything. He scared me with what he could do sometimes, and we had discussed that topic at length; my sense was that he was developing the maturity to know when to hold back. That's not easy for a fifteen-year-old boy, and it was part of why I liked him so much.

I asked him why he was so sure that the token code was the problem, and he said that he wasn't. It could also be that the email program required an RSA key fob, which was a little device that generated numbers every couple of minutes that you had to type into the mail program along with your password. It was similar to a soft token program but was more secure, as you had to be in possession of the physical device. If they had used an RSA key then he would never get in, he said, because the fob would be somewhere in Cuba, in Maria Inés Calderón's possession.

"What about on this side?" I asked him. "Would Segundo have used one?"

There was a long silence. Finally he said, "Doh."

"Is that Spanish?"

"No," he said. "It's Simpson. You're a genius, Vince."

I'll take my technology praise when can I get it, and I basked in the glow of outwitting him, for once. "So now we have to find Segundo's key fob," I said.

"Right," my young associate said. "Get it to me as soon as you find it."

*

Chloe Heffernan had never seen Segundo Pimentel's RSA fob, although she'd seen pretty much everything else. Her husband had gone back to his precinct office, and she and I had taken a moment to talk after I had wrapped up my business on the phone.

I hardly knew the woman, but she looked drawn and on the edge of something. A hit man had recently killed her employer and lover of nine years, and that would explain most of it, but there was something else. It was as if she was begging me to ask her a question, but I had no idea what it was that she wanted me to ask. I did press her about Segundo's six-million-dollar backgammon debt to his half-sister, but she just shook her head. I also asked her why Maria Calderón stood to collect another sixty million from her Florida siblings, but she still pleaded ignorance. Or maybe she was pleading the fifth, and she just wasn't telling me that. Something strange was going on, but all I could get out of her was my twice-washed Nantucket Reds and the dark blue polo shirt, which I thanked her for and donned before getting back into my convertible. I gave her another business card and told her that she could call me anytime. The two of us already shared the secret of her and Segundo's love affair, and I wondered if there were other secrets that Tal Heffernan wasn't privy to, but that I might be, if I had only known what to ask.

I was worried about Chloe. Something was brewing, and it was starting to give off a bad odor like my clothes had before she had so carefully laundered them.

*

South Miami Hospital was practically deserted, and I realized that it was a late Friday afternoon and the hot season was kicking into gear. Florida is unendurable for most people in the summertime. If you

136

lived here you either toughed it out under the air conditioning or you hightailed it to somewhere cooler. I happen to love the Florida summer, including the heat, but I'm a Vermonter by birth, and after enough winters we northern folk wouldn't be uncomfortable in Hell, at least not until we thawed out. And think of the firewood we'd save.

Gustavo Arguelles not only looked better, he could actually speak a few tentative words out of the slot that provided an opening to his mouth between the bandages. The docs had reduced the size of the dressing, and I could see more of his face. He was still very weak, but he could now get up and walk to and from the bathroom, and he was thrilled by the simple accomplishment. I could certainly relate to that—it hadn't been so long ago that I had come out of my own coma and had made the long, hard trek to the john as if I was climbing Everest with Hillary and Norgay. I was delighted and surprised to see him like this, and I pressed the attending doctor to release him and let me take him home.

"I saw Lilian," I told Gustavo. "She was being held captive in a building west of here. The Iturbes mugged me again, and they took me out to where she was."

"She all right?" he whispered through the slot around his lips.

"I think so. They took her somewhere else this morning, before I was awake. I escaped, but I saw the car, and the cops are all over it. This is going to be finished soon."

"How can I help?" he managed to say.

"You just rest up. Roberto and I are on this. We're getting close."

"Who kidnapped her?"

"Lilian? I think it was her half-sister. Maria. Lilian explained some things about the family."

"She hates—" Gustavo started to say, but he began coughing, and it looked incredibly painful. His lungs were fragile, and he had to be in some serious pain just to breathe, let alone cough.

"Take it easy, bud," I said.

Gustavo's breathing calmed down, and he looked up at me. "The woman hates my guts," he whispered. "Lili didn't say?"

"Didn't say what?"

"Maria Calderón and I were engaged," he said. "And then I fell in love with Lilian. Lili and I eloped, a month before Maria and I were supposed to be married. Roberto doesn't know any of this, by the way. He doesn't even know who she is."

Now *that* would certainly create some bad blood, I thought. No wonder Lilian Arguelles had been treated like chattel in this crazy family financial game. Jesus, Mary, Joseph, John, Paul, George, and Ringo. Weren't my cases supposed to be simple? Like, some married dude was shacking up with his au pair, or some angst-ridden teenager took off to the big city, and I could make a few calls, locate them, and get paid? The Pimentels were like one of those Telemundo soap operas that we English-speakers didn't understand, but we still got the drift—everybody was messing with everybody, and I was suddenly lacking the necessary energy to chart out all of the family intrigues.

A nurse entered the room and began to remove Gustavo's things from a closet and pack them into a plastic sack. "You're outta here, Mr. G," she said, smiling. "The doctors just said that it's all right for Mr. Tanzi to drive you home today."

I saw tears forming in my friend's eyes, and I let him have a private moment while I helped the nurse pack up his belongings. I was finally going to bring Gustavo home to my house where he would be with his son. And then I would find his wife, and I would reunite the family who had always treated me like a favorite uncle.

The Arguelles clan was coming back together—and I would make it happen. If I had to knock a few heads, or even stage a minor Cuban revolution of my own, it would be done. I wasn't afraid of some Bryn Mawr-socialist-extortionist-kidnapper, or her Taser-wielding minions, and anyway I had now officially had my fill of this crap. I had a baby to take care of, a marriage to salvage, and I probably also had another shitload of laundry to do when I got home, seeing how the place had been turned into Vinny's Refugee Camp. I would drive Gustavo Arguelles there, make him comfortable, and he would mend, and so would I. My injuries weren't as obvious as his, but I knew that I had taken some serious hits over the last few days—both emotional and physical—and it was now time to rest up for a short while, and then resume the game.

If this were a backgammon game, I would now double my opponent. Because I had suddenly figured out where Segundo Pimentel's key fob was, and if that would help Roberto get access to his aunt's computer in Havana, then maybe we had the beginnings of a plan.

*

"It's a key fob," I said to Bobby Bove. "So it has to be with his car keys. You're holding the car, right?"

"The car but not the keys," he said. "We had to tow it to the impound lot from Middleton's. We couldn't find the keys."

"Send the divers back?"

"They already bitched about the gators the last time."

"It's important," I said. "I'll be in Vero in two hours, and I really need it."

Gustavo's discharge was taking forever, and by the time we made it home it would be dinnertime. I had reached Sonny, who was making a Cuban *ropa vieja* stew with Susanna, which he had described as being everything that I'd had in my refrigerator plus some flank steak. Roberto was on the computer, and Megan was off somewhere. Barbara hadn't been seen.

She had texted me several times since I had left my cellphone at Javier Pimentel's, each time with a variation of the same message: *we need to talk.* She was right, but that didn't mean I felt like talking or that I would be civil to her if we did. Gustavo was still signing paperwork when I took a seat outside his room and finally answered Barbara.

We can talk after you bring the furniture back.

She responded immediately. *It's not that simple.*

Yes it is, I wrote.

I found myself staring at my cellphone, waiting for her reply. An apology, something about Royal, a kind word, whatever. Just not silence.

Since you refuse to talk with me I'll have to tell you this way, she finally wrote. *I've been unfaithful to you.*

Her words hit me like the Taser darts that I'd taken the day before. Maybe worse. There it was, in black and white, right in front of my face on the tiny screen.

I already knew that, I wrote, but I held down the button that would shut the phone off before I could send it. A nurse was wheeling Gustavo out of the room with his belongings in a bag on his lap.

"If you want to go get your car we'll meet you out front," she said. She was one of the younger ones, and she was sporting a new-looking diamond ring on her finger, without an accompanying wedding band.

I pointed to it. "Engaged?"

"Last night," she said, beaming.

Good luck, sweetheart. You're going to need it.

*

Gustavo Arguelles was relaxing comfortably in my bed. I was going to have to take a headcount and decide where everyone else would be sleeping for the night. Susanna had made him a mango smoothie, and he looked a lot happier than anytime I'd seen him since he had been assaulted. Sonny had served the *ropa vieja* to the rest of us shortly after we had arrived, and he and Susanna had gone way overboard on the garlic. I am pretty much immune to the stuff, having grown up with my mother's cooking, but after two bowls of the stew my breath was strong enough to peel wallpaper.

Bobby Bove had called to say that he was on the way to my house with Segundo Pimentel's car keys. The divers had found them in the muck with the help of a submersible metal detector. Segundo had possibly dropped them into the water in his rush to save himself, or maybe his assailant had tossed them there. Either way, it didn't matter now, because we had them, and according to Bobby the little RSA device was still displaying six-digit numbers that would change once every minute. Roberto smiled when he heard the news and said to me: *You and I are not getting any sleep tonight.*

I didn't know about that, because I was truly exhausted. Getting the official declaration of infidelity from Barbara had been a disastrous finish to an already long day that had begun in a foul-smelling slaughterhouse and had gone downhill from there, although Gustavo's release was cheering everyone up. I had taken Sonny aside after the meal to tell him that he was right about his friend Angelo, and he shook his head and said that he was sorry, and he wished he'd never mentioned it, but we both knew that things didn't work like that. If your mate was cheating on you, you usually found out, and it was better for it to come from a friend who cared about you.

Bobby Bove dropped off the key fob and declined my invitation to stay for a beer, as he had a date. A hot young chickadee, as he'd described her, and it made me think of Megan Rumsford and wonder where she was. I had been thinking of booking some P.T. for the first thing in the morning if she could do it, and I had tried calling her cell, but the call went to voicemail. That was probably for the best. I needed to follow through on finding another physical therapist, although I had mellowed on that issue somewhat since Megan had moved in with us and had behaved, relatively speaking, not counting all of the flouncing around in my too-large shirts.

At nine in the evening we were having a typical night at home for my odd little family: Megan was off somewhere, Gustavo was asleep, Sonny and Susanna were in my study drinking Cointreau from snifters and reading aloud to each other, I had my knitting out to see if I could salvage the aborted sweater, or possible plant-hanger, and Roberto was on the computer, attempting to gain access to the private communications of one of the highest-ranking officials in the Cuban government. It would have made a splendid Norman Rockwell painting.

"I'm in," Roberto called from across the room. "This is whacked."

I got up from my chair and sat down next to him for a look. "What is that?"

"It's her bank account," he said. "She's loaded."

"How much?"

"Twenty million in this account, and there's a link to other accounts that I haven't even seen yet."

"What bank?"

"This one's in Grand Cayman," he said, "but there are a couple in Europe that she logs into. She uses the same password for all of them. Typical."

"How did you get in?"

"I sent her a program," he said. "It looks like a software update. She clicked on it, and it installed itself in the background. It's new, and the antivirus programs won't pick it up for a while. I had a guy customize it for me."

"So you can see everything on her computer?"

"Better than that," Roberto said. He was on his third Coke, and he was wide-eyed from the caffeine. "I can control it like I'm sitting there. It's my bitch."

I couldn't help but laugh. "So now you can read all the emails? They aren't scrambled anymore?"

"I think so," he said. "Go get me another Coke."

"Get one yourself," I said. "That computer may be your bitch, but I'm not."

*

Even after it had been unscrambled, the correspondence between Segundo Pimentel and his half-sister in Cuba had been largely unintelligible, at least to Roberto and me. It was a jumbled mix of English and Spanish, as both parties to the emails were equally fluent in both languages. A lot of it was in Legalese, which is a curious tongue that is distinguished by the fact that the few who speak it are permitted to charge $400 an hour to the many who don't.

The term *fideicomiso* kept coming up, as did *beneficiario, tenedor, otorgante, fiduciaria,* and so on, until we knew that we were out of our depth, however good Roberto's Spanish was. This was about money, and about somebody's will, or trust, and most likely about who got what. I was eager to know the details, because I had a suspicion that the knowledge would eventually lead me to Lilian.

Some of their correspondence had been in English, and the meaning was considerably more obvious:

Maria: *You screw me on this and you're dead.*

Segundo: *You push us too hard and I'll blow you sky high. I don't care who you are.*

And later, an exchange between them that was dated the day after Lilian Arguelles' disappearance:

Segundo: *Take me instead, you fucking putona. She has nothing to do with this.*

Maria: *You have one on the bar now, brother. Pay up or lose.*

"One on the bar?" I asked Roberto.

"It's a backgammon term," he said. "That's when your opponent lands on your unprotected piece, and it gets taken all the way to the beginning, and off the board. You have to roll the right number to get back on the board, and you hope that the spaces aren't blocked. The piece is sort of a captive—like my mother."

"You should teach me how to play," I said. "Are you good at it?"

"My mom taught me. She can kick anyone's ass."

"I've been getting my ass kicked all day," I said. "Now I'm going to bed."

*

It was that damn dream again. This time, I at least knew that I was in a bed—the single futon mattress that I had taken out of storage and had set up on the floor of Royal's abandoned nursery where Barbara's cot had been. This was not the cold stone slab of the other dreams. But I still couldn't move.

The same hands touched me. They started at my sides, and then moved to my chest and massaged my nipples between their fingertips. The hands moved down my torso to my groin, found a grip, and began to stroke.

No...not now...too tired...

Shhh, a voice said. Barbara? Had she come home?

I want you, Vince, the voice said. You have no idea how much.

The stroking was having an effect, but I couldn't wake up. I didn't want to. Everything was too complicated. And I hadn't been touched like this in months.

She was going crazy on top of me, and the room was spinning. Too much had happened to me in too little time, and my head hurt where the bullet had entered, which was never good because everything would suddenly go bright white like the angels were coming for me, but I wasn't ready to go, because people needed me here—

OH GOD, the voice was now screaming, and I had suddenly gone from nine-ty percent asleep to ninety percent awake and was sliding off the edge of unconsciousness into a free fall of realization that ended with a shock:

This was no dream.

Which would have been fine if it had been Barbara. Make-up sex was always the best.

But I was fully awake now, and I had just made love—or something—to Megan Rumsford, who lay naked on the bed next to me and was gasping for breath.

SATURDAY

I HAD GOTTEN GOOD AND drunk one night in my freshman year of college and had found myself in bed with a girl the next morning. I didn't know what her name was, or what dorm we were in, or even what she looked like. She slept facing away from me, and her sandy blonde hair was all that I could see—just a section of it that wasn't covered by her bedcovers—and I lay there, mortified, hung over, and not knowing what to do. Finally, I got up as quietly as I could, dressed, and left. For the rest of my one-and-only year as a college student, I would pass by some girl with sandy blonde hair on the campus—there were a lot of them—and I would feel sick to my stomach. That was by far the worst experience that I had had with a woman, and I swore that I would never do anything that stupid again, ever. And I hadn't.

Until last night.

Megan had left the room before I awoke, and I tried to reconstruct what had happened. Had I really been awake? Or was I asleep, and defenseless, and I'd had no idea what was going on, and Barbara wouldn't kill me when she found out, because the whole thing was not my fault?

Nope.

I had been awake. Not at first, but there had been a time when I could have stopped the proceedings, although we were way into it by then. A time when I was aware that it wasn't my wife who was on top of me. But I hadn't stopped it.

And, why not? Was I retaliating against Barbara for her affair? That would be childish, although I'm not immune to being childish. Was I actually attracted to Megan? Hell yes, she was attractive. But that still didn't explain it.

I felt like some primal instinct had taken over, and I had allowed it to. Oh yes, I'd heard every variation of that one when I was a cop. It was *nature*. Men and women just *did this*. You can't fight these urges. In fact, you shouldn't—it's not healthy to bottle up your sexuality.

144

Tell that to a rape victim.

I was totally disgusted with myself, and I wished that I were still a practicing Catholic because I could hightail it to confession and do my penance, but I had never truly bought into that whole scene, not even as a kid. Sin was sin, and it might temporarily lighten my load to confess it to a priest, but that didn't mean that I hadn't done it, or that I wouldn't ultimately pay the price. Instead, I got up off of the futon, entered the bathroom, and turned on the shower. And I would need more than one shower, again, because the stink on my conscience was even worse than the one on my clothes had been, the day before.

*

I was carefully removing a rack of just-baked popovers out of the oven with my mitts when Gustavo shuffled out of the bedroom in his bathrobe and took a stool at the counter next to Roberto, Sonny, and Susanna. "That smell," he said as loud as he could, which was a whisper. "It sucked me in here like Looney Tunes."

"You mean like where the smoke drifts, and Daffy Duck floats off the ground, back to the food?" Sonny asked.

"'Zactly," Gustavo slurred.

"My man Vince makes some dope-ass popovers," Sonny said. "So Gustavo, you can eat all the good shit now?"

"Language, Sonny," Susanna said, frowning.

"I'm going to try," Gustavo said.

"I'll scoop out the middle and cut it up," I said. "That's how I feed them to Royal."

"Sorry, Vince," Gustavo said.

"No trouble," I said. "I enjoy doing it. I miss my little boy."

No one said anything, but I had instantly changed the mood in the room.

"Vince, man," Sonny finally said. "You got too much on your mind. We should all go fishing."

"Nobody's going fishing," Roberto said, looking up from his computer. "We have work to do." He turned to his father. "Dad, Vince and I have a few questions, if you're up for it. After we eat, maybe?"

"I'm up for it," Gustavo whispered, and I saw the look of pride on his face as his fifteen-year-old son stepped up and took control. Roberto was becoming a man, because all of a sudden his parents needed him to. He was in the process of leaving his innocence behind like a molted snakeskin, and it was beautiful to watch. Some kids never grew up, because they had never been tested. This was Roberto's test.

We finished our breakfast without much further conversation. After a while Sonny said, "You guys go out back and talk. Me and Susanna got the dishes."

"Susanna and I," she corrected.

"Hoo boy," he said. "What I meant to say was Susanna got the dishes." He winked at me. "I'm going fishing."

*

Lilian Arguelles had intended to disclaim her portion of the trust, according to Gustavo. Roberto, his father, and I were gathered around the glass-and-aluminum patio table out under the back awning that we had chosen as a place to talk. The morning was still, and was quiet enough for us to hear Gustavo's faint words. "She called it blood money," he told us. "People in Cuba died because of it, and neither of us wanted any part of that. We both have good jobs. We don't need anything else."

Gustavo said that Segundo was the one who kept track of everything, and all that he knew was that a separate trust had been set up by Fulgencio Batista for each of his nine children from the estimated two hundred million dollars that he had left Cuba with after he had been ousted in 1959. Plus interest. Gustavo had no idea what the numbers looked like now, but he said that Raimundo Pimentel had been entitled to the income from his wife's trust after she had died, and when he was gone the principal was to be split equally among Maria Marta Pimentel's children, including Maria Inés. Since Lilian had planned to opt out, that meant that the money would be divided four ways between Javier, Susanna, Segundo, and Maria Inés.

Ah, yes—good old money. The family real estate business was in deep trouble, and sixty million that I knew about was owed to Maria Inés Calderón, who could send out navy ships to pick up coolers full of Ben Franklins, and could kidnap her own half-sister seemingly at will. Throw in Segundo Pimentel's backgammon wagering disasters, and you suddenly had a motive: kill off the old man, distribute the trust, and everybody was flush again. *Habemus pecuniam.*

"Could Segundo have killed his father?" I asked Gustavo. "Or had him killed?"

He took a long sip from the straw of his water cup and put it back down on the glass table. "We used to fish together," he whispered.

"You get to know someone when you go fishing with them. I would say no, but he hated the old man. They all did."

"Why?"

"Long story," he said.

"Take your time," I said.

"They were in Vermont," Gustavo whispered, and Roberto and I had to lean close to him in order to hear. "Up where you come from. A January ski trip, with all the kids. Lilian was like, eleven or something. Raimundo and Maria Marta had a fight, and they had rented a house way out in the woods, and he threw her out in the middle of dinner and locked the door. The temperature was below zero, and she didn't have her coat on. The kids were all crying, but he wouldn't let her back in, and she walked three miles in her slippers to a gas station and then collapsed. She was in the hospital for two weeks with pneumonia, and she was never the same after that. She was sick all the time, until she died."

Roberto looked at me, and then back at his father. "So if Segundo killed his father for the money, then who killed Segundo?"

"I don't know," Gustavo said. "I've been thinking about it. I thought it might be your aunt, Maria Inés, but that would make it more difficult for her to collect what you said they owed her. She's capable of killing somebody though, or having it done. She has her grandfather Fulgencio's genes."

"Why did they even let her back into Cuba?" I asked him.

"She's like the return of the prodigal daughter," he said. "A Batista granddaughter who rejected capitalism and came back to Cuba. She lives in a small house, and she drives a beat-up old Lada. She's a folk hero. But Segundo told me that she's probably the wealthiest woman on the island."

"Not for long," Roberto said, looking up from his open laptop.

"What?" Gustavo and I said at the same time.

The young man closed the lid of the computer. "I just transferred a hundred thousand dollars out of her Cayman account," He said. "That's the limit without a voice print."

"Transferred to where?" I asked him.

"Planned Parenthood," Roberto said. "It's my mom's favorite charity. My aunt probably won't see it for a while, unless she's really paying attention. I just wanted to make sure that I could do it."

"What do you have in mind?"

"Later," Roberto said. "Let's go inside and see if Sonny can fly us to the Keys."

*

Bobby Bove called while Susanna and I were putting away the last few dishes. That's a task that the owner of the house needs to be involved in, or your guests will find new and creative places to put away your strainer or your carrot peeler so that you will never, ever find them again. I dried off my hands and picked up the phone.

"You getting anywhere with that key fob?" Bobby asked.

"Yes. You'll never guess what this is about."

"I've been a cop for thirty-four years," he said. "So it's either sex or money, and I'll take money."

"You got it," I said. "There's a trust, set up by the grandfather. Blood money from Cuba. Now that Raimundo is dead, it gets divided."

"How much are we talking about?"

"Millions. Maybe a lot of millions. The grandfather was Fulgencio Batista."

"The dictator? No shit?"

"I'm wondering if Segundo killed his father. He was in the hole for a lot of money. It looks like he owed it to the half-sister in Cuba, and she's a cutthroat."

"Didn't happen," Bobby Bove said. "I forgot to mention that the divers found a shell casing in the water yesterday. Segundo got killed by a single shot from a Walther PPK. The shell was a .32 caliber, and the hammer mark was from a Walther."

"That's what James Bond carried."

"Yeah, whoever shot Segundo must think he's some kind of cool guy. It's a decent concealed carry weapon, but it's pretty heavy."

"So why couldn't Segundo have shot Raimundo?"

"Because the father was shot with the same gun," Bove said. "And Segundo didn't shoot himself. He was hit from too far away, and we would have found the weapon. You see anybody with a Walther, you let me know. We're talking the same shooter for both jobs."

"Has anybody seen Javier?"

"I just got off the phone with Heffernan. He has people at the house, and the Key West cops are watching the boat. But no, Javier's disappeared, and so have those two gangbangers."

"I wonder how Javier would feel if I borrowed his boat for a while?"

"What? How are you going to get inside? Or start it? It's gotta be locked up tight."

"I know a guy who does locks," I said. "At least I used to."

*

By the time Sonny landed the Piper at the Key West International Airport I felt like my whole body had been twisted into a buñuelo. Sleeping on the futon in Royal's room had been better than my hay bale bed of the night before, but my little after-hours session with Megan had been the wrong kind of therapy, and I was knotted up into a figure eight, both physically and emotionally. Guilt will do that to you.

I'd had some time during the trip to think about it all, and I had decided to stop torturing myself. Barbara had had an affair, and so had I, although mine had been a semi-somnolent one. So we had both screwed up, and it wasn't the end of the world. Couples could get professional help, like I'd encouraged Rose to do for the trauma that she'd been through. Just like cops heard the same things from people all the time, so did therapists, and the best ones could cut to the chase. I knew that counseling worked because I'd seen it with many of the estranged couples I had dealt with as a private investigator: my snooping would expose the problem, everything would go to hell for a while, and then a good counselor would jump in and would help the couple resolve it, assuming that they wanted to preserve the relationship.

We could do that, if Barbara wanted to. But maybe she didn't. Maybe I was damaged goods, and she'd helped nurse me back to a semblance of the man who she had initially fallen in love with, but the effort had cost her too much. The whole issue would normally have been at the top of my list, but getting Lilian back was the only thing on my list now. My troubles with Barbara were going to have to wait.

Rose DiNapoli's flight had beaten us to the airport, and she already had a taxi waiting. She was wearing her customs uniform, and she carried a small bag.

"What's in there?" I asked her, after I gave her a friendly hug.

"My gun, the impoundment paperwork, and a swimsuit," she said. "I wasn't sure what role I'm supposed to play here, customs agent or boat bimbo, so I brought both."

"We haven't figured out your part yet," I said. "But you'd make a pretty convincing bimbo."

She smiled. "I sure hope that was a compliment, because it didn't sound like one."

I introduced her to Sonny and Roberto, and they shook hands. She led us to the taxi, and a few minutes later the driver let Rose and me off at Charter Boat Row while Sonny and Roberto continued on to get some food for the trip. Rose found the local cops who were on duty and showed them the documents that she'd brought, giving the Department of Homeland Security full possession of the Mikelson on the grounds that Javier had used it to illegally transport laundered funds. That happened to be the truth, seeing how Javier had told me that much of the cash that he'd dropped off the Cuban coast on our previous trip was dirty.

I didn't have a bathing suit with me, but I did have every lock picking tool that I owned, and this time I was inside the cabin in less than fifteen minutes. Hotwiring Javier Pimentel's million-dollar boat would be a different matter, though. The ignition wires were threaded through a hardened metal tube, and I had to attach a diamond-coated blade to my Dremel saw which kept shooting little metal fragments into my eyes as I lay on my back under the helm of the flying bridge. This was going to take a while.

"Looking for these?" Ms. DiNapoli said, and I banged my head on the helm console as I sat up. She had changed into a blue-and-green tankini, with the top section visible through a loose, scoop neck T-shirt. She held out a set of keys on a ring with a small float attached. "They were in the master stateroom," she said.

"Doh," I said. "You're very resourceful for a bimbo."

"Thanks, I think," she said, smiling. "I'll put my uniform on again when we get closer. In case we need to let them know that we're not messing around."

I heard somebody board the boat and spotted Roberto and Sonny on the deck below us, holding plastic bags. "Got us some conch fritters," Sonny said. "You missed out the last time, so we got ten orders."

"That ought to do it," I said.

"Don't know about that," Sonny said. "Roberto already ate three of them on the way back."

*

Piloting a seventy-foot boat out of the Garrison Bight was a challenge, and I had come dangerously close to backing the *Mamarta* into one of the power line supports that crossed the body of water near the channel. I'd handled a forty-footer here a couple of winters before, but the Mikelson was so overpowered with its twin diesels that it took me a while to gain control. After a while we were out of the harbor and headed south past Wisteria Island and Sunset Key, into the Florida

Straits. Roberto and Sonny sat next to me at the helm. Rose had claimed a sheltered spot on the deck behind us and was lying on her back in the warm sun. She had shed the T-shirt and was wearing her movie-star sunglasses with her curly dark hair tied up in a tight bun. She looked quite excellent in her bathing suit, and it took all the resolve that I could muster to keep my eyes on where I was going and not whack the million-dollar yacht into a buoy. As if I didn't have enough women problems already. Lord, why do you torment me so?

Tanzi's Tip #9: Whenever you think you've dug yourself into the deepest hole possible, someone can always find you a bigger shovel.

Roberto had programmed the ship's navigation system to take us to a location twelve nautical miles off of the Cuban coast, just outside of the country's territorial waters. It was far too deep to drop anchor there, so if our timing was off, we wouldn't be able to spend the night, and we would have to make the four-hour trip back to the Keys. Everything depended on whether Maria Inés Calderón was checking her email, whether she had access to a fast boat, and whether or not she would believe the story that we had come up with. It sounded pretty good to me, but I'm not an MIT Economics grad, nor a vice president, nor am I sitting on twenty million simoleans in a Cayman bank account.

"Tell me how this goes again?" I asked him, as he worked the touch screen of the GPS.

"I tell her I have the money, and then I give her the coordinates. How fast are you going?"

"Twenty-six knots."

"That should put us there just after six PM," he said. "In an hour or so I'll email her from Segundo's account. The boat has satellite Internet, which is good because we're too far from a tower. I tell her that I'm Javier, and that I have the money, but that we need to talk first."

"You think she'll buy that?"

"We just have to get her on board," Roberto said. "This is Javier's boat, so that will look right. And nobody would have access to her email system except for Segundo, and probably Javier. I think we have a chance."

"So she comes aboard, and I go into my act, and meanwhile a Cuban Navy ship is next to us, ready to blow us out of the water if they don't like us."

"All we need is six words, Vince. *I want to make a transfer.*"

*

We were an hour away from our destination and Sonny was at the helm singing made-up sea shanties in his deep baritone, which was helping to cut the tension and had Roberto smiling. This might have been an enjoyable trip if I hadn't been so worried about how we were going to pull off our planned conference-at-sea with Roberto's aunt. Too much could go wrong.

I was down on the cockpit deck with Rose, sitting across from her in the twin padded fishing seats that someone might sit in if they were actually fishing from the boat rather than dropping off coolers full of cash or running scams on Cuban government officials. I'd found the Elle sweatshirt in the Zodiac tender where I'd hidden on the last trip, and I gave it to Rose, as she was cold but was not ready to give up the swimsuit. It was five o'clock—I call that "ice-rattling time" at my house, and there was a full bar in the galley that was well stocked, but I didn't want to start drinking yet, no matter how beautiful the day or the scenery.

Rose raised her sunglasses and tucked them back into her hair. "So, Vince. You remember when I told you that you looked cute in the priest's collar?"

"Yes. And I accused you of flirting."

"I'm still not flirting. But you said, 'I already have enough trouble at home.' What did you mean by that?"

"Who wants to know?"

"A friend of yours," she said. "Me."

"It's complicated."

"It always is. My ex-fiancé emailed me this morning. He wants five grand for what he calls my half of the deposits."

"Really?"

"Yes. And I think I'm going to send it to him. He's entitled to it. It takes two to screw up a relationship."

"I just said the exact same thing to my physical therapist. She and I were talking about why my wife left."

"Your wife left you?"

"Sort of," I said. "Temporarily, I guess. She's having an affair. And meanwhile, I got in too deep with the physical therapist."

"Oh no."

"I didn't mean to. She crawled into my bed when I was asleep. She's—kind of obsessed with me. Every time I see her, she comes on to me. It's partly my fault, though."

"Some people will stop at nothing," Rose said. "You're a good man, Vince."

"You don't know me. I'm fifty-two years old, and I can still make some colossal mistakes."

"You don't stop making mistakes just because you're old."

"So I'm old?"

"That's not what I meant." She took the sunglasses from her head, folded them, and rested them in her lap. "I'm going to pour you a little rum out of Javier Pimentel's bar. He has the good stuff. The *really* good stuff. We customs agents are very picky about what we confiscate, you know."

"Rose, I shouldn't."

"Don't argue with me," she said. "It's gorgeous out, and you need to relax a little if you're going to pull this off."

Tanzi's Tip #10: Just say yes.

*

We were twelve miles off the coast of Cuba, drifting. I had shut down the twin engines because they gulped fuel, and at the current price of diesel I wasn't about to shell out for any more than the two thousand gallons that the Mikelson already held. I may have taken Javier Pimentel's boat, but I didn't have his credit card.

Roberto was up in the flying bridge, watching the shoreline for activity. Sonny was pacing back and forth on the lanai deck like Captain Ahab. Agent DiNapoli had gone below to change into her uniform and get her sidearm in case there was any trouble, although her automatic wouldn't be much good against a naval gun. I was still sitting in the fishing chair, nursing the last of the rum that Rose had poured me and rehearsing my lines.

"She just emailed, and she's on the way," Roberto yelled from above me, and we let out a collective whoop. Sonny came aft, and I sent him into the saloon to stay out of the sight of any approaching boats. Not long afterward I saw a shape on the horizon, and I decided that I would also go inside, so that when they drew near they would have to guess who was aboard. If Maria Inés happened to spot me through binoculars she might turn around, and our rendezvous would never happen.

The approaching shape grew larger, and to my relief it was not a naval vessel—it was a cigarette boat, one of those noisy, floating dragsters that could make fifty knots or more, and it was coming up fast. I heard the engines throttle down as they drew near, and the

captain expertly maneuvered the arrow-shaped craft alongside our
starboard beam and hailed us. The seas were nearly calm with a light
breeze, and Sonny and I came out to help them tie up to our side,
catching lines while three dark-skinned men fastened rubber fenders
between our hulls to avoid contact between the two expensive boats.
The men were dressed in civilian clothes, but they didn't look like
civilians—they were young, muscular, and agile. If this ended up in a
fight, we just might lose.

Maria Inés Calderón emerged into the cockpit of the cigarette
boat from below decks and then stepped over the rail and onto the
deck of the Mikelson. She was dressed in tailored khaki pants, blue
Top-Sider sneakers, and a white fleece jacket with the sleeves pushed
up to expose a gold Rolex on one wrist and a thick diamond bracelet
on the other. The finance minister looked more like Mitzi from the
Boca Raton Yacht Club than she did a hero of the socialist republic.

She gave me a dismissive look, as if I had blocked her way.
"Where's my brother?"

"Down below. Seasick. Come inside and we'll pour you something."

"I don't drink," she snapped. "I didn't come out here to socialize
while Javier pukes."

"Please," I said, holding open the door to the saloon, and she entered the big teak-paneled room. I closed the door behind me, and it
was just the two of us except for Roberto, who was in the galley
pretending to be absorbed by his laptop.

"Who's the child?"

"He's not a child," I said. "Have a seat."

She sat in one of the overstuffed chairs in the saloon, across a
brass-covered coffee table from where I stood. "Javier is going to put
in an appearance, I presume? I've never known him to be seasick
before."

"What do you want?" I said.

"What do I want? Come again?"

"To make," I said. "You want to make."

"Mr. Tanzi, I don't follow you. Not at all. You told me before that
you represented the Pimentel family, and I know that's false. I believe
you know why I'm here, so let's get on with it, or I'll be leaving."

"What would you prefer?" I asked. "Cash now? Or do we make a
trans—what do you call those?"

"Make a what?"

"A bank trans—" I said. "What's the word?"

"You mean a wire? But you just said you have the cash here?"

"I could trans—whatever it to your boat."

"You're confusing me," she said. "This is nonsense. Don't tell me that you don't have the sixty million."

Goddamn. I was counting, and I was still one word short, no matter what I tried. I just couldn't get her to say it.

"*Transferencia*," Roberto called from the galley. "That's what Mr. Tanzi is trying to say."

"A transfer?" she said.

"Bingo," Roberto said, and he smiled at me. *We did it.* It was all I could do to not burst out laughing, I was so relieved.

"Say again?" I said to Roberto's aunt, just in case the three separate recording devices that we had brought hadn't picked it up.

"You heard me," she said. "What kind of game are you two playing? And where's Javier?"

"Oh, sorry," I said. "Javier couldn't make it. And there's no money."

"I figured as much. I'll just call my men aboard, and we'll settle this."

At that moment Sonny Burrows emerged from below, with his shaved head, gold earrings, and sunglasses. He had removed his shirt, and his arms were crossed over his heavily muscled chest like a boxer. Rose DiNapoli came up right behind him in her ICE tactical outfit, with her weapon at her side. She wore an expression that might have sent a Doberman yelping back to its kennel.

"Are you sure that you can't stay for a drink?" I asked our guest.

"You'll regret this," she said, scowling, as she pushed open the door to the deck.

"Aunt Maria," Roberto called after her. "Be sure to check your email."

Maria Inés Calderón took a long look at my fifteen-year-old friend. "You have no idea who you're dealing with, young man." She turned and climbed back over the rail of our boat to hers and ordered her crew to cast off.

"Neither does she," Roberto said to us.

*

Rose DiNapoli had been sitting next to me on the flying bridge, staring at the open, limitless water and the emerging stars while I steered the big yacht back toward Key West. She had stopped talking, and when I looked over to her I noticed that she was shivering.

"Cold?" I asked her.

She nodded her head in assent. She was still in her uniform and had put the Elle sweatshirt on top of it. I had the windows closed, but the shivering seemed to be getting worse.

"Rose, are you all right?"

"No," she said, in a whisper.

I yelled for Sonny from below, and he came up and helped me get her down the ladder. We led her to a sectional sofa inside the main saloon where Roberto sat at one end, working on the computer. "Get her a blanket," I called to him, and he dashed below into the staterooms. He came back with a pile of bedding, and we wrapped her up and propped her on the sofa with her legs elevated by pillows.

"You got this?" Sonny said, looking at me.

"Yes. Go up and take the helm."

Roberto and I waited at Rose's side while her breathing slowed and her color began to come back. After a while I poured her a glass of water from the galley sink and held it to her lips while she sipped. "I think I've been holding some things in," she said. "Maybe you're right, Vince."

"You are definitely going to go talk to somebody, all right? I insist."

"I guess," she said. "I'm going below. I need some sleep." She rose from the sofa and made her way down the steps to the staterooms.

"What happened to her?" Roberto said, after she had left.

"The Cuban police took her in for questioning," I said. "Your aunt was involved. The cops strip-searched her, and she wouldn't tell me what else, but it was bad. She's been toughing it out, and I think it finally hit her."

He didn't say anything, probably because he didn't have any idea what to say about a situation like that. No one did. Roberto returned to his laptop and got back to work.

I puttered around the galley and cleaned up the empty boxes of conch fritters from Sloppy Joe's, which we had demolished, along with most of a bottle of Brugal Siglo de Oro rum that had probably cost Javier Pimentel more than the new tires that I had recently put on the Beemer. I would need to take the helm from Sonny soon, as we were getting within reach of the coastline, and there would be other boats out.

"How's it going?" I asked Roberto, as I put away the last few drink glasses.

"It's going," he said. "I have it pretty much edited. Once I do, the sky's the limit. Meanwhile, I made a donation for your friend. I like her."

"A donation?"

"Yeah," he said. "My Aunt Maria just gave away another hundred thousand. This one went to RAINN. They have a national rape hotline."

"We could do this all night," I said, smiling at him.

"I know," he said, and he got back to his work.

SUNDAY

SONNY KEPT ME AWAKE FOR the rest of the boat ride, and I did the same for him on the flight home. We took Rose with us to Vero, as it was too late for her to catch a flight to Miami, and she was still in rough shape. We arrived back to the house at three in the AM. I put Roberto on the futon in Royal's room, Rose in the study, and I flopped onto the couch. Gustavo was sleeping soundly in my room, and Sonny and Susanna were having a little welcome home party in the spare bedroom, so I turned on a fan to drown out the noise.

Just before I went to bed Roberto played me back the fruits of our labors on the speakers of his computer. *I want to make a transfer,* a voice said, through the tinny-sounding speakers.

"Is that going to be good enough?" I asked him.

"Let's play it on yours," he said. "Check it out. I just emailed it to you."

I booted up my MacBook, which was hooked up to an audio system. I found the email and clicked on the file.

I want to make a transfer, the voice said again.

It was the voice of Maria Inés Calderón, who would soon be a vice president of Cuba, and it was as if she was in the room standing next to me.

*

I got three fitful hours of sleep that had been interrupted every so often by the pinging of Roberto's computer next to his bed in Royal's room. He had set it up so that whenever Maria Calderón's computer received an email, it would alert him, as her bank would send her a confirmation each time that a transfer had been completed, and then Roberto would go into her email account and delete the messages before she could see them. At around six AM he got the last ping, and we finally both had an hour of real sleep.

Each wire, he had explained, would be for just under five million. That was the Cayman bank's limit for an individual transfer outside of business hours, even with the voice authentication. If you wanted to wire an amount greater than that, you had to wait until the bank opened on Monday morning and talk to a real person.

I had watched him execute the first one: he filled in a form on his laptop, which was actually on his aunt's computer that he was now controlling. After he sent the form he received a secure email with a code, and he called a 24-hour automated voice response system at the bank. He was prompted to enter in her account number and the code, and then the voice response system asked him to say *I want to make a transfer*, which was the identifying phrase that Maria Calderón had recorded into the system when she had first set up the account.

The bank's voice recognition software would then employ a sophisticated program to verify the speaker's voiceprint, which was as individual and distinctive as a fingerprint—and if it passed, the wire transfer would proceed. Roberto explained to me that the software had been around for over ten years and that it was still un-hackable, unless you happened to have recorded Maria's actual spoken words, spliced them together, and then played them back into the phone during the verification call, which he did as I listened. His hacker friends had carefully laid out every step of the process, and he had followed their instructions exactly, but he looked hesitantly at me after the first try with the recorded phrase, and I winked back at him and silently crossed my fingers.

Verified, the automated voice on the other end said, and we gave each other a high five. The next three attempts were just as successful. Now he had to wait until the money had been received on the other end, and then his friends would start moving it around the globe until it was almost impossible to trace.

I had asked him why he trusted his online friends—none of whom he had ever met in person—with nearly twenty million dollars that would reside in their accounts, however briefly, and he had responded that there was a hacker's code, of sorts. None of his friends were into hacking to get rich, or to harm others. Their attraction to it was purely out of curiosity, and to test and refine their skills. The best of them were revered by the others, and I got the feeling that Roberto was one of the exalted ones. They also knew the circumstances of his mother's disappearance, and so this was the right thing to do in their eyes, although it was also theft on a grand scale and could be no doubt punishable by imprisonment, even though the money was intended to be returned to its owner if Lilian was freed, minus the two hundred-thousand-dollar contributions that Maria Calderón had unknowingly made to worthy causes. That part was payback, and it didn't seem like anywhere near enough, but we didn't want her money. We just wanted to scare the crap out of her when she saw the zeros on her bank balance, and then we might finally have the advantage, at least until Monday when the bank opened and the alarm bells went off. Wires could sometimes be reclaimed, and this was a woman who was well versed in finance and wouldn't be fooled for long. So we figured that we had one day, and our plan was to get a little more sleep, have a nice breakfast, and then send her the message that Roberto had already composed:

Hi Aunt Maria. Check your bank balance.

*

"She looked," Roberto said. He was coming out of Royal's bedroom dressed in a baggy pair of pajama shorts and a black T-shirt emblazoned with skulls and some band's logo on it. I couldn't read the name, but it probably wasn't The Carpenters.

"Did she write you back?"

"Not yet, but she logged on fifteen minutes ago. She's got to be going mental."

I poured him a glass of orange juice that I had squeezed in the juicer, waking most of the house up in the process, and he took a stool at the counter. "Good," I said. "What's next?"

"We wait for her to email back. And then we find out where my mother is, or my aunt loses the money."

My cellphone began to vibrate on the countertop, and I picked it up. Bobby Bove.

"I don't think you're going to like this," he said.

"What?"

"Javier Pimentel is dead. Somebody shot him last night, in a hotel room in South Beach."

"You're right, I don't like it." If Javier was now dead, then the millions that the Pimentels owed Maria Inés Calderón might be also at risk, and we didn't need that complication right now. It would be on the news, and his half-sister would surely find out about it.

"You'll be interested to know that we found a shell casing," Bobby Bove said. "Guess what caliber?"

"Thirty-two," I said.

"Right."

"So we have the same hitter, taking out the whole family," I said.

"Do you still have the other sister staying with you?"

"Yes. And she has a twenty-four-hour bodyguard, as of right now."

"Let me know if you hear anything," Bove said, and we hung up.

I didn't even have time to relay the news to Roberto, because, speaking of complications, Barbara Tanzi pulled up in front of the house in her Yukon, got out, slammed the car door and barged into the front hallway of the house. "I want to talk to you," she said. "Outside. Right now."

"Welcome home," I said.

"We'll talk outside," she said. "Unless you want me to embarrass you in front of your friends."

Sonny and Susanna were coming downstairs from the bedroom at that moment, and they stopped cold when they saw my wife's expression.

"Go ahead," I said to Barbara. "Speak your piece."

"All right," she said. "So, Vince. Maybe you can explain to me why you were fucking Megan Rumsford the other night?"

"I'm in the middle of something," I said. "We'll talk about this later."

"We'll talk about it right now."

"Cool down, Barbara—"

"Cool down?" she screamed. "Go to hell, Tanzi. I never want to see you again, and you're never going to see your son again, either." She turned, left the house, and slammed the front door so hard that the windows rattled.

The study door opened, and Rose DiNapoli emerged, dressed in a T-shirt and a pair of black sweatpants that I had lent her the night before. It was probably a good thing that Barbara was already gone. The kitchen was silent except for the ticking of the toaster oven.

"Anybody else want some OJ?" I said.

Rose, Sonny, and Susanna quietly took their seats at the counter, next to Roberto. "I'm sorry, man," Sonny said. "You don't deserve that shit."

"Oh yes I do," I said. "But at the moment I have other things on my mind."

*

Put back what you stole. Then get your uncle to pay his debt. After that we'll talk.

That was the first email message from Maria Calderón, and it was an effective one, just as you would expect from somebody in a leadership position: calm, firm, and nonnegotiable. She apparently hadn't heard about her half-brother's murder yet, unless she was bluffing for some reason. Possibly because she knew who had pulled the trigger? I had changed my mind about whether telling her would hurt us or help us, after discussing it with Roberto, Sonny, and especially Susanna, who hadn't shown the slightest sign of mourning or even surprise at Javier's death. "My brothers took too many risks and had no regard for the law," she'd said. "They learned that from Raimundo."

We decided as a group to inform Maria about the shooting. Roberto tapped at the keyboard.

Uncle Javier was killed this morning in a hotel, so the twenty million may be all that you ever see. I'm sorry for the bad news.

I had to hand it to Roberto; he was respectful, and almost sympathetic in his tone.

Five minutes later a reply appeared:

No deal. I won't respond to your threats.

It's not a threat, Roberto wrote back. *The funds are already gone.*

"Give her an hour," I said. "A time limit. And then tell her you have to go."

One hour to comply, he typed. *Thank you Aunt Maria. I have to sign off now. I'll talk to you in an hour.*

Maria Inés Calderón sent one more message, which I wish that Roberto hadn't seen, because this was a dangerous game that was being played with a powerful, vindictive woman who had kidnapped her sister and had quite possibly murdered both of her brothers:

Just because you're young doesn't mean that you won't suffer when I find you.

You bitch, I thought. Her words made me want to get on the next plane to Havana and kick her ass all the way down the marble-clad stairway of the Ministerio de Finanzas y Precios.

*

I turned the breakfast duties over to Sonny and went into the master bathroom, being careful not to wake Gustavo, who was sleeping that medicated sleep that you get with the kind of painkillers that they had given him.

The shower is one of my favorite places to think. And this was going to be a long shower, because I had a lot to think about. For starters, I had my wife's white-hot outburst to ponder, but that was too big a topic to deal with at the moment, and I had no choice but to compartmentalize it. Also, there was Javier's shooting, but, like his sister Susanna, I wasn't all that shocked or even surprised. My biggest concern by far was Maria Calderón, who Roberto had just robbed and probably humiliated, and people don't always react rationally when you do that. Especially rich people with big egos. The instinct was to fight back, even when you were cornered. If she had been systematically killing off the Pimentel family, then I figured that taking out Vince Tanzi and Roberto Arguelles would soon be added to the list of Things to Do Today that she kept on the side of her fridge.

She probably knew that because the money had been wired it was most likely gone permanently unless we returned it, and twenty million was a lot of money unless she was able to collect from the Pimentel brothers posthumously, which would surely be a long if not impossible process. And, collect what? Her part of the Maria Marta Batista trust? Those things took forever. Ms. Calderón had told me that she'd given Javier until the weekend to cough up sixty million, and the weekend was now. Exactly what was the sixty million dollars, and how did it play into this?

Sonny Burrows opened the door to the bathroom and waved his hand in front of him to clear away the steam. "Vince, you got a phone call," he said.

"I'll call them back," I said.

"She said it's urgent. Woman named Cleo."

"Give me a second," I said. I didn't know anybody named Cleo, but it was eight thirty on a Sunday morning, and I didn't think that it was someone who needed a ride to church. I turned off the water, grabbed a towel, and Sonny passed me the phone. "Vince Tanzi."

"This is Chloe Heffernan. I need to see you."

"What about?"

"Javier Pimentel," she said. "He was killed last night."

"I heard about that," I said.

"I might know who did it. But I'm afraid."

"Where's your husband? You should tell him about this."

"You don't understand, Mr. Tanzi. I'm in my car, and I'm on the way to your house. There are a lot of things that I haven't told you, because I was afraid to, but it's too late for that now."

"Where are you?"

"I'm about half an hour away," she said. "Please don't tell anybody, especially my husband."

"I'll be here," I said. "You can stay with us, and you'll be safe."

Plenty of room at Camp Tanzi.

*

Roberto hadn't heard back from his aunt, and more than an hour had passed. So much for my idea of imposing a deadline. I didn't think that she had forgotten: more likely, she was marshalling all the forces she could for an all-out attack on the people who had taken twenty million bucks from her Caribbean bank account, and I wondered what her strategy would be. For now, nobody was allowed to leave the house, because I didn't want to run the risk of one of my refugees meeting up with the Walther-wielding hitter or anyone else.

Chloe Heffernan had definitely aroused my curiosity, and I was anxiously waiting for her arrival. I had allowed Rose DiNapoli to make a fast trip out to the mailbox to get the Sunday paper in hopes that it would distract our group, but we were all on edge. Even Gustavo, who was now bathed, dressed, and briefed on the recent happenings, looked tense. He had winced when I'd told him about Javier's death, for the same reason that I had—a killer was on the loose, and his victims were all related. I hadn't told Gustavo about Maria Inés Calderón's thinly veiled threat to Roberto, but it wasn't relevant, because nothing bad was going to happen to Roberto, period. It just wasn't.

I heard the crunch of the driveway outside and saw Chloe Heffernan get out of her black Mercedes E-class coupe. Nice ride for a cop's wife, I thought. I wondered how much she had made as a paralegal. Maybe being Segundo's lover had come with some perks.

I met her at the door and immediately regretted my crass speculation about her income and her love life. This was a woman in severe distress. I seemed to have amassed a collection of them over the past several days.

"Quiet place to talk?" she said.

"Out back," I said, and I led her through the house and out the sliding glass door to the patio without any introductions. She took a seat at the table and began to nervously twirl her strawberry blonde hair in her fingers. "Glass of something?" I offered.

"It's too early to start, but I'd like a drink," she said.

"Orange juice? I made some fresh."

"Put something in it," she said. "I think I'm about to destroy my whole life, and I want a real drink."

I returned a few minutes later with a glass of fresh-squeezed orange juice spiked with a shot of vodka. I might have joined her if I hadn't been running on three hours of sleep.

"My husband and I have breakfast every Sunday morning at the S&S Diner on Second Avenue," she said. "Downtown Miami, off of Biscayne Boulevard."

"I know it."

"Tal likes to go out to Dodge Island afterward and walk around. That's where the cruise ships dock. He and I used to go on cruises, a long time ago. We'd wait for the deals."

"So what made you afraid?"

"Have you found Segundo's sister yet?"

"No. We think that his half-sister in Cuba kidnapped her. She's being held as a hostage because the Pimentels owe her some money."

"Sixty million," Chloe Heffernan said. "You found all that on Segundo's tablet, right?"

"Some of it. Not all of it though. What do you know?"

"She was financing them. She'd set up a sovereign loan fund through the Cuban government. The fund was supposed to make foreign investments, and she secretly lent them the money through a bank in the islands, so that they could buy the malls. This was back in 2007."

"Right before the crash," I said.

"Yes. Raimundo paid top prices, and then a few months later everything went to hell. They couldn't make the payments, and so they started a side business laundering cash. Every couple of weeks they would drop off millions in dollars, and she'd sell it and would make a profit. It was all good, and they were waiting for the market to come back, and then she got nominated to be a vice president."

"What was the problem with that?"

"Her ministry got audited," Chloe Heffernan said. She had drained the orange juice and vodka, and leaned back in her chair. "Nobody knew that she had lent Cuban government money to an American enterprise. It was a major problem, according to Segundo. The Cuban bosses kept it quiet, but they gave her an ultimatum—get the money back, or she was out. And Segundo said that they didn't know that she had been pocketing her cut of the profits from the money laundering, which would be even worse if they ever found out."

"This is on the tablet?"

"There are spreadsheets," she said. "They probably look like nothing, but I know how to read them. When I gave you the tablet I hoped that you would bring her down. She's a witch. She screwed Segundo every step of the way, and she even beat him out of millions in backgammon bets, just to rub it in. Segundo died almost penniless. He had pledged every dollar of his share of the family trust to her."

"And then she killed him? Or she had him killed?"

"That's what I thought. Until this morning."

"What happened this morning?"

"After breakfast," Chloe said. "Tal had been on duty all night, or so he said. He told me Javier had been shot. He was almost smiling about it, and then he said, 'The more for you.' I was shocked when I heard that."

"Why?"

"Because Segundo made me his beneficiary," she said. "I'm entitled to his share of his mother's trust, which is now basically nothing because he'd pledged most of it to Maria, but with Javier dead it would be something, because Javier's share would be divided among the others. We're talking about many millions. But I never breathed a word about this to Tal."

"So then you came here?"

"No, then we drove out to Dodge Island. We were walking around where the boats are, and Tal took something out of his jacket and threw it into the water, behind one of the cruise ships. He said, 'I won't need that anymore,' and I said, 'What?' And he said nothing, but I saw it. He had it all wrapped up in a plastic bag, but it was obviously a gun, and it had a thing on the end of it like a soda can. It made a splash when it hit the water."

"And then?"

Chloe Heffernan's freckled face was pale with fear. "And then he said, 'You and I are going to make love tonight.'"

"So?"

"So, we haven't made love in over a year. He goes to prostitutes. I've seen the emails. He likes the young ones, and I guess I have no business arguing with that, seeing how I've been in love with Segundo Pimentel for nine years. But I saw the look on his face."

"Go on."

She was staring at the cement surface of the patio floor, unable to look upward. "I don't think he wants to make love to me," she said. "I think he wants to kill me."

*

It was nearly noon, and we had heard nothing back from Maria Inés Calderón, but Roberto and I had been busy with Chloe Heffernan, examining the spreadsheets on Segundo Pimentel's tablet computer. Susanna Pimentel and Rose DiNapoli were looking over our shoulders, with Susanna translating where needed and Rose helping with the forensic accounting, as that had been one of her duties at ICE.

It was all there, in an Excel file folder labeled "BACKGAMMON66". The files looked innocuous enough, but when Roberto keyed in the password and the RSA fob number like he had with the emails, an entirely new set of spreadsheets was revealed. The spreadsheets contained the meticulously detailed books of a vast money-laundering operation, complete with names, bank account numbers, transaction amounts, and even the discounts and markups that had put some serious coin into the pockets of the parties on both sides. Maria's twenty million had come from it, and Javier and Segundo's rake-off had kept their debt serviced without having to sell any properties, but when the finance minister had needed to call in the sixty-million-dollar principal, they couldn't do it, and Maria Inés Calderón's political future was suddenly in jeopardy. The last thing that Cuba needed was another Batista ripping off the country.

And so, I had finally found out what Segundo had meant when he'd told Gustavo that *this was all about backgammon.* He hadn't meant the game that he loved so dearly.

He had been referring to a much bigger, nastier game involving dirty money, politics, and his own family's financial survival. This other game had not only cost them their entire fortune but had also taken the lives of three of them while a fourth remained captive. It was all laid out in dollars and cents in the file named BACKGAMMON66. At last I now had an explanation.

And, some leverage. When Maria Calderón wrote back, we would be ready.

I was also waiting to hear back from Bobby Bove after a call I had made to him explaining that I needed a diver, yet again. This time I had asked him to hire a private contractor and to go watch the dive himself, and to keep everybody else—including the Coral Gables police—out of the loop for the time being. When I'd told him what they might find, he had gone along with it. Chloe had provided a detailed description of the location: directly off of the stern of one of those floating, ten-deck behemoths that ferried you around the islands and plied you with endless food and cheap drinks while you played the slots, worked on your sunburn, and swapped accounts of your recent colonoscopies with that nice couple from New Rochelle. I had suggested to Bobby that he ask the crew to give him some notice if they were about to motor off, because we didn't want to accidentally turn the diver into a shish kabob. Bobby said he would check in again with me as soon as he got to Miami.

Sonny made us a batch of peanut butter and jelly sandwiches, and I washed mine down with a glass of milk. Still no word from Maria Calderón, but I hoped that she was near her computer, because it was time to end this. I had decided that we would initiate the conversation. I would be the one writing, not Roberto, because I didn't want to run the risk of her terrifying him again with her nastiness.

I had Roberto open up the email account for me, and I began to type.

This is Vince Tanzi, I wrote. *It's time for your answer.*

The answer is no, she wrote back almost immediately.

I typed out my response. *I double you.*

This is not a game, Mr. Tanzi.

But you treat it as if it were, I replied. *Somehow you think that you have the advantage.*

I am a vice president of Cuba, she wrote. *And who are you?*

Just a guy, I responded. *A palestino, like you called your dead brother. But I'm looking at Segundo Pimentel's spreadsheets here, and they're pretty interesting. He kept very detailed records.*

I don't know what you're talking about. Segundo owed me money, that's all.

I'm talking about a file called BACKGAMMON, I wrote. *Bank accounts, deposits, sources, everything. I'll email you a copy. Your name comes up a lot.*

There was no response, and I took advantage of the lull to have Roberto load up the attachment from the tablet. I mailed it off, and we waited by the computer screen for several long minutes.

What do you want?

Ha. Gotcha, lady.

I think that's obvious, I wrote back. *And release her immediately, or the spreadsheets go to the Miami Herald. They have a Cuba desk that would love this.*

Return the funds first or no deal.

If I don't get a phone call from Lilian within half an hour the files go to the media. You'll get your money. We don't want it. Goodbye.

I reached behind the computer and shut the damn thing off. I was shaking, because I was so angry, and so scared. I couldn't predict what Maria Calderón would do next. She might be ruthless enough to make things worse. But I had done the best that I could, and now the only thing to do was wait.

*

The half hour had come and gone, and all I could think of was that I had been operating way beyond my capabilities, and somebody else was going to pay the price for my incompetence, namely Roberto, or his mother, or his father, who had been pacing around my living room like an expectant dad who happened to have his neck in a plastic brace with metal rods bracketing the lower half of his face. Nobody wanted to talk, and we didn't even want to look at each other for fear that we would somehow jinx it, and Lilian would be lost. If she truly was, then I would keep Maria Calderón's money, and I would use it to stage an invasion that would make the Bay of Pigs incident look like kids with sparklers on the Fourth of July.

My cellphone rang in my pocket, and I prayed that it was Lilian Arguelles, but it was Bobby.

"My diver just pulled a Walther PPK out of Davy Jones' locker," he said. "It had a nasty-looking silencer on it, too. And by the way, nobody heard any shooting at Javier Pimentel's hotel. So give, Tanzi. Who's the shooter?"

"This is ugly," I said. I had been a deputy for more than two decades, and it went against the grain to give up a fellow cop, but it was what it was. "Talbot Heffernan. He thought that he was coming into some money, because Segundo Pimentel had named Heffernan's wife as his heir. Our detective friend thought that he was about to score, big time."

"Why was she getting the money?"

"She and her boss had a thing going," I said. "Heffernan must have found out. So he killed Raimundo, and then Segundo, and then his wife is in line for the money. Millions, by the way. And then—and I'm not sure about this part—but I'm guessing that Javier told him he was getting nothing, which was true because Segundo had already spent most of his inheritance."

"Holy crap," Bobby said. "Sex *and* money. A two-fer."

"There's more to this, but right now you need to find Tal Heffernan. His wife saw him dump the weapon, and she thinks that she's next."

"Where is she?"

"Right here," I said. "If you ever need a place to hide, my rates are reasonable."

"I'll pass for now," Bobby said. "So—"

Roberto approached me and interrupted my phone conversation with a frantic wave. He had his own phone to his ear, and he lowered it. There were tears welling up in his eyes, and I had a sick, empty feeling in my stomach, until he suddenly smiled through the tears.

"My mom wants to speak with you," he said, and he handed me his phone.

*

If I had owned a school bus, I would have taken the entire population of my refugee camp along with me, but I had the convertible, with Roberto crammed into the back seat and Rose in the passenger seat next to me. Sonny had stayed behind with Susanna, Chloe, and Gustavo. Before I left I gave him the keys to my gun cabinet, because as elated as I was about Lilian's release, this wasn't necessarily over.

Lilian had been tossed out of a car onto the sidewalk of 10th Avenue in Hialeah in front of an auto parts store that doubled as a junkyard. Her abductors had tied a pillowcase over her head and had cuffed her, and she said that she had a few scrapes but she was OK. The guys in the auto parts store had seen the whole thing and had called 911. I'd called Bobby shortly after we had left the house, and he was also on the way and would beat us there by an hour and a half. Lilian would be taken care of, Bobby promised. He said he would call us as soon as he picked her up. They might go to the emergency room, or to the Hialeah P.D., depending on how Bobby thought she was doing.

I was so excited about seeing Roberto reunited with his mother after two excruciatingly long weeks that I hardly noticed the drive, and the three of us chatted about whatever popped into our heads, told each other jokes, and even sang along at full volume with the Celine Dion CD that Barbara had left in my car and Rose DiNapoli had inserted into the player. Life was not only good, it was friggin' great. You have to cherish the few successes that you are given, because they are all too often fleeting.

Rose was as giddy as I was, and she made silly faces as she mimicked the Quebecois singer, although Rose's singing was so far off key that it was painful. But it didn't matter, because the three of us were drunk with relief, and within a short time we would collect Lilian Arguelles, and I would wrap up the case.

Party time, right?

Tanzi's Tip #11: Don't count your chickens until they're hatched, but keep in mind that after they hatch they run around so goddamn fast you'll never be able to count them.

We met Bobby and Lilian in the lobby of the police station where they were waiting on a bench. Lilian looked pale and weak, but that didn't stop her from jumping up and embracing her son, which was one of those moments when you are glad to be alive and all the badness in the world goes away for a while. She finally released Roberto from their monumental hug, and I was next. Lilian comes up to about my belly button, so I had to stoop to return her embrace.

"I can't ever thank you enough, Vince," she said. "I will never be able to repay you for this."

"You already have," I said. Which was true. Lilian had seen me through some very bad times after Glory had died. "It was your son who made this happen. He's a man now."

"I highly doubt that," she said. "Men pick up their rooms, and I expect to find a mess when I get home."

Roberto laughed, and we helped her out of the police station and into the back of my car. I stood by the door for a moment while Bobby Bove and I talked.

"They tracked his car," he said. "He was driving an unmarked, north on I-95, and he disabled the GPS somewhere around St. Lucie. They radioed him a bunch of times, but he won't answer."

"Get a car to my house," I said. "Send your best people. His wife's in there."

"Yeah, you told me."

"She thinks that he wants to kill her, too."

"You told me that, too," Bobby said. "I'm on this, Vince. You go home and get some rest. You look like you haven't slept in days."

"I haven't."

"It's over. You can relax now. Nice work, man."

"Thanks," I said. But I was a long way from feeling relaxed. Maybe it was simply that I needed to come down from the crazy adrenaline rush that you experience when you have recently been scared shitless.

Or maybe it was something else. Maybe my chickens had hatched, and I hadn't counted them correctly.

*

We dropped Rose off at her bungalow-style house in Fort Lauderdale, which allowed Roberto, Lilian and me to breathe again in the cramped confines of the Beemer. Rose gave me a peck on the cheek through the lowered window of my car, and I promised to stay in touch, to which she said: *you're not getting off that easy, Tanzi,* and I smiled. I was definitely going to be in touch with her supervisor, and I would tell the person that Agent DiNapoli had just helped break up a money-laundering racket that had involved millions, although I would reluctantly keep Maria Inés Calderón's name out of it. I had made a deal with the Devil, and I keep my promises, however distasteful.

We were back at my house by cocktail time. I poured myself one while Gustavo and his wife reunited, and then she began packing up his things. The Arguelles family was going home; they had a lot of catching up to do. Sonny had left a note saying that he had taken Susanna and Chloe over to his place in Gifford to hang out with Venus and Pluto, his two pit bulls who had been cared for by his neighbor while he'd been helping me out. Two deputies were stationed in a car under a leafy palm that shaded the end of my driveway, and they had been told to not let anyone inside the house, not even if they flashed a badge. Bobby Bove had quietly put out a statement about Talbot Heffernan, which was awkward seeing how he was a detective lieutenant, but Bove said that he had already sent the gun to ballistics, and the guys there were coming in on a Sunday evening to make sure that there was a match. If there was, the whole state would be looking for Heffernan.

Bobby had also alerted people to be on the lookout for the Iturbe brothers, who were now driving another van—dark green this time, according to the employees at the body shop in Hialeah who had seen them dump Lilian. Lilian had explained on the trip back that the Iturbes had been her captors from the beginning and had snatched her from her home in Vero, given her the ketamine treatment, and imprisoned her at the slaughterhouse for nearly two weeks until I was taken there, and then they had moved her to a house in Hialeah where she'd been tied up and gagged.

It was Pepe Iturbe who had sent the original message to Gustavo using Lilian's phone, saying *please to not worry. I have met someone.* Pepe's English was almost as wretched as my Spanish, but he had wanted to throw everyone off the trail, and it had worked for about a day. He had also dumped Lilian's phone in the Florida Straits shortly afterward, which had fooled all of us into thinking that she was in Cuba. That one had worked for almost two weeks.

Lilian had also said that the Iturbes had planned to leave me in the slaughterhouse. She said they didn't like me. If I ever saw them again I would tell them how hurt and disappointed I was about that, right after I beat them senseless with a nine-iron.

I finished my drink, which with my lack of sleep had felt like a double, or maybe a quadruple. Roberto and I took his and Gustavo's bags out to my car, and I crammed the whole family into the convertible for the three-block ride to their house. The air was slightly dank when we opened the door, and Lilian said that she was going to get to bed early, and tomorrow morning she would turn the place inside out. I had no doubt that she would, and that it would smell like an operating room when she was finished. After two horrible weeks in the slaughterhouse she would need to purge the experience, and cleaning up was a good start. My cure for trauma was fried oysters, but for Lilian it was Pine-Sol, bleach, and elbow grease.

My phone rang in my pocket. I didn't even want to look. The drink was hitting me, but the exhaustion was far worse, and all I wanted to do was flop into my bed and get about two consecutive days' worth of sleep. Whoever it was, they could wait. But it was Barbara, and I had already held her off for too long. She was right—we had to talk. I needed to explain what had happened with Megan, and there was also the subject of her own affair. I would be so much more ready to tackle this when I was rested, but I pushed the button and answered the call. It was time to get it over with, whatever the consequences.

"I'm sorry about this morning," I said. "And you're right. We need—"

"Where's Royal?" she said. It was more of a scream.

"With you?"

"You didn't take him?"

"I—I don't even know where you live." Royal? No. No way.

"I was out back planting flowers," she said. "The front door was locked, but he was gone when I came back inside."

"How long ago?"

"Just now. Oh please, Vince. This can't be happening. Please."

I ran through my list of who could have taken him. The Iturbes? Was this Maria Calderón having her revenge on me? Talbot Heffernan? Somebody else who had it in for me? There were plenty of people who I had busted over the years, and maybe one of them had just gotten out.

"Give me your address," I shouted into the phone. "And stay put."

*

I have lost some of my mobility since the accident, but I can still drive like a NASCAR racer, even with no sleep, a stiff drink in me, and one hand on the wheel with the other one holding the phone while I called Bobby Bove who was in his car and was on the way back from Miami. I didn't even know what to tell them to look for, except for the green van and Tal Heffernan's unmarked cruiser, but I wanted every law officer in the county looking, and I pleaded with them to set up roadblocks, but it was probably already too late. It took me less than ten minutes to get to Barbara's house-sit, which was located in a faux-Tudor development out by the interstate, and by the time that I arrived I knew that Royal's abductor could already be long gone. I was weeping with frustration, and cursing my stupidity for ever having exposed my family to anything that could have made this happen. I knew that Barbara had been right all along: my work was just too dangerous, and that may be all right for a spouse to live with, but it was unacceptable for a nine-month-old child. How could I be such a goddamned fool?

Barbara still had her gardening clothes on, and her arms were streaked with dirt. She looked at me, tentatively, and I took her into my arms and held her in an awkward embrace. "We'll find him," I said. "I have everyone I know looking."

"What are we supposed to do?"

"We wait," I said. "Let's go inside. I want to look around."

The house had been furnished by its snowbird owner in dark wooden furniture that had probably come from up North and looked out of place. Barbara's things were scattered around the small living room, and I looked into the room where she had set up Royal's crib. It was empty, of course, and it made me sick to my stomach to look at his stuffed animals and elephant-patterned bed sheets. "He was in here?"

"Yes."

"Who else has a key?"

"The owners, but they're in Cleveland," she said. "And the real estate agent who showed it to me."

"Have you called them?"

"No."

"Call them," I said. "Anyone else?"

"No," Barbara said.

Damn. I checked the front door to see if it might have been picked. People who were no good at it often left scratch marks, but there were none. All the windows were closed, and the air conditioning was running. The only way into the house was through the locked front door, or through the back door, and Barbara had been ten feet away planting flowers. I went through all the rooms again and still found nothing, except for a blue silk nightgown that was drying on a hanger, suspended from the shower curtain rod in the tiny bathroom. I had never seen it before, and it was larger than what Barbara might wear.

"Whose is this?" I asked her. She had been right behind me.

"That's Megan's," she said. An odd look came over her face.

"What was Megan doing here?"

"We'll talk about that later," she said. "Royal is missing, Vince. Focus, for god's sake."

"Does Megan have a key?"

She hesitated.

"Barbara? Does she have a key to your house? I know that she lives nearby."

"Yes," she said. "She has a key."

"You'd better tell me what the hell is going on here," I said. Barbara was holding back, and my blood pressure was rising. Our son had been stolen right out from under her nose. I wasn't about to screw around.

"We're lovers," she said, looking away from me, as if she was talking to someone else. "It started at the club. She was giving me a massage, and it—deteriorated. I'm not even gay, Vince, at least I never thought I was. She seduced me, and I let it happen. I can't believe that it started, but then I couldn't stop. And I fell in love with her, which is the worst part."

I was too stunned to say anything, but I happened to know what she meant. Megan Rumsford had seduced me—twice—and I had let it happen, too.

"She was here last night," Barbara continued. "She stayed over. We had a lot to drink, and she told me that you had slept with her, the night before. I was *so* angry, oh my god, I wanted to break your neck I was so jealous. That's when I came over to the house."

"I did sleep with her, but it wasn't anything I'd planned. She came into my room, and I thought it was you at first."

"I believe you," she said. "She's like that. She's crazy sometimes. She'll say some strange things."

"Like what?"

"She said that she wanted you to get her pregnant. She scared me, and I didn't know if she was in love with me or with you, but I started to realize how bad this had become. After I came back from your place I told her that she and I needed to take a break. She was very upset, and she took off. I don't believe I got caught up in this, Vince. I know you'll never forgive me."

"When did you last see her?"

"Megan? This morning," Barbara said. "But Vince, Megan wouldn't—"

"Where is her house?"

"The next block over. You can walk there."

"Show me," I said, and I took my phone out and dialed Megan's number. The call went to voicemail, but by that time my wife and I were running through the streets of the development in the direction of Megan Rumsford's house.

There was no garage, and no yellow Jeep in the driveway. The front door was locked, and I picked up a large paving stone from her walkway and heaved it through a plate glass window, which spewed glass fragments all over the lawn. I carefully climbed in over the jagged edges of the remaining glass and looked around the house. Nobody was home—it was dead quiet, and there was no food out or any other signs that someone was there. Megan had left, and I hoped to God that she hadn't taken Royal with her, but I was already pretty certain that she had. Where had she gone?

I went back outside by the front door, where Barbara was waiting.

"Not inside," I said.

"Where would she take him?" she said. "He'll be a wreck. He'll need diapers, and to be fed—"

"Hold it. Where does she keep her paddleboards?"

"Out behind the house."

I reentered the house and exited by the back door onto a small patio. Two pairs of sawhorses were over to the side, and one of the paddleboards rested on one of the pairs. It was the beginner board—the one that she had let me use. The other board was gone.

I rushed through the house to the front lawn and grabbed Barbara. "Back to your place," I said, and we sprinted around the block to where my car was parked. "You stay here. The deputies should be coming soon."

"Where are you going?"

"Blue Cypress Lake," I said.

"Not without me," she said. "Don't leave. I need to get my things."

She disappeared through the door, and I took the opportunity to take my Glock out of the trunk and attach the holster to my waistband at the small of my back. If Megan Rumsford was crazy enough to steal my baby, she might be crazy enough to do anything.

*

Barbara remained in the car while I went into the building at Middleton's Fish Camp. We had already spotted Megan's Jeep by the boat-launching ramp in the same spot where she had parked it when she and I had gone paddling and I had discovered Segundo Pimentel's dead body in his boat. That seemed like a lifetime ago, and I prayed that everyone would be safe this time. You didn't do bad things to nine-month-old babies. They are not pawns. They are off limits, and anyone who thought or did otherwise would receive the full fury of the nine-millimeter automatic that was strapped to my back.

A heavily tattooed young man in a tractor hat was seated in an office to the side of the main store, staring at a laptop computer screen. He didn't look up when I came in, even though the screen door had slammed shut behind me.

"I need a boat, right now," I said. "This is an emergency." The kid still didn't move his glance. "Did you hear what I said?"

He turned his head toward me, reluctantly. "We don't rent boats after six PM, mister. Y'all out of luck."

I walked up to his desk and slammed the laptop shut. "Listen up, kid. My baby boy just got kidnapped. Get your ass out of that chair and find me a boat. Right now."

The young man turned pale, and for a moment I thought that he might pass out, but he stood up and took a set of keys from the wall. "I'm sorry, mister," he said. "I didn't understand. I'll help you. I heard a baby crying while I was out fishing, and I kinda wondered."

"Where?"

"Moonshiner's Camp. I fish that spot all the time."

"Let's go," I said. "My wife's coming, too. She's in the car."

"Won't take us but a minute," he said. "I got an Air Ranger, seven-hundred-fifty horse. Follow me."

*

The boy's name was Blair, and I knew his grandfather—he had been a deputy when I had first started out at the Sheriff's Department.

That was as far as our conversation had gotten, because once he started the engine of the Air Ranger and the prop blades began to rotate behind us, you couldn't hear anything short of a nuclear attack. Blair took the high seat with the controls, and Barbara and I strapped into two padded chairs in the bow of the boat, which were the marine equivalent of the front seats of a roller coaster. Airboats can go over a hundred miles an hour on flat water, and the evening was calm and still, with a three-quarters moon rising in the east that illuminated our way north to the top of the lake. It would have been an exhilarating ride had I not been terrified—not by the boat, but by what might be happening to our baby son.

I signaled Blair to cut the engines as we drew near. There was just enough moonlight for me to see the dock, which was clear of alligators and was also clear of any paddleboards. Megan Rumsford wasn't here—or at least she wasn't if she had used her board. Segundo Pimentel's bass boat was long gone, and there was no light coming from inside the cabin. But there was a sound. It was the sound of an infant who was very, very unhappy.

"Royal!" Barbara screamed. "He's in there!"

Blair docked the boat and Barbara and I dashed up the wooden steps to the house. I had grabbed a flashlight and lit our way, but Royal's plaintive sobs were already directing us and Barbara snatched him from a cardboard box on the floor of the cabin where he had been imprisoned with nothing else inside it except for a roll of paper towels. She held him to her chest, and his shrieks slowly subsided. Out came the breast, and he latched on for dear life, intermittently heaving huge, gasping sobs while he nursed.

I found some kerosene lamps and lit the wicks while the two of them sat on Segundo Pimentel's rattan sofa. A mother and child reunion, as the song went, and I almost wept with relief.

"I'll be back," I said to Barbara. "You'll be all right now."

Barbara looked up from her nursing child. "Where are you going?"

"To find Megan."

"Please don't hurt her," Barbara said. "This is all my fault."

I wasn't going to make any promises. I didn't respond.

I left the cabin, closing the screen door behind me, and made my way down the steps to the airboat. "Can you run this thing quietly?" I asked Blair.

"Hell yeah," he said. "I got a trolling motor in the well. I could sneak up on a jackrabbit and his ears wouldn't twitch."

"Let's go," I said. "Use the trolling motor. It's not far from here."

*

"I hear you," Megan Rumsford said as we approached the little island with the three-sided building. The moon was behind us, and it reflected slightly on the structure, but I couldn't see where she was. "Don't come any closer."

"It's Vince," I said from the slowly approaching airboat. "Everything is going to be OK."

"No it's not," she said from the darkness. "I mean it. I have your shotgun. I took it out of your trunk."

"Megan—"

"You don't love me, Vince. You made love to me, but you don't give two shits about me. You never did."

I signaled to Blair to move the boat closer. "Let's talk about this. I can make this better for you. I can help you."

"I know," she said. "You were a cop. You dealt with crazy people all the time."

"You're not crazy." The airboat was silently drifting closer to the island, and in a few more seconds I would be able to set foot on it.

"Says who?" she said. "And don't get off that boat or I'll shoot this thing."

"Please don't. Come on, Megan. Help me out on this, OK? I can barely talk, I'm so goddamn exhausted."

"You need me, right Vince? Is that what you're saying?"

"Yes. That's right. I need you."

"Damn right," she said from the darkness. "I healed you, Vince. You were in a coma for almost a month. My physical therapy class came to visit you, a few days after you had been shot. We had a program at Fletcher Allen Hospital, in Burlington. We were supposed to learn how to treat patients who were bedridden, so that their muscles wouldn't atrophy and they wouldn't get bedsores. I was assigned to you, and I'd never seen anyone like you. You were so— still. So quiet, and so beautiful. I massaged you that first night, and I felt something powerful. I don't even like men. All they do is piss me off. But you were different."

"You were in the hospital?"

"You're not listening, Vince. The night nurses got to know me, because I kept coming back, after all your visitors had left, including your wife. I would see her in your room, and I wanted to fucking kill her, because you were mine. Eventually she would leave, and then I had you to myself."

"Megan—"

"I took your sheet off. The nurses never knew about it, because I would shut the door. I was quiet, although I wanted to scream. Sometimes I could get you totally hard, and some days it didn't happen, but you were mine for four weeks. Until you fucking woke up."

"Listen, Megan—"

"Listen, Vince," she said. "You made love to me, and you were supposed to get me pregnant. I was supposed to have your child."

"That was a mistake," I said, and I immediately regretted saying it. The woman was in crisis, and I needed to get her trust—at least enough so that I could subdue her, and end this.

"Goodbye, Vince," she said. "And just so you know, all I ever wanted from Barbara was to get close to you. Touching her was like touching you. But that's over now."

I heard a scraping sound like furniture dragging across a floor, followed by a horrible, muffled scream. Somebody was being strangled, and the life was quickly being choked out of them.

Blair turned on his flashlight at the same time that I did, and we both saw Megan Rumsford's writhing body, her legs kicking wildly while she dangled from an improvised hangman's noose that had been fixed to the roof of the lean-to. I scrambled ashore as quickly as I could, with Blair behind me, and I held Megan's suspended torso while he took a knife from his belt and cut her free. She dropped to the ground, and the air slowly returned to her lungs. Several minutes passed while we sat there, and no one spoke.

"You were so damn handsome," Megan said, as I held her in my arms. "Lying there, so quiet, like you were dead. The perfect man."

My dream. Megan had been the one who had massaged me for the weeks that I'd been in a coma in the hospital in Vermont, after I'd been shot. And then she'd moved all the way to Florida because she was obsessed with me, and it had finally boiled over. She was the source of my recurring dream—or, nightmare. And I was her dream man, because I couldn't open my mouth to spoil things.

Megan Rumsford was mentally ill, for sure. But I knew plenty of women who would have had no argument with her logic.

MONDAY

BOBBY BOVE WOKE ME FROM my slumber five hours after I had returned from the Indian River County Sheriff's building where Megan Rumsford had been processed and put into a holding cell under a suicide watch. Tal Heffernan was in a cell down the row from hers, after having shown up at Sonny Burrows' house with a gun. Venus and Pluto, who usually never moved from the couch, had disarmed Heffernan within seconds, and Sonny had held the detective's own gun on him while Susanna Pimentel called 911.

Sonny and I were at the Sheriff's until three in the morning with Bobby, and I finally went home to an empty house: Barbara had taken Royal back to her house-sit, the Arguelles family had moved out, and Chloe and Susanna had stayed at Sonny's. I was up almost until dawn, coming down from the adrenaline rush and wondering about my future. I was still in shock over what Barbara had said and how close we had come to losing Royal. The strange part was that his kidnapping had had nothing to do with my work. It had been because of Megan's fixation on me, which had also been a complete shock. What was it that had made a young woman—who didn't even like men—develop an obsession over a fifty-two-year-old guy who could barely walk straight? Maybe the shrinks would find out. She would certainly be seeing her share of them when they did her evaluation.

I answered my ringing phone.

"Heffernan wants to talk to you," Bobby Bove said. "I think he's close to confessing to all three jobs."

"Where's his lawyer?"

"He waived his rights, and there's no lawyer. It would really help if you got over here."

"Give me twenty minutes," I said. I took a fast shower, got into a T-shirt and jeans, and was on the road ten minutes later. Vero was busy with morning traffic, and the sun was rising in a lazy ball that was already beginning to bake the streets and sidewalks. The air conditioning at the Sheriff's office felt good. Bobby led me to an interrogation room where Tal Heffernan sat, looking about as bad as a man could look.

"No recording," Heffernan said to Bobby.

"I'll leave you guys," Bobby said, and he shut the door.

Talbot Heffernan looked up at me. It was clear from the dark circles around his eyes that he'd had even less sleep than I had. "Where is she?" he said.

"Chloe?"

"Yes."

"She's with my friend," I said. "Do you want to see her?"

"Not yet," he said. "Goddamn. It's a strange feeling being on the wrong side of this table."

"I've been there too," I said, because I had. "When did you find out about them?"

"Her and Segundo? I've known since the beginning," he said. "I worked for them, Vince. They paid me to look the other way, even including when Segundo was fucking my wife. She thought that I didn't know, but I'm a detective, for god's sake. I figured it out the first week."

"What else did they pay you for?"

"A lot of things," he said. "I knew where the people were who needed to unload cash. The Pimentels paid me a cut, and I pissed it away, and all of a sudden Segundo tells me that he and Javier were about to go under."

"And then Raimundo Pimentel conveniently died," I said. "Because you shot him."

"That was Javier's idea. He hated the old bastard. Raimundo was relentless about Javier being queer, and when he died that was supposed to release millions to the kids. But Segundo had already pissed his money away too, which I didn't know about."

"So you killed him, too," I said.

Heffernan's expression darkened. "You going to be an asshole? I've already been worked over pretty good, Tanzi. You're not here to grill me."

"I'm just wondering why you're telling me this."

His grey eyes narrowed, and he looked like he would either take a swing at me or start crying. "Bobby told me what happened to your wife," he said. "Your first wife, I mean, and then I remembered reading about it in the paper. Her name was Glory, right? She cheated on you, and she got killed? And he also told me what happened last night with your second wife. I just thought that you might understand if I told you something."

"Like what?"

"Like that I love Chloe. I've always loved her, even though she pushed me away almost from the beginning, because she was in love with her boss. And I fucking lived with that for nine years. It destroyed me. There's no way that they won't put me away me for all three hits, I know that, I'm not stupid. So I'm going to cop a plea, and maybe I'll be out in twenty years. But I just wanted to tell one guy who might understand that I have always loved my wife, and I still do."

"Chloe thought that you were going to kill her," I said.

Heffernan looked at me like I had just slapped him in the face. He didn't have an answer.

When I was a deputy I used to sit in this very same room, and I would hear people say some amazing things. Excuses, bullshit, pleas for forgiveness, tears of rage—you could witness the entire spectrum of human emotions in one night, and sometimes from the same person.

Talbot Heffernan had called me in to bear witness to the only thing that he still cared about, which was his love for Chloe Heffernan despite her nine years of infidelity. She was no innocent, and neither was he, and he would be an old man when he got out of jail, if he ever did. I almost felt sorry for him.

But I didn't.

"So you love your wife, and you killed three people."

"They were scumbags," Heffernan said. "Florida was a nice place before those people arrived."

By *those people*, I assumed that he was referring to the Cubans.

"That's funny," I said. "That's what the Seminoles said, five hundred years ago."

SUNDAY

ROBERTO ARGUELLES PULLED INTO MY driveway in his mother's beat-up old Toyota and got out. The car was falling apart, and the silver paint had gone nearly transparent from too much sun and salt spray, but to my now-sixteen-year-old friend it was a freedom machine, and none of us had seen much of him since he had passed his driver's test a few weeks before.

"You going to Royal's party?" he said, as I let him in. "My mom wanted me to remind you." He crossed through the kitchen to the refrigerator and got himself his customary Coke.

"Not sure yet," I said. Barbara and I had gone to three different counselors in the months since we'd separated, and none of them had been worth a damn. My wife had continued to stay in touch with Megan Rumsford, and I could deal with the fact that Barbara had fallen in love with someone else, and that it was a woman, but I just couldn't get my head around how she could maintain a relationship of any kind with the person who had stolen our baby. I felt uneasy every time we were in the same room. Counseling seemed pointless, and I figured that I would have been better off spending the money on oysters.

Barbara was fine about sharing time with Royal, and we were on a schedule where I picked him up every day at eleven, fed him lunch, put him down for his nap, and then when he woke up, he and I would play. Barbara used the free hours to run errands or whatever else she had to do, and when she started school again in September I was hopeful that my time with Royal would expand. I was supporting all of us on my pension and the money was getting tight, but I had picked up a few P.I. jobs—the usual runaways, cheaters, deadbeats, and so on—and the income had helped pay the bills for our two households. It felt good to be back to work, and I had stopped worrying about putting Royal in danger because of my job. If anything, I felt more secure and more able to protect him from threats that could potentially come from anywhere—like from an obsessed, troubled woman who I had thought was my healer and my friend.

"Did you read about my Aunt Maria?" Roberto said. "It's in the paper today."

"I haven't seen the paper."

"She stepped down. They said it was for health reasons. Shortest term ever for a Cuban vice president."

"I wonder if they took her money."

"Nah, it's still there," Roberto said.

"How do you know that?"

"I can still get on her computer," he said. "I check in now and then to make sure she's not going to do anything bad to us."

Roberto and his family had been lying low ever since Lilian's abduction, and it was a subject that we hardly ever brought up. It would be a long time until Lilian didn't think about her captivity every day, or Gustavo forgot about his vicious beating at the hands of the Iturbe brothers, who were behind bars again after a shootout with a brave mall cop in June. Meanwhile, the Arguelles household was spotless, and Lilian had started her job again at the hospital. They were on the mend, but those things took a while.

"So are you going?" Roberto said. "Get dressed and I'll drive you."

I was wearing a pair of pajama bottoms and a day-old T-shirt, and I hadn't shaved. Living by myself was comfortable, and I liked it, but there was crap strewn around everywhere and the place wasn't about to be featured on the cover of *Good Housekeeping* anytime soon.

"I don't have a present," I said.

"All you have to do is show up," Roberto said, and I suddenly realized that he was way more on top of this than I was. The child is father to the man.

Half an hour later we were in Barbara's tiny backyard out behind her rental house. Royal was seated in a chair that was clamped to the side of a picnic table, and he was happily smearing gobs of dark chocolate cake all over himself and anyone who dared go near him. Roberto gave him a stuffed bear that he had picked out, and Barbara opened a stack of other gifts from the mommies of the small cluster of one-year-olds who were also in attendance. Sonny had dropped off Susanna Pimentel, who had remained friends with Barbara, although Sonny still kept his distance from my wife. I mostly stood around while everyone took endless pictures with their phones and posted them to Facebook. I had to admit that Royal looked cuter than hell, but I couldn't wait to get out of there, and Barbara noticed my discomfort. She walked across her carefully tended lawn to where I stood. "Thank you for coming, Vince," she said.

"It's his birthday," I said. "I didn't get him anything. I'm sorry."

"Do you want to take him back with you?"

"Sure," I said. "Are you teaching tonight?"

"Actually—I was thinking of going to visit Megan," Barbara said. "Chattahoochee is five hours from here, so I thought I'd spend the night, and then come back and pick him up tomorrow afternoon."

Chattahoochee was the state mental hospital where Megan had been sent for an evaluation. "How is she?"

"Better," Barbara said. "It was pretty rough at first."

"Are you and her still—"

"I don't know what we are, Vince. I'm sorry. I know it makes you squirm every time it comes up."

"It's none of my business."

"Of course it is," she said. "We're still married."

"I think I'll roll, if this is winding down. I'll go tell Roberto."

"I'll get Royal's things," Barbara said.

Fifteen minutes later Roberto and I had packed my baby son's travel equipment into the tiny rear end of Lilian's hatchback, with just enough room to spare for the three of us. The side window was open, and Barbara kept trying to stuff more things into it, until I warned her that if she crammed in one more diaper, the car would collapse under the weight. We said our goodbyes and drove back to my place, where we unpacked all the gear and scattered it around my house with everything else.

There was a message from Rose DiNapoli on my machine, and I pushed the button while Roberto was outside with Royal.

Hey Tanzi, remember me? You were going to take me out for red snapper, like, a couple months ago? Hey, no rush, right? Listen, I have to drive up to Melbourne on Tuesday, and I thought I'd see if you wanted to get lunch. Unless you're too big a deal now, because you solved three murders. Call me back, OK?

The sound of her voice put a smile on my face. It would be nice to see her. I would definitely call her back.

"I have to go home," Roberto said, as he entered the kitchen with the baby in his arms.

"I'll take him," I said. "Thanks for the ride, dude."

"Not a problem, dude."

Royal was too restless for his nap, and I wasn't even going to bother putting him in the crib. It must be all the sugar, I decided. I felt restless also. The house was suddenly far too empty. The late August sun had nudged the temperature into the mid-nineties, which is when nobody in their right mind would go to the beach, but I packed up our suits, a few towels, a backpack carrier, and my beach chair, and we drove across the bridge to the barrier island with the top down and the wind blowing through Royal's dark, feathery hair. I turned north to Tracking Station Park, an old NASA installation with a nice stretch of beach that would be deserted. Barbara and I used to go there when we had first known each other. That seemed like a long time ago.

I laid out our towels and the beach chair, and then decided to put him in the carrier and walk down to a concrete pier that jutted into the ocean, about half a mile away. I'd been walking the beach every morning; it had taken the place of my physical therapy and was paying off. My limp had improved, I'd dropped a few pounds, and even though my marriage was falling apart in slow motion, I was getting my confidence back. Maybe I just wasn't supposed to be married. I'd tried twice now, and that was probably enough.

Tanzi's Tip #12: Most men lead lives of quiet desperation. Except for the married ones. Then it's loud desperation.

The only people on the beach were a bored-looking lifeguard and a group of high school kids playing with a football. I headed south toward the pier with Royal in the backpack. He liked to pull at my hair, and now and then he'd utter a single word and would repeat it endlessly. At the moment it was *bear*, and I realized that he had dropped the stuffed toy that he'd been carrying—his birthday gift from Roberto—and I turned around to go back and look for it. I scanned the edge of the water, hoping that the toy hadn't gone in and been washed away.

Royal saw it first. "Bear!" he yelled, into my ear. I saw a dark object at the water's edge and jogged, with him in the backpack, until we could retrieve it from the sea. I wrung it out and passed it back to him, and he held it to his mouth, tasting the now salty, wet fabric and cooing.

I turned around and started south, and again he called out the name of his toy. He had dropped it again, and I knew that I was being subtly drawn into his little game.

We spent the better part of an hour playing Royal's version of fetch, in which I was the willing retriever. Somewhere along the way my worries and regrets wandered off to another place, and I was simply here in the milky, white-hot sunshine with my baby boy. After a while we sat down, and I released him from the backpack and watched him crawl around in the sand, talking and laughing and having a good time. The backpack was stocked with an extra diaper, and I changed him on the beach, surprising myself at how automatic the motions had become. I may not be much of a husband, but I was a pretty good dad.

I packed him into the carrier, and we started our way back toward the tracking station. All of the running around and the heat would wear him out, and I would try to get him down for his nap when we got home.

A dark object washed across my feet in the foam, and for a moment I thought that Royal had dropped his bear again. I bent over to pick it up.

It wasn't the bear, or a shell. It was a sea bean. Not as rare as the deer cowrie that we'd found back in May, but it was something that you didn't see that often. Sea beans were drift seeds, and they could originate from anywhere in the tropics. The ocean currents would carry them for hundreds of miles and then deposit them along the beaches up and down the Florida coast. This one was heart-shaped, about three inches across, and it fit neatly into the palm of my hand. If I oiled it, the dark, mahogany-colored surface would polish to the luster of a piece of fine furniture. I passed it back to Royal, who put a corner of it into his mouth.

"Bean," I said.

"Bean," he repeated.

Maybe this was another gift from Glory. It was hard to believe that she had been gone for almost three years now, and I wondered what she would have made of all this. I doubted that she would have cared much for Barbara. But I knew that she would have loved my little boy.

I gathered up the rest of our gear, and we crossed the hot sand toward the parking lot. Royal was clutching his wet bear in one hand and the sea bean in the other.

"Happy birthday, son," I said, as I strapped him into his car seat.

He looked up at me with his big, liquid eyes.

"Bean," he said.

# # #

Acknowledgements

Thanks to my early readers and editors Joni Cole, Deb Heimann, Chelsea Lindman, Isabel Dennis, Sara Dennis, Will Siebert, Bob and Heidi Recupero, Roy Cutler, Betsy Jaffe, Gordon Henriksen, and especially to Roberto Veguez for his invaluable help on things Cuban.

About the Author

C.I. Dennis lives in Vermont and New Hampshire with his family and a whole lot of dogs.

Also by C.I. Dennis:

Tanzi's Heat
Tanzi's Ice
Tanzi's Luck

As Zig Davidson:

Unglued

Cover artwork and concept by Alexander Dennis
Additional cover design and production by Morgan Kinney Designs
Author photo by Peter Lange
Formatting by ebooklaunch.com

www.cidennis.com

BK3 10/17

48245580R00117

Made in the USA
Middletown, DE
13 September 2017

tured; we did not understand. It was the greatest threat to the existence of the United States since the Civil War.

Many books have been written and many movies produced showing the heroism and sacrifice our parents' generation made to save this country. While the young men and women went off to fight a war, their parents stayed home and kept the country going. The anxiety these parents felt must have been incredible. The ability for soldiers to communicate back home was almost non-existent compared to today. Every time a telephone rang or someone came to the front door, the fear of bad news had to arise inside these parents.

After World War II ended, Americans faced more problems in Korea (Hastings, 1988). Despite the great sacrifices of the soldiers fighting in a far-off land under rugged conditions, the Korean War did not really strike fear in Americans. Unlike WWII, there was not rationing of commodities or fears of invasions. It appeared that America had settled down for the "Happy Days" of FDR's campaign promises. But, Americans soon became aware of a new threat—Communism.

In terms of creating fear in the American mental state, there were two very different components: one realistic and one imagined. A realistic fear was the possibility of a nuclear war with the Soviet Union that could destroy mankind. Winston Churchill referred to Eastern Europe as being held behind the Iron Curtain. We were at war, but it was a Cold War, at least for the moment (Gaddis, 2006). During the 1950s and 1960s, books and movies, like *On the Beach* and *Fail Safe*, about the horrible outcomes of a nuclear exchange became popular.

One episode of the popular television show *The Twilight Zone* was a story about a man who worked as a bank teller and loved to read books (Zicree, 1992). At lunch, he would hide in the huge steel vault to read. One day, the vault shook and when he came out, everything in the city, as far as he could see was destroyed. Not a single soul was left standing. He was alone.

At the time, that threat seemed real. Neighbors actually built bomb shelters. In school, students had evacuation drills and practiced getting under their desks (Monteyne, 2011). Meanwhile, images drove our fear of the Communists. Perhaps the most memorable was footage of the Soviet Premier Nikita Khrushchev beating his shoe on the podium of the United Nations and screaming into the microphone, "We will bury you!" News programs also showed the parades in the Red Square with all the soldiers and missiles against the dark, gray sky. Did fear drive Americans? You bet!

That threat of Communism becoming a philosophy that Americans accepted or were forced to accept was the source of political power. "There are Communists everywhere" was the fear line that drove the McCarthy hearing. Richard Nixon exemplified the politicians who initially made their reputations as strong anti-Communist leaders.

There was a pervasive fear that the Communists would brainwash young people. Studies were undertaken to determine how persuasion worked to inoculate the youth from the Communist appeal. The basic research conducted in many of the studies formed the foundation of modern attitude research.

In retrospect, this fear of Communism seems anachronistic. Did people like Senator McCarthy think someone was going to convince a child that his/her parents should give ownership of their comfortable suburban house to the government so they could decide if we could live there? Would a child be in favor of the government taking over a family-owned business to become a government entity? Did they think that the parents of the day, who were part of the generation that won World War II, were not teaching their children, even in many subtle ways, that democracy was the best form of government? Bottom Line: were people like Joe McCarthy insane or just hungry for more power?

The fear of Communism became the rationale for the war of the next generation—Vietnam. The rationale was America had to go to war because of the "domino theory," (i.e., a foreign policy theory that if one key nation in the region fell to the Communists, the others would follow). Former military leaders saying if Vietnam fell, the Communists would take all of Asia, India, and by 1975 they might control Australia.

Many people fondly remember the hippies and anti-war days. What they probably do not remember is public opinion did not turn against the Vietnam War until 1968—some fourteen years after our first involvement. Americans trusted their government and it was not causing stress at home like World War II. We could not just give up and say all those soldiers died in vain. However, as always in America, things change when they start impacting a significant percentage of the population. As the number of casualties increased to the point where everyone knew someone whose family had been impacted by death or injury, public opinion changed.

Vietnam was never officially called a "war." It seemed the military was bogged down without clear direction as to what the U.S. government wanted. Our troops were defending South Vietnam, but had no clear objective. No one was sure what "winning the war" meant. President Nixon became so frustrated that he even considered using tactical nuclear weapons. The fear of Communism became less than the fear of a never-ending battle in which young Americans were seen coming home in body bags. The anti-war movement had moved beyond the young protesters and into the middle class living rooms. The politicians reacted to the dominant fear of the people.

In addition to the anxiety about the war in Vietnam, Americans were trying to deal with a changing social fabric. By the mid-1960s the civil rights movement was visible every night on the nightly news. The old social order was under attack as African Americans began demanding their proper place as U.S. citizens. Of course, to link the two driving fears, Dr. Martin Luther King, Jr., was suspected to be a Communist, or at least that was the belief of J. Edgar Hoover, the FBI director who wire-tapped Dr. King.

By the mid-1970s, America claimed it had met its objective in Vietnam and withdrew, leaving South Vietnam to fall in a matter of weeks. But, the Cold War was far from over. And problems continued on the domestic front. Probably nobody but political junkies remember the 1966 Georgia Governor's race in which the outcome was eventually decided by the Georgia House of Representatives. They elected the infamous segregationist Lester Maddox as Governor. His major achievement in office was riding a bicycle around the Governor's mansion while seated on it backwards. But, if you like weird political elections, this was one for the books and it is worth a little historical read.

Although defeated in the 1966 gubernatorial campaign, Jimmy Carter put together a young team and won the Governor's race in 1970. No one could guess by 1976 Jimmy Carter would be President of the United States. President Carter was the first leader to see the face of a new enemy who would eventually cause this generation as much fear as Hitler caused the greatest generation. Radical young Muslims took over the American embassy in Iran and held 67 Americans hostage for 444 days. Every night, Americans saw Ted Koppel say it was "day x of the American hostage crisis," in a nightly show that eventually became ABC's *Nightline*.

That crisis would be a major factor in President Carter's defeat in 1980. President Carter had the military attempt a rescue mission that resulted in a disastrous accident in the desert. Probably, if President Carter had simply bombed Iran back to the Stone Age, he could have won reelection. But, there are sixty-six families that were glad he valued those American lives more than the American Presidency. Now, Americans had a new fear. It was an enemy that did not act like Americans, dress like Americans, and practiced a religion that most Americans probably barely knew existed. Americans faced a new enemy that blatantly hated us and referred to us as "the Great Satan."

In 1980 President Ronald Reagan, a true populist rhetorician, came to power. As discussed in the development of the Republican Party, his victory was a major turning point in the political context of American politics. This President would not let America forget about the dangers of the Evil Empire abroad or liberals who attacked prayer in school, supported abortions, and defended so-called artists peddling smut. He proposed the ultimate defense system for America—Star Wars. This scheme was going to put satellites in space with laser weapons that could shoot down any nuclear missile headed for the United States. Although most scientists said the present day technology made this a pipe dream and many military experts could suggest ways an enemy could defeat the system, the President drove the fear of the Communists and had millions of American tax dollars appropriated for a research program. The defense contractors were, of course, happy to take the money.

The debate over nuclear war, that had been over-shadowed in the 1960s by Vietnam and Civil rights, was once again the front burner fear appeal for the government. In an effort to cool down the Cold War, members of the U.S. Congress introduced the Nuclear Freeze Resolution. It became a huge debate in Congress.

One of the authors was visiting the office of Congressman Jack Hightower during this debate. Congressman Hightower was a west Texas populist who had always been strong on national defense, but he came from a strong Baptist home and always seemed concerned about man's inhumanity to man.

The room was filled with staffers who worked on policy and the debate was lively. What did this resolution mean? Would it limit our production of bombers? How would it affect our various defense programs? Finally, Congressman Hightower turned to the author and asked what the political expert thought. The author I asked one question, "How will this material affect our national defense?" Congressman Hightower smiled and said, "It won't" The author's response? Vote the way he wanted to vote; we would defend it on either side during the campaign.

The key point here, though, is that the issue was a question of who could best reduce the fears of Americans—people who advocated more nuclear weapons or those who were ready to try to limit the ability of the two Super Powers to destroy the earth. Two years later, that debate seemed irrelevant as reform started in the Soviet Union. Eight years later, the Cold War was over with the Soviet Union crumbling from the inside without a single shot from America. It looked like a fear that hung over the Boomer generation from their childhood had ended.

Americans seemed to have nothing to really fear during the 1990s. The world of .com exploded and it seemed no matter what stock you bought, it made money. The Evil Empire was gone and life was good. Then, the new boogeyman appeared suddenly and shockingly.

The numbers 9/11 are all anyone has to say. This event has scarred the psyche of America as much as Pearl Harbor to the greatest generation. This event sent a shock wave of fear throughout America. When a dramatic event like this occurs, the public is suddenly willing to passively accept almost any action the government says is necessary. The public goes into a hyper-patriotic mode and any action that is perceived needed to increase safety is approved.

In 2005, over four years after the terrorists' attack on the World Trade Center, polls clearly indicated that people believe there will be another similar attack within the next year. This fear was not limited by area of the country, race, income, or age. Early in 2005, 45 percent of American adults said the fear of another terrorist attack was causing them stress, and that was

three-and-a-half years after the 9/11 attacks. A majority of women (51 percent) said this fear caused stress in their lives. More than 40 percent of every
age group said the fear of terrorism caused them stress (Kitchens, 2005a).

Other polls in various locations within the United States showed similar
results. Three years after the attack, a survey of Broward County, Florida,
showed 57 percent of the voters thought the United States would be attacked
within the next year, with 10 percent saying they believed the attack would
be in their county (Kitchens, 2005b). In Louisiana, four years after the attack,
60 percent of the people felt the United States would be attacked within the
next year, while four percent thought that either a family member or themselves would be injured or killed; an additional 13 percent thought Louisiana
would be a target (Kitchens, 2005c). In 2008, in the area around Norfolk,
Virginia, 74 percent of the voters said they thought the United States would
be attacked again within the next year (Kitchens, 2008). The situation has
become so intense that Unger (2013) argued that the United States has lives
in a constant state of emergency in which security is the primary concern.

A comparison of President Bush's rhetoric after 9/11 to Prime Minister
Blair's speech after the attack on the London subways provides some insight
into how the fear factor drives images of a nation at war. President Bush
referred to the attacks of 9/11 as "the enemies of freedom committed an act
of war against our country." Prime Minister Blair referred to the London
attacks as a "horrible murder." Obviously, a society's response to an act of
war is different than to a murder.

President Bush framed the motivation as hatred of American democracy:
"Americans are asking, why do they hate us? They hate what they see right
here in this chamber—a democratically elected government." President Bush
described the terrorists in militaristic terms, saying their goal is to overthrow
existing governments, drive Israel out of the Middle East, and drive Christians and Jews out of Africa and Asia. For a force to accomplish these goals,
they would need a vast army and sophisticated training.

Prime Minister Blair described the terrorists as a global problem and
network of murderers who "attacked twenty-six countries, killing thousands
of people, many of them Muslims." His description referred to these people
as criminals rather than military warriors. And he added, "Neither is it true
that they have no demands. They do. It is just no sane person would negotiate
on them."

President Bush described his vision for defeating the terrorists in strong,
militaristic language:

> Now this war will not be like the war against Iraq a decade ago, with a decisive
> liberation of territory and a swift conclusion. . . . Americans should not expect
> one battle, but a lengthy campaign. . . . Every nation, in every region, now has
> a decision to make. Either you are with us, or you are with the terrorists.

The President made it clear: no nation can be neutral or have any shades of gray. There are only two sides.

Prime Minister Blair presented a much different view of the world:

> We must be clear about how we win this struggle. We should take what security measures we can. But let us not kid ourselves. In the end, it is by the power of argument, debate, true religious faith, and true legitimate politics that we will defeat this threat.

Citizens in a nation at war think, act, and perceive the world much differently than a nation who sees a rogue gang of murderers that must be stopped. We have color-coded alerts to warn us of impending attacks. We are a nation willing to give up some freedom if it means increasing our protection from the enemy, a la The Patriot Act. Dissenting opinion on anything the government wants is labeled as unpatriotic and helping the enemy.

Interestingly, President Bush defined this war as an emotion, and the media took the bait. We have a "War on Terror"—not on terrorists, not on Al-Qaeda, not on acts of terrorism. Our enemy is an emotion, the feeling of terror. An emotion will not be defeated, so this war can be used forever by the government to drive fear within the American public.

Still, even before 9/11, Americans felt the power of fear. The access to cable news on a twenty-four-hour basis and the sophistication of reporting has helped drive us to this psychological state. Before cable news, few stories were deemed worthy of constant coverage. Even with events like Apollo 13's troubled return from space, the networks did not go on twenty-four-hours with one story. The assassinations of John Kennedy, Robert Kennedy, and Dr. Martin Luther King Jr. certainly received hours of coverage, but not continuous daily coverage. Information about fearful events is available every minute of every day, and Americans are addicted to it. Today, we can see pictures of a tidal wave from half way around the world in a matter of hours, if not minutes.

On a personal level, we see Americans reacting to fear. According to surveys by both the NRA and gun control groups, somewhere between 40 percent and 45 percent of American homes have a gun. Twenty-five percent of American homes have a handgun which is only designed to kill one thing—another person. Somewhere between 10 percent and 12 percent of citizens carry guns when they leave the house.

The way we live in our homes is so different than our parents. The front porch has moved to the back, surrounded by a privacy fence. Electronic surveillance systems are more common than not among suburban residents. Neighborhoods are built behind gates and walls, and have their own private police forces.

Americans are addicted to fear. People buy steering wheel locks, no one will park a bicycle without a chain lock. We buy mace and pepper spray, and a record number of people are taking martial arts. We even view reality shows, like Fear Factor, on television to watch people living out one of our nightmares. No doubt. Fear is one of the mainstays of America's psyche today. And, it shades our perception of politics and our leaders.

REFERENCES

Allen, Frederick Lewis (2010). Only yesterday: An informal history of the 1920s. New York: Perennial.

Averbeck, Joshua M., Jones, Allison, & Robertson, Kylie (2011). Prior knowledge and health messages: An examination of affect as heuristics and information as systematic processing of fear appeals. *Southern Communication Journal*, 76, 35–54.

Beaudoin, Christopher E. (2002). Exploring anti-smoking ads: Appeals, themes and consequences. *Journal of Health Communication*, 7, 123–37.

Carraro, Luciana, & Cartelli, Luigi (2010). The implicit and explicit effects of negative political campaigns: Is the source really blamed? *Political Psychology*, 31(4), 617–45.

Clark, Christopher (2013). The sleepwalkers: How Europe went to war in 1914. New York: Harper.

Crichton, Michael (2009). State of fear. New York: Harper

Gaddis, John Lewis (2006) The cold war: A new history. New York: Penguin.

Gagnon, Marilou, Jacob, Jean Daniel, & Holmes, Dave (2010). Governing through (in)security: A critical analysis of a fear-based public health campaign. *Critical Public Health*, 20, 245–56.

Gillon, Steven M. (2011). Pearl Harbor: FDR leads the nation into war. New York: Basic.

Hastings, Max (1988). The Korean War. New York: Simon & Schuster.

Hyunyi Cho, & Salmon, Charles T. (2006). Fear appeals for individuals in different stages of change: Intended and Unintended Effects and Implications on Public Health Campaigns. *Health Communication*, 20, 91–99.

Jackson, Brian (2007). Jonathan Edwards goes to Hell (House): Fear appeals in American evangelism. *Rhetoric Review*, 26(1), 42–59.

Janis, Irving L., & Feshbach, Seymour (1953). Effects of fear-arousing communications. *Journal of Abnormal and Social Psychology*, 48, 78–92.

Jerit, Jennifer (2004). Survival of the fittest: Rhetoric during the course of an election campaign. *Political Psychology*, 25, 563–75.

Kitchens, James T. (2005a). A nationwide survey on terrorism. Orlando, FL: The Kitchens Group.

Kitchens, James T. (2005b). A survey of Broward County, Florida. Orlando, FL: The Kitchens Group.

Kitchens, James T. (2005c). A statewide survey of Louisiana. Orlando, FL: The Kitchens Group.

Kitchens, James T. (2008). A survey of the Norfolk, Va. Area. Orlando, FL: The Kitchens Group.

Latour, Michael S., Snipes, Robin L., & Bliss, Sara J. (1996). Don't be afraid to use fear appeals: An experimental study. *Journal of Advertising Research*, 36(2), 59–67.

McElvaine, Robert S. (2009). The Great Depression: America, 1929–1941. New York: Three Rivers Press.

Miller, Gerald R. (1963). Studies on the use of fear appeals: A summary and analysis. *Central States Speech Journal*, 14, 117–25.

Monteyne, David (2011). Fallout shelter: Designing for civil defense in the cold war. University of Minnesota Press.

Moscato, Sara, Black, David R., Mattson, Marifran, & Blue, Carolyn (2001). Evaluating a fear appeal message to reduce alcohol use among "Greeks." *American Journal of Health Behavior*, 25, 481–91.

Ragsdale, J. Donald, & Durham, Kenneth R. (1986). Audience response to religious fear appeals. *Review of Religious Research*, 28(1), 40–50.

Thompson, L. E., Barnett, J. R., & Pearce, J. R. (2009). Scared straight: fear-appeal anti-smoking campaigns, risk, self-efficacy, and addiction. *Health, Risk and Society*, 11, 181–96.

Unger, David C. (2013). The emergency state: America's pursuit of absolute security at all costs. New York: Penguin

Valentino, Nicholas A., Hutchings, Vincent L., Banks, Antoine J., & Davis, Anne K. (2008). Is a worried citizen a good citizen? Emotions, political information seeking, and learning via the Internet. *Political Psychology*, 29(2), 247–73.

.Weber, K., Dillow, M. R., & Rocca, K. A. (2011). Developing and testing the anti-drinking and driving PSA. *Communication Quarterly*, 59, 415–27.

Zicree, Marc Scott (1992). The Twilight Zone companion. Silman-James.

Chapter Three

The Second Pillar of American Politics

Narcissism

Canadians sometimes tell the following joke: "How many Americans does it take to change a light bulb? Only one. He holds it in the socket and the entire world revolves around him." Do Americans think they live in the most important place in the world? Look at world maps printed in the United States. The United States is always in the center of the map. Why not the prime meridian where longitude is at zero degrees? Or the International Date Line? Neither would be appropriate because Americans are used to thinking of the world from an ego-centric perspective.

Pollsters often ask voters an open-ended question about the most important issue facing the country—the issue they want the President and Congress to deal with and try to solve. The only time foreign or world affairs are mentioned is when we are at war. As a rule, Americans worry, think, and obsess about America. Even in the world today, when both Iran and North Korea are developing nuclear capability, concern for these issues is not mentioned by even one percent of the voters. Iraq and Afghanistan are concerns because our troops are there. But, most people probably cannot name a single foreign leader, with the possible exception of Castro. It is apropos that the United States is best known as U.S.

As children, we are taught a societal mantra that America is the greatest country in the world. No one says why or how, and we just accept the concept. In fact, Lewis (2011) says that America's self-occupation with its own greatness is "one of the most prominent political doctrine in the U.S." (p. 19). Historically, the concept can be traced back to the Puritan era when the early Massachusetts Bay colonists believed that God had created a new land as a "redeemer nation" (Madsen, 1998). The concept grew larger during

Thomas Jefferson's administration with the Lewis and Clark Expedition to the West Coast (Ambrose, 1996). By the early eighteenth century, even most European nations saw the United States as different, if not exceptional (Murray, 2013). By 1845, the concept of "Manifest Destiny" had become part of the concept, i.e., the belief that God had intended for America to expand its influence across the width of the continent (Hietala, 2002). That concept became part of the Western Myth as pioneers traveled in wagon trains to open new communities on the western frontier. By the end of the nineteenth century, a combination of America's geography, ideology, politics, and daily life had set the nation apart from those in Europe (Murray, 2013).

The concept expanded in the twentieth century. America's entry in two world wars altered the balance of power in those conflicts, leading to the defeat of militaristic regimes in Germany and Japan. The Cold War that followed World War II, fueled by fears of Communism (McDougall, 2013), enhanced a belief about America's exceptionalism around the globe and in world history (Pease, 2009). Brothers John Foster Dulles (Eisenhower's Secretary of State) and Allen Dulles (head of the CIA at the same time) orchestrated a propaganda campaign on American patriotism as they plotted to expand American ideals across the globe (Kinzer, 2013).

President Ronald Reagan expanded that international perspective to American exceptionalism with his view of the nation as one that was designated by God for greatness (Dunn et al., 2013). Reagan's program for promoting American democracy eventually developed into a $100 million industry that promoted American ideals abroad (Heidt, 2003). Following the 9/11 attacks on the World Trade Center and the Pentagon, the concept of American exceptionalism got redefined again by President George H. W. Bush, who used the concept as part of his justification for invading Iraq and instituting a security state in the nation (Pease, 2009; Unger, 2013) and for the subsequent "war on terror" (Rojecki, 2008; Esch, 2012).

After that, the concept became a mantra for Republican politicians (Gamble, 2012; Silk, 2012), as illustrated by former GOP Speaker of House Newt Gingrich (2011), who described the United States as "A nation like no other." And, while the message is often associated with Republicans, Democrats use it too. Shane (2012), for example, wrote, "Is America the greatest country? Candidates had better say so." And he added, that the ploy allows candidates to avoid discussing major issues because "the reason talking directly about serious American problems is risky is that most voters don't like it" (p. SR6).

Some have argued that America's national narcissism is a key premise behind the efforts of some Republicans to question whether President Barack Obama was born in the United States (Kumar, 2013). Yet, while Republicans have criticized President Obama for not having the same "crusader exceptionalism" that describes their form of national narcissism, Obama has continued the tradition with his own form of "prophetic exceptionalism" about America that involves "the possibility of equality, solidarity, and unity among people from around the globe" (Gorski & McMillan, 2012, p. 41). In fact, Obama successfully used the idea of American exceptionalism in his 2008 presidential campaign (Ivie & Giner, 2009) and in his subsequent presidency (Pletka, 2013). In addition, Americans' pride in their nation was further enhanced when the Obama administration ordered and successfully killed Osama bin Laden (Hasian, 2012).

Statistics, however, indicate that most of the people who believe that America is special have never crossed the ocean to see another country. We are still a nation where a large percentage of people do not see other cultures. The U.S. Department of Transportation reports that between 1990 and 2000, Americans made a record 27 million trips overseas (International Tourism . . . , 2000). However, even if every one of those trips were made by a different person, it would mean only about 1 in 10 people have been overseas. That statistic is unlikely because some people have traveled overseas on business and European vacations more than once in a decade. With the population of the United States being around 300 million people, we can conclude that less than ten percent of U.S. citizens have traveled overseas.

Looking at our history and geography, our national narcissism is somewhat understandable. The nation covers a huge land mass due to the foresight of President Thomas Jefferson. Stephen Ambrose (1996) pointed out that President Jefferson thought the United States needed to control all the land from the Atlantic Ocean to the Pacific Ocean or this continent would develop like Europe, with a number of different countries and cultures. At the time of Jefferson's presidency, the French controlled the Gulf Coast and claimed land to the headwaters of the Missouri River. This was in spite of the fact that no European explorer had traveled to that area. The Spanish still had a strong presence on the Pacific Coast and west of Louisiana, and the British were firmly in the Canadian provinces.

If America had developed in a way that reflected Europe, a person from the East Coast might have traveled through ten countries with five or six different languages before reaching the West Coast of the continent. But, that did not happen. America became a geographically large country, with people from other nations all over the world coming to settle here. Hence, our nation is commonly referred to as a "melting pot." In some ways, that term applies; in others, it is a myth that seems like we have not completed the melting and are more like a tossed salad (Smith, 2012). Many Americans cling to their ancestral past, and, as a result, ethnic neighborhoods still exist in every major city in America. People fondly remember "the old country" and show great pride in the place from where they or their family immigrated.

Still, we don't always view other citizens as equally American. Examples of racism, with one group showing hatred for another, are evident in the news virtually every day. One reason for the problem is that many Americans feel swamped by the large number of immigrants coming into the nation from other cultures (Barone, 2001). Obviously, this indicates not everyone believes we are all equal and the same. A 2005 *Wall Street Journal*/NBC survey reported that President George Bush's approval rating among African American voters was two percent. Their analysis indicated that the African American voters felt that the Federal government's failure to get help to the people of New Orleans, in the aftermath of hurricane Katrina, was an indication of racism.

On the other hand, the melding of religious, cultural, and racial groups is occurring in America. Most U.S. citizens of foreign dissent identify themselves and their culture as purely American in nature (Felto & Gardyn, 2001). The U.S. Census Bureau says interracial marriages in the United States have more than doubled since 1980, up from 651,000 to 1.4 million. The Bureau is bemoaning their efforts to racially classify people. What race is the child of a man whose parents are African America and Hispanic and a woman who is Asian American and Caucasian? Additionally, in the Jewish Community, since 1985, 52 percent of Jewish children are marrying out of the faith (Rosenblum, 2003).

It is fairly amazing immigrants from so many different backgrounds have developed such a strong and exclusive view of themselves as a nation and their role in the world. Some writers believe this national narcissism is a national hangover from the nineteenth century idea of "Manifest Destiny." This phrase, originated by New York journalist John L. O'Sullivan in 1844, expressed a belief the United States had a divinely inspired mission to expand and spread its form of democracy and freedom (Hietala, 2002). This idea fueled the westward expansion of the United States. It was a factor behind the Mexican–American War of 1846, in which the United States captured California and New Mexico from Mexico (Greenberg, 2013). This rationale was also used during the displacement of Native Americans (Miller, 2011). In the twenty-first century, it was the underlying concept that President George W. Bush used to justify the war in Iraq, i.e., he believed it was our national duty to spread democracy—a theory outlined in one of his favorite books (Sharansky & Dermer, 2006).

Manifest Destiny not only drives our national narcissism, but it plays very well into another pillar of the American psyche—religiosity—which will be discussed later. This idea would seem outlandish to European and Asian countries who have had centuries of history that include invasion, occupation, and changing national borders. How absurd it must seem to countries in the Middle East whose borders were drawn by the British after World War I without any consideration to history and culture, but mainly a concern about oil resources. But, as we examine our national behavior, it is hard not to conclude that the idea of American manifest destiny is part of our national consciousness. As Americans, we generally think we are so different and so special. Let's look at some examples.

Americans like to say we celebrate diversity, but there are many signs we want to be all the same and part of our Manifest Destiny. An important part of any national identity is language, and Americans support having one official language—English (Baron, 1992). This insistence is in spite of the British observation that we have not spoken English for generations. There is even a lobby group, U.S. English, Inc. that pushed a bill in Congress to make English the official language, a move that was part of a larger English-only movement. Their website cites a 2004 national survey by Zogby International that indicates 82 percent of Americans support making English an official language, while only 16 percent oppose the measure and two percent are unsure. These results are not strongly partisan or regional. 92 percent of Republicans support the proposal, but 76 percent of Democrats also support it. More than 80 percent of Americans in every part of the country support this proposal (U.S. English, 2004). This movement is representative of an attitude that Thompson (2008) label "language chauvinism" and merely reinforces negative images of Americans to citizens of other nations.

It is amusing to see how Americans behave abroad. Not only do Americans think English should be our official language, but they expect everyone in every other country to speak English. That is just one of the problems faced by Americans who travel abroad for the first time; they often find that they cultural expectations of the country they visit catch them by surprise (Gruber, 2012). Even universities fall victim to cultural centrism when they send students abroad to study or professors go abroad to teach (Dolby, 2007; Getty, 2011). As Dolby concluded, "Although universities often promote study abroad through paradigms that emphasize global awareness, national sentiments and identity are still fundamental elements of how Americans see and position themselves in the world, particularly in the post—September 11 context" (p. 141). In the past, even American diplomats and their staffs are often unprepared for the cultural and political situations to which they are assigned (Kondracke, 1979).

Not surprisingly, the citizens of many other nations have negative attitudes toward the United States even as they hold positive attitudes about the individual Americans they know (Nada, 2010). The issue is severe enough that the federal government has considered launching programs to improve our national image (Devarics, 2008) and President Barack Obama delivered a major speech to address the issue (LaFranchi, 2008).

One of the common negative attitudes that other nations associate with Americans is that of cultural arrogance (e.g., Cohen & Tucker, 2006). Perhaps Americans are treated rudely abroad because we expect everyone to cater to us in terms of language and culture. We fulfill their stereotype that we are arrogant Americans. If we are traipsing around France, is it too much for the French to expect us to know some basics of their national language?

During a short stay in Italy, one of the authors and his wife tried to find a bus to get back to their hotel. In their best Italian, which was not very good, they tried asking a ticket seller nearby for some assistance. He smiled and in perfect English answered, "Bus 321 is over there on the left." Can you imagine finding average workers in this country who could communicate with foreign visitors in their native language? Unlikely.

Americans expect every other country to follow our lead. One of the arguments advanced by the Bush Administration when it was arguing for war in Iraq, was that we should not ask anyone's permission. Further, extremists within the Republican Party have shown little or no respect for the United Nations and have pushed for the United States to withdraw from the United Nations. That overall goal hasn't come to fruition, but they have taken incremental steps. For example, in 1995, Republicans in the House passed legislation to reduce U.S. payments to the U.N. for peacekeeping operations (Towell, 1995). In 2004, House Republicans opposed the U.N.'s "Law of the Sea" Treaty, despite support for the plan from the Bush White House (Skomeck, 2004). In 2011, the GOP attempted to tie U.S. support for the U.N. to America's foreign policy goals (MacFarquhar, 2011).

When France refused to join the invading coalition in Iraq, Republican Members of Congress took their anger out on France (Cogan, 2004; Hoffman, 2004). The party played public relation stunts like renaming French fries to Freedom fries in the House cafeteria (Kiely, 2003; Rawson, 2003; Swartz, 2009). In the long run, though, France seems to have made a smart decision. France now has no national debt from that war, no obligation to pay for rebuilding Iraq, its soldiers were not killed in the conflict, and the weapons of mass destruction used to justify the invasion were never found.

One definition of narcissism is that it is a psychological condition characterized by self-preoccupation. In nationalistic terms, this manifests itself with a total preoccupation with flags and nationalistic bumper stickers. French writer Bernard-Henri Levy (2005) spent a year in the United States, traveling and writing his observations for *Atlantic Monthly* magazine. His first observation was about our obsession with the American flag:

> In the end, it's the American flag that dominates. One is struck by the omni-presence of the star-spangled banner, even on the T-shirts of the kids. . . . It's the flag of the American cavalry in westerns. It's the flag of the Frank Capra movies. It's the fetish that is there, in the frame, every time the American president appears. It's the beloved flag, almost a living being. . . . It's a little strange, this obsession with the flag. It's incomprehensible for someone who comes from a country where the flag has, so to speak, disappeared, where any nostalgia and concern for it is a sign of an attachment to the past that has become almost ridiculous (p. 56).

As well as supporting English as the official language, Americans also support a law that punishes people who burn the flag, a protest that was shocking during the Vietnam War era. Like the English language group, there is a lobbying group called the Citizens Flag Alliance. Opinion Research Corporation's poll for this group showed 81 percent of Americans would support a Constitutional Amendment to make it a crime to burn a flag (Citizens Flag Alliance) Further, Americans spend a lot of money buying flags, banners, and emblems of the flag. The U.S. Economic Census says Americans spend about $349 million annually on items with images of the American flag.

Another sign of America's national narcissism is the bumper sticker that that reads, "God Bless America." Why not, "God Bless the World"? This bumper sticker is a clear indication that our culture has a deep-seated hold on the Manifest Destiny idea.

The psyche pillar of narcissism also has become part of us as individuals, enhanced today by modern technology. Everyone has cell phones, Blackberries, and laptops We are never off work. While for some people, the work schedule is closely connected with the consumerism part of the American psyche, discussed in the next chapter, many people simply love the feeling that they are indispensable. Not surprisingly, many Americans are simply working too much (Sorohan, 1984). The problem is so severe that some employers have to consider their potential liability from having workers who work too much (Kobayashi & Middlemiss, 2009).

Some political consultants include as part of their sales pitch to candidates the statement, "I am available 24 hours a day, seven days a week." What difference does that promise make? What could a campaign possibly do at 3:00 a.m. that would make any difference in the outcome of any election?

The United Nations International Labor Organization once determined that Americans put in more hours than anyone else (Anderson, 2001). They noted that the average Australian, Canadian, Japanese, or Mexican worker was on the job roughly 100 hours less than the average American in a year, or almost two-and-a-half weeks less. The Brazilians and British work 250 hours less or five weeks less than Americans. Germans work 500 hours less, or over three months less than Americans. In other words, the dream that machines would give us more time to be with our families or develop interests, other than work, has happened in other industrialized countries but not in the United States. In one national survey in 2007, 69 percent of people who have a full time job said their work was a significant source of stress in their life (Kitchens, 2007).

The pillar of narcissism has driven politics into a total exercise of self-interest appeal. When Ronald Reagan asked his famous question, "Are you better off than you were four years ago?," his campaign showed an understanding of the growing American narcissism. He did not ask if the nation was better off, if your state was better off, or if your community was better off. His message was are You better off? If you are not better off, then it is the leaders' fault and they should be thrown out of office.

Former Senator Bob Dole attempted an appeal like this but it was not as effective. Then First Lady, and now Secretary of State Hillary Clinton (1996) wrote a book about raising children entitled, It Takes A Village. The title is based on an old African value that every adult in a village has a responsibility to help raise every child in the village and to be an example for that child. In his attempt to position himself as the "family candidate" during his convention speech, Senator Dole made the sarcastic remark, "Mrs. Clinton, it takes a family to raise a child." The underlying premise of this statement, as a criticism to the idea that all adults in a community have responsibility, is that other people's children are not your problem or responsibility in any way. It is also an allusion to the idea that a "family" consists of both parents who take responsibility for their children. With the large number of single parent families and blended families based on second marriages, this 1950s stereotypic idea does not really resonate with the voters.

Political candidates sometimes forget the campaign is really about the voters, not the candidate. Each voter will listen to the communication and evaluate it in terms of the relevance and importance to their everyday life. Voters will evaluate if the information reinforces the idea America is the greatest country and that the voters' individual beliefs and values are the correct ones. If they don't make that evaluation, the candidate loses.

REFERENCES

Ambrose, Stephen (1996). *Undaunted courage: Meriwether Lewis, Thomas Jefferson, and the opening of the American West*. New York: Simon & Schuster.

Anderson, Peter (2001, August 31). Study: U.S. employees put in the most hours. CNN.com.

Baron, Dennis (1992). *The English-only question: An official language for Americans?* Princeton, NJ: Yale University Press.

Barone, Michael (2001). *The new Americans: How the melting pot can work again*. Washington, DC: Regnery.

Citizens Flag Alliance, http://www.cfa-inc.org.

Clinton, Hillary Rodham (1996). *It takes a village*. New York: Simon & Schuster.

Cogan, Charles (2004). The Iraq crisis and France. *French Politics, Culture & Society*, 22(3), 120-134.

Cohen, Warren I., & Tucker, Nancy B. (2006). America in Asian eyes. *American Historical Review*, 111, 1092–119.

Devarics, Charles (2008, July 10). Proposal seeks to improve America's image abroad. *Issues in Higher Education*, 25(11), 12.

Dolby, Nadine (2007). Reflections on nation: American undergraduates and education abroad. *Journal of Studies in International Education*, 11(2), 141–56.

Dunn, Charles W., Ceasar, James W., Herclo, Hugh, & Arkes, Hadley (2013). *American exceptionalism: The origins, history and future of the nation's greatest strength*. Lanham, MD: Rowman & Littlefield.

Esch, Joanne (2010). Legitimizing the "War on Terror": Political Myth in Official-Level Rhetoric. *Political Psychology*, 31(3), 357–91.

Felto, John, & Gardyn, Rebecca (2001). An All-American melting pot. *American Demographics*, 23(7), 8–10.

Gamble, Richard (2012, Sept). American Exceptionalisms. *American Conservative*, 11(9), 12–15.

Getty, Laura J. (2011). False assumptions: The challenges and politics of teaching in China. *Teaching in Higher Education*, 16, 347–52.

Gingrich, Newt (2011). *A nation like no other: Why American exceptionalism matters*. Washington, DC: Regnery.

Gorski, Philip S., & McMillan, William (2012). Barack Obama and American Exceptionalisms. *Review of Faith & International Affairs*, 10(2), 41–50.

Greenberg, Amy S. (2013). *A wicked war: Polk, Clay, Lincoln and the 1946 invasion of Mexico*. New York: Vintage.

Gruber, Criag (2012). Culture, courage, and collectivism: An insider's guide to culture in American schools. *Culture & Psychology*, 18, 417–24,

Hasian, Marouf (2012). American exceptionalism and the bin Laden Raid. *Third World Quarterly*, 33, 1803–1820.

Heidt, Stephen J. (2013). Presidential rhetoric, metaphor, and the emergence of the democracy promotion industry. *Southern Communication Journal*, 78(3), 233–55.

Hietala, Thomas R. (2002). *Manifest design: American exceptionalism and empire*. Ithaca, NY: Cornell University Press.

Hoffman, Stanley (2004, February 16). France, the United States & Iraq. *Nation*, 278(6), 16–19.

International Visitors (Inbound) and U.S. Residents (Outbound) (2000). Office of Tourism Industries, Washington, DC: U.S. Department of Commerce.

Ivie, Robert L., & Giner, Oscar (2009). American exceptionalism in a Democratic idiom: Transacting the Mythos of Change in the 2008 Presidential Campaign. *Communication Studies*, 60(4), 359–75.

Kiely, Kathy (2003, April 1). Angry lawmakers focus on unhelpful allies. *USA Today*, 4A.

Kinzer, Stephen (2013). *The brothers: John Foster Dulles, Allen Dulles, and their secret world war*. New York: Times Books.

Kitchens, James T. (2007). Nationwide survey. Orlando: The Kitchens Group.

Kobayashi, Tamie, & Middlemiss, Sam (2009). Employers' liability for occupational stress and death from overwork in the United States and the United Kingdom. *Common Law World Review*, 38(2), 137–62.

Kondracke, Morton, (1979, March 31). Ugly American redux. *New Republic*, 180(13), 12–15.

Kumar, Hari Stephen (2013). "I Was Born . . ." (No You Were Not!): Birtherism and Political Challenges to Personal Self-Authorizations. *Qualitative Inquiry*, 19(8), 621–33.

LaFranchi, Howard (2008, December 12). Obama plans major speech in Muslim world to 'reboot' America's image abroad. *Christian Science Monitor*, 101(13), 25.

Levy, Bernard-Henri (2005, May). In the Footsteps of Tocqueville. *Atlantic Monthly*, 56.

Lewis, V. Bradley (2011, November 3). American Exceptionalism. *America*, 205(9), 19–22.

MacFarquhar, Neil (2011, January 26). G.O.P. renews call to tie U.N. funding to U.S. goals. *New York Times*, A9.

Madsen, Deborah L. *American exceptionalism*. (1998). Jackson: University Press of Mississippi.

Marling, Karal Ann (1996). *As seen on TV: The visual culture of everyday life in the 1950s*. Boston: Harvard University Press.

McDougall, Walter A. (2013). The unlikely history of American exceptionalism. *American Interest*, 8(4), 6–15.

Miller, David W. (2011). *The taking of American Indian lands in the Southeast: A history of territorial cessions and forced relocations, 1607–1840*. Jefferson, NC: McFarland.

Murray, Charles (2013). *American exceptionalism: An experiment in history*. Lanham, MD: Asi Press.

Nada, Ayman (2010). Has the American image abroad changed during the last decade? Examining the changes in the Egyptian public attitudes about the USA (1999–2008), Paper presented at the annual meeting of the Southern Political Science Association.

Office of Tourism Industries (2000). International Visitors (Inbound) and U.S. Residents (Outbound). Washington, DC: U.S. Department of Commerce.

Pease, Donald E. (2009). *The new American exceptionalism.* University of Minnesota Press.

Pletka, Danielle (2013). Think Again: the Republican Party. *Foreign Policy*, 198, 42–47.

Rawson, Hugh (2003). The road to freedom fries. *American Heritage*, 54(3),12.

Rojecki, Andrew (2008). Rhetorical Alchemy: American Exceptionalism and the War on Terror. *Political Communication*, 25(1), 67–88.

Rosenblum, Jonathan (2003, June 20). The end of the chain. Jewish Media Resources. http://www.jewishmediaresources.com/592/the-end-of-the-chain

Shane, Scott (2012, Oct 21). The opiate of exceptionalism. *New York Times*, SR6.

Sharansky, Natan, & Dermer, Ron (2006). The case for democracy: The power of freedom to overcome tyranny and terror. Washington, DC: PublicAffairs.

Silk, Mark (2012). American Exceptionalism and political religion in Republican politics today. *Review of Faith & International Affairs*, 10(2), 33–40.

Skomeck, Carolyn (2004, March 27). Despite White House backing, U.N. 'Law of the Sea' treaty hits growing GOP resistance. *CQ Weekly*, 62(13),761.

Smith, David Michael (2012). The American melting pot: A national myth in public and popular discourse. *National Identities*, 14, 387–402.

Sorohan, Erica Gordon (1994). Too much work, too little time. *Training & Development*, 48(8), 11–12.

Swartz, Salli Anne (2009). From French fries to freedom fries: Notes from Paris. *International Law News*, 38(3), 1–15.

Thompson, Cooper (2008, Fall). Language chauvinism: The ugly American revisited. *Diversity Factor*, 16(4), 1–3.

Towell, Pat (1995, February 18). House votes to sharply rein in U.S. peacekeeping expenses. Congressional Quarterly Weekly Report, 53(7), 535–37.

U.S. English, Inc. (2004), http://www.us-english.org/inc/official/survey/national.asp

Unger, David C. (2013). *The emergency state: America's pursuit of absolute security at all costs.* New York: Penguin. (2005, October 13).

Chapter Four

Pillars of the American Psyche

Consumerism

As David Halberstam (2012) pointed out in his book *The Fifties*, America became an economy based upon consumerism after World War II. Prior to that time, America was in the Great Depression. There was little money and few goods. At the end of World War II, America had a large number of manufacturing plants available that had been geared to the war effort. Afterward, the tank factories could go back to making domestic cars. Uniform textile mills could begin making cloth for fashion. The experimental chemical labs could now go back to making plastic, cosmetics, and toys. Beyond the goods, however, Madison Avenue learned the power of a new emerging medium—television. With this new, mass media, advertisers could reach millions of people and the reactions were clear. The consumer economy had begun.

Two important concepts related to consumerism are relevant to the political process. First, if the economic growth and stability depend on consumption, then society must continually encourage the population to consume. Therefore, you need more, new, and better stuff. Comedian George Carlin (2009) did a routine that was a commentary about American consumerism. He said you have stuff so you buy a house. As you get more stuff, your house gets full so you buy a bigger house. Now, you need more stuff to fill up the house, so you buy more stuff. He continues this progression on and on (p. 215).

The statistics on our willingness to drive ourselves into debt, as a result of our consumerism frenzy, are staggering. While Americans revere the idea of fiscal responsibility and conservatism, our lifestyle indicates just the opposite. CNN Money observed that the American consumer has become deeply addicted to spending, running up ever higher level of debt to live in a fashion that is beyond their means (Lahart, 2003). *Frontline* reporter Lowell Bergman (2004) noted that, "with more than 641 million credit cards in circulation and accounting for an estimated $1.5 trillion of consumer spending, the U.S. economy has clearly gone plastic."

Companies spend millions in advertising to get consumers to buy more. Automobile dealers offer a zero-money down payment. Furniture companies advertise a no-payment plan for a year. Telemarketing companies call constantly to get you to borrow money against the equity in your home. It is a "what's-my-monthly-payment" society. The result is that the average family is in debt by $8,000.

In this environment throughout the 1970s and into the twenty-first century, Republicans attacked the Democrats as wild spenders. Their attack was, "Your family must live within the family budget. Your government should do the same." The truth was and is that families are not living within their budget. Most families are living well beyond their means and are deficit spending as much as the federal government. Likewise, the Republicans were seen as the party of spending discipline. However, the Reagan administration's record deficits were replaced by the Clinton's balanced budgets only to be replaced with George Bush's new record deficits. Meanwhile, under Democratic President Barack Obama, the excessive spending has continued. While Tea Party Republicans made some public relations efforts to cut government spending (Weisman & Parker, 2013), mainstream Republicans joined with Democrats to restore most of the cuts that had previously been made. Essentially, the moderates of both parties agreed that money was needed in the economy to maintain the politics of consumerism (Hulse, 2013).

Lest the above analysis sounds like an indictment of the GOP, keep in mind that Democrats also engage in consumerism as a political technique. They merely choose a different approach. The basic Republican approach to political consumerism is to reduce taxes, thus putting more money into the pockets of citizens; that, in turn, allows them to spend more on consumer goods. The Democratic approach is to increase government spending, thus creating more jobs and putting more money into the pockets of consumers. Their basic approaches are polar opposites, but their goal is the same. Both parties assume that more spending by voters is a plus for the political system.

Even that most sensitive of issues, race relations, is influenced by consumerism. Jones (2014), for example, argued that the nation's racial problems are really due to economic exploitation that began with slavery and continues today in the form of economic disadvantages for poor African Americans. Newman (2000) argued that economic issues were behind much of the Civil Rights movement of the 1950s and 1960s. Vavrus (2000) argued that consumerism influenced political choices via its impact on lifestyles, and that this was particularly true for women voters. Turner (1995) argued that consumer analysis was a major contributor to political flux in the United States. Even the traditional issue of military spending is ultimately tied to the economic well-being of areas and the manufacturers who contribute to local economies (Borch & Wallace, 2010).

Much of the expansion of consumerism is because products (and therefore advertising) are aimed at kids and teens. Consider the development of one product, such as the "tennis shoe." While the term "tennis shoe" was the dominant name of the product in the 1950s and 1960s, those of the Boomer generation remember them as basketball shoes. They were the shoes your parents were required to buy for physical education in high school, even if you did not participate in the few organized sports teams that were available. Later, the term "athletic shoes" became more dominant and the price increased accordingly.

In the 1950s, the decision of which product to purchase was only a two-dimensional problem. You could have either black or white, high top or low cut. If you were really fashion conscious, you would decide between Converse or Keds. The cost of all of them were about the same, around $10. You normally bought these shoes at department stores, such as Sears.

Today, there are entire stores dedicated to selling "athletic shoes." There are numerous shoes for specialized activities—running shoes, walking shoes, tennis shoes, basketball shoes, softball shoes, soccer shoes, and cross training shoes. Of course there are five to ten brands and styles of each shoe. One side of the store is for men, the other side is for women. And, of course the colors and styles depend upon the shoe endorsement from a super-star. If the shoe is endorsed by a famous athlete, it will obviously be more expensive too. It may not be better for your feet in terms of support on your ankles or arches, but it is more prestigious. But, how could a nine-year-old possibly play basketball unless he is wearing the same shoe as Shaq? Even considering the inflation rate for the past fifty years, it is hard to believe that PE shoes now cost hundreds of dollars.

In addition to the sophistication of one product, think back twenty years and consider all the new products that are available. Two decades ago, there was no mass consumption of fax machines (which are almost obsolete now), iPad's, DVD's, cell phones, Blackberries, and tablets. These are just a few of the thousands of new consumer products to hit the market since the new millennium.

POLITICAL CONSUMERISM

Some academic research has looked at the role of political consumerism in the political process (e.g., Micheletti, Follesdal, & Stolle, 2008; Newman &

Bartels, 2011). Some consumers specifically choose the products they purchase (or avoid) based on political ideologies or issues (Banaji & Buckingham, 2009). As such, political consumerism can be defined as "the use of consumer power to influence politics" (Stroomsnes, 2009, p. 303). Overall, political consumers have more trust in other citizens, are heavily involved in charities, and score high on measures of political efficacy (Stolle, Hooghe, & Micheletti, 2005). Political campaigns have been known to target voters based on consumer habits, as in the famous designation of "soccer moms" in the 2000 election (Vavrus, 2000). More recently, an increasing number of campaigns have targeted young voters' consumer habits based on their behavior on the Internet (Ward & de Vreese, 2011).

THE BROADER ISSUE OF CONSUMERISM

Political Consumerism is a down-up approach to politics, with the intent of the action being to use consumer behavior by ordinary individuals to influence decisions by corporations and politicians. Form the most part, though, consumerism is a broader national factor that impacts how political parties address voter concerns. As noted earlier, both parties take a different approach—approaches that are so diverse that they lead to political stalemate.

The criticisms of the Republican approach is relatively simple, i.e., the "trickle down" method of tax cuts has little benefit for the average person but rather benefits high income individuals. The only major result of trickle-down politics is that it reduces governmental revenues. In Kansas, in 2012, the state adopted two tax reduction techniques (Barro, 2014). First, the state legislature cut tax rates and raised the standard deduction on state income taxes. Then they eliminated any taxes on self-contracting income, i.e., that which is reported on 1099-MISC tax forms. This latter law was designed to encourage small businesses that rely on such income. The idea was that cutting those taxes would lead to more job creation and thus offset the tax revenue that would be lost by the tax cuts. It didn't work. The next year, the state projected that they would get $651 million in state income tax, but the actual number that came in was only $369 million. Those who benefitted from the tax cuts merely accepted the cuts and kept the money to themselves.

The Kansas example is only one which demonstrates that trickle-down economics rarely trickle down to low income voters (Frank, 2007). As commentator Paul Krugman (2014) wrote, "Republicans . . . are having a hard time shaking their reputations for reverse Robin-Hoodism, for being the party that takes from the poor and gives to the rich" (p. A19). Similarly, *New York Times* columnist Ross Douthat (2014) wrote that "policies championed on the right . . . have often made it harder for low-income men to find steady work and stay out of prison, and made women understandably wary of marrying them" (p. SR13).

There is some agreement with this criticism from within the Republican Party itself. Republican commentator Joe Scarborough (2013), for example, argued that Ronald Reagan "rose to power as a Main Street conservative with more in common with Eisenhower and Nixon than people generally recognize" (p. 117). Scarborough called for a return to an ideological view that was friendly to middle America.

Given the ineffectiveness of past trickle-down policies, many Republicans turned to a call for balanced budgets, with the idea that the budget could be balanced by austerity techniques that targeted cuts in unnecessary spending (Cohn & Davis, 2005; McGahey, 2013). This approach labels Democrats as "big spenders" whose policies only increase the national debt (e.g., Cohn, 2005). That, in turn, leads to a gradual building up governmental debt that will have to be repaid by future generations (Siegel, 2014). The Democratic response is simple: Their approach puts more money into the pockets of low- and middle-income Americans, putting more money into the American economy, and thus increasing the nation's gross national product. In the end, the result is increased tax revenue for the government. As a result, there is often a drive to increase government spending in down economic times, under the assumption that increased government spending will stimulate the economy (e.g., Hitt & Mullins, 2009).

Easterly (2014) argued that neither the Democrats nor the Republicans understand global economics. Instead, he argued that governments are inherently biased against the poor, leading to an increased financial gap between the rich and the poor. In his view, the problem exceeds that of any specific nation, but is due to the technocratic nature of global government itself. Still, there is an assumption in his argument that the very nature of government leads to unchecked powers against the poor. Which approach is the best? That's the essence of the debate. However, there is research that argues that different global nations take differing approaches to addressing the issue. Generally, in opposition to Easterly's arguments, Simmons and Nooruddin (2006) found that on an international level, democracies generally increased spending on public services because that helped to meet the needs of a large portion of society, while non-democratic governments could remain in power by simply responding to economic elites.

It is unclear whether Americans really demand these things or if the demand is artificially driven by marketing and advertising. Which is the cause and which is the effect is only a philosophical question. The results are the same—everyone wants more of everything.

REFERENCES

Banaji, Shakuntala, & Buckingham, David (2009). The civic sell. *Information, Communication & Society*, 12(8), 1197–1223.

Barro, Josh (2014, June 29). Yes, if you cut taxes, you get less tax revenue. *New York Times*, BU6.

Bergman, Lowell (2004, November 23). Secret history of the credit card. PBS, http://www.pbs.org/wgbh/pages/frontline/shows/credit/etc/synopsis.html

Borch, Casey, & Wallace, Michael (2010). Military spending and economic well-being in the American states: The Post-Vietnam War era. *Social Forces*, 88, 1727–752.

Carlin, George (2009). *Last words*. New York: Free Press.

Cohn, Jonathan (2005, March 21). Hey, big spender. *New Republic*, 232(10), 6.

Cohn, Peter, & Davis, Susan (2005, February 8). Leaders pledge austerity, eye cuts through reconciliation. *Congress Daily*, 3–4.

Douthat, Ross (2014). More imperfect unions. *New York Times*, (p. SR13).

Easterly, William (2014). *The tyranny of experts: Economists, dictators, and the forgotten rights of the poor*. New York: Basic Books.

Frank, Robert H. (2007, April 12). In the real world of work and wages, trickle-down theories don't hold up. *New York Times*, C3.

Halberstam, David (2012). *The fifties*. New York: Villard Books.

Hitt, Greg, & Mullins, Brody (2009, February 2). Pressure grows to boost size of stimulus package. *Wall Street Journal*, 253(26), A4.

Hulse, Carl (2013, Dec. 14). Boehner's jabs at activist right show G.O.P. shift. *New York Times*, A1, A13.

Jones, Jacqueline (2014). *A dreadful deceit: The myth of race from the Colonial era to Obama's America*. New York: Basic Books.

Krugman, Paul (2014, Jan. 13). Enemies of the poor. *New York Times*, A19.

Lahart, Justin (2003, October 3). Spending our way to disaster. CNN Money.

McGahey, Richard (2013). The political economy of austerity in the United States. *Social Research*, 80, 717–48.

Micheletti, Michele, Follesdal, Andreas, & Stolle, Dietlind (eds.) (2008). *Politics, products, and markets: Exploring political consumerism past and present*. Piscataway, NJ: Transaction Publishers.

Newman, Benjamin J., & Bartels, Brandon L. (2011). Politics at the checkout line: Explaining political consumerism in the United States. *Political Research Quarterly*, 64, 803–17.

Newman, Kathy M. (2000). The forgotten fifteen million: Black radio, the "negro market" and the civil rights movement. *Radical History Review*, 76, 115–35.

Scarborough, Joe (2013). *The right path: From Ike to Reagan, how Republicans once mastered politics—and can again*. New York: Random House.

Siegel, Fred (2014). *The revolt against the masses: How liberalism has undermined the middle class*. New York: Encounter.

Simmons, Joel, & Nooruddin, Irfan (2006). Openness and the Political Economy of Government Spending. Paper presented at the annual meeting of the International Studies Association.

Stolle, Dietlind, Hooghe, Marc, & Micheletti, Michele (2005). Politics in the Supermarket: Political Consumerism as a Form of Political Participation. *International Political Science Review*, 26(3), 245–69.

Stroomsnes, Kristin (2009). Political consumerism: A substitute for or supplement to conventional political participation? *Journal of Civil Society*, 5, 303-314.

Turner, James S. (1995). The consumer interest in the 1990s and beyond. *Journal of Consumer Affairs*, 29(2), 310–27.

Vavrus, Mary Douglas (2000). From women of the year to "soccer moms": The case of the incredible shrinking women. *Political Communication*, 17(2), 193–213.

Ward, Janelle, & de Vreese, Claes (2011). Political consumerism, young citizens and the Internet. *Media, Culture & Society*, 33(3), 399–413.

Weisman, Jonathan, & Parker, Ashley (2013, Sept 28). Shutdown looms as Senate passes budget bill. *New York Times*, A1, A11.

Chapter Five

The Fourth Pillar of the American Psyche

Religiosity

Many of the initial settlers from Europe —such as the Puritans (McKenna, 2007) and the Pilgrims (Marty, 1985)—came to the American continent as religious refugees and that religious influence continued into the Colonial Era (Kidd, 2007). That heritage led the founding fathers to include a plank for religious freedom, i.e., the separation of church and state, into the U.S. Constitution (Lambert, 2003). That attitude was a direct by-product of the motivations that brought the settlers to the New World. Those early religious groups were not initially seeking a place that embraced religious diversity or tolerance. These settlers came from societies where people believed there should be one official religion in a country. If citizens organized a religion that was different from the official religion, then the government punished and persecuted the dissenters. The original American colonists brought these attitudes with them. They founded colonies based upon their religious beliefs and would persecute anyone who disagreed with their religious doctrines. The Puritans, for example, believed that the "true" faith was known only to "visible saints" and others represented false religions (Morgan, 1963). That resistance to other ideas eventually led Roger Williams to settle Rhode Island as a haven for religious freedom—a concept eventually adopted by the founding fathers (Barry, 2012).

Organized religion has always been an important institution in America. Churches were the central place in many towns where people gathered not only to worship, but to consider the issues of the day. During the Revolutionary War, ministers on both sides launched arguments from the pulpits and published their sermons for distribution throughout the colonies (Van Tyne, 1913).

Church (2002) noted in his "biography" of the Declaration of Independence that the document was based at least partly on religious principles. Gaustad (1987) argued that the founding fathers viewed religion as playing a major role in preserving the social mores of the new nation. The Bible, in particular, has had a major influence on the life of the nations (Miller, 1956; Tuveson, 1968) and on the nation's public discourse (Johnson, 1985; Sandeen, 1982). In the nineteenth century, the concept that Americans were really God's chosen people erupted onto the American public in the idea of Manifest Destiny (Cherry, 1998) This idea says it is our duty to God to spread our form of Democracy across the world. This current of religion in the nation's history continued through the beginning of the twentieth century with orators such as William Jennings Bryant (Cherny, 1994; Kazin, 2007; Leinwand, 2007) and the Prohibition Era of the 1920s (Carter, 2012). In the modern era, the civil rights movement of the 1950s and 1960s centered around the role of churches in the African American community (Johnson, 1986).

While different forms and denominations of churches have emerged, declined, or been reinvented over our 230-year history, this does not necessarily mean people adopt the ideas the institutions are promoting. Religiosity means the numerous aspects of knowing, believing, and behaving based on the assumption of the existence of a higher power. The evidence from the opinions, beliefs, and attitudes Americans provide to social science researchers clearly demonstrates religiosity is a strong part of the American psyche and plays an important role in politics (see, for example, Miller & Wattenberg, 1984).

In terms of identification, 76.5 percent of Americans identify themselves with a Christian group. Researchers note, however, "There appears to be a considerable gap between "identification with" a religion and reported "membership" or "belonging" to an institutional embodiment of that faith." An additional 3.7 percent of the population identifies with non-Christian religious groups, such as Judaism, Buddhism, etc. Only one percent of the respondents openly identify themselves as agnostic or atheists. Further, while some Christian groups decry Americans' secular nature, Americans do not view themselves in this manner. When asked, "When it comes to your outlook, do you regard yourself as religious or secular?" Seventy-five percent responded religious and 16 percent responded secular (Kitchens, 2008).

Surveys which examined religiosity, in terms of beliefs, indicated similar results as the survey that asked people to identify themselves religiously. A *FOX News* poll in 2004 indicated that 92 percent of Americans said they believe in God (Blanton, 2004). In terms of religious concepts, 84 percent of the respondents said they believed in Heaven, 74 percent believed in Hell, and 71 percent of the respondents believed there is a Devil. One interesting finding is that younger people are more likely to believe in Hell and the Devil than older people. A *Newsweek* survey around the same time found many of the same results, with 80 percent of the respondents saying they believe God created the universe and only 10 percent saying they did not believe God created the universe. The other 10 percent were uncertain ("Where we stand on faith," 2005).

While we have a Constitutional separation of church and state, America has never had a separation of politics and religion. From ministers driving revolution against England, Abolitionist preachers admonishing the evils of slavery, and African American churches being the center of civil rights movements, religion has always been involved with politics, in questioning the morality of certain issues. These issues are national and local, as well as, old and new. For example, creation versus evolution has been fought since the famous 1926 Scopes trial in Tennessee (Harrison, 1994; Hostetler, 1998; Marsden, 1980). These matters are still far from being settled today. In 1999, the Kansas State Board of Education deleted the teaching of evolution from the State's science curriculum. Other states, such as Texas, Nebraska, California, Louisiana, and New Hampshire, are having similar battles.

No issue has brought the right-wing Christian movement to the forefront in politics more than legalized abortion (Francome, 1980; Fried, 1988). This concern has become a single-issue vote and a litmus test for groups to either help or attempt to defeat political candidates (Joffe, 1997). In his book, *What's the Matter with Kansas*, Thomas Franks (2004) pointed out how the religious fervor over legalized abortion has made voters ignore their downward economic plight, handed to them by the Republican Congress and White House, to work tirelessly for Republicans who want all legal abortions banned. This so-called life agenda has encouraged these groups to oppose stem cell research (Deckha, 2008), to get involved in a family's agonizing decision involving Terri Schaivo (Kaplan, 2007), and to rail in Congress against human cloning (Stolberg, 2001).

The latest morality drama was played around the issue of gay marriage. In 2004, 64 percent of Americans opposed gay marriage and 32 percent supported allowing it (Gilgoff et al., 2004). This issue was put on the ballot in several states before the 2008 election. Of particular note was Ohio, one of the key battleground states in the 2004 Presidential election. The Republican assumption was that this issue would help them to turnout conservative voters. Polling in Ohio during the campaign clearly indicated the heat of this issue. 71 percent supported banning gay marriages. In addition, a plurality said homosexuality was a lifestyle choice, not something predominately determined by genetics (Kitchens, 2008).

Since then, public support of gay marriage has increased. By 2012, support had increased to 49 percent, while opposition had dropped to 40 percent;

still, the nation remained divided on the issue (Connelly, 2012). The 2013 Supreme Court decision that struck down much of the Defense of Marriage Act, thus supporting gay marriage, served to intensify the debate as opponents promised to keep the issue going. In the week following the decision, support for gay marriage had grown even higher (up to 55 percent) while opposition had dropped to 40 percent (Page, 2013). Still, it remained a divisive issue, but the shift in support of gay marriage seem to be a result of its framing as a fairness issue rather than a religious issue as it was during the preceding decades.

Despite the nation's historical and Constitutional separation of church and state, voters want to mix religion and politics. In a Pew Charitable Trust nationwide survey, when Americans were asked if churches should express views on political matters, 52 percent said yes and 44 percent said no. When asked how they felt about the amount of expressions of faith and prayer by political leaders, 41 percent said politicians expressed too little about faith and prayer and only 21 percent said they expressed too much.

The latest incarnation of religious influence had its roots in the 1970s and 1980s, largely from television preachers. The broadcast preachers of the 1950s, who were considered rather laughable by most of the American public, built a communication empire in the 1970s and 1980s that constantly injected their religious take on political issues and current events. The first of these efforts came under the leadership of Reverend Jerry Falwell and his Moral Majority organization, who built a strong following among audiences in the nation's sun belt (Williams, 2010). That effort failed, largely due to it lacked broad-based support and had an ineffective grassroots organization (Wilcox, Rozell, & Gunn, 1996). The Moral Majority finally shutdown its organization in 1988, but its role was picked up by Pat Robertson and his Christian Coalition (Wilcox, DeBell, & Sigelman, 1999).

Pat Robertson's 700 Club on his Christian Broadcasting Network reached more than one million households per day and was seen in 96 percent of America's television markets ("Christian Broadcasting Network"). Robertson used his program as a political pulpit and, by the 1988 election, became a major figure in the Republican Party (Penning, 1994). He also had a broader influence on the national media and the issues that it covered (Huckins, 1999). Robertson once told his audience that Hurricane Katrina hit New Orleans because Ellen DeGeneres was chosen to host television's Emmy awards (New Orleans is her hometown) (Duke, Ihssen, & O'Brien, 2012). Similar to Senator Joseph McCarthy's list of "communists," Robertson claimed his employees at the network put together a list of 283 nominees, presenters, and invited guests at the Emmy's known to be of sexually deviant persuasions. Robertson's political strength was significant enough that he influenced the 2000 Republican platform (Schnabel, 2013).

Another religious player in politics is James Dobson. His *Focus on the Family* radio show was syndicated to more than 700 stations across the country ("Christian Evangelicals Proclaim," 2004). He and other politically active non-traditional Christian leaders are often seen on the talk shows and attending political functions.

The influence of the religious right reached its peak during the administration of George W. Bush from 2000 to 2007 (Green, 2009). In Bush, the evangelical community not only had a member of their group in the White House, but his administration openly used religious appeals in its rhetoric (Schroepfer, 2008). Part of Bush's domestic program was faith-based initiatives for community action (Carlson-Thies, 2009). That religious base, teamed with Bush's handling of the crisis following the 9/11 attacks, kept the Republicans in the White House for two consecutive terms. They lost only when the nation's financial problems, including a massive collapse of Wall Street and the banking system, shifted the discussion from religion and patriotism to the pillar of consumerism.

Religion was not a major factor in the 2008 election. The Republican nominee, John McCain, was not an active church-goer, although his vice-presidential nominee Sarah Palin had strong appeal among evangelical voters (Hart, 2013). Of the two nominees, Democrat Barack Obama was more active in religious meetings, but his religious association with controversial preacher Jeremiah Wright was more of a distraction than an asset (Walker & Smithers, 2009). By the 2012 election, the Republican nominee was Mitt Romney—a Mormon whose religious beliefs did not excite evangelical voters (Powell, 2012).

Still, being a Christian has now become "cool." Young people are being entertained by Christian rockers and there is a Christian rock radio station in most major markets (Adedeji, 2006). Religion has always been part of the American psyche. Now, being clearly part of a religious group is a necessity to be accepted as part of what's "in," both for teens and their parents. Instead of finding the discussion of religion and politics as uncomfortable, politicians are now finding it a necessity. Voters can be persuaded with arguments about the morality of public policy.

THE PHARISEE EFFECT

While religion can be a strong motivation for supporting a political candidate, any candidate who overuses religion as his motivational base is at risk of going too far. An extensive use of religion can trigger a voter backlash known as the Pharisee Effect. The label is based on a biblical parable of the Pharisee and the Publican in which Jesus criticizes a Pharisee for being too public with his prayers (Luke 18:9-14). The Pharisee's mistake is that his loud public prayers were intended to enhance his own image rather than being an honest expression of internal religious devotion, leading Jesus to rebuke him with the remark that "everyone that exalteth himself shall be abase" (Luke 18:14). Similar language is used to criticize the Pharisees in the book of Matthew (particularly Matthew 23:12), with the section adding the description that the Pharisees "outwardly appear righteous unto men, but within ye are full of hypocrisy and iniquity" (Matt. 23:28). The Pharisee, it would be argued, was so openly religious that he was subject to charges of insincerity and hypocrisy. The same thing can occur with the use of political appeals in politics.

This phenomenon was first described by Powell and Neiva in 2004. It was subsequently tested in an Alabama gubernatorial campaign involving Judge Roy Moore ("The Ten Commandments Judge") (Powell, Neiva, & Fuller, 2008). Specifically, the Pharisee Effect hypothesizes that excessive religious appeals subject the user to negative evaluations regarding the speaker's intention or motivations. These potential negative evaluations fall into one of five different categories: (1) self-serving motivations, (2) hypocrisy, (3) inappropriateness, (4) fanaticism, or (5) a "holier-than-thou" attitude.

(1) Self-serving Motivation

The speaker is using a religious appeal for their own purposes, rather than to promote a religious purpose. In this sense, the Pharisee Effect could be somewhat similar to the psychological concept of "intentionality." Intentionality assumes that observers make judgments regarding whether a person engages in a specific behavior for (1) the purpose of achieving a specific outcome and (2) with the belief that the behavior can achieve that consequence (Malle & Knobe, 1997). If the intentionality of the act is viewed as self-serving, the positive attributions that could be obtained from the use of the appeal could be negated. From this approach, the sin of the Pharisee was that he was seeking public recognition for his spirituality; he was, as Duke (1995), "praying with a sideward glance" that monitored public reaction to his prayer (p. 923).

(2) Deception, or Hypocrisy

The speaker is viewed as basing their appeal on a set of religious values that they themselves do not personally hold. Biblical scholars typically identify hypocrisy as the major mistake of the Pharisee in the passage from Matthew 23 (Eddy, 2001; Mason, 1990; Weinfeld, 1990). Hypocrisy has been studied as a psychological phenomenon that reflects an inconsistency between behavior and one's moral principles (Batson & Kobrynowicz, 1997; Batson, Thompson & Chen, 2002) that is related to self-deception (Batson & Thompson, 1999; Statman, 1997) and dissonance reduction (Stone et al., 1997). It may exist in different forms, including pretense, inconsistency, complacency, and blame (Crisp & Cowton, 1994), but is generally viewed as an indication of dishonesty (Bulka, 1976). Gailli (1994) argues that hypocrisy is a constant professional threat for those in religion, and the argument could just as easily be made for anyone in public life. Political hypocrisy, in particular, is a favorite news story for journalists (Hoyt, 1999). Political opposition groups also like the theme, regardless of the group's political ideology. Liberal groups have attacked the right-wing Christian Coalition with charges of hypocrisy (Gilbert, 1993). During the controversy over President Bill Clinton's sex life, for example, one of the Republicans (Congressman Bob Livingston) criticizing the President resigned after it was revealed that he too had engaged in extra-marital affairs (Carlson, 1998; Hosenball & Murr, 1999; Smith, 1998). The information became public after publisher Larry Flynt charged that Livingston and other Republicans were being hypocritical for criticizing Clinton for "sins" that they also had committed (Hosenball & Murr, 1999).

(3) Inappropriateness

Bucy (2000) argued that one dimension that the public uses to evaluate its leaders is that of the appropriateness of the leader's messages and behavior. In some instances, the appeals may be so strong as to be viewed as inappropriate behavior in a nation that values church-state separation (Gedicks, 1995). In fact, some theorists argue that religious arguments are inappropriate in public debates (e.g., Greenawalt, 1988; Nuehaus, 1984; Thiemann, 1996), with one describing religious messages as a "conversation stopper" (Rorty, 1994, p. 1). Carter (1993) argued that "public culture more and more prefers religion as something without political significance, . . . never heard, rarely seen" (p. 9). Hostetler (2000) essentially described an instance in a 1995 speech delivered by Congressman Glenn Poshard in which the congressman responded to an attack from the Christian Coalition by talking of his own religious beliefs; Hostetler further argued that Poshard was hindered because of a "prejudice against religious discourse" in such a situation (p. 88). Similarly, Senator Joseph Lieberman was criticized for airing his religious views, with one commentator describing Lieberman's leadership style as "the religiosity, the sanctimony, the self-absorption" (Nordlinger, 2000, p. 34). Another noted that, in his first campaign speech as the Democrats Vice-Presidential nominee, that Lieberman "invoked God thirteen times" (Gellman, 2000, p. 10). Such comments indicate that the appropriateness of religious discourse is highly dependent upon the context in which it is used. In some instances, including that of political campaigns, religious messages may appear to be out of context.

(4) Fanaticism

Members of a religious community are faced with a constant contradiction in that devoutness is valued positively, and the more devout the better. But one must be devout without being extremely devout. While extreme devoutness might be valued within the religious community, it is viewed negatively and labeled fanaticism outside of that community (Joelson, 1989, 1990). Bruce (2000) argued that any religious involvement in politics that is based on fanaticism or zealotry is doomed to failure since the psychological character-istics associated with zealotry (certainty and dogmatism) "because they create unrealistic expectations and thus generate their own sources of disap-pointment" (p. 263). For outside observers, though, the presence of the "un-realistic expectations" serves to further identify the zealot as a religious fanatic and thus outside the mainstream of both religion and politics. Such reactions prompted Darsey (1997) to comment that "only madmen talk to God" (p. 126). Thus Johnson, Tammey, and Burton (1990) argued that this factor also makes it difficult for religious candidates to reach a broader spectrum of voters because their religious base creates a paradoxical situation for them. Their moral values provides them an initial base of volunteers and financial support, but the fanaticism label keeps them from reaching a broad range of voters.

(5) The "Holier-than-thou" Attitude

This may have been the real "sin" of the Pharisee in the parable, i.e., the purpose of his loud boastful prayer is to let others know that he is an ex-tremely pious and religious individual. He comes across as a self-satisfied individual who is proud to be so religious and—even more so—not one of those common sinners who represent most of the other inhabitants of his community. This attitude is consistent with social psychological definitions of the "holier-than-thou" attitude, i.e., the rating of the self to be better on religious attributes than others (Rowatt et al., 2002; Taylor, 1999). Willimon (2002) described this attitude as "the sin of smugness" (p. 11), while Galli (1994) considered it a problem faced by the "professional holy . . . (that) can be hazardous to your spiritual health" (p. 106). Thus Liut (1998) criticizes the Pharisee, noting that as we overhear his prayer, "we learn nothing about who God is, what God does; but we come to know the man" (p. 932). As with hypocrisy, there is some debate within the field of psychology as to the extent to which such attitudes are the product of self-serving assessments or a by-product of self-deception (Epley & Dunning, 2000), but that factor has little impact on the negative public impression that is created by such a persona. Public reaction to a holier-than-thou attitude is usually negative, as evidenced by the glee that so many people take when a religious icon is revealed as a hypocrite.

CONCLUSIONS

Religion is a complicated pillar of American politics. Religious beliefs reflect moral values that have been around since the initial settlement of the New World. Those values and beliefs influenced the founding fathers and have been involved in American politics, to some degree, ever since. Religion played a role in the founding of the nation and in key historical events like prohibition and the civil rights movement. That trend may have reached its peak during the administration of George W. Bush, when Christian evangelicals played a major role in helping Bush win the presidency.

Still, the politician who uses religion as the only pillar of a campaign risks a potential voter backlash. Overuse of religion can trigger images related to the politician's motivations and possible perceptions of hypocrisy, inappropriateness, fanaticism, and a "holier-than-thou" attitude. If that happens, the political candidate loses.

REFERENCES

Adedeji, Femi (2006). Essentials of Christian music in contemporary times: A prognosis. *Asia Journal of Theology*, 20, 230–40.

Barry, John M. (2012). *Roger Williams and the creation of the American soul: Church, state and the birth of liberty*. New York: Viking.

Batson, C. D., & Kobrynowicz, D. (1997). In a very different voice: Unmasking moral hypocrisy. *Journal of Personality & Social Psychology*, 72, 1335–348.

Batson, C. D., & Thompson, E. R. (1999). Moral hypocrisy: Appearing moral to oneself without being so. *Journal of Personality & Social Psychology*, 77, 525–37.

Batson, C. D., Thompson, E. R., & Chen, H. (2002). Moral hypocrisy: Addressing some alternatives. *Journal of Personality & Social Psychology*, 83, 330–39.

Blanton, Dana (2004, June 18). More believe in god than heaven. *FOX News*. Retrieved from http://www.foxnews.com/story/2004/06/18/more-believe-in-god-than-heaven/.

Bruce, S. (2000). Zealot politics and democracy: The case of the new Christian Right. *Political Studies*, 48(2), 263–82.

Bucy, E. P. (2000). Emotional and evaluative consequences of inappropriate leader displays. *Communication Research*, 27, 194–226.

Bulka, R. P. (1976). Honesty vs hypocrisy. *Judaism*, 25, 209–16.

Carlson, M. (1998, December 28). The Clinton in us all. *Time*, 152(26), 94.

Carlson-Thies, Stanley W. (2009). Faith-based initiative 2.0: The Bush faith-based and community initiative. *Harvard Journal of Law & Public Policy*, 32, 931–47.

Carter, Paul Allen (2012). *The decline and revival of the social Gospel: Social and political liberalism in the American Protestant churches 1920–1940*. New York: Literary Licensing.

Carter, Stephen L. (1993). *The culture of disbelief*. New York: Basic Books.

Cherny, Robert W. (1994). *A righteous cause: The life of William Jennings Bryan*. Norman: University of Oklahoma Press.

Cherry, Conrad (1998). *God's new Israel: Religious interpretations of American destiny*. Chapel Hill: University of North Carolina Press.

Christian Broadcasting Network, http://www.sourcewatch.org/index.php?title=Christian Broadcasting_Network

Christian Evangelicals Proclaim 'Now Comes the Revolution' (2004, November 4). http://www.democracynow.org

Church, F. (2002). *The American creed: A spiritual and patriotic primer*. New York: St. Martin's Press.

Connelly, Marjorie (2012, December 8). Support for gay marriage growing, but U.S. remains divided. *New York Times*, A1.

Crisp, R., & Cowton, C. (1994). Hypocrisy and moral seriousness. *American Philosophical Quarterly*, 31, 343–49.

Darsey, J. (1997). *The prophetic tradition and radical rhetoric in America*. New York: New York University Press.

Deckha, Maneesha (2008). The gendered politics of embryonic cell research in the USA and Canada: An American overlap and Canadian disconnect. *Medical Law Review*, 16, 52–84.

Duke, P. D. (1995, October 11). Praying with a sideward glance. *Christian Century*, 112, 923.

Duke, Anna, Ihssen, Brenda Llewellyn, & O'Brien, Kevin J. (2012). Natural disasters as moral lessons: Nazianzus and New Orleans. *Journal for the Study of Religion, Nature & Culture*, 6, 56–70.

Eddy, G. T. (2001, May). Harlot and Pharisee. *Expository Times*, 112(8), 275–76.

Epley, N., & Dunning, D. (2000). Feeling "holier than thou": Are self-serving assessments produced by errors in self-or social prediction? *Journal of Personality and Social Psychology*, 79, 861-875.

Francome, Colin (1980). Abortion politics in the United States. *Political Studies*, 28, 613–21.

Franks, Thomas (2004). *What's the matter with Kansas: How conservatives won the heart of America*. New York: Henry Holt.

Fried, Amy (1988). Abortion politics as symbolic politics: An investigation into belief systems. *Social Science Quarterly*, 69, 137–54.

Galli, M. (1994). Perils of the professionally holy: Trying to be a godly leader can be hazardous to your spiritual health. *Leadership*, 15, 106–14.

Gaustad, E. S. (1987). *Faith of our fathers: Religion and the new nation*. San Francisco: Harper & Row.

Gedicks, F. M. (1995). *The rhetoric of church and state*. Durham: Duke University Press.

Gellman, M. (2000, December) Joe Lieberman as Roschach test. *First Things: A Monthly Journal of Religion & Public Life*, 108, 9–11.

Gilbert, R A. (1993). *Casting the first stone: The hypocrisy of religious fundamentalism and its threat to society*. Shaftesbury, England: Element Books.

Gilgoff, Dan, Walsh, Kenneth T., Samuel, Terrence, & Ewers, Justin (2004, April 8). Tied in knots by gay marriage. *U.S. News & World Reports*, 136(8), 28–30.

Green, John C. (2009). American faith-based politics in the era of George W. Bush. *European Political Science*, 8, 316–29.

Greenawalt, K. (1995). *Private consciences and public reasons*. New York: Oxford University Press.

Harrison, S. L. (1994). The scopes 'monkey trial' revisited: Mencken and the editorial art of Edmund Duffy. *Journal of American Culture*, 17(4), 55–63.

Hart, D. G. (2013). *From Billy Graham to Sarah Palin: Evangelicals and the betrayal of American conservatism*. Grand Rapids, MI: Wm. B. Eerdmans.

Hostetler, Michael J. (1998). William Jennings Bryan as Demosthenes: The Scopes Trial... *Western Journal of Communication*, 62(2), 165–80.

Hosenball, M., & Murr, A. (1999, January 18). Who's on Larry's list? *Newsweek*, 133(3), 29.

Hoyt, M. (1999). The hypocrisy flag. *Columbia Journalism Review*, 37(6), 62.

Huckins, Kyle (1999). Interest-group influence on the media agenda: A case study. *Journalism & Mass Communication Quarterly*, 76, 76–86.

Joelson, J.R. (1989). Religious fanatics and censorship. *Humanist*, 49(3), 33.

Joelson, J. E. (1990). God, save us from the ideologues. *Humanist*, 50(1), 35.

Joffe, Carole (1997). Abortion as single-issue politics. *Society*, 34(5), 25–29.

Johnson, J. T. (Ed.) (1985). *The Bible in American law, politics, and political rhetoric*. Philadelphia: Fortress Press.

Johnson, S. (1986). The role of the black church in black civil rights movements. In S. Johnson & J. Tamney (Eds.), *The political role of religion in the United States*. Boulder: Westview Press.

Johnson, D. Tamney, J. B., & Burton, R. (1990). Factors influencing vote for a Christian Right candidate. *Review of Religious Research*, 31, 300.

Kaplan, Kalman J. (2007). Zeno, Job and Terry Schiavo: The right to die versus the right to life. *Ethics & Medicine*, 23, 95–102.

Kazin, Michael (2007). *A Godly hero: The life of William Jennings Bryan*. New York: Anchor.

Kidd, Thomas S. (2007). *The great awakening: The roots of evangelical Christianity in Colonial America*. New Haven, CT: Yale University Press.

Kitchens, James T. (2008). A statewide survey of Ohio. Orlando: The Kitchens Group.

Kitchens, James T. (2009). National survey of voter Opinions. Orlando: The Kitchens Group.

Lambert, Frank (2003). *The founding fathers and the place of religion in America*. Princeton: Princeton University Press.

Leinwand, Gerald (2007). *William Jennings Bryan: An uncertain trumpet*. Lanham, MD: Rowman & Littlefield.

Luti, J. M. (1998, November 14). General principles. *Christian Century*, 115(27), 932.

Malle, B. F., & Knobe, J. (1997). The folk concept of intentionality. *Journal of Experimental Social Psychology*, 33, 101–21.

Marsden, George M. (1980) *Fundamentalism and American culture: The shaping of twentieth-century evangelicalism, 1870–1925*. New York: Oxford University Press.

Marty, Martin E. (1985). *Pilgrims in their own land: 500 years of religion in America*. New York: Penguin.

Mason, S. (1990). Pharisaic dominance before 70 CE and the Gospels' hypocrisy charge (Matt 23:2-3). *Harvard Theological Review*, 83, 363–81.

McKenna, George (2007). *The Puritan origins of American patriotism*. New Haven, CT: Yale University Press.

Miller, Arthur H., & Wattenberg, Martin P. (1984). Politics from the pulpit: Religiosity and the 1980s elections. *Public Opinion Quarterly*, 48, 301–17.

Morgan, Edmund (1963). *Visible saints: The history of a Puritan idea*. New York: Cornell University Press.

Nordlinger, Jay (2000, December 31). Orthodox Democrat. *National Review*, 52(25), 34–38.

Neuhaus, R. J. (1984). *The naked public square*. Grand Rapids: William B. Eerdman's Publishing.

Page, Susan (2013, July 2). Same-sex marriage at record approval. *USA Today*, 1A.

Penning, James M. (1994). Pat Robertson and the GOP: 1988 and beyond. *Sociology of Religion*, 55, 327–44.

Powell, Larry (2012). Will Mormonism keep Mitt Romney out of the White House? *Journal of Contemporary Rhetoric*, 2(2), 39–43.

Powell, Larry, & Neiva, Eduardo C. (2004). The Pharisee Effect: When Religious Appeals Go Too Far. *Journal of Communication and Religion*, 29, 70–102.

Powell, Larry, Neiva, Eduardo C., & Fuller, Jessica (2008). A look at the excessive hypothesis of the pharisee effect: The "ten commandments judge" in the Alabama republican primary. *North American Journal of Psychology*, 10, 251–64.

Rorty, R. (1994). Religion as conversation stopper. *Common Knowledge*, 3, 1–6.

Rowatt, W. C., Ottenbreit, A., Nesselroade, Jr., K. P., & Cunningham, P. A. (2002). On being holier-than-thou or humbler-than-thee: A social-psychological perspective on religiousness and humility. *Journal for the Scientific Study of Religion*, 41, 227–37.

Sandeen, E. R. (Ed.) (1982). *The Bible and social reform*. Philadelphia: Fortress Press.

Schnabel, Landon Paul (2013). When fringe goes mainstream: A sociohistorical content analysis of the christian coalition's contract with the American family and the republican party platform. *Politics, Religion and Ideology*, 14, 94–113.

Schroepfer, Helen Daley (2008). Pursuing the enemies of freedom: Religion in the persuasive rhetoric of the Bush administration. *Political Theology*, 9, 27–45.

Smith, J. M. (1998, December 19). The adultery wars. *New York Times*, 148(51376), A15.

Statman, D. (1997). Hypocrisy and self-deception. *Philosophical Psychology*, 10, 57–75.

Stolberg, Sherly Gay (2001, August 1). House backs ban on human cloning for any objective. *New York Times*, A1.

Stone, J., Cooper, J., Wiegand, A. W., & Aronson, E. (1997). When exemplification fails: Hypocrisy and the motive for self-integrity. *Journal of Personality & Social Psychology*, 72, 54–65.

Taylor, B. B. (1999). The evils of pride & self-righteousness. *Living Pulpit*, 1(4), 39.

Thiemann, R. F. (1996). *Religion in public life*. Washington: Georgetown University Press.

Van Tyne, Claude H. (1913). The influence of religion and sectarian forces in the American Revolution. *American Historical Review*, 19(1), 46-44.

Walker, Clarence E., & Smithers, Gregory D. (2009). *The preacher and the politician: Jeremiah Wright, Barack Obama and race in America*. Charlottesville: University of Virginia Press.

Weinfeld, M. (1990). The charge of hypocrisy in Matthew 23 and in Jewish sources. *Immanuel*, 24-25, 52-58.

Where we stand on faith (2005, September 5). *Newsweek*, 146(9/10), 48–49.

Wilcox, Clyde, DeBell, Matthew, & Sigelman, Lee (1999). The second coming of the new Christian right: Patterns of popular support in 1984 and 1996. *Social Science Quarterly*, 80, 181–92.

Wilcox, Clyde, Rozell, Mark, & Gunn, Roland (1996). Religious coalitions in the new Christian right. *Social Science Quarterly*, 77, 543–58.

Williams, Daniel (2010). Jerry Falwell's Sunbelt politics: The regional origins of the Moral Majority. *Journal of Policy History*, 22, 125–47.

Willimon, W. H. (2002, August 28). The sin of smugness: A time for regret. *Christian Century*, 119(18), 11.

Wolfe, Tom (1980). *In our time*. New York: Farrar, Strauss & Giroux.

Chapter Six

Why Voters Frighten Politicians

"I don't see why we need to stand by and watch a country go communist due to the irresponsibility of its people. The issues are much too important for the Chilean voters to be left to decide for themselves." —Henry Kissinger (1970).

Americans both hate and love government. They like many government services, but they hate much of what government represents. And that hatred is something that can scare politicians.

Why do voters direct so much hatred toward a government that they consider the best in the world? There are lengthy lists of cliches and urban legends used to justify that hatred while also maintaining the hyper-patriotism Americans exhibit to the country. These include such cliches as: government wastes money; the government paid $600 for a hammer; the government takes my money and no one cares how it is spent; all politicians are crooks—if they are honest when we elect them, they become crooks after they are elected; the government is just a pointy-headed bunch of bureaucrats that do not understand average people; and we need to run government like a business.

Of course, some of this criticism is based in reality. A 1997 audit of Medicare uncovered $23 billion in overpayments (Pear, 1997). The lobbying scandal involving Jack Abramoff (Samuel, Pound, & Streisand, 2005) reinforced the belief that most politicians are dishonest or can be bought off. On virtually every survey, if voters are asked to name the most important quality they seek in a candidate for public office, the word "honesty" is always at the top by a huge margin. As Congress scrambled to convince the public they are not a bunch of crooks by passing a lobbying reform bill, the new Republican majority leader was creating more damage.

Representative and later Speaker of the House John Boehner (R-Ohio) and other Republicans defended the relationship between Members of Con-

gress and special interests groups (Lipton, 2010). Boehner said it was important for Congressmen to understand industries because attending meetings of
industry groups helped with legislation. Of course, the press pointed out that
he had been given more than $150,000 in travel by special interests groups
and gone to golf resorts from Scotland to California (Jeffrey & Bauerlein,
2011). Such behavior only reinforced the public's perception that all politicians are crooks.

Now, the urban legend that most people have heard: There is a woman
who drives a Cadillac and is sometimes seen with her poodle at the grocery
store buying cigarettes and beer or wine with food stamps. She has been seen
in every state. In some places, that are not too politically correct, they mention that she is an African American. This story was first presented to the
American public in a 1976 campaign speech by Ronald Reagan in which he
talked about a fictional "welfare queen" who had stolen $150,000 from the
government by using 80 aliases, 30 addresses, a dozen social security cards,
and four fictional dead husbands ("'Welfare queen' becomes issue . . . ,"
1976). That anecdote was likely triggered by an earlier Top Ten country song
called "Welfare Cadillac," written by Guy Drake (1970). The story is a
typical "dependency narrative" aimed at attacking those who are viewed as
taking money from the government (Cassiman, 2006). This legend has been
thoroughly debunked (Seccombe, 2010), with at least one scholar saying the
story was created as a way to stigmatize welfare (Kohler-Hausman, 2007).
Regardless, the legend persists.

It is somewhat amazing that the people who invent such an urban legend
can ignore so much reality. Our government works seamlessly in so many
areas that we do not even notice that the government is doing anything. For
instance, when you buy gasoline for your car, the pump reads you have a
gallon. How do people know it is not nine-tenths of a gallon? How do they
know it was really gasoline? When people pulled through the drive-thru to
grab a burger, did they ever think, "This might not be beef. This might poison
me and I might die?" Probably not. When people drive on those wide-lane
Interstate highways, do they ever say the government should never have built
these roads? No. The public loves the benefits from the government, but they
rarely notice them.

This point was driven home to one of the authors in his own neighborhood. He was playing on a tennis team and one of his teammates was prais-
ing the candidacy of George W. Bush and quoting his anti-tax television
spots. He argued that the government needed to cut taxes because it was his
money. Government just wastes money, and it was his money that the
government was wasting. When asked why he did not belong to the private
tennis club less than two miles away, he responded that it was too expensive.
"It cost more than a grand a month," he said with disgust. When asked how
much it cost to belong to the tennis club at the public park, he confessed it

was $50 for a family membership for the entire year. The author just looked at him and said, "Now, do you understand why we pay taxes?" Unfortunately, he probably did not get the message.

As much as Democrats object to the idea, with a little research, you can find government waste, abuse, and fraud. But, if you examine any large corporation or institution, you will find as much or more waste and fraud as in the government. Why? Because all large organizations are composed of people. No person is perfect. Since organizations are made of imperfect people, there are going to be imperfections. It is hard not to smile when you watch the documentary *Enron: The Smartest Guys in the Room* and see both President Bushes on a video birthday card to an executive saying that Enron is a model for corporations of the future (Cox, Friedman, & Edwards, 2009). And, while Enron was a high profile example, such mismanagement is a potential problem in most big companies (Bryce, 2005).

Academic research on voters who hate government has generally fallen into three broad categories—political cynicism, political skepticism, and the hostile media phenomenon. Political cynics generally hate politics and politicians, and they often cut themselves off from political activities. Political cynicism is associated with decreased interest in political campaigns and in civic participation (Capella & Jamieson, 1997). This cynicism is not the same as political apathy. Political apathy is a lack of interest in the political process; political cynics, conversely, have participated in the political process, but they have grown distrustful of that process. Political cynics become so distrustful of politics that they quit paying attention to political messages. As a result, they remove themselves off from politics, since they don't trust the political system or the politicians in it.

That low level of trust distinguishes political cynicism from political skepticism (Capella & Jamieson, 1997; Pinkleton & Austin, 2001). The core factor influencing political skepticism is doubt, not lack of trust (Tsfati & Cappella, 2005). Political skeptics pay attention to political messages, but they simply don't believe much of what they hear. They process the information in the message, but they question its truthfulness. That leads them to make delayed decisions, i.e., they don't decide whether they agree with a new political message until they have time to gather more information and evaluate it. Skeptical voters are highly active voters, but slow to act or react. They refuse to accept political messages at face value, but actively seek additional evidence that supports, refutes, or modifies the initial information. They stay involved in the political process, but they don't quickly take sides. Their skepticism typically expands beyond politics to the realm of advertising, where they are skeptical about price claims or other points advocated by a retailer (Hardestry, Carlson, & Beardeen, 2002).

Quite often, people who hate politics also hate political media. More specifically, they often blame the media for negative coverage about their favorite candidate, a phenomenon known at the Hostile Media Effect. Scholars sometimes trace this effect back to the 1970s and the reelection campaign of President Richard Nixon and his label on-going disagreement with the press (Liebovich, 2003). Nixon pursued a strategy in which he changed references to journalism from "the press" to "the media," under the assumption that the later terms had no connotations of objectivity (Nolan, 2005). The campaign was aided by Vice President Spiro Agnew and his "nattering nabobs of negativism" description of the media (Barone, 1996; Hart, 1994). Research on the hostile media effect has found that perceptions media bias exceeds that of reality (e.g., Kyun & Yorgo, 2007), but exceptions are made of cable channels such as Fox News and MSNBC (Coe et al., 2008), which deliberately seek biased audiences. In addition, Stadler (2009) found the perceptions of hostile media were rarely based on what people heard or saw in the media, but rather what they heard about the media from other people. Such research led Matheson and Durson (2001) to conclude that hatred for the media was largely a perception based on in-group bias. For those who hate political media, though, that doesn't matter. They have an easy scapegoat to blame for political problems and their hatred of politics in general.

Given so much hatred directed toward politics and the political system, many politicians are justifiably worried about how voters will respond to them. Not all, however, hate government. A significant number still like their government and its services. For example, while former Republican Congressman Dick Army of Texas said there was no place in a free society for Social Security (McIntire, 2001), Republicans in Congress have not pushed to eliminate it. When Medicare was first proposed, the American Medical Association (AMA) screamed "socialized medicine." They were unwilling to believe a number of senior citizens simply did not go to the doctor because they could not pay for it. It took less than a year for the AMA to discover that the basic assumption for Medicare was correct. There were many older people who never went to the doctor because they could not afford to go. Social Security and Medicare are now sacred cows to the American people and no politician would seriously propose eliminating them.

Some events clearly show that Americans expect government to rescue them. Consider the aftermaths of hurricanes Katrina, Rita, and Sandy. As the former head of FEMA (Federal Emergency Management Agency) testified before Congress, the nature of the American disposition was clearly demonstrated. Michael Brown, or "Brownie" as President Bush referred to him, testified that FEMA had been reduced in staff and financial resources by conservatives in Congress. Thus, he did not have the needed resources to do his job after Hurricane Katrina hit New Orleans. Brown tried to blame the local governments, saying they did not meet their responsibility. During the same news program, the media produced a FEMA document which said they knew the state and local government would be overwhelmed with a major hurricane. In fact, public trust in government significantly declined following the aftermath of Hurricane Katrina (Nicholls & Picou, 2013). That led to a point of political irony: a conservative Bush appointee, Brown, testified before Republican members of Congress, who also voted for less government at FEMA, and all these conservatives tried to place blame somewhere else because the public was in an uproar because the Federal government could not respond with enough resources to handle the crisis (Block, 2006).

The New Orleans debacle was a classic example of people wanting to reduce the size of government but simultaneously demanding that more government intervention was needed. The Republicans in power had aggressively tried to cut the size of many agencies in the federal government (although expanding some others). The result? A massive disaster that only a strong federal government could handle, but a government that was not equipped to meet public expectations. By the time of Hurricane Sandy in 2012, FEMA seemed to be prepared to handle the problem (Krugman, 2012), but Congress (mostly Republicans in the House) was still slow to allocate disaster aid for the area.

Such problems have been created by the attitude that government is bad and we need to get government out of our lives. For example, the following problems were reported on the news during a single three-week period in 2005 and they include:

(1) Most of the National Guard troops were out of the country. Why? Because playing to the idea of government being smaller, there were simply not enough troops to invade and manage the aftermath of a war in Iraq. A number of sources reported that the Bush administration was informed of this fact by military advisors, but it was ignored. When it was obvious that more forces were needed, they had the choice between a draft and taking the National Guard from the states. A draft would have meant an expansion of government power and loss of public support for the war. Thus the only real option was to use the National Guard. Of the 4,000 men and women in Louisiana's National Guard, their commander told the news media that 3,000 of them were in Iraq. Welcome to smaller government. Overall, 40,000 National Guard troops, which accounted for 50 percent of the combat load, were in Iraq in 2005 (Freedberg, 2006).

(2) New Orleans was in chaos after Hurricane Katrina (Whoriskey & Gugliotta, 2005). The people who could not evacuate were given conflicting instructions as to where to go: the Super Dome or the convention center. Frustration and anger lead to violence. As the Insurance Commissioner of Louisiana told one of the authors, "New Orleans is now the law of the Pecos. You better have a gun." Many observers openly questioned the ability of the government to handle the crisis (Sullivan, 2005).

(3) After trying to blame local officials, state officials, the bureaucracy and finding his poll numbers continuing to sink, President Bush said we can't

play the blame game. The downsizing of government was exactly what President Bush and his Party promised the voters during the 2004 election.

Those examples all came from the George W. Bush administration, but plenty examples of governmental dysfunction are also available from Barack Obama's tenure in office. Consider these events:

1. The federal government went four consecutive years with no budget. Partisan bickering resulted in no real effort to address budget needs for four years as the two sides fought over cutting spending and raising taxes (Schlapp, 2013).
2. The House of Representatives rejected a new Farm Bill after negative votes from both Republicans and Democrats. Democrats voted against the proposal because they argued that it cut too deeply into the Food Stamp program. Republicans voted against it because they argued that it didn't cut enough (Nixon, 2013).
3. Congress was unable to pass an immigration package. The failure to pass this legislation came even though it had support from elected officials in both parties. Some in Congress objected because it might be viewed as amnesty bill for illegal aliens. Some wanted tougher control of the borders. As a result, nothing happened.

The head of the Veterans Administration had to resign under pressure after reports that veterans were waiting for months to see a doctor at VA hospitals. Some veterans died before they had a chance to keep their appointment. Overall, the scandal raised serious questions about the quality of care that was provided for the nation's vets.

Ironically, trust in government soared after the terrorist attacks in September, 2001 (Heatherington & Husser, 2012). The voters reelected Bush by more than three million votes, and the President claimed he had a "mandate" for his policies. However, less than a year after his reelection, the voters were upset because there was not enough government to address the hurricane situation (Hsu & Goldstein, 2006). Eventually, trust in government reached such a low level that one observer questioned whether the public could trust government again (Madrick, 2012).

Do these voters' conflicting attitudes about government mean they are stupid? No. It means that most Americans are not political scientists, journalists or political junkies. They are busy people with busy lives who receive contrasting messages on a daily basis. If these messages were analyzed, it would show that they are often contradictory, but sometimes the uninvolved voter simply accepts them both. Psychologists call this phenomenon cognitive dissonance, and it's a common aspect of political attitudes (e.g., Lashley, 2009).

How do voters decide which side of the message is going to be the basis of their reactions at any given time? That depends on their personal situation at the moment. Former Speaker of the House Tip O'Neill is credited with creating one of the most frequently used political clichés, i.e., "All politics Is local." That saying was probably true during the time of O'Neill's politics, but political realities are different today. Now, all politics are personal. The voters have shifted their attitudinal anchors from issues to identity politics (Monroe, Hankin, & Van Vechten, 2000). They are more concerned about ideology than about pragmatic performance.

Voters are bombarded daily with messages from advertisers, issue messages, and groups looking for support. Try this experiment. The next time you are filling up your car with gas at the convenience store, see if you can count the number of persuasive-oriented messages you see. Odds are that you will finish filling up your car before you finish counting the messages. Americans get messages only in small bites because they won't take the time to analyze complex messages. Between junk mail, television ads, telemarketing, and visual messages, people have to filter communication and selectively let information into their minds to evaluate. People test communication against one question—Why should I care?

There are messages that people care about. People care about their money. People care about their children. People care about their family's safety. People care about their jobs. People care about their homes.

Average people do not care about governmental processes. Average people do not care about inside politics. Average people do not care about why a politician thinks he/she is the best leader. Average people do not care about government programs, Congressional committee meetings, or white papers from policy groups.

Voters truly pay attention only when an event is so large and has such an impact, either physically or emotionally on the public that everyone knows about it. One of the authors has a friend who said he never reads the newspaper or watches the news. When asked why, he said, "if something important happens, someone will tell me." His observation reflects the average voter. A 9/11, a hurricane, or a tragedy with the space shuttle will result in so many channels of information talking about it, basically everyone will know the details of the story. On a day-to-day basis, however, information comes to people in small bites, slogans, and symbols like the golden arches.

When Americans are deciding upon the person to be President, they do not seek in-depth information. In 2000 and 2004, less than half the number of people who voted watched the Presidential debates (Rutenberg, 2004). In 2004, FOX News did not even cover the second debate because there was a conflict with a baseball playoff game. While participants in focus group research will tell pollsters they want more information about the candidates for public office and how the candidates plan to solve problems, most will not spend an hour-and-a-half learning about Presidential candidates. Imagine how much less information seeking the voters do about candidates for Congress or the state Legislature?

Voters also tell pollsters they hate political television ads, especially the negative ones. Yet, while voters will not watch an hour-long debate of two Congressional candidates, they will see the television ads for those candidates and those ads will persuade them. The average U.S. home has a television on six hours and forty-seven minutes per day and the average American will see more than two million television ads by the age of sixty-five (Herr, 2012)

Thus the American electorate, the people who political candidates must persuade, is overworked, over-stressed, and sitting in front of their televisions. They are not having political discussions with family and friends or going to debates at the local Rotary Club. They are bombarded with advertisements and handling information in small bites. They both love and hate government and do not see any need to be consistent in their political opinions. These are the people the political parties must persuade to put them in control of the most powerful nation on earth.

Thus the reason that politicians fear the voting public. Those voters hold sets of contradictory attitudes that can shift, during any election, and change the balance of power among the parties. The winner of one election can be the loser of the next. There is little political security, regardless of which party you support.

REFERENCES

Barone, M. (1996, September 30). The rise and fall of Spiro Agnew. *U.S. News & World Report*, 121(13), 28.

Block, Robert (2006, February 11). Katrina hearings put new pressure on White House. *Wall Street Journal*, 247(35), A3.

Bryce, R. (2005). *Pipe dreams: Greed, ego and the death of Enron.* New York: PublicAffairs.

Capella, J. N., & Jamieson, K. H. (1997). *The spiral of cynicism: The press and the public good.* New York: Oxford.

Cassiman, S. A. (2006). Of witches, welfare queens, and the disaster named poverty: The search for a counter narrative. *Journal of Poverty*, 10(4), 51–66.

Coe, K., Tewksbury, D. Bond, B. J., Drogos, K. L., Porter, R. W., Yahn, A., & Zhang, Y. (2008). Hostile news: Partisan use and perceptions of cable news programming. *Journal of Communication*, 58, 201–19.

Cox, P. L., Friedman, B. A., & Edwards, A. (2009). Enron: The smartest guys in the room— Using the Enron film to examine student attitudes toward business ethics. *Journal of Behavioral and Applied Management*, 10(2), 263–90.

Drake, G. (1970). Welfare Cadillac. Royal American Music.

Freedberg, S. J., Jr. (2006, March 11). Reservists coming home. *National Journals*, 38(10), 63–64.

Hardesty, D. M., Carlson, J. P., & Bearden, W. O. (2002). Brand familiarity and invoice price effects on consumer evaluations: The moderating role of skepticism toward advertising. *Journal of Advertising*, 31(2), 1–15.

Hart, R. P. (1998). *Seducing America: How television charms the modern voter.* Thousand Oaks, CA: Sage.

Heatherington, Marc, & Husser, Jason A. (2012). How trust matters: The changing political relevance of political trust. *American Journal of Political Science*, 56, 312–25.

Herr, N. (2002). Television & health. The Sourcebook for Teaching Science, http://www.csun.edu/~vceed002/health/docs/tv&health.html.

Hsu, S. S., & Goldstein, A. (2006, Feb 2). Administration faulted on Katrina; GAO report blames bungled responses on failures that started at the top. *Washington Post*, A5.

Jeffrey, C., & Bauerlein, M. (2011, Sep/Oct). Boehner's handicap. *Mother Jones*, 36(5), 2.

Kissinger, H. (1970). Public comments on Chile, prior to Augusto Pinochet's U.S.-supported / CIA-facilitated military coup against Chile's democratically-elected President Salvador Allende.

Kohler-Hausman, J. (2007). The crime of survival: Fraud prosecutions, community surveillance, and the original 'Welfare Queen.' *Journal of Social History*, 41, 329–54.

Krugman, P. (2012, November 4). Sandy versus Katrina. *New York Times*, A27.

Kyun, S. K., & Yorgo, P. (2007). Study of partisan news readers reveals hostile media perceptions of balanced stories. *Newspaper Research Journal*, 28(2), 99–106.

Lashley, M. (2009). The politics of cognitive dissonance: Spin, media and race (ethnicity) in the 2008 U.S. presidential election. *American View of Canadian Studies*, 39, 364–74.

Liebovich, L. W. (2003). *Richard Nixon, Watergate & the press: A historical perspective.* Westport, CT: Praeger.

Lipton, E. (2010, September 12). G.O.P. leaders tightly bound to lobbyists. *New York Times*, A1.

Madrick, Jeff (2012, April 9). Can we trust government again? *Nation*, 294(15), 11–13.

Matheson, K., & Dursun, S. (2001). Social identity precursors to the hostile media phenomenon: Partisan perceptions of coverage of the Bosnian Conflict. *Group Processes & Intergroup Relations*, 4(2), 116–25.

McIntire, R. S. (2001). Armey's austerity. *American Prospect*, 12(14), 6–7.

Monroe, K. R., Hankins, J., & Van Vechten, R. B. (2000). The psychological foundations of identity politics. *Annual Review of Political Science*, 3(1), 419–48.

Nicholls, Keith, & Picou, J. Steven (2013). The impact of Hurricane Katrina on trust in government. *Social Science Quarterly*, 94, 344–61.

Nixon, Ron (2013, June 21). House defeat of Farm Bill lays bare rift in G.O.P. *New York Times*, A12, A15.

Nolan, M. R. (2005). Orwell meets Nixon: When and why 'the press' became 'the media': *Harvard International Journal of Press/Politics*, 10(2), 69–84.

Pear, R. (1997, July 17). Audit of Medicare finds $23 billion in overpayments. *New York Times*, A1.

Pinkleton, B., & Austin, E. (2001). Individual motivations, perceived media importance, and political disaffection. *Political Communication*, 18, 321–34.

Rutenberg, J. (2004, November 2). First debate draws large TV audience. *New York Times*, A10.

Samuel, T., Pound, E. T., & Streisand, B. (2005, August 29). Snake eyes for 'Casino Jack.' *U.S. News & World Report*, 139(7), 34–40.

Schlapp, Mercedes (2013, March 29). Obama and Democrats offer no real budget path. *U.S. News Digital Weekly*, 5(13), 19.

Seccombe, K. (2010). *So you think I drive a Cadillac? Welfare recipients perspectives on the system and its reforms* (3rd ed.). Boston: Pearson.

Stadler, D. R. (2009). Political orientation, hostile media perceptions, & group centrism. *North American Journal of Psychology*, 11(2), 383–400.

Sullivan, K. (2005, Sept 4). How could this be happening in the United States. *Washington Post*, A12.

Tsfati, Y., & Cappella, J. N. (2005). Why do people watch news they do not trust? The need for cognition as a moderator in the association between news media skepticism and exposure. *Media Psychology*, 7(3), 251–71.

Tsfati, Y., & Peri, Y. (2006). Mainstream media skepticism and exposure to sectorial and extranational news media: The case of Israel. *Mass Communication & Society*, 9, 165–87.

'Welfare queen' becomes issue in Reagan campaign (1976, February 15). *New York Times*, A51.

Whoriskey, P., & Gugliotta, G. (2005, August 30). Storm thrashes Gulf Coast; Dozens are reported dead in one Mississippi County. *Washington Post*, A1.

Chapter Seven

Republicans versus Democrats

The Democratic Party and the Republican Party have developed along different paths. Further, the events that shaped the two parties are different than the historical events that shaped the country. Regardless, in the modern era, both American political parties can trace their present incarnations to six elections—1964, 1980, 1992, 2004, 2010, and 2012.

1964: JOHNSON VERSUS GOLDWATER

By 1964, the late President Kennedy and President Johnson had started the country on a radical new course. After the "happy days" of the 1950s, with the steady and father-figure President Dwight Eisenhower, the 1960s began a period of rapid change. Political consultants often point to the 1960 Presidential campaign as the beginning of modern political campaigns (Donaldson, 2007), because television became recognized for its potential power to influence electoral politics. Perhaps no political event has ever been the subject of more study than the Kennedy-Nixon debates (White, 1964).

During the period between 1960 through 1964, the Kennedy/Johnson administration pushed the federal government into a much more active role in American life. Civil rights legislation which guaranteed and protected African Americans' right to vote and equal access to public facilities was passed. A universal health care plan for senior citizens was introduced that would eventually become Medicare (Helm, 1999). NASA began its manned space flight program in an effort to beat the Soviets in a race to the moon. Federal funding for public education was greatly increased. The nation had been frightened to near panic by the Cuban missile crisis and the Cold War almost went hot (Dobbs, 2009). Against this backdrop, the 1964 Presidential election rolled around.

The Democrats did not have a primary contestant. Their sitting President, Lyndon Johnson, had stepped into the Presidency as a shocked nation tried to make sense of the assassination of their young President, John F. Kennedy (Swanson, 2013). Johnson chose a traditional liberal, U.S. Senator Hubert H. Humphrey, as his vice presidential candidate (Johnson, 2009).

The Republicans lined up three candidates who reached from right to left of the political spectrum. On the left was Governor Nelson Rockefeller of New York, the moderate was Governor William Stanton of Pennsylvania, and the conservative was Barry Goldwater of Arizona. Their nominee was the conservative U.S. Senator, Barry Goldwater. Senator Goldwater was a strong voice against communism and big government (Middendorf, 2008). He believed in maximum individual liberty. Later in his political career, Goldwater expressed extreme dislike of fundamentalist Christian groups, like the Christian Coalition because these groups desired government intrusion in individual's lives (Goldberg, 1995).

While polling was still a relatively new science, and distrusted by many politicians, all the gauges of public opinions suggested a landslide was going to occur. One of the undocumented stories from this campaign concerns President Johnson's refusal to have a live, televised debate as occurred in the 1960 Nixon–Kennedy election. According to legend, a young aide asked the President, "Mr. President, I do not understand. All the polls say we have a large lead. When Senator Goldwater tells the voters where he stands, everyone will know he is too conservative to be President. I do not understand why we would not debate him?" The President turned to the young aid and said, "Son, you have to understand about live TV debates. You might just say oral sex when you meant Australia."

There were no Freudian slips, and it was a devastating landslide defeat for the Republican Party. Senator Goldwater only won five Southern states, basically as a backlash to the civil rights legislation, plus his home state of Arizona. Senator Goldwater lost the popular vote by 15 million votes, and received less than 40 percent of all popular votes cast. For the Democrats, it was confirmation the voters liked the direction of the government. So, it was full steam ahead and focused on running the government. Despite the beginning concerns about a little war in the distant land of Vietnam, everything had come up roses for the Democrats.

For the Republicans, the loss was a rejection of the basic tenet at the foundation of the Republican Party. At the time, the national Republicans had one idea that kept the Goldwaters and the Rockefellers in the same political party, i.e., big government is bad for business. If it is bad for business, it is bad for America. Americans do not like big government. Big government will limit the individual's freedom. Yet, the American voters had overwhelmingly supported a President and party that was expanding the national government in every direction.

However, his campaign is still viewed by many as the beginning of the modern conservative movement (Middendorf, 2013). After this defeat, the Republicans set out on a mission to find a way to sell the message of conservatism. In the decade of the 1970s, the Republicans began attempts to redefine conservatism in two different dimensions—the fiscal definition and the social definition. The effort on redefining the concepts in a way that would persuade a majority of Americans to support the ideas led to the creation of think-tank groups to work on ways to present their message and reach out to voters.

Several new organizations were founded, many of them still very much a part of the extreme right-wing of the Republican Party. In 1972, Phyllis Schlafly created the Eagle Form to fight what she called "radical feminism" in the form of the Equal Rights Amendment (Critchlow, 2005). Ms. Schlafy's group continues in strong operation today. She writes a syndicated newspaper column and has a three-minute radio commentary five days a week that is carried on more than 450 radio stations.

The Heritage Foundation was founded in 1973 (Edwards, 2013). This group's mission statement says they believe in "individual liberty, free enterprise, limited government, a strong national defense, and American values." This group is credited with redefining the estate tax as the "death tax."

In 1974, Paul Weyrich and beer magnate Joseph Coors founded the Committee for Survival of a Free Congress, now known as the Free Congress Foundation (Gizzi, 2010). It was founded for the purposes of examining public policies in social and family areas and to conduct studies of the electoral process. These men wanted to create a new political activist group that was to the political right of the Republican Party, which they viewed as being too moderate.

Direct mail fund raising guru Richard Viguerie founded the National Conservative Political Action Committee or NCPAC in 1975. This group was to become the real political campaign operation of the right wing. In the 1980 election cycle, this operation targeted six United States Senators and fourteen members of the United States House of Representatives for defeat. By using third-party negative attacks, they are given credit for defeating four of the Senators and twelve members of the U.S. House (Kitchens & Powell, 1986).

In 1979, Reverend Jerry Falwell created the Moral Majority to push fundamentalist Christians to action in the political arena (Webber, 1981). It disbanded in 1989, with Reverend Falwell saying he was devoting more time to Liberty University. The Moral Majority's agenda included the censorship of media outlets that promoted what the Moral Majority labeled as "anti-family" programming. In 1989, the organization morphed into the Christian Coalition led by Pat Robertson (Watson, 1999).

In 1977, one interesting conservative group was founded by Edward H. Crane, the CATO Institute (Boaz, 2009). The CATO Institute's mission statement says it seeks "to broaden the parameters of public debate to allow consideration of the traditional American principles of limited government, individual liberty, free markets, and peace." This group is unlike many of the other groups because they are truly interested in public policy related to economics, not in hot button social issues. They are as likely to criticize a Republican as a Democrat. On their Web site they say, "We reject the bashing of gays, Japan, rich people, and immigrants that contemporary liberals and conservatives seem to think addresses society's problems."

All of these conservative groups tested messages, examined new policies, and began taking aim at a broader base of voters. The next critical election rolled around.

1980: CARTER VERSUS REAGAN

The 1980 election was the first time right-wing groups began producing paid communication with groups called "independent expenditure campaigns" (Smith et al., 2010). These groups were supposedly independent of any candidate and were forbidden by law from coordinating with candidates. However, enforcement of this idea was virtually impossible. They were the attack force against the Democrats.

James Earl Carter, the unlikely Naval Academy graduate, peanut farmer and former Governor of Georgia, was elected as President in 1976. He rode to Washington as an outsider in the wake of the Watergate scandal that had forced Richard Nixon to resign as President (Bourne, 1997). The conservative movement inside the Republican Party was stifled by Jimmy Carter. He openly talked about being a born-again Christian and a Southern Baptist. He campaigned on trust and promised to never lie to the American people. After impeachment hearings and a war in Vietnam that seemed to never end, the American people seemed to say they were ready for some gentle Southern style.

However, the world events did not give President Carter or the country a chance to take a breath and relax. As the 1980 election approached, President Carter was being hamstrung with runaway inflation, OPEC's attempt to hold America hostage at the gas pump, and America feeling like the country was helpless in the face of young Iranians storming the American Embassy in Tehran and holding sixty-seven Americans hostage (Wright, 1996).

As the election approached, President Carter was challenged on the political left from his own party by Senator Edward Kennedy. Having a sitting President challenged from within his own party is a political aberration in

American politics. It did not help the public perceptions of President Carter in any way.

The Republicans had a contest that became one of the most significant struggles for the Republican Party. In hindsight, this indicated the battle for the American electorate and how it was going to be different than at any other time in the twentieth century. Representing the far-right and the newly empowered Republican social conservatives like the Moral Majority was former Governor Ronald Reagan. Representing the traditional business Republicans and the moderate wing of the party was former Congressman and CIA chief George H. Bush.

The campaign was spirited. Governor Reagan promised to balance the federal budget, increase defense spending, and cut taxes. Although it was never clear how this would be accomplished; the far right rejoiced. At one point, George Bush referred to this economic plan as "voo-doo" economics. Despite the harsh tone of the primary campaign, the two contenders cut an alliance between the two wings of the Republican Party and George H. Bush accepted the Vice-Presidential spot on the Republican ticket.

When Ronald Reagan received sufficient delegate support to win the nomination, most strong Democratic loyalists were overjoyed and thought the election was over. They felt Ronald Reagan would be another Barry Goldwater; far too conservative for the country. This situation might be referred to as one of those times when you should be careful what you wish for, as you might get it.

From the day Ronald Reagan was nominated to the day he left the Presidency, Democrats and at least some of the press complained that he would simply misstate facts to suit his purpose of the moment. When anyone directly called him on it, he would just smile, shrug and continue telling his version of reality. The public did not seem to mind and it points to the truism that it is not always about the facts. President Reagan earned the nickname of the "Teflon President" because no one could make anything bad about him stick to his image. Democrats hated Ronald Reagan for the same reason Republicans hated Bill Clinton. Both were truly great communicators who could win elections.

The 1980 election is one of the most important elections in the development of the Republican Party for one main reason. Ronald Reagan changed the basic message of the Party. Until 1980, the basic Republican message was big government is bad for business. Ronald Reagan made the new Republican message "big government is bad for you." For years, the Democrats had won elections by making big business the enemy of the average worker. Big business had one ally—the Republican Party. In 1980, Ronald Reagan changed the equation. Big government became a worse enemy than big business.

In his debate with President Carter, Ronald Reagan asked the rhetorical question, "Ask yourself. Are you better off now than you were four years ago?" There are tremendous implications to this question. First, it is the point at which all politics was no longer local. Politics became personal. Ronald Reagan argued that the voters' decision should be based on their personal well-being. He did not ask, is America better off? Is your state better off? Or, is your community better off? Second, Ronald Reagan clearly implied, stated, and argued that if you were not better off, it was because the big federal government had hindered your progress. (Kazin, 1995)

Ronald Reagan blamed the bureaucrats who were greedy and needed the hard-earned money of the taxpayer to expand power and give undeserved benefits to those who did not work. Ronald Reagan was not openly racist, but this rhetoric in the ears of Southern white voters meant the government was taking their money and giving it to African American citizens who did not work.

President Carter won only seven states plus the District of Columbia. While Ronald Reagan won a bare majority of 50.8 percent, President Carter won only 41 percent of the vote. John Anderson won 6 percent with the minor candidates winning the few remaining percentages. But, in addition to taking the White House, the Republicans took control of the United States Senate. Congressman Jim Wright was moving into the Speaker of the House position, and the battle lines were drawn. With Congressman Wright's leadership, the Democrats over-rode the veto of the Public Works Bill and the Clean Water Act. While the great communicator President Ronald Reagan could whip up the right wing fever, Congressman Wright's skills at managing the U.S. House of Representatives kept the policies of the government balanced and aligned with mainstream America.

However, the die was cast. The theocrats of the Republican Party had grabbed control of the Republican Party if not the government of the nation. The new message for the Republicans had worked. They were ready to attack big government, and they controlled two of the three major law making institutions.

Congressman Newt Gingrich of Georgia took the role of irresponsible bomb thrower and eventually brought Congressman Wright's career down with legal technicalities and the Republican propaganda machine. The *Washington Post* joined the attack on Congressman Wright and the Democrats in control of the House. The Post actually appeared to be on a crusade to change the control of the U.S. House of Representatives feeling that thirty years was enough control for Democrats. The Republicans produced their "Contract for America" and the propaganda war for the theocrats continued.

1992: BUSH VS. CLINTON

From 1968 to 1992, the Republicans won five out of six presidential elections. Their only loss was the 1976 win of Democrat Jimmy Carter, and voters quickly knocked Carter out after only one term. Ronald Reagan followed with two consecutive terms for the Republicans, then George H. W. Bush, kept the office with the Republicans by defeating Michael Dukakis in 1988.

As the 1992 election approached, the Republicans seemed poised to win another round. They had an incumbent president running for reelection, and the Democrats were having major problems with establishing a national message. The party apparatus seemed to be controlled by the extreme left and party efforts to expand the message to the middle class was met with resistance by party leaders. That in-fighting was a product of long-term pattern within the party and was one reason the party had been so unsuccessful in the previous three presidential campaigns (Harwood, 2014).

Into that vacuum stepped a young southern governor who campaigned in the primaries as "a different kind of Democrat." Bill Clinton's campaign focused on the economic dissatsifaction that had occurred during Bush's four years (Grant, 1993), talking about jobs and the economy in a way that made it personal for low- and middle-income voters (Kunde, 2009)

2004: BUSH VERSUS KERRY

The third critical election in terms of defining the political parties is the 2004 election. For the Democrats, this election should have felt like an earthquake, rated a 7 on the Richter scale. The truth is, the 2000 election should have felt this way, but the Democrats were convinced the Presidential election was stolen and they made slight gains in Congress. They failed to understand what was really happening.

During the decade of the 1990s, the Republican propaganda machine grew stronger, and it was paying off in terms of elections. In 1992, while Bill Clinton was winning the Presidency, the Democrats lost ten seats in the House of Representatives. In 1994, the control of the U.S. House of Representatives went to the Republicans for the first time in forty years. The House of Representatives has been in Republican hands ever since except for a two-year period after the Barack Obama election. By 1994, 53 percent of the U.S. Senators were Republicans.

The election of 2000 gave the Democrats a ray of hope; although it turned out to be false hope. The Democrats picked up four U.S. Senate seats, so the split in the U.S. Senate was 50-50. They also picked up two seats in the U.S. House of Representatives. However, it remained under Republican control.

The 2004 election created a situation the Democrats had not seen since 1932. John Kerry lost the Presidency to George W. Bush. The Republicans moved to a 55-44 advantage in the U.S. Senate (with one independent). The Republicans picked up three seats in the U.S. House of Representatives, giving them 53 percent of the seats. For the first time in seventy-two years, the Democrats did not control either house of Congress or the White House. For the very first time, Democrats had no power to pass laws, control the agenda, or veto Republican initiatives. The Democrats ability to make laws during seven decades of having at least some power in Washington was gone. For the first time in nearly a century, Democrats were irrelevant in the legislative process.

As bad as the government side of the political equation was for the Democrats, the political side was even worse. The Democrats held a basic premise about electoral politics since 1932. The Democrats believed their agenda more closely matched the majority of voters than the Republican agenda. Therefore, winning campaigns was really a matter of voter turnout. If enough people voted, then Democrats would win. In the 2000 Presidential election, just over 105 million votes were cast, and the election was too close to call. The results eventually had to be decided by the courts. In 2004, more than 122 million votes were cast. With the largest voter turnout in history, the basic assumption for the Democratic Party would indicate Americas would be seeing President Kerry on television. But, George W. Bush won reelection by more than three million votes.

For the first time in nearly a century, the Democratic Party faced the fact that elections were not just about turning out voters. They had to try to win the electorates' hearts and minds. This election was as devastating for the Democrats as 1964 was for the Republicans. The unanswered question at this point was how would the Democrats respond? The opportunity was sitting on the table because the Republicans got what they wanted. They had the power and were a disaster in terms of governing. Inside the Republican Party, the tail, a.k.a. the extreme right, was wagging the dog.

2010 MID-TERM ELECTIONS—WELCOME TO THE TEA PARTY

In 2008, Barack Obama became the first African American President and the Democrats gained control of both the U.S. House and U.S. Senate. The 2008 election contest was close for most of the race. While the Democrats had chosen a young, charismatic African American candidate, the Republicans had chosen a much respected U.S. Senator and Vietnam War hero John McCain. The "fresh face" of Obama was gathering support and fascinated voters. Even so, going into the Republican convention, the outcome was not decided.

The Republicans made a high risk strategic move and McCain picked Alaskan Governor Sarah Palin as his Vice Presidential candidate. Governor Palin had the liabilities of being unknown and from one of the two states not part of the lower 48 states. However, she was an attractive woman in her forties which matched up generationally with Barack Obama and trumped the fact the Democrats did not have a woman on the ticket (Barnes, 2008). In addition, Palin was known as a strong conservative with strong anti-abortion views. McCain, always know as a centrist, could shore up the right wing of his own party with Palin on the ticket. The day after her nomination, Rush Limbaugh pronounced on this talk show, "We finally have a candidate that believes in guns, God, and babies."

The Republicans ticket was doomed more by current events than their campaign strategy. On September 29, 2008, the Dow Jones Industrial Average dropped by 3260 points, a decline of 29 percent in the index. The major reason for the drop was a crash of the housing market. Through a series of schemes, the mortgage bankers were loaning money to consumers that they knew could not pay the mortgages. The Wall Street investment bankers were bundling good loans with bad and selling them as all good mortgages. An excellent account of the events can be found in Michael Lewis' (2010) book *The Big Short: Inside the Doomsday Machine.*

The collapse of the financial markets and the actions of the Obama administration to the crisis gave birth to a new populist movement, the TEA Party. The party's acronym stands for Taxed Enough Already. This movement is somewhat different than other populist movements in America and its impact is still being played out. Historically, populist movements arise during times of economic hardships. William Jennings Bryan's Populist Party in the 1890s and Huey Long's Share Our Wealth in the 1930s are good examples. In his book, *The Populist Persuasion: An American History*, Michael Kazin finds common elements to populist movements in America. Two of the main elements are an attack on the banking establishment and the government's support of it, and an element of racism, as demonstrated by George Wallace's "Working man" rhetoric during the 1960s and 1970s. The Tea Party movement has some of the same elements, but it has some unique elements.

The beginning of this movement is generally attributed to a comment made by a CNBC correspondent, Rick Santelli. When President Obama announced his mortgage relief plan to help consumers who could not pay their mortgage, Santelli, speaking from the floor of the Chicago Mercantile Exchange, called the action a plan to "subsidize mortgage losers." The clip of his angry speech went viral on the Internet, probably representing the first time a social movement was created by social media. His appeal aroused average people who had seen billions of tax dollars go to financial institutions who had created the crisis. Unlike previous American populist movements that focus their ire on big business and bankers, the Tea Party focused anger on the federal government and argued the free market would solve the problem. Looking back to the 1980 election, President Reagan convinced the public that big government was more of a problem than big business. Thirty years later, the message still worked. Over a span of only a few months, Tea Party groups begin organizing throughout the country, communicating through social media and cheered on by conservative commentators such as Glenn Beck. Governor Sarah Palin resigned as Governor of Alaska to become the voice of the Tea Party.

In 2009, the Democrats were busying moving government in the direction they wanted to go and handed the Tea Party two issues to help their movement continue. The concern over healthcare insurance was a major talking point for Barack Obama. Democrats railed against the insurance industry on issues denial of coverage for pre-existing conditions and forcing you people off their parents' policies as soon as they finished college. Instead of moving on a few issues, the Congress wrote the Health Care Reform Act, commonly called Obamacare. The law was somewhere between 10,000 and 20,000 pages of regulation changes. Before voting for it, some Democrats admitted that they had not read the law.

The conservative media went on the attack accusing the Democrats of a government takeover of the healthcare system, and even charging the law set up "death panels." The claim was the law would deny health care to senior citizens and mentally retarded children. Tea Party leaders organized protests across the country, including in Washington, DC, Congresswoman Michele Bachman (R-MN) called for people to take off work to attend the protests (Kindy, 2009). When member of Congress returned home for the August recess, they were met with angry constituents at town hall meeting (Urbina, 2009).

The other issue that fed the Tea Party movement was immigration reform. This issue became the racist component that Kazin points out is a common element in populist movements. Labeling immigration reform as "amnesty for illegal aliens" became a rallying cry. Heading for the 2010 elections, the populist movement had a clear and simple set of messages for the campaign.

One unique feature of this populist movement is related to its financing. One reporter referred to the Tea Party as an Astroturf movement—meaning a fake grassroots movement (Monbiot, 2010). This charge came because it was discovered the Koch brothers, millionaire industrialists, had provided millions of dollars for the movement. The Koch brothers have been associated with libertarian and anti-government groups for years. However, big business had never financed a populist movement. Other evidence also indicates that the major tobacco companies were providing funding for the Tea Party Movement (Jarvis, 2013).

As the 2010 election approached, the Tea Party began fielding candidates. The Tea Party candidates did not take aim at only Democrats. They entered Republican primary elections, even against incumbent Governors and U.S. Senators (Espo, 2010). Any Republican who was viewed as a "compromiser" with President Obama and the Democrats was not safe.

The Democrats entered the 2010 elections arguing they had kept their promise to change America. As political analyst Charlie Cook pointed out, the election was an up-and-down election on the Democrats (Cook, 2010). The national polls showed that only 30 percent of the electorate felt the country was headed in the right direction. This attitude is always critical for whether the electorate is happy and will likely return incumbents, or unhappy and will vote incumbents out of office.

The Republicans won a huge victory, regaining 63 seats in the U.S. House, the most since 1948. In the U.S. Senate, the Democratic margin was cut from a 58-seat to a 40-seat advantage to a 51-seat to a 47-seat advantage. But, where did the Tea Party fit into this equation. Tea Party candidates won 39 seats in the U.S. House of Representatives and five U.S. Senate seats. In the U.S. House, 62 percent of the freshman class were members of the Tea Party movement. Because the Tea Party is part of the Republicans movement, other Members of Congress started falling in line with the Tea Party ideas to protect their political careers from a primary election. Today, estimates of Tea Party sympathizers who are in Congress range as low a 55 to a high of 144. Whatever the exact number, it is clear this political movement is a force in the Republican Party.

REFERENCES

Barnes, Robert (2008). McCain Picks Alaska Governor; Palin First Woman on GOP Ticket. *Washington Post*. August 30, 2008.

Boaz, David (ed.) (2009). *Cato Handbook for Policymakers (7th. ed.)*. Washington, DC: Cato Institute.

Bourne, Peter G. (1997). *Jimmy Carter: A comprehensive biography from Plains to post-presidency*. New York: Scribner.

Critchlow, Donald T. (2005). *Phyllis Schlafly and Grassroots Conservatism: A Woman's Crusade*. Princeton, NJ: Princeton University Press.

Cook, Charlie (2010). Storm clouds gathering for the democrats. *The Washington Quarterly*. October, 2010.

Dobbs, Michael (2009). *One Minute to Midnight: Kennedy, Khrushchev, and Castro on the Brink of Nuclear War*. New York: Vintage.

Donaldson, Gary A. (2007). *The First Modern Campaign: Kennedy, Nixon and the Election of 1960*. Lanham, MD: Rowman & Littlefield.

Edwards, Lee (2013). *Leading the Way: Ed Feulner and the Heritage Foundation*. New York: Crown.

Galbraith, John Kenneth (1962, March 2). *Letter to President John F. Kennedy*. Published in John Kenneth Galbraith (1969). *Ambassador's Journal*. Chicago: Houghton Mifflin.

Gizzi, John (2010, February 15). Free Congress Foundation. *Human Events*, 66(7), 26.

Goldberg, Robert Alan (1995). *Barry Goldwater*. New Haven, CT: Yale University.

Grant, Alan (1993). The 1992 US presidential election. *Parliamentary Affairs*, 46(2), 239–54.

Harwood, John (2014, July 5). Shut out of White House, G.O.P. looks to Democrats of 1992. *New York Times*, A13.

Jarvis, C. (2014). *The United States of dysfunction*. Houston: BKSC Media Group.

Johnson, Robert David (2009). *All the way with LBJ: The 1964 Presidential Election*. Cambridge: Cambridge University Press.

Kazin, Michael (2009).*The Populist Persuasion: An American History*. New York: HarperCollins.

Kindy, Kimerly (2009, August 25). Tea Party protest organizers target health care reform. *Washington Post*.

Kitchens, James T., & Powell, J. Larry (1986). Critical Analysis of NCPAC's Strategies in Key 1980 Races: A Third Party Negative Campaign. *The Southern Speech Communication Journal*. p. 208.

Kunde, Margaret (2009). Ronald Reagan and Bill Clinton: Personalizing the economy. Paper presented at the annual meeting of the National Communication Association. Chicago.

Lewis, Michael (2010). *The Big Short: Inside the Doomsday Machine*. New York: W.W. Norton.

Marmor, J. R. R. (2000). *The politics of Medicare (2nd ed.)*. Chicago: Aldine Transaction.

Monbiot, George (2010, October 25). The Tea Party Movement: Deluded and Inspired by Billionaires. *The Guardian*.

Middendorf, J. William (2008). *A glorious disaster: Barry Goldwater's presidential campaign and the origins of the conservative movement*. New York: Basic Books.

Smith, Melissa M., Williams, Glenda C., Powell, Larry & Copeland, Gary A. (2010). *Campaign finance reform: The political shell game*. Lanham, MD: Lexington Books.

Swanson, James L. (2013). *End of days: The assassination of John F. Kennedy*. New York: William Morrow.

Urbina, Ian (2009, June 14). Why the august recess should scare immigration reform backers. *National Journal*.

Watson, Justin (1999). *The christian coalition: Dreams of restoration, demands for recognition*. London: Palgrave Macmillan

Webber, Robert E. (1981). *The moral majority: Right or wrong*. Wheaton, IL: Crossway Books.

White, Theodore H. (1964), *The Making of the President 1960*. New York: Atheneum.

Wright, James (1996). *Balance of power*. Turner Publishing Company. Atlanta.

Chapter Eight

The Republican Party

Disaster Inside and Out

"I am frankly sick and tired of the political preachers across this country telling me as a citizen that if I want to be a moral person, I must believe in "A," "B," "C" and "D." Just who do they think they are? And from where do they presume to claim the right to dictate their moral beliefs to me? And I am even more angry as a legislator who must endure the threats of every religious group who thinks it has some God-granted right to control my vote on every roll call in the Senate. I am warning them today: I will fight them every step of the way if they try to dictate their moral convictions to all Americans in the name of conservatism." —Republican United States Senator Barry Goldwater on the Christian Right (1981)

Ever since the election of George W. Bush as president in 2000, the Republicans have had trouble using their standard argument: "It's the Democrats fault." The election of Barack Obama in 2008 provided some ability to use that argument again, but they still controlled the House of Representatives. Some of the "blame" rhetoric returned when Obama was sworn in, since it provided the GOP with some room to attribute the problems of America on those "liberal Democrats." Their argument was hampered, however, the massive debt problems and economic free-fall that occurred during the Bush administration. As of this writing, the nation is still dealing with the resulting problems.

Still, the election of Obama triggered a major reaction by factions within the Republican Party. Hatred for the president resulted in the rise of the Tea Party Republicans who based their movement on anti-tax, pro-family attitudes that were so far to the right that they bothered establishment-type conservatives. Meanwhile, business interests in the Republican Party have financed a right-wing propaganda machine like history had never seen (Smith & Powell, 2014). Both groups met with some success, but also some failures. The Tea Party developed their following by using Facebook to establish in-group identification (Morin & Flynn, 2014). This loose collection of voters is often credited with the Republicans gaining control of the House of Representatives in the 2010 midterm election, but their candidates did poorly in the 2012 elections. Some were so extreme that they allowed Democrats some easy senatorial wins and kept the Republicans from winning control of the Senate. Similarly, establishment Republicans raised hundreds of millions of dollars for the 2016 presidential campaign, but were unable to unseat President Obama (Smith & Powell, 2014).

Many problems for the Republicans can be traced back to the eight years in which George W. Bush led the party from the White House. After the 9/11 attacks in 2001, for example, America had support and sympathy from around the globe. Further, when the American military launched into Afghanistan, not even the government of Iran, a neighboring country which shares an equal disdain for the United States, objected. Then, the Bush administration ignored the advice of the military and invaded Iraq (Gordon, 2012). According to a number of books and articles about the decision, the Bush administration (particularly Vice President Cheney and Secretary Rumsfield) had wanted to invade Iraq since the beginning of President Bush's first term. The invasion was strongly supported by Cheney and based on the argument that Iraq had weapons of mass destruction, an allegation that turned out to be false (Gelman, 2008). Eventually, even President Bush stopped listening to his Vice President (Baker, 2013). Still, years after the Bush administration was over, Cheney (2011) continued to press and support that argument. Rumsfeld (2011) has similarly insisted that the invasion was justified in the face of mounting evidence to the contrary.

The second problem that the Republicans created was a huge budget deficit during the administration of George W. Bush. When President Bush took office, there was a debate about what should be done with the budget surplus left by President Bill Clinton—a surplus projected to be $5.6 trillion over the following ten years (Peterson, 2010). The Republicans wanted a tax cut, while the Democrats wanted to invest the surplus into social programs. With a Republican in the White House, the Republicans won that debate. By 2005, the Congressional Budget Office projected that the budget deficit for the year was $317 billion dollars; that followed a record deficit in 2004 of $413 billion dollars. Both sets of numbers seemed of minor importance by October 2008 when the banking industry collapsed and triggered a nationwide recession.

Some Democrats believe the budget deficits were part of a Republican strategy to justify cuts in Federal programs and thus cutting the size of the federal government. However, under President Bush, the size of the Federal government actually grew tremendously (Bartlett, 2006). Instead of cutting the size of government, the Bush administration seemed more interested in (a) maintaining low tax levels for the wealthy, or cutting them even more (Kennedy, 2004), or (b) providing money from the Social Security pool to Wall Street investors (Altman, 2005). The latter proposal died from lack of public support, but the former became a long-term goal for the Republican Party that extended well past the Bush administration. The issue arguably contributed to the election of Barack Obama, who campaigned against tax cuts for the rich in opposition to proposals supported by the Republican candidates in both 2008 and 2012. In any event, the fiscal policy of the Republicans was virtually non-existent, a problem that many Republicans recognize but seem helpless to address in the face of strong opposition from within their own party.

The third problem facing the Republican Party is that many of its members base their support for a candidate on that candidate's religious beliefs. This government-by-theocracy approach alienates many middle-of-the-road voters; and, if it goes too far, it can also alienate a number of Republican voters (e.g., see the discussion in chapter 5 on the Pharisee Effect). In some instances, it has led to the nomination of unelectable candidates (e.g., Powell, 2012), or at least hurt the ticket overall, as happened when Sarah Palin was named the vice-presidential nominee for John McCain in 2008 (e.g., Powell & Hickson, 2014).

Further, if a Republican tries to demonstrate a willingness to move more to the middle on any interest, that person can incur the wrath of the religious right. President George W. Bush, for example, received significant support from the religious right in his 2000 election, but almost immediately got into trouble with the group. During Bush's first post-election press conference, Bush dodged a question about the support he got from the religious right; the move prompted James Dobson, founder of Focus on the Family, to criticize the newly elected Republican for not crediting evangelical voters for his victory (Gilgoff, 2008). It was just one example of how the right wing of the Republican Party keeps a tight control on its messages (Prior, 2014).

The religious wing of the Republican party was particularly visible on two notable occasions. One involved the case of Terri Schiavo and the question of whether she should remain on life support despite to hope of recovery. While it is understandable that her parents found it hard to give up a child, fifteen years of court battles came down on the ruling that her husband had the right and responsibility to make the decision about continuing life support. As her autopsy later proved, he and numerous doctors were clearly correct in diagnosing her as being in a vegetative state (Perry, Churchill, & Kirshner, 2005). Ms. Schiavo was beyond help by any imaginable medical knowledge. An autopsy could not even be performed for a number of days because her brain was severely destroyed and liquefied.

Regardless, the religious right maintained their protests for thirteen days, received extensive media coverage by doing so (Perry, 2006), and brought the issue to the floor of Congress (Gilgoff, 2008). Republican office holders took to the floor of the Congress invoking Ms. Schiavo's name (Kirkpatrick & Stolberg, 2005). The political overtones of their speeches became apparent when Florida Senator Mel Martinez drafted a memo on how the Republicans could use Ms. Schiavo's cause and make it a central political issue ("Verbatim," 2005). When confronted with the memo, the courageous Senator blamed the staff (Kirkpatrick, 2005). He just happened to be passing it out on the floor of the U.S. Senate. This rabble rousing created a media circus outside Schiavo's hospice facility. The result, argued Gilgoff (2008) was that neither the Democratic party nor the Republican Party benefited from the issue. As he wrote, "It was another example of the Christian Right's agenda being subverted by activists and lawmakers for the sake of symbolic action" (p. 125).

In March 2005, an ABC poll found 70 percent of Americans called Congressional intervention in this situation inappropriate and 58 percent strongly held this view. Even people who called themselves conservatives or evangelical Christians were split on the issue. By a margin of 67 percent to 19 percent, Americans felt the politicians were getting involved because they thought it was good politics, not because they were concerned about a principle ("ABC poll", 2005). In Florida, the state legislature and Governor Jeb Bush also got into the act and met with similar public reactions. A Florida statewide poll in the spring of 2005 indicated 70 percent of Florida voters said the legislature should not have gotten involved in the Terri Schiavo case. They agreed with the statement this act was a clear attempt by the legislature to take away basic individual freedoms and get government involved in personal family decisions (Kitchens, 2005). Most of the politicians behind the actions quickly realized they had misjudged their constituents and went silent. The exception was Governor Jeb Bush, who publicly attempted to smear Ms. Schiavo's husband and insinuated that he may have murdered her.

A second major example of the over-reach of the religious right came when Justice Sandra Day O'Connor resigned from the Supreme Court. The extremists of the religious right demanded that the President to pick someone who would legislate their agenda from the bench. When the President nominated his personal lawyer and friend, Harriet Miers to the Supreme Court instead, the right wing reacted in anger (Vining, 2011). She had no credentials to prove her loyalty to their cause, and they would not take the president's word that she shared their ideology. As Gilgoff (2008) wrote, the Miers' nomination was viewed by the religious right as a vindication of "fears that the four horsemen [former Attorney General Ed Meese, George H. W. Bush's White House counsel C. Boyden Gray, Federalist Society executive vice president Leonard Leo, and evangelical legal advocate Jay Sekulow] had insulated the White House from the conservative base" (p. 231). Eventually, President Bush was forced to back down, withdrawing Harriet Miers' name from the nomination even before she had a hearing in the U.S. Senate (Bush, 2005). It was a clear signal there were ideological differences between the two wings of the Republican Party.

By the end of the second administration of President George W. Bush, public opinion polls indicated that the voters of the nation had a low opinion of the incumbent. His approval ratings were only in the mid-thirties, and only one-in-four Americans thought the country was headed in the right direction. An NBC/Wall Street Journal poll found that there was no good news on either the foreign or domestic front. But, the President is not taking all the heat. When asked about Congress, only 29 percent of Americans approve of the job they were doing, while 52 percent disapprove ("NBC poll", 2005).

Had this occurred in 1980, analysts would likely predict the Republicans would lose 50 seats in Congress. In 2006, the Republicans did indeed lose seats in the House, a loss that they attributed to "the party's strategy of playing to its base rather than reaching out to moderates" (Gilgoff, 2008, p. 124). And, that was an accurate assessment of their problem. Further, the Republicans did successfully take over the House in 2010 (Bullock & Hood, 2012, Carson, 2013).

However, gaining a majority in the House didn't help Republicans gain control of power in the House, due to their internal fighting over ideology. Further, the Republican edge in House seats is not likely to change soon. Because of the skillful waging of redistricting battles, there are very few competitive seats for Congress. Both Democratic and Republican analysts generally agree that there are only about 25 competitive seats in the U.S. House of Representatives, and that number is too few to shift the balance of power in Congress to the Democrats. However, with the Republican Party effectively split into two distinct ideological camps (Phillips-Fein, 2014), getting a majority of members in the House to support any legislation is difficult.

Further, the Republicans have another internal disaster brewing. The business groups pulled the fundamentalist religious groups into the conservative movement in the 1970's, hoping to take advantage of the grassroots organizations that came with those groups. However, as Hadden and Swann (1981) noted more than twenty years ago, "when you lock horns in social conflict, it's good to have God on your side" (p. 137). Those words were prophetic. While the anti-tax, pro-big business groups wanted to have these church groups declare cultural war on the Democrats, they never intended these groups to become the majority of the Republican Party, dictating candidates and policy. However, that ended up happening. The nation's largest business group, i.e., the Chamber of Commerce, adopted a policy of supporting only Republicans in a plan that lasted through the 2012 election; that changed in

2014 after they realized that they had supported Tea Party candidates who did not share the pro-business attitudes of traditional Republicans—some of whom replaced pro-business Democrats (Nocera, 2014). In 2014, the Chamber again started supporting pro-business Democrats (Nocera, 2014). Further, the Tea Party's ideological rigidity have made it and, as a result the Republican Party, unappealing to voters of racial minorities—thus making it even harder for Republicans to win national elections (Knowles et al., 2013; Zeskind, 2012). That problem could increase in future presidential elections, particularly if Davis (2013) is correct in labeling the 2012 presidential campaign as "the last white election" (p. 5).

Currently, polling data of surveys taken in "red states" where Republicans have control indicates that a majority of Republicans identify themselves as either fundamentalists or evangelical Christians. In every case, more than 40 percent of Republican voters regularly listen to Christian radio, either for music or inspirational messages. A majority of these voters also listen to conservative talk radio for information about current affairs and politics. These voters make up a majority of core Republican voters, and they have learned how to flex their muscle. Republicans still have control of the House of Representatives, but they have little power to institute a Republican agenda in Congress. Their problem is that Republican officeholders can no longer dodge issues like the abortion, prayer in school, and anti-homosexual laws. The religious right cannot be convinced to slow down, even if public opinion polls indicate that their positions are not acceptable to most Americans. That means that the party itself has an internal "identity crisis" that it does not know how to fix (Saunders, 2014, p. 9).

The religious right-wing knows that it is now virtually impossible for a Republican candidate anywhere in the country to win a Republican primary without the support of their voters. What started as a way to expand the Republican Party and to find a pro-business message appealing to a broader spectrum of voters has resulted in Republicans becoming a party controlled by ideological fanatics (Hassett, 2010; Williamson & Skocpol, 2012). Krugman (2014) calls it an "incompetence dogma," and he wrote that the Republican Party finds itself with "a firm conviction that the government can't do anything useful—a dogmatic belief in public-sector incompetence—is now a central part of American conservatism, and the incompetence dogma has evidently made rational analysis of policy issues impossible" (p. A23).

In the final analysis, the Republican Party has created a situation in which its nominees may be unacceptable to broader, general election voters. And, even if those candidates win in November, they go to Congress to participate in a process in which there are at least three distinct ideological groups—all disagreeing about how to handle the problems of the nation. The ultimate result is stalemate, with neither party able to establish or develop a clear vision for the future of the nation.

REFERENCES

ABC news poll (2005, March 21). *ABC News*. New York.

Altman, Nancy J. (2005). *The battle for Social Security: From FDR's vision to Bush's gamble.* New York: Wiley.

Baker, Peter (2013). *Days of fire: Bush and Cheney in the White House.* New York: Anchor.

Bartlett, Bruce (2006). *Imposter: How George W. Bush bankrupted America and betrayed the Reagan legacy.* New York: Doubleday.

Bullock, Charles S., & Hood, M. V. (2012). The Tea Party, Sarah Palin, and the 2010 Congressional elections: The aftermath of the election of Barack Obama. *Social Science Quarterly*, 93(5), 1424–435.

Bush, George W. (2005, October 31). Statement announcing the withdrawal of Harriet E. Miers to be an Associate Justice of the United States Supreme Court. *Weekly Compilation of Presidential Documents*, 1608.

Carson, Jamie L. (2013). Strategic politicians, partisan roll calls, and the Tea Party: Evaluating the 2010 midterm elections. *Electoral Studies*, 32(1), 26–36.

Cheney, Dick (2011). *In my time: A personal and political memoir.* New York: Simon & Schuster.

Davis, Mike (2013). The last white election. *New Left Review*, 79, 5–52.

Fausset, Richard (2014, July 26). *Move to center divides G.O.P. in N. Carolina.* New York Times, A1, A13.

Gelman, Barton (2008). *Angler: The Cheney vice presidency.* New York: Penguin.

Gilgoff, Dan (2008). *The Jesus machine: How James Dobson, focus on the family, and evangelical America are winning the culture war.* New York: St. Martin's Griffin.

Goldwater, Barry M. (1981, September 16). Speech in the U.S. Senate. Washington, DC.

Gordon, Michael R. (2012). *The endgame: The inside story of the struggle for Iraq from George W. Bush to Barack Obama.* New York: Vintage.

Hadden, Jeffrey K., & Swann, Charles E. (1981). *Prime time preachers: The rising power of televangelism.* Reading, MA: Addison-Wesley.

Hassett, Kevin (2010, May 4). Arizona pushes GOP far to the white. *Birmingham News*, 5A.

Kennedy, Diane (2004). *Loopholes of the rich: How the rich legally make more money and pay less tax.* New York: Wiley.

Kirkpatrick, David D. (2005, April 7). Schiavo memo is attributed to a senate aide. New York Times, A20.

Kirkpatrick, David D., & Stolberg, Sheryl Gay (2005, March 22). How family's cause reached the halls of Congress. *New York Times*, A1, A18.

Kitchens, James T. (2005). A statewide poll of Florida. *The Kitchens Group*. Orlando.

Knowles, Eric D., Lowery, Brian S., Shulman, Elizabeth P., & Schaumberg, Rebecca L. (2013). Race, ideology, and the Tea Party: A longitudinal study. *PLoS One*, 8(6), 1–11.

Krugman, Paul (2014, June 27). The incompetence dogma. *New York Times*, A23.

Morin, David T., & Flynn, Mark A. (2014). We are the Tea Party!: The use of Facebook as an online political forum for the construction and maintenance of in-group identification during the GOTV weekend. *Communication Quarterly*, 62, 115–33.

NBC/Wall Street Journal poll (2005, September). *NBC News*, New York.

Nocera, Joe (2014, July 26). Chamber lost its way in right turn. *New York Times*, A19.

Perry, Joshua E. (2006). Biblical biopolitics: Judicial process, religious rhetoric, Terri Schiavo, and beyond. *Health Matrix: The Journal of Law-Medicine*, 16(2), 553–630.

Perry, Joshua E., Churchill, Larry R., & Kirshner, Howard S. (2005). The Terri Schiavo case: Legal, ethical and medical perspectives. *Annals of Internal Medicine*, 143(10), 744–48.

Peterson, Peter G. (2010). *Running on empty: How the Democratic and Republican parties are bankrupting our future and what Americans can do about it.* New York: Farrar, Straus & Giroux.

Phillips-Fein, Kim (2014). The business lobby and the Tea Party. *New Labor Forum*, 23(2), 14–20.

Powell, L. (2012). Will Mormonism keep Mitt Romney out of the White House? *Journal of Contemporary Rhetoric*, 2(2), 39–43.

Powell, L., & Hickson, M. (2014). Sarah Palin and the rhetoric of victimage: From pit bull to victim. *Journalism and Mass Communication*, 4(1), 13–25.

Prior, Francis B. (2014). Quality controlled: An ethnographic account of Tea Party messaging and action. *Sociological Forum*, 29(2), 301–17.

Rumsfeld, Donald (2011). *Known and unknown: A memoir*. New York: Sentinel.

Saunders, Paul J. (2014, March/April). The GOP's identity crisis. *National Interest*, 130, 9–19.

Smith, Melissa M., & Powell, Larry (2014). *Dark money, Super PACs, and the 2012 election*. Lanham, MD: Lexington.

Verbatim (2005, April 18). *Time*, 165(16), 19.

Vining, Richard L. (2011). Grassroots mobilization in the digital age: Interest group response to Supreme Court nominations. *Political Research Quarterly*, 64(4), 790–802.

Williamson, Vanessa, & Skocpol, Theda (2012). *The Tea Party and the Remaking of Republican Conservatism*. New York: Oxford University Press.

Zeskind, Leonard (2012). A nation dispossessed: The Tea Party Movement and race. *Critical Sociology*, 38, 495–509.

Chapter Nine

The Democratic Party

Searching for Unicorns

For centuries, people sought to capture a unicorn. There was no doubting its existence. References to unicorns are made in the writings of Aristotle, Genghis Khan, and even the Bible. These creatures were thought to bring good fortune to the person who could capture one. The horn of the unicorn was believed to be an antidote to virtually all poisons. The beautiful unicorn would signify the birth of a great leader.

Perhaps in the twenty-first century, we would think anyone who was chasing a unicorn is out of touch with reality. But, in the political arena, it seems many Democratic politicians running for office look for a magical unicorn. And, they often commit hundreds of thousands of dollars, and sometimes millions of dollars, looking for a magical beast to take them to power and reverse the Republican trend.

The vast majority of people who seek public office never try to systematically study how and why someone is elected. Because of this lack of knowledge, the candidates for office often fall prey to consultants selling the equivalent of political unicorns. There are no formal credentials. Anyone can hang out a shingle and call himself a political consultant, pollster, media consultant, or general campaign guru, regardless of their lack of qualifications. This factor has lead to an industry where there are some very successful people who are great salesmen and very poor consultants.

As the Republican approach to campaigns altered the context of American politics in the 1980s, Democrats saw their power slipping away. The Democrats and their allied interests wanted a quick fix. They wanted a piece of magic to return them to the position of power they once knew. They want a magical unicorn to fix the nightmare.

Part of the continued success of people who are not very good consultants is that they know how to sell the unicorn. Democratic candidates, Democratic Party operations, and interest groups who are aligned with the Democratic Party hold certain beliefs in the magic, so they want to hire people who tell them the magic is real. There are several common varieties of unicorns Democratic interests seem more than willing to buy.

THE UNICORN WITH THE SILVER BULLET

Candidates often ask polling consultants to find a "silver bullet" in a public opinion poll. The candidate wants the one sentence—the one turn of a phrase—that will make the voters reject the opponent and embrace his or her candidacy. Unfortunately, that unicorn rarely exists. The opponent rarely casts the one vote or utters the one phrase that changes the dynamics of the campaign. Normally, the opponent is not engaged in some antisocial behavior that the voters will view as making him unfit for office. There is rarely one thing contrasting the candidate and the opponent that makes it an easy choice for the voter.

Campaigns at all levels fall into the search for this mythical message. The 2004 presidential campaign of Senator John Kerry indicated how a candidate can get hung up on one message. As a result, they not only miss messages that should be used, but fail to properly deliver the intended messages. In Kerry's case, he thought the magic unicorn was his military service in Vietnam. In the end, not only did this message not win the election for him, but the Bush campaign was able to undermine it with an independent group that put out the swift boat ads (Reyes, 2006). Meanwhile, public opinion research indicated Kerry had a problem. Focus groups conducted with undecided voters and voters leaning toward voting for President Bush had a consistent finding: The only positive things they knew about John Kerry was that he served in Vietnam and he was then a U.S. Senator. The only other consistent image comments from the groups were from a Bush campaign attack ad, i.e., several people said John Kerry was a "flip-flopper" on issues (Kitchens, 2004). A week before the election, *Newsweek* published an article pointing out the Kerry strategists had made the Vietnam factor the central message and intentionally ignored his record as a U.S. Senator. Senator Kerry's record in the U.S. Senate was purposely excluded including his "groundbreaking investigation into money laundering, drug dealers, terrorists, and secret nukes" (Wolfe et al., 2004, p. 38)

Not only did the Kerry campaign make the mistake of believing his service in Vietnam versus President Bush's getting into the National Guard (to avoid the war) was a silver bullet, they did not even explain to the voters why they should care. They never translated the information as to how this piece of biographical information, while a good way to introduce the candidate, was at all relevant to how he was going to help, serve, or represent anyone in a way that should concern them.

In politics, as in any other choice people are asked to make, a variety of information is filtered through a maze of values, beliefs, and perceptions and the outcome is an opinion. The opinion may be changed as new information and images are provided to the voter. Or, new information may be rejected if it too strongly challenges an important attitude or belief. As a result, the outcome of an election rarely comes down to one statement, one event, or one piece of opposition research that will cause a majority of voters to accept one candidate and reject another.

THE UNICORN WHO CAN ORGANIZE AND OUTVOTE THEM

Republicans spent more three decades getting the definition of their political party down to four words: Less Taxes, Less Government. This "bumper-sticker" philosophy plays well into one side of the voters' perceptions discussed earlier. Voters want to pay less in taxes and they believe government wastes money. On the other hand, they want a fully functioning government that provides Social Security checks, Medicare payments, keeps a first-class military force, and knows how to handle a natural disaster such as hurricanes. Polling data consistently reflect this bipolar response of the voters.

Democrats always took comfort by looking at polls with a laundry list of issues and coming to the conclusion: "More people agree with our issues, so all we have to do is get more people to vote and we win." This major premise has been the foundation of the Democratic Party logic since Franklin Delano Roosevelt was president. At times, it has also been very successful, as demonstrated by the wins at the presidential level by Barack Obama in 2008 and 2012. But in 2004, the Democrats suffered a loss equivalent to the landslide defeat of Barry Goldwater in 1964. On election day, 122,293,337 voters cast their votes—16 million more votes than in the 2000 election. Based upon the assumption that increasing voter turnout assured a Democratic win, Kerry should have won. But, George W. Bush won reelection by more than 3 million votes.

THE UNICORN WITH ENOUGH FACTS TO WIN THE ELECTION

One problem with many campaigns is they believe elections are only a battle of facts. Knowing facts and the details of public policy is important for a candidate, *but* facts are not the basis of voting behavior. Voters do not view the candidates and say, "I agree with candidate A on three issues and candidate B on two issues, so I am going to vote for candidate A." Even a brief examination of psychological research on how people make choices will dispel this notion.

In one sense the reliance on turnout to win elections has turned the Democrats into a party of technicians. In addition, the Democrats seem to be much more the party of lawyers than the Republicans. Both technicians and lawyers think in a linear fashion. Most lawyers, for example, go to court believing the judge will decide a case based on the facts of the case and the law.

More importantly, the Democrats *want* to be the party of facts, ideas, and the champion of the debate. However, Democrats only have to look back to the big debates of 2004 to see the flaw in this thinking. The ABC news poll, after the first Bush-versus-Kerry debate, showed 45 percent of likely voters felt Senator Kerry won the debate and 36 percent thought President Bush won the debate (Langer, 2004). The second appearance was a town hall meeting-style, joint appearance that did not really even simulate a real debate of issues. The third debate was back to the traditional style. The CNN/USA Today survey, conducted shortly after the debate, indicated 53 percent of the likely voters said Senator Kerry won the debate and 39 percent said President Bush won ("Bush, Kerry . . . ," 2004). Still, despite the public perception that Kerry won two of the three debates with the incumbent President of the United States, these perceptions did not translate into voters changing their candidate preference. The reality Democrats must come to grips with is that issues are vehicles to talk about the candidate as a person. There are seldom situations where one public policy or problem is so dominant the election is a referenda on that issue. Command of facts is a prop for a campaign. For example, a candidate for governor must be able to name the ten largest employers in his state if he is going to talk about jobs, but, this command of facts does not win votes. It is the impression of competence coming from a command of facts that is important for the candidate to provide to the voters.

THE UNICORN WITH MAGIC VOTER DELIVERY SYSTEM

Most consultants can relate any number of times that a candidate has said something like, "I just got the support of Joe Jones over in Smith County. He'll deliver that county for me." In reality, why should a candidate could believe that one person has the power to deliver the votes from an entire county? The folly of this attitude emerges from the belief in old political machines and the flawed premise that big turnout means Democrats win. It is commonly referred to as the "two-step process" where opinion leaders get information and then pass it down to the regular people. In this age of mass communication, this over-simplified system of opinion leadership rarely exists or works.

In the early 1980s, The Kitchens Group conducted some extensive polls for a business group in North Carolina. The business leaders were convinced the working class people were conservative. Since they also viewed themselves as conservative, the business leaders were convinced if they escorted a candidate through their factories, shops, and business headquarters, all of the employees would get the message: "This is our candidate." When the poll was completed, the business leaders were shocked. While their blue collar employees did consider themselves conservative, it was not conservative in the way the business leaders defined conservative. In fact, they opposed tax cuts for executives. They did not want the government to "get off the back of business" in terms of workplace safety. They did not believe if their boss got a tax cut it would mean more investment in the company that would increase their pay and quality of life. The blue collar workers did not believe the executive running the companies really cared about them at all. Therefore, the message of the opinion leader had exactly the opposite effect as the intended one. The workers saw a candidate with the boss and thought, "I'll never vote for that guy" (Kitchens, 1983).

Even the traditional Democratic organizations running strong endorsement campaigns for candidates, such as labor unions, have seen their impact diminish. In the 2000 and 2004 elections, most organized labor unions worked hard for the Democratic nominee, but, their endorsements did not automatically lead to their workers' support. In 2004 alone, the AFL-CIO and its affiliated union poured hundreds of millions of dollars into the campaign to defeat George W. Bush. The Service Employees International Union (SEIU) alone brags that it is spending a cool $65 million in support of the Democratic Party Presidential ticket (Kelber, 2004). But the effort simply didn't work. Quite the contrary. Polling data from that election found that Democrats did not even win a majority of votes from union households ("Unions couldn't deliver . . . , 2004)

These examples don't mean that there are no groups where voters will take a strong cue from their leadership. In many places in the South, there are strong African American groups who have leaders the people feel they can trust. The Republicans have countered the traditional Democratic dependency on organizations with organizations of their own. The National Rifle Association and religious groups know where to find their supporters and how to provide them with information. Since the party has shifted to appealing to social conservatives, they have used the same techniques as the Democrats have used for years. The by-product of the Republican action is to nullify traditional Democratic organizations' impact in some elections.

In his book, *What's the Matter With Kansas*, Thomas Frank (2010) points out that traditional union workers in Wichita whose unions fought for good paying jobs switched sides and backed Republicans who were helping ship those jobs overseas. Why? Because they are also strong religious voters and

many are gun owners. The ability for other groups to deliver a more persuasive message than the unions have now persuaded people to vote against
their economic self-interest.

Still, that's only a piece of the political puzzle. If Democrats continue to
buy into the idea that individuals can "deliver" a large block of voters, they
are chasing a myth. For groups to be effective, the candidates must first win
the hearts and minds of the group members with good messages. The real
value of these groups is the potential for volunteers, money and the ability to
increase voter turnout among their group. However, if any candidate thinks
the groups can deliver in the face of a poor message, the candidate is wrong.

The judgment a candidate must make is whether the people saying they
have an organization and can help voter turnout really has a system that can
help the campaign, or if those people are simply looking for a little cash for
their pockets. The bottom line is, even if the group leadership supports a
candidate, it will not translate into support of the individual group members
unless the message is right for the individual voter.

THE UNICORN WITH THE MAGIC SPELL OF CONVENTIONAL WISDOM

Former political consultant and now successful novelist Mike McClister had
a common statement that he introduced to candidates at the beginning of any
campaign: "if it is conventional wisdom that we should do certain things in
this campaign, then you can count on it being wrong." In every campaign,
there are people who have learned some conventional wisdom about running
political campaigns, and they try hard to get the candidate to buy into it.
Unfortunately, they are often successful. Further, based on the authors' expe-
riences, this particular myth appears more common among Democrats than
Republicans. Here are some examples of some conventional wisdom that can
be heard by Democratic candidates in every part of the country and at every
level of politics.

*Never mention your opponent's name, because it will increase his or her
name identification.* In reality, name identification does not equate to winning an election. Even today, Adolf Hitler's name identification is close to
100 percent in the United States, but if he returned and tried to run for public
office, he would have no chance of winning. It is not unusual to hear news
commentators push this conventional wisdom, offering the opinion that a
candidate has an advantage because he or she has name identification. However, name identification is only an advantage if the name also brings a
positive image into the mind of the voter. Only at the lowest level of the
ballot, such as a local judicial race, is name identification a major factor.

Campaigns from the state legislature to the White House are more about the candidate's message than simple name identification.

You must have a good sign program to win. The idea of having a massive sign program for a campaign may be the biggest waste of money in politics. Why? See the above comment about name identification. Signs do not carry a message, and their only major function is to increase name identification, and—as noted above—you can't win many races just on name identification.

Consider this true story of two candidates, for the same statewide position in Louisiana during the same election year, that one of the authors had to evaluate. The first candidate came to the meeting and said he knew he had a big lead. He had spent nearly all his campaign funds on billboards, 4' x 8' signs, and yard signs. He pointed out his opponent did not have a single sign. He was killing the opponent in the sign war.

The second candidate said he had spent very little of his campaign money. His plan was to have a strong television blitz during the final three weeks of the campaign. He was starting to purchase the air time and would have as much advertising on television as the leading candidates for Governor.

It was easy to predict which candidate was going to win. The first poll in the race found that both candidates had about the same level of name identification, i.e., the candidate who spent all his money on signs was no better off than his opponent on that factor. But all of the first candidate's money was gone. The candidate, Richard Ieyoub, ran his television and became the Attorney General of Louisiana.

People are different here. Any time a political consultant from another state arrives at a campaign, some pusher of conventional wisdom will say, "Well, people are different here." There are indeed differences in the political ideology of people in different states, with some states having more Democrats and some having more Republicans. And there are also some local cultural elements that are distinctive to some areas. Beyond that, however, polling data consistently shows that people in different states hold similar values. As a nation, we are more alike than different. The persuasion techniques used by political campaigns or commercial advertisers that work in one place will work in another place.

Our attitudes and values have been greatly dictated by the development of Western civilization. We all use Aristotelian logic, even if we do not know it. As children, we are taught to think in logical sequences, such as "If I touch the hot stove, then I will be burned," or with the use of classical deductive logic, i.e., major premise, minor premise, and conclusion, such as "All German Shepherd puppies grow up to be big dogs. Spot is a German Shepherd puppy. Therefore, Spot will grow up and be a big dog." The reasoning process is common in all Western culture. For this reason, we sometimes have trouble understanding Eastern cultures who do not think in these classical logic sequences. There may be different customs or traditions in different parts of the country. There may be ethnic or racial subcultures in parts of the country. But, anybody who has been in this country for more than a generation has probably been assimilated in a way of thinking and perceiving the world that is similar to the rest of America.

We have to have (a specific campaign trinket). In every state, there seems to be a group of trinket salesmen who are ready to pounce as soon as a candidate announces for office. These people are really good salesmen. They sell candidates and their campaigns a variety of items, most of which are a waste of money. Take T-shirts, for example, buying a few T-shirts for people walking door-to-door or volunteering at the campaign headquarters is fine, hundreds, and in some cases, thousands of T-shirts is a waste of money. T-shirts are as useless as signs stuck on the side of the road. Worse, they are expensive to buy. Further dollars often go for a T-shirt that will be only worn by someone already supporting the candidate. T-shirts are merely yard signs made of cloth.

Still, T-shirts seem really sane compared to some other trinkets, such as sponges printed with the candidate's name, nail files, refrigerator magnets, and books of matches. Possibly the most unusual item for any campaign was in the 1993 campaign for governor between legendary governor Edwin Edwards and avowed racist David Duke. The Edwards campaign spent a lot of money to pay for fly swatters with a logo saying, "Swat Duke."

THE UNICORN WHO IS THE ULTIMATE GURU

Every campaign and organization with a problem is looking for the guru who can turn things around. Every campaign cycle, some consultant becomes "hot property" because of great success in the previous cycle. The campaigns falsely believe if they hire a certain pollster or media consultant, large contributing groups will give them money because they know they will win with this consultant. And, political consultants selling their wares certainly would not do anything to dispel the myth. Regardless, the truth is that political consultants are like jockeys, and you don't win the Kentucky Derby riding a mule. However, even if the candidate is a thoroughbred, the consultants must be able to guide them around the track. The most successful campaigns normally involve a team of good professionals and a dedicated candidate. In a team approach, a good idea can come from any member of the team and there is no professional jealousy.

However, even with a great team and a good candidate, a campaign for public office may not be successful. Winning and losing campaigns happens because of many factors, not the least of which is the political context or the way the voters are viewing the world at the moment. No example is better than the defeat of George H. W. Bush by Bill Clinton in the 1992 Presidential election. Clinton almost won the Democratic nomination by default. At the beginning of primary season, the Gulf War was on and President Bush's approval ratings were around 90 percent. It looked like the entire country was rallying around the President and the thought of confronting him in an election seemed like a suicide mission to most potential Democratic candidates.

Then, the war ended, the troops came home, and the economy took a downturn. Suddenly, public opinion turned on the President. One of the most quoted political clichés was born from Clinton's campaign manager James Carville when he said he kept a sign in his office that read: "It's the economy, stupid!"

Were President Clinton's consultants geniuses and President Bush's consultants idiots? Doubtful. How did the Bush consultants, just four years earlier, make President Bush the only sitting Vice President ever to win the Presidency? The truth is the consulting team on both campaigns was comprised of highly competent professionals in this business. The country had Republican Presidents for twelve years and there was a slight economic downtrend. Bill Clinton was probably the best campaign politician the Democrats had fielded at that time. The Clinton campaign was well executed, and it all added up to a win. But, there was no one magical guru.

Success for the Democratic Party in the future depends upon the party's ability to stop searching for unicorns. The magic does not lie in one message, one person, one extra voter per precinct in Ohio, or conventional wisdom from the past. They must clearly define their message in understandable language to win the hearts and minds of the voters.

REFERENCES

Bush, Kerry hit each other on domestic issues (2004, October 14). *CNN/USA Today Poll.*

Frank, Thomas (2010). *What's the matter with Kansas?: How conservatives won the heart of America.* New York: Metropolitan Books.

Kelber, Harry (2004, October 13). Labor's Role in 2004 elections is limited to supplying money and spear carriers, *The Labor Educator.*

Kitchens, James T. (1983). A poll of blue collar workers in North Carolina. Orlando: The Kitchens Group.

Kitchens, James T. (2004*). Focus group results on undecided voters in the 2004 presidential campaign.* Orlando: The Kitchens Group.

Langer, Gary (2004). Poll: Kerry Wins Debate, But No Change. *ABC News,* http://abcnews.go.com/section/politics/Vote2004/debatepoll040930.html.

Reyes, G. Mitchell (2006). The Swift Boat Veterans for Truth, the politics of realism, and the manipulation of Vietnam remembrance in the 2004 presidential election. *Rhetoric & Public Affairs, 9(4),* 571–600.

Unions Couldn't Deliver Votes for Kerry (2004, November 4). *FOXNews.com.*

Wolfe, Richard, Gegax, T. Trent, Bailey, Holly, & Hosenball, Mark (2004, October 25). Kerry by the book. *Newsweek, 144(17),* 38–41.

Chapter Ten

Practical Lessons

Why Some Candidates Don't Win

The four pillars are the driving forces to the psychology of the voters. When political candidates or political parties activate these forces, they are normally successful. When they do not activate these forces, campaigns usually fail. When the four pillars are used to analyze some recently past and potentially future campaigns, the current state of politics in America can be better understood—particularly in terms of why candidates don't win.

THE 2004 PRESIDENTIAL CAMPAIGN: GEORGE W. BUSH VERSUS JOHN KERRY

Democrats assumed George W. Bush would be easy to defeat in 2004. They reached that conclusion because they focused on him as a person, not President Bush as a leader. President Bush was often criticized in the press for misusing words (or inventing new words) (Finn, 2004). He was portrayed as a man who was not very intelligent and being run by an evil Vice President Dick Cheney. The economy was still in poor shape from the downturn that occurred after the attacks on 9/11.

The Democratic Presidential nominee was U.S. Senator John Kerry (Kranish, Money, & Easton, 2004). Senator Kerry was a Vietnam War veteran who had volunteered and served as an officer. The Democrats felt this was a real strength because Democrats are generally seen as less supportive of defense spending. The conservatives often define this policy position as merely a lack of patriotism. In the wake of the attacks on 9/11, being willing to wave the flag was a must for any candidate for public office.

Political opponents of George W. Bush called him a draft dodger because he was in the reserves. Democrats pointed the John Kerry's record as a hero of the Vietnam War while claiming Bush got into the reserves during the Vietnam War using the family's political connections (Apple, 2004). There were even questions about his service in the reserves.

The Bush campaign had one major strength and one major weakness. The strength was they understood the pillar of fear and how to use it. The Democrats underestimated the psychological impact of the attacks on 9/11 or were too politically correct to use a strong fear appeal about a future attack. In 2004, polls indicated that Americans did not question whether another attack would come; the only question was when. Additionally, 41 percent of Americans believed it was likely that they or a member of their family would be a victim of a terrorist attack (Gallup, 2004). Cheney boldly claimed, "If Kerry is elected, the terrorists will attack." This appealed to both the fear and narcissism pillar.

In April 2004, the news media reported that American interrogators were using aggressive techniques, or torture, to question prisoners at Abu Ghraib prison in Iraq. Democrats decried torture as an interrogation technique. The Republicans defended the techniques as necessary to stop future attacks. A majority of Americans told pollsters they did not approve of the techniques. However, some of these reactions were based upon a socially desirable response pattern. That is, Americans do not think that support of torture is socially acceptable. However, the fear of a terrorist attack being imminent was still high. The Democrats were put in the position of failing to support anything necessary to defend the homeland.

The Democrats believed they could gain an advantage with presenting the military service record of John Kerry. They had commercials which showed John Kerry in Vietnam with his troops. The Democrats' overall attack could be translated into John Kerry is a patriot and George W. Bush is a coward.

The Republicans took the Kerry strength and used it as an attack point. An independent group produced and aired television commercials that became known as the "swift boat" ads. John Kerry commanded a riverboat in the Mekong Delta, known as swift boats. The commercial presented men who served with Kerry in Vietnam questioning his command and leadership during their missions. This attack was effective at neutralizing the Democratic advantage on the narcissism pillar. During the campaign, it became Kerry, not Bush, defending his service to the country. The technique was so effective, using hard personal attacks in political campaigns has become known as "swift boating" ("Swiftboating," 2007).

In the end, George W. Bush won the election by a bigger margin than he won in his first election as President. This campaign is a classic example of a campaign understanding how to drive the electorate using the pillars of fear and narcissism.

THE 2008 PRESIDENTIAL CAMPAIGN:
BARACK OBAMA VERSUS JOHN MCCAIN

The Republican Party faced a challenge in the 2008 election. President George W. Bush was completed his second term and couldn't run again, but his popularity had dropped as the wars in Iraq and Afghanistan became increasingly unpopular (Stolberg & Myers, 2008). Peter Baker (2008) wrote that Bush was "arguably the most disliked president in seven decades" (p. 29). Republican legislators running for reelection found that they had to distance themselves from him to increase their reelection chances. Republican nominees for president tried to run on other issues that appealed to their partisan base, while the Democrats, with Hillary Clinton and John Edwards as the major candidates, focused on their opposition to the wars that were blamed on Republicans. A third candidate, Barack Obama, was also running, but he was given little chance of winning—even by African American voters (Steele, 2008). Meanwhile, the voters seemed more concerned about another problem: a stagnant economy that had led to economic hardships for many workers, including the middle class (Andrews, 2008; Broder, 2008; Page & Risser, 2008). As Kevin Sack (2008) wrote, the voters' "politics are driven by the powerlessness they feel to control their financial well-being, their safety, their environment, their health and the country's borders" (p. A16).

Initially, Barack Obama campaigned on his vote against the invasion of Iraq, distinguishing himself from Hillary Clinton who had voted for the war. Eventually, though, Obama switched to the economic pressures facing the middle class (Leonhardt, 2008). In the end, Arizona Senator John McCain beat out Rudy Guiliani, Mitt Romney and others to win the Republican nomination (Bumiller, 2008), while Illinois Senator Barack Obama surprised pundits by running away with the Democratic nomination (Kristol, 2008).

The 2008 campaign started as a generational campaign—the older, war hero who carried the Republican banner versus the new generation and anti-war candidate of the Democrats. Obama selected Joe Biden as his running mate (Healy, 2008a), and also picked up campaign help from his former opponent, Hillary Clinton (Healy, 2008b). McCain pulled a surprise and selected Alaska Governor Sarah Palin as his running mate, and that choice dominated the news for a while and helped McCain solidify support among religious conservatives (Cooper & Bumiller, 2008) and those whose voting was based on patriotism (i.e., narcissism) (Friedman, 2008), but her appeal with swing voters diminished following ridicule by the press and devastating impersonations on TV's *Saturday Night Live by comedian Tina Fey (Fairbanks, 2008). Meanwhile, the underlying problems with the economy remained (Krugman, 2008). The Republicans tried to keep a focus on abortion* as an issue, an approach that relied on the religiosity pillar of politics (Seelye, 2008a). But that issue simply wasn't getting any traction with the voters, partly because of their personal economic concerns and partly due to the media's focus on Sarah Palin.

The Republicans tried to repeat their 2004 success by using the pillars of fear and narcissism. The result was a series of false attacks (often through alternative media) that attacked Obama for being either a radical liberal, a Muslim, and/or someone who was not born in the United States (Rutenberg & Bosman, 2008). To the disappointment of the GOP, these lines of attack only worked with the hardcore base, while most voters turned their attention to other issues—including the economy. This issue was sparked by an increasing unemployment rate that exceeded six percent in August (Uchitelle, 2008). The basic issue for voters was whether George W. Bush and the Republican Party should be blamed for the slow economy, or whether the tax-and-spend policies of Democrats should be blamed for not doing enough to get the economy back on track.

Eventually, an outside event dominated the final days of the campaign—the failure of several large banks and other financial institutions (Broder & Cooper, 2008; Hulse, 2008). The ultimate remedy advocated by both candidates was a government-sponsored bailout of those institutions (Cooper & Zeleny, 2008). Obama, though, had the edge as many voters blamed Republican-led policies toward big business for the problem (Cave, 2008; Nagourney & Zeleny, 2008). That situation caused Healy (2008c) to write that "Obama wraps his hopes inside economic anxiety" (p. A21). Meanwhile, the McCain campaign launched an attack based on Obama's association with a 1960's radical, William Ayers (Seelye, 2008b)—an attack based on the pillar of fear. It didn't work. Obama's reliance on consumerism and the economy dominated and resulted in the election of the first African American president in the history of the nation.

THE 2012 PRESIDENTIAL ELECTION:
PRESIDENT BARACK OBAMA VERSUS MITT ROMNEY

The 2012 election opened with the United States still mired in a sluggish economy and high unemployment rates. The Republican Party sensed and opportunity, especially if they could select a nominee who could challenge the president on the consumerism issue. The Republican primary season opened with a series of candidates hoping to capture the banner for the party.

From mid-2011 through the early part of 2012, a series of Republican candidates surged briefly into the spotlight only to fall under the glare of media attention. Early front-runner congresswoman Michele Bachmann had the advantage of being the darling of religious conservatives in the caucus state of Iowa, but fell victim to a series of gaffes and the perception that her religious views were out of the mainstream eventually knocked her out of contention (Bruni, 2011; Burke, 2011). Pizza businessman Herman Cain had a brief flirtation with Republican voters until rumors of illicit affairs with several women derailed his bid (Henry & Jackson, 2011). Congressman Rick Santorum inherited the conservative mantle and did well in the Iowa Caucus, but he had trouble raising money to continue his campaign. Former Speaker of the House Newt Gingrich appealed to some Republicans, but his past problems with an ethics violation and a history of serial adultery eventually doomed his chances (Saunders, 2011). Texas governor Rick Perry entered the fray and seemed to have potential, but a series of poor debate performances doomed his chances (Shear, 2011).

The eventual nominee was Mitt Romney, the man who finished second for the nomination in 2012. Romney got the nomination despite one major problem, i.e., Republican concerns that his Mormon religion would not sit well with many voters (Powell, 2012; Powell & Hickson, 2013). The fact that the billionaire was also seen as an example of Republican big-money interests didn't help either (Brooks, 2012; Krugman, 2012a).

The Obama campaign's major strategy was to blame the sluggish economy on the previous administration of Republican George W. Bush, arguing that electing Romney would lead to a return of the Republican policies that created the problem. That argument was enhanced by the fact that, despite the slow recovery, most voters felt more economically secure than when Obama took office (Lowrey, 2012). As Douthat (2012) wrote, "Americans don't yet trust the Republican Party given how little the party seems to have learned and changed since 2008" (p. SR11).

A number of side issues emerged during the election but, as election day approached, the focus returned to that of the economy (Page, 2012). That issue continued to benefit Obama, as the nation's economic news was buoyed by an improving housing market as the election approached (Schmit, 2012). Meanwhile, Romney's economic positions drew criticism from the media, with economist Paul Krugman (2012b) writing that Romney's economic plan "is a sham. It is a list of things he claims will happen, with no description of the policies he would follow to make those things happen" (p. A27). In the end, the pillar of consumerism was the major issue of the campaign, and Barack Obama was reelected.

GOVERNOR CHRIS CHRISTIE:
HOW A TRAFFIC JAM SLOWED A PRESIDENTIAL CAMPAIGN

In 2013, New Jersey Governor Christie was viewed as the front runner for the Republican nomination for President in 2016 (Moore, 2013). He was a Republican who won in a northern Blue state. His populist style seems to strike a chord with the middle class voters in New Jersey. The former federal prosecutor brought straight talk to issues, but also had a likable side to his personality. He seemed like a regular guy.

The extreme right did not like Christie. His cardinal sin was his refusal to attack President Obama after Hurricane Sandy destroyed significant areas of the New Jersey coast. While the right wing did not like it, most Americans saw a public official who was working in a bipartisan manner to solve a serious problem. Many political analyst felt Christie had the philosophy and appeal to win a national election.

Then came the "Time for Some Traffic Problems" scandal. In September 2013, at the height of Governor Christie's reelection campaign for Governor, the George Washington Bridge, which connects Fort Lee, New Jersey and New York City, closed two lanes for "a traffic study." The closure of these lanes caused massive traffic jams, delaying workers from their jobs and school buses from getting to school. Democrats began speculating that the lane closure was a retaliation by the Christie campaign against the Democratic Mayor of Fort Lee Mark Sokolich because he would not endorse Christie's reelection bid (Flegenheimer, 2014).

For months, Governor Christie treated press questions about the lane closure's connection to campaign politics as a non-issue. He joked about the guy in the bright orange vest putting out traffic cones was really him. Then began the worst nightmare a politician can have. In January, the press released emails between top Christie staffers and Christie appointees confirming the lane closings were, in fact, a politically motivated act against the Democratic mayor. Governor Christie made all the moves that political pundits would advise clients when the scandal broke. He fired everyone involved (Zernike & Santora, 2014) and spent almost two hours apologizing for the incident (Barbaro, 2014). He stood and answered every question the press gave him. It was a classic and strategically sound attempt for damage control.

How is it possible that the actions of staffers that seem like an exaggerated sophomoric prank could derail the campaign of the person who potentially would be the next President of the United States? At the time of this writing, the 2016 Presidential campaign had not started in earnest. The debate of whether or not this scandal can disqualify Governor Chris Christi continued. Still, this incident had potential to derail the Governor's campaign? An analysis using the four pillars will show how this scandal can be used to persuade voters to reject Governor Christi as unacceptable.

The first line of attack that can be made against Governor Christi is using the pillar of religiosity, i.e., the concept of right and wrong. This incident reflects some of the worst stereotypic descriptions about politicians, such as they misuse power to their own benefit, they don't really care about people, they have no real morals. One of the most damaging stories from the incident is that emergency workers could not get onto the bridge and a woman died. Even if Governor Christi could not be directly tied to ordering the stunt, opponents will point out he surrounded himself with people who don't know right from wrong. As might be predicted, people caught in the scandal will claim that Governor Christi knew about the plan in an effort to save themselves (Zernike, 2014).

The second potential line of attack on Governor Christi would use the pillar of consumerism. Thousands of workers could not get to their jobs. Many of them were not paid because they were not at work (Brumfield, 2014). A class action suit was organized to sue the state of New Jersey to recover lost wages for the people who missed worked. The attack would be based on the argument that Chris Christi said he cares about working people, but this incident could be used to say he was willing to make people lose their pay to play politics. In addition, if the lawsuit is successful, the opponents will argue that Christi's political stunt cost the taxpayers millions of dollars. The conclusion will be drawn that Chris Christi cared more about politics than the taxpayers, driving the attitudes around the pillar of consumerism.

The third line of attack on Chris Christi would use the pillar of fear. His opponents will argue that Americans cannot trust Chris Christi to keep them save. The argument would be: What would happen if Chris Christi and his people used this poor of judgment in the time of national crisis, such as another terrorist attack or major economic crisis? The natural psychological reaction is to mistrust someone you fear. The attack will tie the strongest fears of voters to the traffic jam issue, and in this context, raise a specter of mistrusting his judgment.

The fourth pillar of narcissism can also be engaged to attack Governor Christi—an attack that will charge that Governor Christi is not "one of us." The attack will associate Governor Christi with the "political class." That is, Governor Christi is not like you and me, or this incident would never have happened. Attack language could be framed around the idea that leaders who love their state and their country do not engage in this unpardonable behavior. To make matter worse, Governor Christi never took the issue seriously, was unsympathetic to the problems the traffic jam caused, and only became serious about what had happen to us when there was no denying the fact that incident was a political dirty trick played by his highest and closest advisors.

The images, hearings, and lawsuits created by this famous planned traffic jam will make it impossible for Governor Chris Christi to escape and find a positive message for himself. Opponents in either a primary or general election will understand how to exploit this situation.

All of the examples in this chapter refer to actual or potential presidential campaigns. They were chosen for illustrative purposes because of their national influence. However, the examples can easily be expanded to state and local campaigns. If a candidate or campaign does not understand the four pillars of politics, winning an election becomes increasingly difficult.

Chapter 10

REFERENCES

Andrews, Edmund L. (2008, Feb. 4). It's the economy again, and some see similarities to 1992. *New York Times*, A18

Apple, R. W. (2004, July 28). Navigating two wars and a minefield. *New York Times*, P1.

Baker, Peter (2008, August 31). The final days. *New York Times Magazine*, 26–33, 46, 49.

Barbaro, Michael (2014, Jan. 10). His apology, done his way. *New York Times*, A1, A20.

Broder, John M. (2008, Jan. 12). With economy slowing, all speeches turn to it. *New York Times*, A10.

Broder, John M., & Cooper, Michael (2008, Oct. 8). Economic struggles dominate presidential debate. *New York Times*, A1, A17

Brooks, David (2012, January 13). The C.E.O. of politics. *New York Times*, A19.

Brumfield, Ben (2014, January 10). Legal woes lurk for Gov. Chris Christie over bridge traffic jam scandal. *CNN*.

Bruni, Frank (2011, July 24). Much ado about Michele. *New York Times*, SR2,

Bumiller, Elisabeth (2008, Feb. 6). McCain's political rebound defied popular wisdom. *New York Times*, P1.

Burke, Daniel (2011, September 3). Bachmann's 'prophecy' has company with belief in signs. *Birmingham News*, 1F, 2F.

Cave, Damien (2008, Oct. 4). Economic crisis fuels Obama in tight ground war for Florida. *New York Times*, A1, A16.

Cooper, Michael, & Bumiller, Elisabeth (2008, August 30). Alaskan is McCain's choice: First woman on G.O.P. ticket. *New York Times*, A1, A11.

Cooper, Michael, & Zeleny, Jeff (2008, October 1). Both Obama and McCain make push for bailout. *New York Times*, A24.

Douthat, Ross (2012, September 30). Obama's new normal. *New York Times*, SR11.

Fairbanks, Amanda M. (2008, Sept 16). Finding her inner Palin. *New York Times*, A21.

Finn, Andy (2004). http://andyfinn.us/bush_league/bushisms1_mispronunciation.htm.

Flegenheimer, Matt (2014, Jan. 10). To congestion-bound New Jerseyans, messing with traffic may be ultimate sin. *New York Times*, A21

Friedman, Thomas L. (2008, Oct. 8). Palin's kind of patriotism. *New York Times*, A25.

Gallup Poll (2009). http://www.gallup.com/poll/4909/terrorism-united-states.aspx

Healy, Patrick (2008a, August 25). Tasks for Biden this fall: Travel and attack McCain. *New York Times*, A12.

Healy, Patrick (2008b, August 27). Clinton rallies her troops to fight for Obama. *New York Times*, A1, A15.

Healy, Patrick (2008c, Oct. 9). Obama wraps his hopes inside economic anxiety. *New York Times*, A21.

Henry, Ray, & Jackson, Henry C. (2011, November 29). Woman says she had long affair with Cain. *Birmingham News*. 3A.

Hulse, Carl (2008, Oct. 5). Bailout votes and the economy threaten to overwhelm other issues. *New York Times*, A28.

Kranish, Michael., Money, Brian. & Easton, Nina J. (2004). John F. Kerry, The Boston Globe Biography, *Boston Globe*.

Kristol, William (2008, Feb. 11). Obama's path to victory. *New York Times*, A25.

Krugman, Paul (2008, August 18). It's the economy stupor. *New York Times*, A21.

Krugman, Paul (2012a, January 13). America isn't a corporation. *New York Times*, A19.

Krugman, Paul (2012b, October 26). Pointing toward prosperity? *New York Times*, A27.

Leonhardt, David (2008, Feb. 2). Obama emphasizes middle-class relief more than deficit reduction. *New York Times*, A11.

Lowrey, Annie (2012, September 28). Economy still weak, but more feel secure. *New York Times*, B1, B9.

Moore, Martha T. (2013, November 6). Christie's next stop may be 2016). *USA Today*, 2A.

Nagourney, Adam, & Zeleny, Jeff (2008, October 5). Economic unrest is shifting electoral battlegrounds. *New York Times*, A1, A24.

Page, Susan (2012, October 22). Obama casts Romney as outdated. *USA Today*, 4A. .

Page, Susan, & Risser, William (2008, February 5). Economy's slide has voters on edge. *USA Today*, 1A–2A.

Powell, Larry (2012). Will Mormonism Keep Mitt Romney out of the White House? *Journal of Contemporary Rhetoric*, 2(2), (2-12), 39–43.

Powell, Larry, & Hickson, Mark (2013). Mitt Romney, Mormonism, and the 2008 presidential election. *Journalism and Mass Communication*, 3, 87–100.

Rutenberg, Jim, & Bosman, Julie (2008, August 13). Book attacking Obama hopes to repeat '04 anti-Kerry feat. *New York Times*, A1, A14.

Sack, Kevin (2008, Jan. 24). Voters showing a darker mood than in '00 race. *New York Times*, A1, A16.

Saunders, Debra K. (2011, December 15). Newt gives Demos plenty to attack with. *Birmingham News*, 9A.

Schmit, Julie (2012, Oct. 18). Housing surge looks solid. *USA Today*, 1A.

Seelye, Katharine Q. (2008a, August 31). G.O.P. holds to firm stance on abortion. *New York Times*, A19.

Seelye, Katharine Q. (2008b, October 12). McCain campaign sustains the focus on Obama's links to a 1960s radical. *New York Times*, A22.

Shear, Michael D. (2011, September 10). Perry stumbles on number of justices. *New York Times*, A16.

Steele, Shelby (2008). *A bound man: Why we are excited about Obama and why he can't win*. New York: Free Press.

Stolberg, Sheryl Gay, & Myers, Steven Lee (2008, Feb. 10). Republicans weighing benefits of Bush's embrace. *New York Times*, A21.

Swiftboating (2007, October 27). Time, 107(17), 18.

Uchitelle, Louis (2008, Sept 6). U.S. jobless rate climbs past 6%, highest since '03. *New York Times*, A1, A13.

Zernike, Kate (2014, Feb. 1). Christie linked to knowledge of shut lanes. *New York Times*, A1, A3.

Zernike, Kate, & Santora, Marc (2014, Jan. 10). Christie moving to limit damage in Bridge scandal. *New York Times*, A1, A20.

Chapter Eleven

Why Some Public Figures Can't Lead

"Sometimes I wonder whether the world is being run by smart people who are putting us on, or by imbeciles who really mean it." —Anonymous, but often incorrectly attributed to Mark Twain

Losing an election is often caused by not understanding the four pillars of politics. Still, winning an election is no guarantee that an elected official will be able to provide leadership to the public. The problems here are based upon the idea of checks and balances that dominate our constitutional government and the increasing role that money plays in modern campaigns.

To prevent too much power in the hands of one person, our founding fathers deliberately divided the government into three distinct branches— executive, judicial and legislative—with each branch providing some balance to what the leaders of the other two might do. What the founders did not anticipate, however, was the amount of animosity that could be generated by two major parties who approached the four pillars from totally different orientations. Over the past decade or more, the result of that balance has been stalemate and inactivity. While the examples in this chapter are again from the national level, the principles also apply to many states.

THE UNITED STATES CONGRESS WITH NO HOPE FOR LEADING

Congress is in such total gridlock that in his 2014 State of the Union address, President Obama promised the American people he would lead the country forward, with or without Congress (Milligan, 2014). While the two major political parties have always been combative, until the last few years the leaders of both parties have found a way to compromise and make major strides on both foreign and domestic policies. President Nixon with a Democratic Congress opened relationships with "Red China" (MacMillan, 2008). President Reagan with a Democratic House and Republican controlled Senate passed a major and sweeping change in the tax system (Matthews, 2013). President Clinton passed welfare reform with bipartisan support (Hamilton, 2007).

So, why has Congress become dysfunctional? There are two reasons—a mathematical reason and an attitudinal reason—and both reasons are tightly intertwined. The mathematical reason is tied to the one truly bipartisan issue that still exists in Congress—the Congressional redistricting process. Every ten years, following the U.S. Census, all 435 U.S. House of Representatives District lines are redrawn. The original intent of the process was to insure that then number of people each U.S. Representative represented was approximately the same, and states with larger populations had the appropriate larger number of representatives.

The process also helped to account for geographic shifts in the population. For example, in 1980, year period, the state of Florida went from being the seventh largest state by population to the fourth largest state by population. During the same time, the population of Pennsylvania declined and it went from being the fourth largest state to being the sixth largest state. The district lines of both states were drawn by the legislatures in each state. It is not unusual for Members of Congress to send paid staff or outside consultants to lobby for the lines defining their district. It is also very common for the two major political parties to suggest the definition of particular districts to the members of their party serving in the legislature.

Modern technology has also changed the process. In 1982, districts were hand-drawn on precinct maps with magic markers. Today, with advanced algorithms and detailed voter data-bases, the lines of Congressional districts are drawn virtually down to the voter household. In addition, civil rights litigation required legislatures to produce "minority access" districts. This step was taken to stop legislatures from fracturing African American or Hispanic populations in a way that diluted their strength as a voting bloc and made it impossible for an African American or Hispanic to be elected to Congress (Miller et al., 2013).

The goal of Congressional incumbents is to have a district where the voters are so supportive of candidates from their own party that a general election challenge will be viewed as virtually impossible (Drew, 2013). Most of the money for Congressional campaigns is generated from special interest groups in Washington. These groups are constantly analyzing the Congressional races to determine where they need "to play." This means that groups who are most likely to support Democrats, such as organized labor and trial lawyers, will not give money to a Democrat which they view as having little chance of winning. By the same token, groups who primarily fund Republicans, such as the Chamber of Commerce, will not give money to a Republican they feel has no or little chance of winning. These groups study voting patterns and read expert analysis of races from sources such as The Cook Political Report.

For the 2014 elections, political experts estimated only 15 to 30 of the 435 Congressional seats will have a serious contest in the general election (Silver, 2012). When incumbents know they are safe from a serious general election challenge, they know there is a 99 percent chance of being reelected. While a member of the same party could challenge them in a primary election, this has been almost impossible until the recent split in the Republican Party between the Tea Party wing and the established wing of the party (Lipton, 2014). Primary challenges are so difficult because there is an unwritten rule during political meetings that the job of the party is to protect the incumbent.

The ultimate result of this redistricting is that most districts are not only partisan in nature, but they also often reflect the ideological extremes of both parties. In such a system, moderates—who account for the bulk of voters in the nation—can be underrepresented As Black and Black (2007) argued, the result is that the parties as represented in Congress have both been reduced to minority status with approximately equal levels of support. The resulting dysfunction has led to what conservative columnist David Brooks (2014) calls a "spiritual recession" in which neither party has faith in its ideological core, and, "Without the faith, leaders grown small; they have no sacred purpose to align themselves with" (p. A23). With no sense of purpose, the two parties have also lost the willingness to compromise. As Archibald (2014) noted, "That's not civic leadership. It's a competitive team sport" (p. 26). Similarly, Friedman (2014) wrote that "Today, we would be best served in meeting our biggest challenges by adopting a hybrid of the best ideas of left and right—and the fact that we can't is sapping our strength" (p. SR11). Bruni (2014) was even more cynical when he wrote, "Behold Congress, the saddest costume party there is" (p. SR3), while Wehrman (2014) simply wrote, "There's a whole lotta politics, but there's not much policy" (p. 15). Not surprisingly, the public has become disenchanted with this situation, leading to a national sense of "chronic disillusionment" as voters become increasingly disappointed in the ability of the government to function (Dowd, 2014, p. SR11).

Since most major interest groups always have legislation that they want to pass or stop, there are two pressure points that keep interest groups from funding challengers. The parties can pressure their leadership to withhold or push legislation in opposition to the interest groups desire as a way to discourage or punish them for funding a challenger. Second, the Member of Congress can use his or her legislative power, legislative procedures, or a legislative deal to punish a group who is funding an opponent.

Once an incumbent feels safe from the opposition party, the goal become to make the core voters of his or her own party happy. Primary elections normally have a small percentage of voters participating. These voters are the true believers who expect their candidates to take a hard line on their issues. This is the point where the four pillars and attitudes associate with the strong partisans comes into play.

To understand how the nation came to this situation, it is important to understand a bit of the history of news media. Prior to cable television, there were only three networks; ABC, NBC, and CBS. These networks and all the local television stations were bound by the Federal Communications Commission's "Fairness Doctrine" which required that news coverage had to report both sides of public issues in a fair manner. If a television or radio station editorialized about a public issue, the other side must be provided with equal time to present their side of the issue. Failure to abide by the fairness doctrine could lead to a loss of the broadcast license. Because network affiliated local television stations were highly profitable, they were not interested in having their license challenged over a political debate (Simmons, 1978).

In 1980, cable television was starting to explode. The laying of coaxle throughout the country meant the creation of many new networks, including news, sports, and entertainment. In 1982, the Reagan administration eliminated the fairness doctrine. The rationale was that the number of networks were now virtually unlimited, resulting in enough news outlets that all political positions could have a voice and these outlets could have total First Amendment freedom of speech rights (Ruane, 2011).

For the past two decades, the extreme conservatives have had a news network that reports news with their point of view, FOX News, and liberals have had a news network that reports the news with their point of view, MSNBC (Carr, 2013). Studies of information seekers indicate that people want to receive information that reinforces their current attitudes, not information that challenges their preconceived beliefs (Klapper, 1960).

This phenomenon has meant that conservatives and liberals become more convinced that their view of the world is correct and the other side's view is totally wrong. Further, that's unlikely to change in the near future. On the Republican side, the Tea Party forces are not a fringe group within the Republican Party that can be ignored. These populist groups, though opposed to the Republican establishment, are the top Republican fund-raisers while groups like Karl Rove's American Crossroads struggled after the lost in 2012 to Barck Obama and the Democrats (Confessore, 2014b). On the Democratic side, the left wing will continue to push its agenda with an aim of getting moderates to cater to their positions. The result: The extreme sides of both parties will continue to have a major impact on the functions of those parties. Even those news outlets which try to stay in the middle have been influenced.

Rosenthal (1993), for example, argued that the mainstream national media have increasingly seen their function as analyzing, rather than simply reporting the news.

The chart below shows how the four pillars are diametrically interpreted by the two extremes.

CONSUMERISM

Democrats: The wealth in the country needs to be redistributed. There is too much wealth concentrated in the top one percent of the population. Government must find a way to regenerate the middle class. Government should increase taxes on the rich.

Republicans: Government takes money from the people who create jobs and those who work to give it to people who will not work. Government hurts the middle class by taking their money. Taking more in taxes from anyone hurts the economy.

FEAR

Democrats: The enemy is a group of people who want to limit the rights of certain Americans, enslave the working class, and use fear of foreigners to keep the military industrial complex draining resources needed for domestic programs.

Republicans: There are forces in the world who hate us because we are a democracy. The most important job of the government is to protect us. We need more military and stronger laws to limit foreigners from entering the country. If we have to forfeit some part of our rights for national security, we are willing to do it.

RELIGIOSITY

Democrats: We should have a strict interpretation of the separation of church and state. All religions should be accepted as part of America. There are forces who are trying to impose their religious values on us by restricting women's reproductive right and opposing the rights of gays to marry and have full rights in society. America should be concerned about what is fair for all people.

Republicans: America was founded on Judeo-Christian beliefs, morals and values. These beliefs are the basis of our laws and create order in our society. America has gone too far in limiting the display of Christmas trees and prayers at public events. Liberals want to pass laws which destroy the basic structure of the family. This behavior has caused many great societies to fall, and it could destroy America.

NARCISSISM

Democrats: We are intellectually sound in our policies. We represent thinking people, not people who act with knee-jerk emotions. We believe our communities have a responsibility to take care of the people who cannot take care of themselves. In our view, what makes America great is embracing a multi-cultural society where differences are not only accepted but celebrated.

Republicans: America is a nation built upon people who are exceptional. We are superior to most societies because of our dedication to work. We should not radically change our society. If people want to be a part of our society, they should speak English. We believe in the individual. The individual should be free to excel. No one should have the government take from one person's success and give it to someone who does not earn it for themselves.

The two factors of redistricting and media catering means that both Republicans and Democrats must reflect the extreme right and extreme left of the party to be elected. There is little doubt about the outcomes of most general elections—only party primaries. This structure has created a number of factors which makes political leadership difficult. First, the term "compromise" has become a dirty word for true partisans. There are now numerous examples of incumbents who have been defeated because they acted in a "moderate" or "compromising" manner. For example U.S. Senator Richard Lugar (R-Indiana) was defeated because of he was considered too bipartisan (Farrell, 2012). In the 2014 election cycle, U.S. Senator Mitch McConnell, the Republican majority leader, was challenged in the primary election for his failure to "be conservative enough," as was U.S. Senator Lindsay Graham in South Carolina (Newton-Small, 2014). Similarly, in interviews with four lawmakers—two Republicans and two Democrats—who retired after 2014, the *New York Times* reported that all four noted the inability of Congress to compromise as a source of gridlock in Washington (Hulse & Pear, 2015).

This uncompromising position of both parties has divided the states and regions of the country into primarily dominated by one of the two parties. Currently, there are no Republican members of the U.S. House of Representatives from the New England states. Likewise, there are virtually no Southern white Democrats in the U.S. House of Representatives. The Democrats from the South are dominated by African American and Hispanic representatives representing districts that are overwhelmingly dominated by voters from these ethnic groups.

Additionally, the rules of both Houses of Congress make it impossible for either party to have a functioning majority. The entire House of Representatives has to run for reelection every two years. Up until the last redistricting in 2011, there was a shift of power almost every two years during the 21st century. However, ever since that redistricting, the number of limited districts that are really "swing" districts has decline to the point that the shift of power will be less frequent.

The U.S. Senate requires the vote of 60 U.S. Senators to end debate. Neither of the two parties has had 60 U.S. Senators since the Democrats had 61 Senators in 1977 to 1979. Thus for 33 years, neither party has had a functioning majority of 60 U.S. Senators. However, during much of the 1980's and 1990's, the U.S. Senate was functional because Senators found a way to compromise. A bipartisan effort provided America with legislation such as major reforms such as the Child Tax Credit, amendments to the Clean Air Act, and the Strategic Defense Initiative.

If the President vetoes a bill passed by Congress, it requires a two-thirds vote of both houses of Congress to override the veto. That scenario has become increasingly difficult to achieve; especially when Members of Congress are afraid that working with the members of the other party could mean a defeat in the next primary. An examination of the White House and Congress since 2000 clearly indicates the nature of this gridlock:

- In 2000, Republican George W. Bush won the Presidency. When he took office, the U.S. House had 212 Democrats, 221 Republicans, and two independents, while the Senate was split with 50 Democrats and 50 Republicans.
- The 2002 mid-term elections changed the composition of Congress slightly. The House ended up with 205 Democrats, 229 Republicans, and one independent; the Senate had 48 Democrats, 51 Republicans, and one independent,
- In 2004, Republican George W. Bush was reelected as President. The House had 202 Democrats, 232 Republicans, and one independent. The Senate had 49 Democrats, 49 Republicans and two independents.
- The 2006 election saw little change in power. The House was composed of 233 Democrats and 202 Republicans, while the Senate had 49 Democrats, 49 Republicans and two independents.
- The election of Democrat Barack Obama as president in 2008 saw an increase in Democratic legislators, but still not enough to ensure no gridlock. The House had 257 Democrats and 178 Republicans, while the Senate had 51 Democrats, 47 Republicans, and two independents.
- After the 2010 mid-term elections, the power in the House of Representatives shifted to the Republicans and gridlock was virtually ensured. The House had 193 Democrats and 242 Republicans, while the Democrats had

a small majority in the Senate: 51 Democrats, 47 Republicans and two independents
- In 2012, Barack Obama was reelected as President, but Republicans retained control of the House with 233 members compared to 200 for the Democrats. The Senate remained under Democratic control with 53 Democrats, 45 Republicans and two independents.

Thus neither party has had a comfortable and over-whelming majority since the turn of this century. President Obama had a two year period (2008–2009) with a significant majority, but still did not have the 60 partisan votes in the U.S. Senate to truly have control. The result is a picture of a Congress in gridlock; and no party or political institution leads during gridlock.

Further, that gridlock is likely to continue. Thirty-six of the fifty states have legislatures and state officers that are dominated by one party (Confessore, 2014a). With legislatures dominated by one party, it will be impossible for the minority party to have influence in drawing Congressional districts. When the people elected to public office are only concerned about representing a set of values in an uncompromising manner, the values that they see define American, leading the country becomes impossible.

THE GROWING ROLE OF BIG MONEY

The final factor that has led to political dysfunction is the growing role of big money in political campaigns. That change started in January 2010 when the United States Supreme Court made a historic ruling in a case known as Citizens United v. FEC (Smith et al., 2010), a ruling that provided campaigns with the ability to form political action committees funded by unlimited donations from corporations and individuals. That ruling led to the development of "Super PACs," in which candidates could solicit unlimited funds from high-dollar donors (Smith & Powell, 2013). Hypothetically, the raising and spending of these Super PAC funds could not be coordinated with the campaigns themselves, but the barrier separating the two has been at best a thin façade. Candidates or high campaign executives often help to raise those Super PAC funds. Further, while there is supposed to be no coordination between the two in expenditures, campaigns and Super PACs often operated out of the same offices at the same addresses.

As a result, the total cost of running a campaign escalated to the point that it has been described as "obscene amounts of money" are now required (Faulk, 2014, p. 6). Many candidates find themselves raising money for their campaign and for related Super PACs. Millions of dollars could flow into the PACs. In 2010, the Democrats did not use such PACs because of their ideological objection to the ruling. That resulted in Republicans taking control of the House of Representatives. Since then, both parties have actively used them in campaigns. Thus, people like hedge fund manager Tom Steyer donates millions of dollars to PACs for Democrats (Confessore, 2014c), while the Koch brothers (Charles and David) do the same for Republicans and conservative causes (Schulman, 2014). For political consultants, the change has meant that it is now more profitable to work for a Super PAC than for a campaign. For the public, though, the result is that politicians of both parties find that they rely more on money from big donors than from average voters. And, while representatives of both parties deny that it influences their political decisions, that money has at least an indirect impact since all incumbents know that they need to raise more money from the same donors for the next election.

WHERE DOES THIS LEAD IN THE FUTURE

While predicting the future is a hazardous business, there are several possible paths based upon history. Scenario 1: Continued gridlock for the next fifteen to twenty years. The strength of the Tea Party and the conservative movement in the country comes from people in the Boomer generation who are white and middle class. They truly feel that they are "Taxed Enough Already." They are not, like many others, accepting social changes such as gay marriage. At this point, these voters control politics in the deep South, some western states, and are a force in the Midwest. They control a sufficient number of Congressional seats and U.S. Senate seats that the liberals cannot win a functioning majority.

In twenty years, many in this generation will die and a number of changes may occur. The Boomers are the last generation who remember racial segregation in the United States. Desegregation occurred when this generation was coming of age. Today, one-in-five marriages are "inter-racial." The younger generation does not view the country in terms of race. Likewise, the memory of women's lib, the Vietnam War, and anti-draft rallies will disappear. When that occurs, the values of generation X and the millennials will become dominant in America. Whether this generational passing leads to a more moderated society is impossible to predict, but it is clear that they see the errors of their parents.

Scenario 2: Another major crisis. During the first year of this century, American suffered a huge blow to the perception of its strength when the 9/11 attacks occurred. In 2008, the economic collapse of the housing market created havoc in the middle class because people took out loans they could never repay. But, the lending institutions encouraged it. As a result, we are no longer a society that feels totally safe from terrorists' attacks or an economic collapse. As the Republicans learned in 2008, you may not be responsible for the crisis, but if you are in power when it occurs, the voters will punish you. If there is another crisis, the voters could give the party out of power a ruling majority, which would break the gridlock in Congress and move America in one direction or another.

Scenario 3: A major structural change in American Democracy. American-style Democracy is difficult and has not been embraced by other countries when given the opportunity. The Soviet Union collapsed and many people thought democracy would take hold. However, Russia is now run by a political strong man who is basically a dictator. Several years after the collapse, a majority of people in that nation still want a dictator, not democracy. Looking at the results of the U.S. war in Iraq, it would be impossible to argue that the U.S. gave them a functioning democracy. The "Arab Spring" has not lived up to a democratic expectation.

The United States has not had a war of survival since World War II. We assume the citizens are devoted in their love of our democratic system. But, if the system does not work, at least in their perceptions, what will they tolerate or embrace? A broken economic system brought a communistic government to Russia and fascists to power in Hitler's Germany. We should never assume gridlock is good. Without compromise on the interpretation of the basic values, the world's greatest experiment may undergo significant changes. Examples of such changes could include, but are not limited to, term limits, increased public financing or matching funds to offset independent groups, a return of the fairness doctrine, or no two-term limit for Presidents.

Currently, the four pillars of politics form the basis of our national system of democracy. But that system has led to a situation in which many candidates have no chance of winning. Even worse, those who do win find it difficult to provide leadership to the nation and its states. Both candidates and public officials find themselves more fearful of the extreme voices in each of their parties. As a result, politicians are more interested in pandering to those interests rather than addressing the problems of the day. Meanwhile, neither party is providing effective leadership, a situation that Street and DiMaggio (2012) described in terms of national representation by "radical Republicans" and "dismal Democrats" (p. 549)

Late in the 20th century, Michael Janeway (2001) predicted that our democratic system would become increasingly dysfunctional as the nation's media and politicians increasingly appealed to the base instincts of voters. Janeway (2004) later blamed part of the problem on a trend that he traced from the Roosevelt administration to that of Lyndon Johnson in which power brokers grew increasingly manipulative and highhanded. But the problem does not seem to have stopped with the Johnson administration. Instead, the nation's leaders have become increasingly focused on winning reelection instead of serving the public. The problem has been apparent in the administration of President Barack Obama; even though the president criticized Republicans for kowtowing to special interest groups, his own administration was full of lobbyists and former lobbyists who represented similar special interests (Malkin, 2014).

Beinart (2001) argues that the ineptness is due to the polarization of the parties and the resulting loss of influence by moderates. Columnist John Archibald (2014) may have aptly described the problem when he wrote that "Politics is seldom about leadership anymore—if it ever was. It's about manifest ideological destiny. Seize power and hold it" (p. 26). Regardless, at some point, the nation needs candidates who will address the issues facing the nation and leaders who can provide leadership on those issues. Similarly, political scientist Richard Skinner (2008/2009) argued that the problem can be traced back to Ronald Reagan and a trend that Skinner labeled the "partisan presidency" (p. 605), a trend that reached full bloom in the twenty-first century and the presidency of George W. Bush.

If it was bad under Bush, it seems to have gotten worse under President Obama. It has reached a point where partisanship is now a toxic element in the political process. Historically, our democratic system is based upon the concepts of competition during election campaigns, but collaboration after the elections. That second stage has vanished, but both parties continuing the partisan competition while they serve in office. The victim of all this fighting is the ordinary American, the lower- and middle-class voters who work and seek a better life (Herbert, 2014). As commentator Michael Gerson noted:

> America is in desperate need of a politics of repair, not a politics of demolition and rebuilding. We need leaders who take populist discontent seriously, but direct it toward projects of practical reform. . . . The proper response is the renovation of institutions that allow us to live a decent, compassionate, orderly life together. This is the dignity and importance of the political profession. (p. 22)

That's a worthy goal, indeed. What if our government could become a mechanism for improving the lives of ordinary Americans. What if Republicans and Democrats could still express their ideological differences, yet unite in a common goal of improving the life of its citizens? What if a candidate possessed both the skills to be elected and those need to provide leadership? Is such a process possible? Not in the current political environment.

REFERENCES

Archibald, J. (2014, September 3). The problem with our politics. *Birmingham News*, 26.
Beinart, P. (2010, March 1). Why washington's tied up in knots. *Time*, 175(8), 20–24.
Black, E., & Black, M. (2007). *Divided: The ferocious power struggle in American politics*. New York: Simon & Schuster.

Brooks, D. (2014, June 27). The spiritual recession. *New York Times*, A23.

Bruni, F. (2014, Feb. 16). Let our lawmakers hide! *New York Times*, SR3.

Carr, D. (2013, October 12). It's not just political districts. Our news is gerrymandered, too. *New York Times*, B3.

Confessore, N. (2014a, Jan. 12). A national strategy funds state political monopolies. *New York Times*, A1, A20-A21.

Confessore, N. (2014b, February 2). Fund-raising by G.O.P, Rebels outpaces party establishment. *New York Times*, A1.

Confessore, N. (2014c, May 18). Billionaire expands activism to Senate races. *New York Times*, A18.

Dowd, M. (2014, July 6). Who do we think we are? *New York Times*, SR1, SR11.

Drew, E. (2013, September). The strangle hold on our politics, *Huffington Post*.

Farrell, J. (2012, April 7). Lugar: Too bipartisan for Washington? *National Journal*, 2.

Faulk, K. (2014, May 7). Is justice for sale? *Birmingham News*, 6.

Friedman, T. L. (2014, Jan. 5). Compromise: Not a 4-letter word. *New York Times*, SR11.

Gerson, M. (2014, Dec. 17). Populist Democrats, Republicans should embrace politics of repair. *Birmingham News*, 22.

Hamilton, N. (2007). *Bill Clinton: Mastering the presidency*. Washington, DC: PublicAffairs.

Herbert, B. (2014). *Losing our way: An intimate portrait of a troubled America*. New York: Doubleday.

Hulse, Carl, & Pear, Robert (2015, Jan. 3). Departing lawmakers bemoan the decline of compromise. *New York Times*, A11.

Janeway, M. C. (2001). *Politics of denial: Press, politics and public life*. New Haven, CT: Yale University Press.

Janeway, M. C. (2004). *The fall of the house of Roosevelt: Brokers of ideas and power from FDR to LBJ*. Columbia: Columbia University Press.

Klapper, J. (1960). *The effects of mass communication*. New York: Free Press.

Lipton, E. (2014, January 4). Tangled role in G.O.P. war over Tea Party. *New York Times*, A1, A10.

MacMillan, M. (2008). *Nixon and Mao: The week that changed the world*. New York: Random House.

Malkin, M. (2014, August 15). Obama administration is full of lobbyists. *Birmingham News*, 24.

Matthews, C. (2013). *Tip and the Gipper: When politics worked*. New York: Simon & Schuster.

Miller, W. J., & Walling, R. (eds.) (2013). *The political battle over Congressional redistricting*. Lanham, MD: Lexington.

Milligan, S. (2014, January 31). Obama is ready to go it alone. *U.S. News Digital Weekly*, 6(5),4.

Newton-Small, J. (2014, January 13). Races to watch in '14. *Time*, 183(1), 24.

Rosenthal, T. (1993). *Strange bedfellows: How television and the presidential candidates changed American politics, 1992*. New York: Hyperion.

Ruane, K. L. (2011). *Fairness doctrine: History and constitutional issues*. Washington, DC: Congressional Research Service.

Schulman, D. (2014). *Sons of Wichita: How the Koch brothers became America's most powerful and private dynasty*. New York: Grand Central Publishing.

Shear, M. D., & Landler, M. (2012, November 2). Storm-imposed intermission over, both campaigns rush back onto stage. *New York Times*, A12.

Silver, N. (2012, November 160. Democrats unlikely to regain House in 2014. *New York Times*.

Simmons, S. J. (1978). *Fairness doctrine and the media*. Berkeley: University of California Press.

Skinner, R. M. (2008/2009). George W. Bush and the partisan presidency. *Political Science Quarterly*, 123, 605–22.

Smith, M. M., & Powell, L. (2013). *Dark money, Super PACs, and the 2012 election*. Lanham, MD: Lexington.

Smith, M. M., Williams, G., Powell, L., & Copeland, G. A. (2010). *Campaign finance reform: The political shell game.* Lanham, MD: Lexington.

Street, P. L., & DiMaggio, A. R. (2012). Beyond the Tea Party: Dismal Democrats, radical Republicans, debt ceiling drama, and the long right tilt in the age of Obama. *Critical Sociology*, 38, 549–63.

Wehrman, J. (2014, June 8). Broken Congress: In the House. *Birmingham News*, 15.

Index

About the Authors

James T. Kitchens (PhD, University of Florida) is the owner of The Kitchens Group, a political consulting firm based in Orlando, Florida. He has an extensive background in political polling for a variety of clients. His clients include former Speaker of the U.S. House of Representatives Jim Wright, former Alabama Governor Fob James, and dozens of congressional clients. Dr. Kitchens was also an assistant professor at Texas Christian University (TCU) and authored a number of academic articles before becoming a full-time political pollster.

Larry Powell, PhD, is a professor in the Department of Communication Studies at the University of Alabama at Birmingham (UAB). He is co-author of *Campaign Finance Reform: The Political Shell Game* (Lexington Books, 2010) and lead author of *Political Campaign Communication: Inside and Out* (Pearson, 2012) and *Interviewing: Situations and Contexts* (Allyn & Bacon, 2006). He is also co-author of *Organizational Communication for Survival* (5th ed., Pearson, 2013), and several other books. He and co-author Melissa Smith have recently completed another book for Lexington Books, *Dark Money, Super PACs and the 2012 Election: How the Citizens United Ruling Changed the Campaign Finance Game.*